City
of
Veils

Zoë
Ferraris

ABACUS

First published in Great Britain in 2010 by Little, Brown
This paperback edition published in 2011 by Abacus
Reprinted 2011, 2012, 2013 (twice), 2014

A CIP catalogue record for this book
is available from the British Library.

ISBN 978-0-349-12213-7

Typeset in Caslon by M Rules
Printed and bound in Great Britain by
Clays Ltd, St Ives plc

Papers used by Abacus are from well-managed forests
and other responsible sources.

MIX
Paper from
responsible sources
FSC   FSC® C104740
www.fsc.org

Abacus
An imprint of
Little, Brown Book Group
100 Victoria Embankment
London EC4Y 0DY

An Hachette UK Company
www.hachette.co.uk

www.littlebrown.co.uk

Zoë Ferraris lived in a conservative Muslim community in Jeddah, Saudi Arabia. Her first novel, *The Night of the Mi'raj*, is available in Abacus paperback.

'A double whammy: a riveting portrait of an extraordinary society and a satisfying police procedural to book' *Daily Mail*

'A tautly plotted crime novel, set in the fascinating and alien world of Saudi Arabia' *Sunday Times*

'Thrilling, with plenty of twists and turns. What makes this novel really extraordinary is Ferraris's knowledgeable and sensitive depiction of a place where religion, used as a blunt instrument, has given rise to a stultifying, paranoid and sex-obsessed society. Highly recommended' Laura Wilson, *Guardian*

'An impressive performance ... She expertly weaves an excellent whodunit into an engrossing portrait of a vibrant society, full of sexual, religious, political and moral contradictions ... The plot is lively, tortuous and satisfying, but it's the brilliant backdrop that takes the novel to a higher level' *The Times*

'At one level this is a fascinating crime novel with an astonishing denouement during a sandstorm in the desert ... But *City of Veils* does more than that, providing unique insights in to the minds of men brought up to fear women and the desire they inspire' Joan Smith, *Independent*

Also by Zoë Ferraris

The Night of the Mi'raj
Kingdom of Strangers

City
of
Veils

I

The woman's body was lying on the beach. 'Eve's tomb', he would later come to think of it – not the actual tomb in Jeddah that was flattened in 1928, to squash out any cults attached to her name, nor the same one that was bulldozed again in 1975, to confirm the point. This more fanciful tomb was a plain, narrow strip of beach north of Jeddah.

That afternoon, Abu-Yussuf carried his fishing line down the gentle slope to the sand. He was a seasoned fisherman who preferred the activity for its sport rather than its practical value, but a series of lay-offs at the desalination plant had forced him to take up fishing to feed his family. Sixty-two and blessed with his mother's skin, he had withstood a lifetime of exposure to the sun and looked as radiant as a man in his forties. He hit the edge of the shore, the hard-packed sand, with an expansive feeling of pleasure; there were certainly worse ways to feed a family. He looked up the beach and there she was. The woman he would later think of as Eve.

He set his tackle box on the sand and approached carefully in case she was a crazy, half-dressed woman who would sit up and wipe her eyes and mistake him for a *djinn*. She was lying on her side, her dark hair splayed around her head like the tentacles of a dangerous anemone. The seaweed on her cloak looked at first like some sort of horrible growth. One arm was tucked beneath the body, the other one was bare and it rested on the sand in a

1

pleading way, as a sleeper might clutch a pillow during a bad dream. Then he saw that the hand was mutilated; it looked burned. There were numerous cuts on the forearm. Her bottom half was naked, the black cloak pushed up above her waist, the jeans she was wearing tangled around her feet like chains. His attention turned to the half of her face that wasn't buried in sand. Whole sections of her cheeks and lips were missing. What remained of the skin was swollen and red, and there were horrible cuts across her forehead. One eye was open, vacant, dead.

'*Bism'allah, ar-rahman, ar-rahim*,' he began to whisper. The prayer spooled from his mouth as he stared. He knew he shouldn't look, he shouldn't *want* that sort of image knocking around in his memory, but it took an effort to turn away. Her left leg was half-buried in the sand, but now that he was closer, he saw that the right one was cut around the thigh, the slashes bulbous and curved like tamarinds. The rest of the skin was unnaturally pale and bloated. He knew better than to touch the body, but he had the impulse to lay something over the exposed half of her, to give her a last bit of dignity.

He had to go back up to the street to get a good mobile signal. The police came, then a coroner and a forensics team. Abu-Yussuf waited on the street, still clutching his fishing rod, the tackle box planted firmly by his feet. The young officer who first arrived on the scene treated him with affection and called him 'uncle'. *Would you like a drink, uncle? A chair? I can bring a chair*. They interviewed him politely. *Yes, uncle, that's important. Thank you*. The whole time, he kept the woman in his line of sight. Out of politeness, he didn't stare.

While the forensics team worked, Abu-Yussuf began to feel crushingly tired. He sensed that shutting his eyes would lead to a dangerous sleep, so he let his eyes drift out to sea, let his thoughts drift further. *Eve*. Her real tomb was in the city. It had always seemed strange that she was buried in Jeddah, and that Adam was buried in Mecca. Had they had a falling out after they were exiled from the Garden of Eden? Or had Adam, like so many men today, simply died first, giving Eve time to wander? His grandmother, rest her soul, once told him that Eve had been 180 metres tall. His grandmother had seen Eve's grave as a girl, before the King's Viceroy had demolished the site. It had been longer than her father's entire camel caravan.

One of the forensics men bent over the body. Abu-Yussuf snapped out of his reverie and caught a last glimpse of the girl's bare arm. *Allah receive her.* He leaned over and picked up his tackle box, felt a rush of nausea. Swallowing hard, he looked up to the street and began to walk with an energy he didn't really have. *Uncle, can I assist?* This was another officer, taller than the first, with a face like a marble sculpture, all smooth angles and stone. The officer didn't give him time to protest. He took Abu-Yussuf's arm and they walked up together, taking one slow step at a time. The going became easier when he imagined Eve, a gargantuan woman stomping across cities as if they were doormats. She could have taken this beach with one leap. Pity it was only the modern woman who had been rendered so small and frail.

2

24 hours earlier

In the loading garage of al-Amir Imports, the great bustle of activity drowned out the sound of Nayir's mobile, which went unnoticed in his pocket. There were tents to be folded, rations to be stored, and water to be measured, not to mention that the GPS navigation network still hadn't been brought online. While the younger Amir brothers were raising a fuss about the static on the screens of their hand-helds, an assistant came rushing up to warn Nayir that the servants had forgotten to stock salt tablets.

Nayir went straight to the Land Rover in question – mobile still happily jangling – and foraged in the boot for the missing tablets. He found table linens and silverware, two boxes of cigars, a portable DVD player, and a satellite dish – none of which he had approved for the trip. Men brought whatever they wanted to the desert, but the satellite dish was going too far.

'Take this stuff out,' he ordered. 'Don't tell anyone. Just do it.'

'Where should I put it?' the assistant asked.

The sweat ran in rivulets down Nayir's back. 'I don't care. Just make sure they don't notice it's missing until we're gone.' He took a handkerchief from his pocket and wiped his face. The garage, like many belonging to the super rich, was air-conditioned, but it made no difference. The heat bled into everything. 'And send a servant to buy salt!' These men were going to have daily doses of salt tablets whether they liked it or not. He didn't want them coming home on stretchers, dying of dehydration.

Nayir grabbed a water bottle and headed for the door. Behind him, twelve Land Rovers sat in regal formation, each attended by detailers, fussed over by mechanics, lovingly attended like pashas of old by the eager hands of slave labour (this more modern type of slave imported from Sri Lanka and the Philippines), and all for a five-day jaunt to the desert so that the male half of a large and obnoxiously rich family of textile importers could later brag to their friends and neighbours about shooting wild foxes, eating by campfires, and generally 'roughing it' at the edges of the Empty Quarter. The trip had originally been planned to last a fortnight, but because of the great chaos of schedules and commitments – each Amir son with his own boutique to manage, investors to please, workers to boss around – their desert adventure had slowly been whittled down to five days. *Five*. Nayir counted them in his head: Days one and two, to the desert. Day three, piss in the desert. Days four and five, drive home.

He remembered the preparations for long-ago trips, taken to far more difficult locales in the company of greater men than these. Packing sandbags and live pigeons for archaeological digs with old Dr Roeghar and Abu-Tareq. 'Why are we bringing *sand* to the desert?' Nayir had asked, back then a boy of eight. 'To give us ballast in case of a storm,' Dr Roeghar had replied. Nayir had not understood the word 'ballast' and he had had to refer to his uncle's English–Arabic dictionary. When he finally understood, the idea conjured such a wild, windswept image of the desert that he could hardly suppress his excitement. Then he reached the real desert, so treacherously hot that he and the other children had to cover their faces for the first time, ingest water at ritual intervals like medicine, and discover the indignity of salt tablets at work in the gastrointestinal system.

He'd worn his first pair of sunglasses that year, and been teased

5

by Abu-Tareq's daughter Raja' for looking American, so he'd taken them off and never worn sunglasses again. Young, beautiful Raja' with the bright green eyes. She swore that she'd marry him someday, and he believed it, to his later, quiet embarrassment. During the day, they slept side by side in his Uncle Samir's tent on an old mattress of straw that smelled incongruously green and chemical. Machines loomed above them, set on folding wooden tables. He and Raja' always curled up like twins, face-to-face, with dust on their cheeks and sand in their hair. They locked legs sometimes, and once he tied pieces of string to her hair while she slept, and then tied the whole bundle with a longer string to his own hair. Occasionally, when they woke, he'd find that her fingers had become entangled in his hair, which was long and often knotted from the wind. The wind would wake them at dusk, and they'd hear the camp stirring, and the coolness of the evening would beckon them outside. Everything would be forgotten as they raced off to play.

It was hard now to imagine that he'd once been so close to a girl, close enough to sleep on the same mat and call each other 'best friend'. At eleven, Raja' had become a 'woman', and her mother had draped her in a veil and sent her off to be with her sisters. He never saw her again. The next winter Dr Roeghar's dig had gone on without her, and Nayir soon became mature enough to feel ashamed of any lingering thoughts of her face.

Nayir drank half the bottle of water and resisted the urge to pour the other half over his hair. Their Bedouin guide, Abdullah bin Salim, was standing just outside the garage, unperturbed by the heat. He was staring at the traffic on the boulevard. It was the same look he wore when studying the winter pastures of the Empty Quarter, a look of contemplation and challenge that said: *What do you have for me this year?*

He frowned as Nayir approached. 'Are you sure about this?' Abdullah asked.

Nayir wanted to remind him that he said that every year, no matter what kind of people they were taking to the desert. 'I have to admit,' he said, 'they don't seem ready.'

Abdullah didn't reply.

'Listen,' Nayir said, 'I'm sure it will be all right.'

Abdullah's eyes remained on the boulevard. 'How do you know them?'

'Through Samir. He's known the father for twelve years.'

'These people aren't Bedouin. They never were. Just looking at them, you can see they were *sharwaya*.' Sheep herders, not the 'real' Bedouin whose lives were tied to camels. It was an insult, but Nayir had heard this remark before as well. The families they took to the desert were seldom good enough for Abdullah. And perhaps it was true that they could never actually survive in the landscape their forefathers had inhabited for 6000 years, but in the greater scheme of things, it was enough that they would try.

Nayir nodded politely. 'You're probably right. So let's teach them how to be real Bedouin.' His mobile rang again and this time he answered it. He listened patiently to his uncle, made a few replies, and once he was finished, excused himself from the preparations and headed quickly to the car park for his Jeep.

3

As Miriam Walker made her way to the back of the plane, she could see that the flight to Jeddah was going to be tedious. It was packed with holiday travellers. There were too many overhead items, too many nervous stewards scurrying down the aisles looking for space. She felt a familiar combination of dread and excitement. She was looking forward to seeing Eric again – she'd been gone for a month – but this simple walk down the aisle marked a return to a world where she would stay indoors for weeks at a time. As the line trudged forward, she pushed ahead, anxious to buckle herself in as if the seatbelt would prevent her from stepping off the plane and turning her back on it all.

Miriam had been assigned a seat next to a man, it turned out. It seemed that Saudia ought to have restrictions against seating women next to strange men, but apparently not. The man stared as she approached, a knowing look in his eye. He had the dark eyes and olive skin of an Arab man but a shock of natural blond hair. The contrast made him surprisingly handsome. Miriam's cheeks brightened. A sidestep put her behind a tall man in a turban. Slowly, casually, she straightened her shoulders and licked her front teeth. Another brief glance told her he was still staring. They were technically in New York, but she could feel Saudi Arabia draping over them with every blast of recycled air. She ran a hand through her hair and thought: *Enjoy your last bit of freedom, curly locks.*

She slid into her seat and shot him a casual smile, practised to hide a crooked incisor. He greeted her with a satisfied look. To stall him from talking, she rummaged in her handbag, made a show of forcing it beneath the seat in front of her and spent a few minutes inspecting the contents of the seat pocket. She found an unexpected treat there – a silk drawstring bag that must have been left by the passenger before her. In it was a toothbrush, a bar of soap, a tortoiseshell comb and a small bottle of Calvin Klein perfume. Escape. She smirked.

As the plane backed out of the gate, Miriam felt herself tense. *No going back now.* She never used to be afraid of flying, but travelling to Saudi had done something to her. As they lumbered down the runway, her instincts took over. Palms cold, forehead wet, chest tight. The plane would never go fast enough to rise off the ground. Everyone stared at the windows and walls, which were shuddering violently. An overhead compartment burst open, spilling jackets and a coffee tin on to a passenger's head. She wondered why anyone would bring Folgers to Jeddah.

'Do you know,' the man beside her said, 'on the old Saudia flights, they used to say Mohammed's prayer for journeys over the loudspeaker?' He spoke with a clear American accent, which surprised her somehow. She had thought he was Arab.

'Oh really?' She gave a nervous laugh.

'Another tradition lost.' He seemed almost amused.

They felt the pull of their bodies resisting the rise. A man across the aisle began cursing. Miriam wanted to hush him but she was hinged in a twilight of prayer, hoping they wouldn't fall out of the sky. With a bounce, the plane levelled. It seemed to stop in mid-air and float like a walrus on top of a balloon. A mechanical lullaby hummed in her head. It was night. That and fear combined to make her feel crushingly tired. The only way to escape the terror of flying was to surrender to the void of unconsciousness, but there was no alcohol on Saudia flights, and the dark nestle of sleep would only come closer once they turned out the lights. She shut her eyes, hoping to deter her neighbour from starting a conversation, but he pressed the call button. *Bing.* The steward appeared, looking annoyed. Her neighbour leaned past her, almost touching her breast with his shoulder. 'Excuse me,' he said. He asked for two empty cups.

'One for me,' he told the steward, 'and one for my girlfriend.'

☽

From the pocket of his jacket, he produced two small bottles of wine. Miriam's chest tightened.

'You know that's—'

'Forbidden,' he said. 'Yes. But what are they going to do, kick us off the plane?' He smiled at her, poured out two glasses and tucked the bottles in the seat pocket. He gave one glass to Miriam. She shook her head but he insisted. 'Come on,' he said, 'I'm sure the worst they'll do is make us flush it down the toilet.'

She felt like a teenager again, and she found herself doing just what she'd done back then. She picked up the wine glass. 'Thanks,' she said, taking a sip. It was a welcome palliative. *Actually, the worst they'll do is arrest us and throw us in prison when we land.*

'First trip to Jeddah?' he asked.

'No. My second.' Miriam saw the television flicker on, a big arrow showing the direction of Mecca and the time of the next prayer: five hours away, local time. The stewardess came by with amenity kits, followed by a steward passing out coffee and dates. Miriam quickly hid the wine glass beneath her tray table, but neither of them seemed to notice or care. 'What about you,' she said, 'is this your first trip?'

'No. By the way, I'm Apollo.' His smile was teasing. 'Apollo Mabus.'

'Great name,' she smiled back. 'I'm Miriam.'

'Is that a Southern accent I hear?'

'I'm from North Carolina.'

'Ah, I'm from New York.' He said it the way people say 'Checkmate'. She was a lesser species, Elvis perhaps, living in a trailer on processed cheese food and grits. The slight was so common, so predictable that it might have been imagined, but her cheeks flushed anyway and she hid the sting by taking a long sip of wine.

'And what do you do?' he asked.

'I'm a doctor.' She glanced at his reaction, saw his face stiffen, and decided she didn't like him as much as she thought. She certainly wasn't going to clarify that she had a doctorate in music. 'And you? You look like the academic type.'

He raised his eyebrows. 'How's that?'

'Well, you're squinting, which means you probably left your glasses somewhere. And you've got a big callus on your third finger and ink stains on your thumb.' He was trying to hide his discomfort with a look of amusement. The wine was warming her up. 'But you don't seem the tweed jacket type, and those are some pretty big biceps, so tell me, what kind of academic pumps iron?'

'When you spend a lot of time at a desk,' he said slyly, 'you need to do something to get the blood pumping.' She thought it was a cheesy thing to say. She took another sip of wine.

'So what brings you to Saudi?' she asked.

He set his elbows on the armrests and she watched him play with his watch strap, turning it around his wrist. 'I'm a professor of Middle Eastern Studies. My speciality is Quranic scripture. This trip is for research.'

'Ah.' The first rush of alcohol hit her, and she felt a wave of dizziness. Something on the TV caught her eye and she glanced up to see that the in-flight movie had been censored. Women's arms and hair moved across the screen in blurred grey patches.

'What about you?' he asked. 'What brings you to Jeddah?'

'My husband found a great job—'

'Of course.' He interrupted her with a smirk. 'I didn't think you'd be going into the country by yourself.'

Although she had just spent the past four weeks complaining loudly to her sisters, her father, her nieces and anyone who would listen about the miseries of being a kept woman in Saudi Arabia, she found herself prickling.

'I think it's very brave of you,' he went on, 'sitting it out in Saudi so that your husband can advance his career. Or are you only in it for the money?'

'Both,' she said as flippantly as she could manage. It wasn't strictly true. Eric had taken the job as bodyguard – or rather as 'executive protection specialist' – even though most of his military training had been as an engineer. He had said he wanted to get out of that, into something more practical and engaging, but he could have worked in security anywhere. She didn't like that he'd chosen Saudi Arabia, even if it was only for a year.

'And how long have you been there?' Mabus asked.

'Six months.'

'Impressive,' he said. 'Most women don't last that long. Western women, that is – and if they do, it's with the assistance of drugs. But I suppose you live on the compound?'

Miriam looked at her cup. 'No.'

'Really? That's unusual. Do you have a dedicated driver?'

She pursed her lips, shook her head. This was dangerous territory, and she fumbled desperately for a clever way to change the subject but she was feeling muddled by the wine.

'Tell me,' he soldiered on, oblivious to her discomfort, 'what do you do with yourself all day when you're not allowed to leave the house, drive a car, or even ride a fucking bicycle?' He said it loudly enough that Miriam looked around, expecting a few horrified stares. No one seemed to notice.

His questions had triggered a familiar sensation of self-pity and

12

suppressed rage, and now she was sweating. She didn't want to think of her confinement any more, and he was a bastard to ask. Did he want to hear a little whining? She wouldn't give him the satisfaction.

He broke her silence with a laugh, an explosion that shot the adrenalin through her. 'That's a wonderful answer,' he said, 'an answer by demonstration.' Then his face grew serious. 'It's no place for a woman.'

Miriam nodded. Anything she might say would only fuel his diatribe.

'They hate women,' he said, leaning closer to her. 'They fear them and they hate them, and do you know why? Because women are smarter, more biologically gifted and have always had power over men.' She could smell the wine on his breath, mingling with the crisp woodsy scent of his cologne; it reminded her of a bedroom, closed air, the smell of a man.

'There's an old Islamic saying,' he went on, 'that heaven is crowded with beggars, and hell is overflowing with women.' She frowned at him. 'And you haven't been through the worst of it, believe me.'

'What do you mean?' she asked.

'Now that you're ready to go back to the States, good and ready, you'll find that your husband has fallen in love with the place. I've seen it a dozen times. Men love Saudi Arabia about as much as their wives seem to hate it.

'If you really want to keep your husband's heart,' he went on, 'then remind him that the religious Saudis believe in the "duty of dissociation" from infidels. This means they have a duty to keep you at a distance. They believe that relating to infidels – that's you – actually removes the person from the realm of religion. They might be hospitable to your husband, they might give him tea and dates, but they'll never accept him, not there. It's more xenophobic than anywhere else on earth. Here's the Quran for

13

you: *Ye who believe, Take not into your intimacy, Those outside your ranks, They will not fail to corrupt you.*'

'I'm sure that—' ... *not everyone believes that*, she was going to finish, but it was as if he knew she would try to moderate him, and he interrupted quickly.

'They say that the Quran is the word of God,' he said, 'and that everything that was written in it is exactly as it was when the message was passed to the Prophet Mohammed. *Exactly as it was*. Even though it was written down by dozens of different people – and translated from Aramaic. But never mind that, they're so damn proud that not a single diacritic mark has been changed in the holy book since it was written. Did you know that?'

'Sort of,' she lied.

'And are you really going to sit there and tell me that they're not backward? What if I told you the Bible was the word of God, and that the way it is today is exactly how God intended it, and not a single thing has been changed, would you believe me?'

She felt thoroughly annoyed, afraid to speak in case it should provoke him, afraid of the awkwardness of more interruptions and potentially explosive rage. No one was watching them, but she felt as if the whole plane were listening. She reflected morosely that for someone with such a concern for women's rights, Apollo Mabus had silenced her as effectively as any scornful Saudi had ever done.

The effects of the wine had worn off in the adrenalin rush, and now she was coming down from that as well. Mabus went on, less angry now, but he seemed to feel it his holy duty to make sure she understood just how cruel and backward the country was, and how foolish she was for allowing herself to put up with it, especially for a man. She let the sound lap over her and wondered where all of his rage came from. The curious duality of his appearance – part Arab, part Western – did not point to an equally intriguing depth of personality. In fact, he seemed to have been flattened somehow; he was the two-dimensional stereotype of a bigoted American.

She thought about Eric, about his dogged appreciation for Saudi culture, for Islam, and how much stronger it had become over the past few months. She had come to Saudi expecting – half-hoping, half-fearing – that the intensity of this country would finally turn him off, but in fact his affection for it had only grown stronger.

'I think you've got it wrong,' she finally said, cutting Mabus off mid-sentence.

'Oh?' He looked surprised.

She was sinking inside, filled with the terrible dread one feels when one has just committed to an argument that can't be supported – certainly not when the mind is fuzzy with alcohol.

'Yes,' she said, still not certain how she would proceed until the words came tumbling out. 'I didn't come here for my husband. I came for myself. I wanted to see how other people lived. I wanted to understand it.'

'And what do you understand now?'

She looked at him, perhaps too sharply. 'That I hate zealots.' She picked up her wine cup, snapped open her seatbelt and stood up, catching his look of offence as she did.

The stewards had vanished. No one stood in the rows, and the lights had been dimmed. Miriam stumbled through the small partition set up to give Muslim travellers a space to pray in and pushed her way into the toilet, fumbling with the folding door.

Bolting the latch, she sat on the toilet seat and put her face in her hands. Her ribcage was thumping. She rubbed her forehead until the beating stopped.

Don't be stupid. What's wrong with you? He's obviously a crackpot. As she stood up, she saw herself in the aluminium door – she seemed squat and dismal in a grey skirt from Penney's, long enough to be modest, now with a liver-shaped stain on the front where she had, inexplicably, spilled wine on herself. Her reflection was warped so that her head was tiny and her feet were large. She looked like she felt – ugly and helpless.

She filled the basin with water, splashed her face and dried it with a stiff paper towel. Mr Apollo. She wished someone would send him to the moon. She stared at her hands and no matter how hard she tried she couldn't feel Eric. She could hardly even picture his face, just the general features like the colour of his hair and the shape of his shoulders.

The smell of Mabus's breath seemed to linger around her, only now it was the rancid smell of old wine. She bent over the sink and rinsed out her mouth, washed her hands, and smoothed down her hair. She washed again and again, because she found it soothing and she wanted to get rid of the smell of the wine. She was, after all, going back to Saudi.

☽

Encumbered by a black burqa covering her face, Miriam clutched her handbag to her chest and stumbled down the narrow walkway to immigration while men rushed around her in a blur of white. Mabus had been eyeing her as they'd got off the plane, so she'd put her burqa down, hoping to avoid a conversation with him.

Twice she tripped on the bottom of her cloak, the second time accidentally jostling a man who made a low hissing noise in response. She stopped. Let them rush past until all of them were gone. Then she'd lift her veil and indulge in the luxury of vision.

The hallway grew quiet and she pulled up her burqa. Outside, the last brush of sunset was fading from the sky. The monster Saudia jet that had brought her from New York glowed green in the tarmac lights. Three stories high, it flouted the skies in the same way the *Titanic* had once flouted gravity.

She withdrew her mobile from her bag and glanced at the

screen: no calls from Eric. She hoped that meant he'd left work on time and would be waiting for her at immigration.

She fumbled behind the other stragglers down a series of carpeted hallways and into the enormous customs hall, lit fluorescent white, where passengers queued in immigration lines like orphans in a soup kitchen. Aside from the religious sites, this was one of the places where Saudis rubbed shoulders with their foreign workers – their Filipino janitors, Egyptian taxi drivers, and Indonesian housegirls.

Getting into line for what promised to be an interminable wait, Miriam adjusted her attire – a floor-length black cloak, a simple headscarf to cover her hair, and a burqa, a rectangular piece of black fabric to cover her face. The burqa fastened at the back of her head with a piece of Velcro, but somehow hers never managed to stay on. Some women wore their gear with innate ease. They swanned through the streets, happily in rhythm with the grain of their fabric, swishing along. Among strangers, they simply cut strides through the crowd. They knew that men would retreat from them like courtiers from a passing queen, reverent, wary of touching them. They had X-ray vision, they could see through black, see the kerb coming up, see the teenage driver careening down the alley, see every single item in a gift shop window without ever having to lift their burqas.

And then there are the women like me, Miriam thought, the ones who seemed to get stuck in their cloaks like plastic dolls in clingfilm on a hot summer day. Always fussing and adjusting, yanking, tripping, catching their headscarves before they slid to the ground. Not to mention that her burqa had no slit for the eyes, just a thinner patch of fabric through which she could sometimes discern large shapes. Eric had bought it for her. He hadn't noticed the eye-slit detail until he had brought it home and she had put it on. Embarrassed but amused, he had encouraged her to think of it as sunglasses. *Bastard*.

Despite herself, she smiled at the memory.

'You don't *have* to wear a burqa, Miriam,' he had said. She knew that, but there were times when she actually preferred it. It gave her a sense of privacy. Anyway, she simply adjusted to the problem by pulling the fabric down so that it only covered her nose and mouth. When she did this, it left her forehead exposed, but it was better than nothing.

Half an hour later, she dropped her passport in the well beneath the bullet-proof window and reluctantly removed her burqa so the guard could see her face. She felt suddenly exposed and could feel the stares of the men around her. To the right of her, a husband and wife were going through the checkpoint, and she noticed that the wife didn't raise her veil.

The guard compared her face at length to the picture on her document. It couldn't be that hard to match the face to the picture, but she waited him out and reminded herself that he had every right to take his job seriously.

'Point of origin?' he asked, rubbing his finger beneath his nose.

'North Carolina, USA.'

'Date of return to America?' he asked.

As soon as possible. 'January.'

'Will that be a holiday or a permanent return?'

'A permanent return.' She blinked. 'God willing.'

The guard looked up. 'God willing.'

He flipped through the twenty-four pages of her passport, then rubbed his nose and blew little bursts of air out of his nostrils. 'Well, Mrs Walker—'

'*Dr* Walker.'

'Mrs Walker.' He closed the passport and passed it through the cage. 'You have no work permit yourself. I'm sorry, but you're not allowed to enter without your hu—'

'My husband's here. I'm sure he's on the other side of the barrier right now.'

The guard glared at the top of her head. 'And this ... *husband* ... where does he work?'

'SynTech Corporation,' she said, feeling the stare of the man in line behind her. 'His name is Eric Walker. He's in th—'

'Who is his sponsor?' The guard turned to his keyboard.

'His name is Mr Mohammed al-Saeed.'

The guard typed something and then studied his computer for an interminable time before he frowned. He motioned her through with a jerk of his chin.

She wasn't in the mood to thank him.

☽

'Ma'am, please place your belongings here.' The customs officer pointed to a specific spot on the table. 'Here,' he repeated. She felt like she was taking part in a pre-school game to test her fine motor skills. He couldn't be older than fifteen. There was no hair on his face, and his eyes were liquid with youth. There was something ridiculous about him, an arrogance inappropriate to his age. His AK-47 swung down off his shoulder and he hitched it up the way a woman adjusts a handbag.

She heaved her suitcase on to the table. The officer unzipped it and, after a thorough inspection, asked her to remove the books. She piled them on the table, but he slid them into a plastic bin and swept them away.

'They're only thrillers,' she mumbled. She'd been careful not to pack books with pictures of people on the covers, which would have been considered too indecent. She could have bought the same books on the black market here, but she didn't want to cross the law. She closed the suitcase and locked it.

They checked everything but her handbag, a beige leather affair with a fake Gucci stamp. It was really a bag of toiletries masquerading as a handbag, a foil for potential bag-snatchers; she kept her money in her shoe. Walking through the metal gates, she wondered why they hadn't asked to inspect it. Perhaps they were afraid of handling tampons or lipstick. Now even her handbag was indecent, but she clutched it, her last port of privacy.

Miriam sighed. *Almost there.* She scanned the crowd on the other side of the barrier but there was no sign of Eric. Heading towards the entrance lounge, she became aware that her white face was visible to every man in the room. They never met her gaze, but on the periphery of her vision she could see them staring. *Well, too damn bad.* If she put on her burqa, Eric might not be able to recognise her.

Between herself and the white partitions of customs there was only one figure – a uniformed guard striding briskly in her direction. He carried a semi-automatic on his shoulder and although he averted his gaze, his trajectory indicated that he was aiming for her. She froze. People stared from the other side of the barrier. It almost seemed that the guard might walk past her, he was marching so rapidly, but instead he seized her arm and yanked her into his stride. She offered no resistance but gripped her suitcase and scurried beside him, amazed by the strength of his grip.

'Where are you taking me?' she stammered, receiving a prompt, non-verbal answer as he flung open a door near the passport lines. She saw a dark, depressing room. Three women were sitting on metal chairs, looking wilted in the heat. The guard pushed her into the room, and she stumbled, losing hold of her suitcase. It thudded on the stone floor a second before the door shut behind her.

4

Detective Inspector Osama Ibrahim leaned into the boot of his car, rummaging for his field shoes while surreptitiously watching the old fisherman drive away. He wasn't sure it was a good idea to let him drive off alone, he had seemed so shaken – and who wouldn't be, finding a body like this one? But there was something about the old man that had stirred his pity and reminded him of what his father would have been like, if he had lived longer.

He remembered a shaft of green light, the golden halo of the mosque's interior reflecting all around them. Madinah, the Prophet's tomb, peace be upon him. His father's soft whisper came back to him suddenly: *You're not allowed to touch it, it's forbidden to worship the grave, because that's what Mohammed wanted, sallā llahu'alayhi wa sallam.*

The association of his father's memory with the gruesomeness of a murder scene felt sacrilegious, and he might have written it off as the quirk of an anxious mind, but it had happened too often. He'd been working homicide cases for the past five years, and certainly seen corpses, but his father was the only person whom he'd ever seen die, actually been there to witness the passage from life to death. Or, if he were being specific, *barzakh* came next, the state of cold sleep after physical death but before the spirit ascends from the body, when the questioning angels, Munkar and Nakir, come to interrogate the dead. Of course that was silly, but he liked to imagine it.

21

He walked down the sand, feeling naked without Rafiq. His partner was still on leave. He wished to hell there were some way he could have brought Faiza, but a woman had no reason to be here and it would only have raised questions in the department.

The beach was roped off at a generous distance with crime scene tape, but beyond that even greater barriers existed where the forensics team had set up an impromptu field office at the back end of a van, and where men were noisily talking and buzzing between the patrol cars and unmarked vehicles parked haphazardly up and down the road. There wasn't much traffic here, especially this early in the morning, but they'd put up a road-block to keep out the curious.

The old man who'd found her had referred to her as Eve, and now the name was stuck in his mind. Strangely, the site where Eve was lying, although surrounded by workers, was almost serene. Osama approached with caution. *Please, not another house-maid*, he thought. Only the forensic tech's face revealed what he thought: a great, upswelling pity, as if it were his own sister lying there.

Osama had once been very proud of the country's murder rate – it was one of the lowest in the world. He had always believed that the harshness of their punishments had the intended deterrent effect. But that was before he'd joined homicide.

The number of murders was rising, and many were shocking enough to make him feel that the country was going to hell. Last year, a man had chopped off his one-year-old nephew's head in a supermarket right in front of the boy's mother and a handful of shoppers. He'd actually managed to sever the entire head. In the fruit and vegetable section. He'd been having an argument with the boy's parents; they'd angered him, and that was his revenge.

Osama forced himself to look at the body. There was no ringing in his ears, but the brutality of the scene made his skin prickle. Her hands had been destroyed by some kind of burn; they might have been dipped in hot oil. The skin was swollen and blistered, an angry red. The year before, the police had found a woman's burned corpse stuffed into an abandoned fridge in the Aziziya district, right in front of the Department of Women's Education, but that wasn't his jurisdiction and he hadn't seen the body, only heard that it was still smouldering when they found it.

This was a different kind of horror. Osama knelt beside her gently, careful not to touch. The tide was at her feet, soaking the bottom of the jeans that were still tangled around her ankles. They had set up sand barriers to keep the water back while they worked, but that was merely for convenience. From the look of the corpse, she had been in the water for a while.

Eve was lying on her side, one arm exposed, the hand open like that of a person about to supplicate in prayer. Her face was a mutilation of tissue and skin – probably from fish, although it was hard to be certain. The lower half of the black cloak she was wearing was tangled around her waist. One of the sleeves was torn. And the scarf that had perhaps been covering her hair was wound around her neck like a garrotte. Had she been strangled?

The coroner, Ibrahim, was staring down at the body with a faraway look in his eyes.

'Washed up on shore this morning,' he reported. 'This beach is busy. Someone would have noticed if she'd washed up last night.' Although the coroner shared the name of Osama's father, Osama often noted that the two men had little else in common. This Ibrahim, who was soft and dough-faced and missing an ear, had served as one of Osama bin Laden's *mujahideen* in Afghanistan back in the '80s. For that the officers gave him respect, but Ibrahim's behaviour could be abrupt and crass, and sometimes downright menacing. Osama tried not to feel like an upstart. He was only thirty, the department's youngest detective inspector, as Ibrahim often liked to point out.

'The water's pretty warm,' Osama said. 'She would probably

have died what – seven days ago?' Ibrahim scowled, prompting Osama to ask: 'Do you want to revise that?'

Ibrahim glared at him. 'Not until we cut her open.'

'Cause of death?' Osama asked.

The coroner jutted out his chin, an unmistakable sign of annoyance that said: *I'll tell you when I know, now leave me the hell alone.*

Osama had to admit there were too many options. She might have drowned, or died from loss of blood from the many stab wounds covering her body. Perhaps she had been choked by the fabric around her neck. The burns probably wouldn't have killed her, but it was possible that the pain from the burns had rendered her unconscious and caused her to drown after someone had thrown her in the ocean.

'These burns look pre-mortem,' Osama went on.

'Yes,' Ibrahim said, then he added, almost as an afterthought: 'I've seen worse.'

Osama was giving up. He knew that anything he asked now would be subject to future revision anyway. Ibrahim was always tense at a crime scene, especially when women were involved.

'And I'm guessing that her hands were dipped in something,' Osama said. 'Kitchen oil, maybe?'

Ibrahim walked away without an answer.

Osama turned to Majdi, who was kneeling in the sand a few feet away.

'What has forensics got for me?' Osama asked.

Majdi was combing a quadrant of sand with a gloved hand, his glasses sliding down his sweaty nose. He looked up, but like a child who can't stop playing, he compulsively turned back to the sand and kept combing. 'Up the shore, behind you a bit, we've got a spot of your usual beach detritus – cigarettes, bottles, pieces of polystyrene – but not much of it, frankly. And I'm not finding anything here. It looks like nothing else washed up on shore with her.'

'Are you certain she washed up?'

'Yeah.' Majdi glanced at the girl's body and Osama knew what he was thinking: *A sea-bloated corpse isn't proof enough for you?* 'Well, you never know,' Majdi said. 'I've already been in touch with the coast guard; they're faxing us the ocean current reports for the past two weeks. We should be able to get an approximate location of where she entered the water, but I can't make any promises.'

'Any ID on the body?'

'No,' Majdi said. 'There's no mobile phone, no ID card or anything. You saw the condition of her hands. I hold out a little hope for fingerprints, but just a little.' He gave a dry rasp and shook his head.

Osama began to feel the dread of having to deal with Missing Persons. The reports were almost all of women – housemaids mostly – who had left their employers because of bad pay, brutal conditions, sexual or psychological abuse, or in some cases just *because*. Slavery had been outlawed in the kingdom in 1962, but that hadn't changed the fact that it still existed in some quarters under the less charged name of domestic help. There were about 15,000 runaway housemaids in the country, plenty of them in Jeddah, and more than half unreported. Even if there were only two, that would still be too many single women running around without money, food, shelter, or proper domestic visas. If Eve had been killed by her employers, chances were they wouldn't have reported her missing. *Please, not another housemaid.* Rationally, he knew it was no worse than any other kind of murder, but with housemaids there was the added horror of the victim being so far from family and home, and, in most homicide cases, of having been physically, sexually, or emotionally abused, or at the very least subjugated by strangers who considered themselves superior.

Osama glanced at the body again. Her jeans were caked in sand and salt. 'The water wouldn't have torn her jeans off like that. Someone tried to rip them off.'

'Yes,' Majdi said.

'Do you think you'll find any hairs or fibres on them?'

'Maybe.' Red-faced, Majdi got to his feet and wiped his hands together. 'Of course the sea water washed almost everything away, but I'll do a third check when we get back to the lab.' He gave a weak smile. 'She's also wearing a Metallica T-shirt.'

Osama looked at the body again. 'Housemaids don't usually wear Metallica T-shirts,' he said with a twinge of hope.

5

Nayir knew he wouldn't be able to eat, but he offered to make dinner anyway. His uncle was looking pale, and he felt that the older man could use the company. Earlier that day Samir had learned of the sudden death of his friend Qadhi.

'The police won't tell me anything,' Samir said, after half an hour on the phone with them.

Nayir was standing at the counter, mashing aubergine with a fork, preparing one of the two cold dishes he knew. It seemed to get hotter every week, which was difficult to believe considering the already scandalous temperatures. Nayir's appetite, typically reliable, had shrunken by degrees so that now he only ate when he felt weak, or when Samir began commenting on his appearance.

'Perhaps you'll be able to find out more in the morning,' Nayir said.

'Hmmph. Are we ready to eat?' Samir asked.

'Not yet, I have to pray first.'

'Oh.' His uncle's face fell. 'Why don't you wait until after dinner? It'll be more satisfying then anyway.'

'Prayer time is now,' Nayir said, glancing at the clock. He left the room before his uncle could give him another lecture on the perils of taking one's religion too seriously.

'Eating ought to be like prayer to you,' Samir called after him. 'You need the nourishment.'

Once Nayir returned, they began the meal. A few months ago he might have been willing to fake a robust appetite to appease his uncle. But he was tired of pretending, and what with the sweat trickling down his back, he could barely manage to sit comfortably in the old vinyl chair. He couldn't tell any more if this lethargy was caused by the heat or by a more general discontent which, Samir had rightly noted, seemed to be getting worse.

Samir took a piece of bread from the stack on the table, and ate in the room's heavy silence. 'You know,' he said finally, 'you might have better luck at getting some answers about Qadhi's death than I. You could talk to the coroner's office.'

Nayir was fairly certain that he'd kept his face in control, but the mention of the coroner's office instantly stirred a memory of Katya.

'It's only been a day,' he told his uncle. 'Maybe the police need time to get their paperwork in order.'

Samir grunted. 'You know, when your parents died, it took them six months to figure out what had caused the crash.' He looked at Nayir with sympathy, aware that this was always a sensitive subject. Nayir wanted to tell him not to worry. The conversation was triggering a much more recent pain.

He hadn't spoken to Katya in eight months. At first, she had continued to call him every week or so, but each call only seemed to push him further into an association he couldn't justify – a relationship with a woman who was neither his relative nor his wife. The investigation into Nouf Shrawi's death was over; Katya's engagement had been broken as a result. And he knew from experience that the pleasure of seeing Katya in person was offset horribly by the anxieties that invaded him whenever he was alone with her. Without the approval of her father, Nayir could not continue to see her, and winning genuine approval would have been impossible. Nayir could never admit that he had been seeing Katya alone, and yet not to admit it was the worst kind of lie. In either case he would be a blackguard in her father's eyes, should the truth come out. And it must have come out. Her escort knew they'd been seeing each other. He must have told her father.

Given what had passed between him and Katya, any modest, concerned parent would dismiss Nayir at once. He was certain that *that* was the right thing to do, and he was equally certain that he couldn't take the rejection. It would have made permanent the very separation Nayir had imposed upon himself, in the half-hope that it wouldn't last forever.

But then Katya had stopped calling. She must have realised his position. She knew him, after all, and more importantly, she knew her father.

Or perhaps she'd simply stopped wanting to see him.

'. . . So will you check it out?' Samir's words brought Nayir back to the present.

'What?' he asked with a note of alarm. 'Check what out?'

Samir looked exasperated. 'I was hoping you would go to the coroner's office and ask a few questions. You know people there.'

'But I don't.'

'You're going to tell me that you can solve a whole murder by yourself, and yet you can't go down to ask a question about an old family friend for me?'

Nayir was taken aback. He hadn't solved Nouf's murder on his own, he had solved it with Katya's help. And he had never intended to get involved in the first place. He was a desert guide, he had only been investigating as a favour to his friend Othman.

'The Shrawis,' he tried to explain to his uncle, 'that was completely different.'

'I know you're concerned with seeing justice done. You've shown that you're willing to work hard, even fight, to see that it's accomplished. That is rare indeed. And now you're acting like—'

'It's not rare,' he snapped, fighting to maintain control. 'There are people who do it every day.'

29

Samir took a bite of bread with dignity. He chewed slowly, watching Nayir, before saying: 'I am very proud of what you've done.'

Nayir, who was about to erupt for a tangled mass of reasons that he didn't dare analyse, was suddenly cut short. His uncle never said those words to him, at least never so directly, and although they had fallen on angry ears, this did not diminish their significance.

Nayir abruptly stood up to refill the water jug and took his time before returning to the table. He had hardly touched his plate, and the lump of food now looked repulsive.

'Of course I'll go,' Nayir said gruffly. 'I'll see what the coroner has to say.'

Samir nodded with satisfaction. Nayir began clearing off the table, taking away plates, even the one Samir was using. He busied himself with wrapping everything up and putting it in the fridge before it spoiled – which wouldn't take long in the forty-five-degree heat.

'You are getting thinner,' Samir observed from behind him, oblivious to his nephew's anger. 'You know, you don't even look like yourself any more.'

Nayir didn't respond, and that silenced Samir. But a little while later the words carried him out the door and into his car, where they echoed uncomfortably in the cramped space.

☾

The Corniche was uncharacteristically empty. No families picnicking or strolling down the long boardwalk. Despite being dusk, it was still dangerously hot outside, and the air was so thick that it felt to Nayir as if it were actually slowing down his Jeep. He half-expected to look over and see the ocean boiling.

In one of the last phone conversations he'd had with Katya, she'd told him that she'd been promoted to a different branch of

30

the Ministry's forensics department, where she was going to be given more responsibility. Instead of being confined to a basement coroner's office, she'd be working in a new police building downtown. Everything was new – the machines, the offices, all of the technology was up to date. Nayir wanted to ask if the attitudes were new, too, but instead he got right to the point. 'Will you be working directly with men?'

This was met by silence. 'Yes,' she said finally. 'I'm sure I will.' After that, she'd gone cold. The rest of the conversation had been awkward. He felt guilty, but it genuinely bothered him that she'd be working with strange men. Then again, who was he to complain? He wasn't her husband.

She hadn't called him since. He understood why. She had contented herself with believing how backward he was, how his religious convictions kept him from treating her the way she wanted to be treated. She had finally given up on him. At first he had simply accepted it. He had unhitched his boat and gone out on the water and lain on the deck staring at the glorious stars. He could have stayed there for days, overcome with an unrepentant laziness, away from people and their discomforts. There was no call to prayer to break his thoughts, and for once he was glad. He realised then that the thing he loved most in the world was solitude, and that perhaps he wasn't the sort of man who should be married in the first place. But sailing back to the marina, he knew that solitude would never satisfy him. And the words of the Prophet rang in his mind: *Marry those among you who are single.*

Someone cut him up and he honked angrily, speeding up to tailgate the reckless driver. Then he realised what he was doing and slowed down. *Allah*, he prayed, *guide me from this anger. I don't know where it comes from. I don't know how to cure it.*

But another voice struggled for space in his head. It said: *You know exactly how to cure it. This anger is a punishment for your coldness towards Katya. You did to her exactly what Fatimah did to you!*

It wasn't true, of course. The situation wasn't as simple as that. Fatimah and he had been introduced through a mutual friend for the express purpose of courtship. It turned out that Fatimah was being courted by other men as well, and she chose her future husband without ever telling Nayir what she was up to. But Katya was different. They hadn't been courting; they had been solving a crime. They had *had* to work together, and any closeness they experienced had been grounded in their thoughtlessness and sin.

Then why did this separation hurt so much?

Because I want a wife, he told himself.

No matter which way he thought of it, nothing changed the fact that being with Katya was a *zina* crime. The Prophet Mohammed had said: *Not one of you should meet a woman alone unless she is accompanied by a relative.* Did injunctions come any clearer than that? In case there was any doubt, the Prophet had also said: *Whenever a man is alone with a woman, Satan is the third among them.* Thinking this, Nayir couldn't help picturing her poor escort, Ahmad, who had sat in the Ferris wheel cabin behind them at the funfair on their one real date.

Back at his boat, he set a pot of water on the stove before he realised that hot tea was the last thing he wanted. He went into the bedroom to change and found himself staring dumbly at the porthole. He regretted telling Samir that he would go to the coroner's. He could just as easily call and speak to an examiner. It wasn't as if he had to be there in person.

The past few weeks had been nothing but humid, restless nights, full of longing. The worst agony came when she broke into his dreams. The days were no better, time stretching as long and empty as the desert. And no one wanted to go to the desert. The Saudis had hunkered down for the summer, taking refuge in their air-conditioned sitting rooms, their private swimming pools and cool shopping malls.

Before going to bed, he performed *istiqara*, the recitation of special prayers before sleep to produce an answer in a dream. He had never tried it before, but Imam Hadi had recommended it to him once, telling Nayir: 'Sometimes you have to search very seriously for the answers you need. Allah will not make it easy for you.' The *istiqara* was no anxious bedtime prayer but a cleansing, altering-of-consciousness-before-falling-unconscious method of prayer from which one should expect an answer of the highest precision. According to Imam Hadi, it was the process which assisted Niels Bohr in his discovery of the atomic structure and which helped René Descartes formulate the scientific method. Nayir figured that such a powerful tool ought to help him through the rather modest matter of deciding whether to go to the coroner's office in the morning.

Just before dawn, he dreamed he was in a gigantic room full of sweets. There were plates of baklava, Jordan almonds, Turkish delight. The more he looked, the more there was to eat: dates and nuts caked in sugar crystals and dipped in honey, glazed pastries waiting in a patient row, sherbets that never melted. Painfully hungry, Nayir sat on the stone floor and ate the sweets on every side while a dusting of powdered sugar drifted over him like snow. He ate and ate until he felt sick, and then he went to the corner to vomit.

It didn't take Niels Bohr-level intelligence to interpret the meaning of that particular dream: he was in grave danger of indulging himself. The answer was no.

6

Miriam was sitting on a bench against the wall, feet pulled up, arms curled around herself. The airport air was chilly and now she was shivering and afraid, and hating herself for it. She had no idea how much time had gone by. An hour, two hours? She couldn't remember when they'd brought her in, and it was too much trouble to figure it out. She'd tried calling Eric on her mobile a dozen times, but he hadn't answered. So she waited. She couldn't call the neighbours or her friends; Eric was the only one who could give her permission to enter the country.

The only person who came in was an airport worker. He brought a bottle of water and asked if there was anything she needed. *Tampons*, she wanted to say. *A side of pork and a bottle of wine*. But she'd said no and gone back to staring at the walls, only later noticing that he hadn't offered anything to the other women in the room.

After a while, the other women were collected, and Miriam was left alone. Now she was wondering which was worse: being worried about Eric or about herself. She felt like a child again, the one feeling she hated above all others. Everything about this country was designed to infantilise women. She'd said so a hundred times. But it hadn't changed anything.

She sat on the bench for what felt like another hour. *But damn me to hell if I'm going to check my watch*. She would not resort to an open display of waiting. To the world – even that composed of four blank walls – she was here by choice. Someone outside was waiting for *her*.

Finally the door opened, the guard poked his head inside and motioned her out with a wiggle of his hand. She took her time standing up, righting her suitcase, adjusting her cloak and making sure the burqa wasn't going to slip off her nose. She glanced at the door and saw a sign she'd missed before. It said in English: *Unclaimed Women*.

When she came into the hall, Eric was standing beside the guard. He was a whole foot taller than the officer, and he stood as he typically did when dealing with shorter people: shoulders hunched, head bowed, one hand compulsively reaching up to run through his close-cropped blond hair, all of which made him seem confused and slightly lost, which was seldom truly the case. Right now he looked upset about something. She wanted to ask what was wrong, but she didn't want to embarrass him in front of the guard. He was also wearing a new shirt – indigo blue, not his usual colour. The silky fabric reminded her of Saudi men.

The guard shifted his machine gun to the other shoulder and put a final signature on a piece of paper, which he handed to Eric along with his passport and work permit. They traded her like runners passing a baton: *Now it's yours – run!* Eric grabbed her suitcase, clutched her hand. They hurried out of the building, through the glass doors and on to the street, where the Ford pick-up sat parked at the kerb. The air was like a slap. It was like opening an oven to take out a pie, except that this oven was full of diesel fumes and dust. She gagged and pressed her burqa to her nose.

Eric heaved the suitcase into the boot and Miriam stumbled into the passenger seat, careful not to hit her head on the frame. Once she shut the door, the climate relaxed, as if someone had drawn a curtain on the world. He started the car. The air inside was still slightly cool from his drive to the airport, and when the air conditioning came on, she turned the vents to blow directly at her face, and heaved a sigh of relief. Eric spun a lazy arc into the opposite lane, heading back to the motorway.

'So . . . double-checking here.' He glanced in her direction. 'You *are* my wife?'

She took off her burqa. 'Your Stepford wife. You know, the one you left for airport security to handle.'

'Jesus, Miriam,' he whispered, running a hand through his hair. He took a deep breath. 'I'm so sorry.'

'What happened?' she asked.

'I'm really glad you're back.'

'What. Happened.' She knew she was about to lose her temper, but she was determined to hold off as long as she could.

He looked abashed. It took him a moment to speak. 'I got the time mixed up. Miriam, I'm—'

'You *forgot* the *time*?'

'I was so busy at work . . .' He trailed off, lamely. 'Please forgive me. I'm sorry, it won't happen again.'

You're damn right it won't, she thought. But despite herself, she couldn't stay angry, she was too relieved to see him. She turned to the window and tried to calm herself down. Traffic was flowing smoothly; the streets were whizzing by.

Taking a deep breath, she said: 'So how've you been?'

'The usual. How was your trip?' he asked, attempting to soften her up.

'Good,' she said. Unable to stop herself, she added, 'Too short.'

He wasn't going to take the bait. 'I missed you. A month is too long.'

'Mmmmh.'

He took her hand, surprising her. 'But I managed to find a second wife, so it wasn't so bad.'

'Oh?' She gave a half-smile; she'd play along. 'Hence the new shirt.'

'Actually, one of my clients gave it to me. His wife's family owns a fabric bazaar in Riyadh. This client is one of these hot-shot princes who wants a bodyguard just so he can feel important.'

It galled her that Eric's work wasn't earth-shatteringly important; that she was putting up with everything here so he could guard one of Saudi Arabia's five hundred princes, and one who didn't need protection in the first place.

'Anyway, my new wife,' he went on teasingly. 'The good news is, she's Saudi, and she does all the cooking and cleaning, so now you're off the hook.' He shot her a sly look. 'I'm saving *you* for other things.'

'Well, you know I *am* your kept woman.'

Eric hit the brakes, veered on to the shoulder, and cut dramatically across a rocky stretch of sand, stopping beside a row of scrub. His fists gripped the wheel, and for a moment she thought she'd gone too far.

Leaning over, he took her face in his hands and kissed her. 'Don't be angry at me any more,' he whispered. 'It's only five more months, and then we're going back. I promise.'

She shut her eyes. She wanted to tell him that it wasn't her dread of the next five months, it was what had already happened in the previous six: the fear, the frustration, the constant worry. This country was slowly crippling their marriage, and she was afraid that by the time they got home, it would be too late.

But she'd already said these things. He'd already failed to understand them. She leaned back against the seat and said the words that had been echoing in her mind for months: 'I'd really just like to get home.'

☾

They drove the rest of the way in darkness, punctuated by the occasional pink neon sign announcing all-night schawarma parlours by the side of the road. Miriam's stomach grumbled for food, but she didn't want to stop.

37

Disorientation gripped her as the pick-up turned on to the road which led to their neighbourhood. From the outside, it was a stranger's land, a man's land. Her knowledge of it was limited to the walls of her building and the occasional brisk walk to the shop.

Now she saw the view that she didn't often get, a sprawling neighbourhood teeming with immigrants from Sudan, Somalia and other Muslim countries, men who spent their days picking up rubbish – but not in their own part of town. There were Saudis, too, in their white robes and scarves. A young man wearing a base-ball cap over his headscarf walked past their car and spat near the fender. Miriam grimaced, thinking that these men spat too much to be descended from people who believed in conserving body fluids. But these weren't Bedouin, and this wasn't the desert. This was Jeddah, humid port, stewing in the endless moisture of the sea.

When they'd first moved into their flat, Eric had convinced her that it was safer than living on a Western compound. But the unspoken reason for them living here was that he hated the seg-regation of Americans. He respected Muslim culture and wanted to be a part of it, at least while they were here. He spoke Arabic from his years in the military, and two tours in Iraq had taught him that there was more to the Muslim way of life than a handful of extremists and some hookah smoke. It went against everything he believed in to cloister himself in an English-speaking compound, even if it was the only place where women could wander around freely, walk their poodles, and lounge around their swimming pools.

In the beginning, she had pushed hard to live on a compound, arguing that he could see all of the city he liked, while she could spend time in more familiar territory. But he wouldn't have it. According to him, there were two types of compounds. The bigger ones were enormous, with upwards of five hundred homes and all the amenities an American could hope to have, including shopping complexes for military personnel. But why live in Saudi Arabia if you were just going to rent a slice of America? The smaller compounds had a wider variety of people, even Muslims, but they weren't reliably safe. Ever since the bombings in Riyadh in 2003, all compounds were required to have heightened security – that is, until some of the smaller ones began evicting their Western tenants. If they got rid of the American and European residents, they didn't have to pay for the security any more. Two friends of Eric's had been evicted in the past six months and been forced to move to more expensive homes across town. So that was the choice – living in mock-America, or living somewhere more integrated where you might be kicked out for being American. Miriam would have liked to live at the sprawling Arabian Gates compound, because fake or not, she wanted some freedom.

'It's one of the biggest al-Qaeda targets in Jeddah,' he had told her. 'We can't live there.'

The pick-up turned on to a narrow street, a dusty splinter, slowing down as they approached their building. It was much like its neighbours, boxy and stucco-white, except that theirs was the tallest on the block; a plaster wall enclosed the roof, adding an extra ten feet of height. Black wooden panels shuttered every window, and the front door, studded with upholstery tacks, looked as if it could resist a tank.

They drove past. It was always difficult to find parking on the little street, but especially at night. It took an effort of will for Miriam to stop herself from griping about it. Instead she stared numbly out the window as they crept through the streets, first circling their block, then the surrounding blocks one-by-one. Eric approached the problem methodically, eliminating one block at a time. After only a few minutes she was utterly lost and couldn't remember which direction their flat was in. All the streets ran together. Some were full of homes, others full of shops, all unfamiliar at night.

Finally, they parked in the middle of a block. Miriam climbed out of the car and a dull, black pain spread behind her eyes. She was exhausted.

As they walked back to the flat, she tried to prepare for the shock of confinement. When Eric was at work, she found it difficult to leave the house. There was a time when he'd encouraged her to get out more often – 'for your own good' he'd say – but she'd learned from experience that it was a terrible idea.

'You're American,' he said once. 'They won't bother you.'

'I'm a woman. That's all that counts.'

Early on, every time she left the house, she drew the neighbours' attention. Hearing footsteps in the hall, they poked their veiled faces out of their doors and warned her that unescorted women could be picked up by the religious police and sent to jail. *They* had problems with the religious police, they said, it would be twice as bad for a Western woman!

At least that's what she thought they said. Talking with most of the neighbours was a game of pantomime and guesswork. Miriam thanked them and went out anyway. On the street, she felt safe and terrified by turns. Some days she could wander freely, going where she liked as long as she wore her cloak and headscarf, keeping her burqa at the ready in case she started to feel too exposed. Sometimes people stared blatantly, even occasionally stopping to gawk at her. Sometimes women would greet her politely. But on other days she would encounter resistance. Men would notice that she was out alone and they would stop her by whistling and even standing in front of her, blocking her passage. They would tell her to go home. They warned her that it wasn't safe to be out. She believed them. Even though she was never arrested as her neighbours had promised, she felt more and more unsafe as the weeks went by. She began to think that it was only a matter of time before something horrible happened.

They finally reached the building and ascended the wide marble staircase. She stopped at the second-floor landing to listen for noises from the Assad household, but it seemed they'd gone out – probably to a relative's wedding or funeral. The women seldom left the house at night for any other reasons.

Miriam followed Eric up the stairs. Before turning the key, he admitted that he hadn't had time to clean.

'You haven't cleaned for a month?'

'Well, I did do *some* work.'

She slid through the door and glanced around, at the bare white walls, the cold stone floors. Truth was, there wasn't much to clean. While Eric dragged her suitcase into the bedroom, she wandered into the kitchen. Except for a tin of fava beans and some stale pita bread, the cupboard was emptier than she'd left it, and for a moment it seemed unfamiliar. Someone else's kitchen. Paint curled from the cabinets. The hob, thick with grease, wore a bonnet of carcinogens and barbecue scum. Eric had written 'bio-hazard' on the dirty oven window. *Jerk*, she thought, forcing a smile. Once white, the linoleum looked like cauliflower mould, its tiles guttered with rivers of grime.

Eric appeared in the doorway. 'I'm going for food.'

'That's okay, I'm not that hungry.'

'I always know when you're hungry.' He reached in his pocket and pulled out his keys, pointed them at her. 'You start chewing your lip. Leave the door locked. I'll be right back.'

She watched him leave. 'Hurry back,' she said, but he was already gone.

☽

Miriam inverted her handbag on the table and sorted through the debris. Receipts, bus tickets. She tossed out sweet wrappers and American pennies and extracted a sheet of folded paper that she'd received from the consulate when they'd renewed her visa. It was a State Department warning. She'd read it before, but she scanned it again to refresh her memory.

American women should exercise extreme caution in matters concerning personal security. Maintain a low profile, reduce travel in the kingdom, and report any suspicious activity to the US Embassy at once.

The religious police, known as Mutawwaiin, have the same powers as normal police. To ensure that conservative standards of conduct are observed, the Mutawwaiin harass and arrest women for the following infractions:

– drinking alcohol
– wearing trousers or other Western clothing
– eating in public restaurants
– driving a car or riding a bicycle
– dancing, listening to music, or watching movies in public
– associating with a man who is not a husband or family member.

Women mingling in public with unrelated men may be charged with prostitution, which can be penalized by arrest and death.

The penalty for drug trafficking is death. Saudis make no exceptions. US officials have NO POWER in Saudi courts to obtain leniency for American citizens in any circumstances.

When she first read this note, she'd been chilled by its severity. She remembered with a sting that when they'd decided to come to Jeddah she'd dreamt about nomads and dark men on horses, swords sheathed in leather and hawks soaring above their white-turbaned heads. Saudi was romantic, if you were a man.

She crumpled the paper and tossed it in the bin. Now she was back – officially back – and although she'd only been home for twenty minutes, she was already waiting for Eric to return, to come back from the shop, back from work, from a world she was afraid to enter without him. Wait, wait some more. Her suitcase was jammed with distractions she'd never engaged in back in the States: cross-stitching, embroidery, knitting needles. She was going to knit in the desert. Someday she'd laugh, but right now it wasn't funny. *Look at that*, she thought, *I'm even waiting to laugh*.

From the bottom of her handbag, she scooped out the remaining handful of junk and found a small piece of plastic among it. She threw the junk aside and inspected the item. It looked like the memory card from a digital camera, but it wasn't hers. Distractedly, she put the card in her pocket and decided to ask Eric about it when he got back.

))

Heavy with dread, Miriam opened the back door and clattered up the staircase to the roof. At least here she could pretend that she was still in the States, in a world that granted her fresh air, sunshine, and her own set of keys. To the east, a pair of stars sparkled blue on the horizon. She leaned against the wall and took a whiff of a night that was heavy with jasmine and the frankincense smoke rolling up from a neighbour's window. It was a comforting smell. She thought instantly of Sabria, her downstairs neighbour, and how much she enjoyed sitting with her in the smoke-filled room, drinking coffee and talking.

But as the minutes ticked by, the suffocating heat tightened its clamp around her. She thought again of the American compound – swimming pools sounded like paradise now.

Five more months.

She noticed that Eric had hung out his laundry – days ago, judging from the stiffness of the fabric and the fact that the sun had bleached the tops of his shirts. A thump on the other side of the roof made her turn. She saw the neighbour's roof-access door swing open and a girl's face peeked out.

'Sabria!' she said.

The girl grinned and came rushing over to embrace her. Miriam went forward, stumbling on a clothesline and cursing with a laugh. 'I'm so glad to see you!'

Sabria kissed her cheeks, squeezed her shoulders and frowned. 'You were gone too long! What am I going to do when you leave for good?'

'You'll have to come with me.'

'And leave my family? Are you kidding?' She grinned. Precisely how her family drove her crazy was one of their favourite topics of discussion. Sabria lived downstairs with her parents, six sisters and a profoundly devout older brother. She was the oldest of the girls, and much of the burden of housework and childrearing had fallen on her shoulders until she cast it off a few months ago when she took a job working in her aunt's beauty boutique. Her parents did not approve.

'We're just about to leave for my cousin's wedding,' Sabria said. 'Everyone's going. My parents already left, but I forced my cousin Abdullah to stay behind because I wanted to see you. I thought you'd be home earlier.'

'That's so sweet.' Miriam felt an irrational swelling of tears. 'We were held up at the airport. Don't hold up your plans on my account. I'll see you tomorrow.'

'Yes, but I wanted to let you know: I'm getting married next month.'

'*What?* To whom?'

'My cousin Omar.'

'Congratulations.' Miriam felt her throat constrict. 'Is he the one who lives in Riyadh?'

'Yes, the one I told you about.' Sabria glanced nervously at the clothesline.

'Are you happy about the wedding?'

'Yes, I am, it's just . . .' She shrugged. 'It's happening so fast.'

Miriam nodded. She took a dim view of how anxious Sabria's parents were to marry off their girls.

She heard a clatter in the kitchen below. 'Listen, Eric's home,' she said. 'Can you come down for a few minutes? He brought dinner, and I'm starving.'

'No, Abdullah's going to leave without me if I don't get down there.'

'Oh, right.' Miriam hugged her again. 'Come up when you get back.'

'I will.' As Sabria trotted back to the door, Miriam was reminded how young she was. Seventeen on the outside, and – most of the time, at least – twelve on the inside, with rare and beautiful flashes of maturity.

'Have a safe trip!' Miriam called out, and a muffled response came up from the stairwell. She smiled and grabbed the laundry tub. They didn't have a washing machine. She cleaned their clothes by hand, and although she complained about the constant housework, deep down she was grateful. It gave her something to do.

She hastily collected Eric's laundry – cursing at the clothes pegs, which had somehow ruined one of his white shirts – and then made her way downstairs.

The smell of hummus and schawarma wafted from the kitchen door. She dropped the tub on the counter and went straight to the table, peeling the tin foil from a take-away tray and dipping her finger in. She tore a slice of pita from a giant round and shoved it in her mouth.

'Errrk?' She swallowed. 'Honey, come eat!'

She heard no response. 'Eric?' A hard swallow. The fly zapper crackled like rounds from a machine gun and she jumped, dropping her bread on the floor. She stooped to retrieve it and took a deep breath. It was probably a lizard; they fried longer than mosquitoes.

She unwrapped a schawarma and sat down to eat, pleased that the meat was still hot. 'I'm eating without you!' She opened a water bottle and took a long drink.

She heard a noise echoing up the hallway, then the distinctive shuddering of the windows in the kitchen as the building's front door slammed shut. She set the sandwich on the table and went to the living room.

The front door was open.

She crossed the room and peeked out, but the hallway was dark.

'You left the door open!' She shut the door and headed back to the kitchen but paused to listen. No sound from the bathroom. She went to investigate and found the bathroom door open, the light off. She switched it on and tore back the shower curtain, exposing a meadow of mildew.

'Eric?' The narrow hallway muted her voice. In the bedroom, her suitcase lay undisturbed on the bed. The table lamp glowed, but a sudden confusion gave her the shivers. She switched on the overhead light. Checking behind the door, she almost laughed at herself: when was the last time Eric hid behind a door to surprise her – their honeymoon?

'Eric, are you here?'

No response. Heading back to the front door, she heard a car starting but decided that the engine was too loud to be theirs. It was probably Abdullah and Sabria leaving for the wedding. She went out the front door and into the men's sitting room, which overlooked the street. Except for the lamplight filtering in through the shutters, the room was dark. She fumbled for the lights, found a table lamp and switched it on. The bulb was ancient and covered in dust but it shed enough light for her to navigate around the coffee table, over the embroidered pillows and mouldy teacups. She peeked out the window. There was no one on the street.

Don't panic, she told herself, trying to believe that her anxiety was really about herself, her fears, *her* claustrophobia. She'd been this way before – edgy, even paranoid, like the time his car had broken down on the motorway and she thought he'd abandoned her for another woman. He'd come home in a taxi to find her sprawled on the sofa, weeping. Miriam Walker, PhD – hear her roar.

She went back to the kitchen and forced herself to fold his laundry. The schawarma blessed her with an immediate food coma that beat back her panic. He must have gone back to the restaurant for some reason. It was within walking distance. Perhaps he'd left his wallet there. His keys weren't on the table where he usually left them. He would have taken them to unlock the door – except that he'd forgotten to *shut* the door. She was going to tease him mercilessly when he got back.

Four hours later the anxiety returned. By then, she had tried calling his mobile a dozen times, but it went straight to voice mail, and the frustration of not being able to reach him was ratcheting up her panic. It was too late to call his friends. She was certain anyway that if he had gone to see them, he would have told her. She kept thinking back to their conversation in the car on the way home, analysing it for unusual behaviour, something that would make it obvious that he had run away. The longer she thought about it, the more her imagination began twisting his words, his expressions, even the meaning of his new blue shirt.

At one in the morning, she realised she was too exhausted to worry any more. She sat down on the sofa, where she eventually slept, eyes flitting open every once in a while to gaze at the unlocked, unopened door.

7

Every afternoon around a quarter to five the downtown streets died in the stifling air. Heat rose in waves from the oily pavement and hung, grey and putrid, in the diesel-choked sky. On a quiet side street, notable for the proliferation of dry goods stores that had collected there, jumbling atop one another like honeybees, only the distant sound of a flushing toilet indicated life behind the shuttered windows and closed shop doors. The street, long and narrow, tapered to an ignominious end, where a decaying, lime-green grocery shop came face to face with a public fountain. Right now, the shopfront was completely covered by a large iron grille. The metal bars were black, hot to the touch, and sticky with moisture. And behind them stood Nayir Sharqi, waiting to be set free.

'Asr prayers had rung from rooftop speakers twenty minutes ago, and like all good shopkeepers, this one had promptly pulled down his gates and locked them. Unlike most owners, however, he had then hurried off to the mosque, leaving Nayir in the darkness holding two tins of fava beans and a jar of coffee.

Normally, Nayir would have avoided such a predicament by being more attentive to the call to prayer, but 'asr had sneaked up on him today. And the shopkeeper had done what he needed to do, locking the shop at once in case the religious police should catch him doing business during prayer time. In case Nayir should be the sort of man who would leave without paying.

Nayir had used the time to do his own devotion, opening a bottle of Evian and performing his ablutions behind the cash register, where the carpet would soak up his run-off. Then he'd knelt on the hard stone floor right next to a low shelf of packaged tobacco and tried very urgently to turn his mind to prayer, but today his body was only going through the motions, while his mind, like a bat, flitted silently and swiftly through a dark cave of thought.

If there was one thing he'd learned in the past eight months, it was that it was no use trying to conquer his guilt. He had tested every strategy he could think of, but no matter how often he sought guidance from Allah, no matter how fully he felt his convictions, the guilt remained full and fierce.

Close the door, lower the veil, shut the mouth. His own thoughts about women echoed back to him. Wasn't that what *he* had been doing all these months? Shutting himself out? For a blinding second, his eight months of guilt crystallised in this brilliant revelation. His justifications for not calling her were flimsy excuses. His reasoning was reduced to nothing more than an outward show of religiosity, empty of meaning. Wasn't true Islam about showing love to others? About giving generously and fully, even when it meant giving the last of yourself? Wasn't true Islam about showing respect? And how was he respecting Katya by never explaining why he had let her drift away? By leaving her to guess? It had been an indecent thing to do.

But the argument disintegrated right before his eyes, because what would happen if every man took the liberty of 'showing love to others' every time he met a woman? What would happen if every man abandoned the dictates of courtesy and respect to a woman's family just because he could argue that Islam was about charity, and he needed to give love? That was about as stupid as you could get.

He finished the prayer and his mind returned to his

surroundings. A locked cage. A hard stone floor. He pushed himself up and, leaving money on the counter for the Evian, the beans and the coffee, went to the front of the shop and stood at the grille. Nothing moved on the street. He tried rattling the cage but there was no one to hear it. Ten minutes later the shopkeeper returned, looking pleased with himself as he unlocked the gate and lifted the grille with a screech. Nayir left without explanation.

It took him ten minutes to reach the police building. He was halfway down the block before he noticed that women were coming out of the side entrance of the building. He stopped, ducking into a nearby doorway, and peeked out. The women dispersed quickly, climbing into waiting cars, hustling down the street in pairs. The street was empty again.

He was moving closer when a final woman came out of the building. He froze, his stomach dropping all the way to his shoes as he recognised Katya's walk. Her burqa was down, and she was alone.

The time was now. He had to act, but he couldn't. Was it really her? His heart was racing and he felt dizzy. She turned to look down the street and when she saw him, she froze too. Her eyes locked on his face. He would have given anything to see behind her burqa now, just for a second so he could know what reaction had flashed across her face upon seeing him again after so many months. Her eyes betrayed only a flicker of surprise.

He went towards her unthinkingly. He noticed that she was clutching her handbag, but the rest of her seemed relaxed.

'I can't believe it,' she said when he was close enough. She sounded amused, but beneath it he detected a nervousness. 'I thought I'd never see you again.'

There was something cold in the words, as if she'd simply put him in a drawer and locked him away. He fumbled, fishing for any response but coming up with nothing.

'How are you, Nayir?'

'Good.' He had to clear his throat. 'I'm good.'

'You've lost weight.'

He nodded. An expectant silence went by.

'It's nice to see you again . . .' she said hesitantly, with something like a question mark at the end.

He felt like an idiot. 'I'm sorry—' He twitched. Her name had nearly slipped out. It didn't feel right to say it any more. 'I'm sorry. I came to ask you something.'

She kept her eyes locked on his, but they showed curiosity. She still wouldn't lift her burqa and he had an irrational, frightening urge to reach over and lift it himself. He tucked his hands into his pockets.

'It's actually about a friend,' he said. 'Who died.'

All the kindness in her eyes vanished. He felt his chest tighten.

'I see,' she said curtly.

The anger in her eyes was unmistakable now. He wanted to say anything to make it right again, but he was attempting to speak a language he didn't understand and with it came all of the humiliated fumbling of the undereducated. Never had he felt so utterly dumb.

He blurted out the first thing that came to mind: 'I'm only doing this for my uncle.'

It was clear that it had been the wrong thing to say. She seemed to be trembling beneath her cloak, some low vibration of rage. She took a breath and clutched her bag more tightly, and that's when he saw it. A ring. On her left hand.

He looked away but he couldn't find anywhere to rest his gaze. The ring was everywhere – a small diamond, an ornate gold band. He saw it on the pavement, the buildings, the cars. The silence between them dragged on so painfully that he had no choice but to fill it.

51

'You're engaged now?' he asked, trying for casual and failing miserably. When she didn't reply, he offered his congratulations.

Her mobile rang. She fumbled in her bag and answered it. 'Excuse me,' she said and turned away.

Nayir was lost in a desert memory. This often happened when something blew apart inside him. An overload of emotional currents sent him back to a world where his body was not the earth-ridden, lumbering form that crouched along the pavement beneath a blinding sun, but rather a kind of vessel for the expansiveness of the world. Typically, he felt this way only in the desert, where the vastness made him feel smaller than he actually was.

Omran, his favourite desert guide as a child, had bragged once that he could make the desert sing. He took Nayir a few kilometres outside the camp, to where the dunes lay in a rippling, spotless infinity. They climbed the highest dune, which was so steep that Omran had to rope himself to Nayir to keep the boy from falling and setting off an avalanche.

When they reached the top, they perched on a narrow swathe of sand that formed the upper rim of a magnificent crescent dune. Its great amphitheatre was the biggest he'd ever seen. It curved sharply down to a smooth little gully. No prints of any kind broke the wind-stroked surface.

'No matter what happens,' Omran said, 'you stay here. I'll need you to run and get help if I don't come back. All right?' Nayir nodded, and Omran bent closer. 'You're about to see magic, so be careful who you tell. You know the words of protection from the *djinn*?'

'Yes.'

'Good. This is our secret, okay?'

'Okay.'

Omran untied the rope that bound them together and in one startling movement, he leapt straight over the edge of the dune.

Nayir saw him suspended for an impossible moment, then he dropped twenty feet. His legs plunged into the sand with a super-natural *BOOM*.

The force of the sound knocked Nayir backwards. He landed on his rear and started sliding down the dune's lee side but scrabbled on to his stomach and crawled back to the crest.

Then he heard it, the sound of a small aeroplane flying towards him, only the note was wrong. In place of a roaring engine he heard a woman's ululation, which became an unearthly scream. There wasn't a Bedouin in the world who didn't have a certain respect for a wicked *djinn*, a *shaytin*. He saw the *djinni* swirling above him, made of smoke and hot metal, their great black mouths opening wider to spew bullets of sand and blistering fire. Six years old at the time, too young to believe in physics, Nayir began to cry.

On his belly he crawled to the edge of the dune and saw Omran still sliding down the ridge like a knife slicing into a large, soft cake. The wind kicked a wall of sand into Nayir's face. He tasted grit in his mouth, instinctively shut his eyes and spat. Then the sound changed. The shrieking stopped and he heard a groan. When the cloud of sand cleared, he saw Omran struggling at the bottom of the valley. He was on his knees, facing Nayir, but his arms were elbow-deep in the sand. He was struggling. It looked as if some creature under the surface was eating his forearms.

'Omran!' Nayir shouted, scrambling to his feet.

The ground gave way and Nayir found himself sliding, slipping and thoroughly falling down the dune, part avalanche, part wild, hawk-like plunge. And with the fall came a screeching noise. It rose from deep within the earth, where his legs were shearing through the sand. The vibrations shook him, travelling up his legs and torso, shuddering through his neck and face. There were so many *djinni* in the sound that he felt possessed by them. But these *djinni* were short, stunted versions of the former. At some moment in the fall, he realised that his body and the sand were the sources of the noise. That he was the *djinn*, afraid of himself.

For once, it wasn't his Uncle Samir who did the explaining. It was Omran, who was forced to do so when Nayir came back to Samir's tent shouting about the singing dunes. Omran sat at the table and, in his adult voice, said that the shear stress of a body sliding through the sand caused synchronous vibrations in the sand that produced high frequency sounds. The crescent shape of the dune acted as an amplifier. He gave a typical range of Hertz and even drew a sketch. All very scientific. Samir nodded, pleased to hear something from a man who knew his physics. Feeling deflated, Nayir stopped listening and went outside into the night.

Only when he'd reached the bottom of the dune did his ear finally recollect the mysterious sound he'd produced and cling to it giddily, repeating it in his mind as a child repeats Quran. The notes were somehow his, as surely as his cells held their essence of life. Occasionally in adulthood those sounds would flash through him, a haunted echo of his own groping in the world.

Watching Katya talk on her mobile, he wished he could explain what he was thinking. That not every fall is a senseless crash. That even in our most awkward moments there's a chord of transcendence. And that no amount of scientific explanation will suffice to reveal what a simple fall down a hill of sand will do. She was whispering into her phone, looking down the street. Only momentarily did she glance at him with what looked like a nostalgic twinge. Finally, she hung up.

'I'm sorry, Nayir,' she said.

She was letting him go. Or she was telling him to go. It was all the same thing. He knew he deserved it. But he also knew that he could not accept it. That he'd had enough of this particular suffering. That what had just happened was not a waking memory, but a kind of *istiqara* – an answer from Allah to the prayers he had been so fervently whispering these past eight months. The path he had chosen was not the right one, but now he would put it right, even if it meant going to her father, making a fool of himself by telling the truth, and proving his unworthiness to her entire family. Did it matter? Wasn't it only his own ego that needed crushing, his own pride that had kept him from declaring his intentions eight months ago, back when she had been so willing to hear them?

His thoughts had a hysterical edge to them now. He realised he was sweating profusely, and that his hands were wet.

'I've got a busy night,' she said, her head down.

Strangely, her persistent rejection brought his confidence back. 'So who's the very fortunate husband-to-be?'

She looked up. 'Oh! I'm not getting married,' she said, her voice confused. 'This is Othman's ring . . .' She trailed off.

The relief came so quickly that it hurt. So she was still wearing Othman's ring even though their engagement had ended months ago. 'Ah,' he managed. 'My mistake.' He gave her a pointed look. 'It was my mistake.' He saw a softening in her eyes. It amazed him that what began pouring urgently through his heart was an even more expansive desire than he'd realised, the urge to be with her no matter what. 'The case I came here to ask you about may not be a case at all.' A flicker of her eyes showed that he'd caught her attention. He explained about Qadhi's death. 'I was hoping you could tell me about the cause of death and put my uncle's mind to rest.'

She thought for a minute.

'I'll see what I can do.' It was spoken with the kind of brusque-ness that indicated an inner turmoil of her own. He found it easy not to take it personally. She glanced nervously up and down the street again, and he realised that she probably didn't want her escort Ahmad to see them together.

'Can I call you?' he asked, nearly laughing at the irony of the question.

'No,' she said. 'I'll call you.'

He felt the first stab of fear. She wasn't going to call him. She was going to do to him just what he'd done to her. And he would deserve it.

She read the concern in his eyes. 'I promise,' she said sternly. 'So you'd better have your mobile *on*.'

8

Once Nayir was out of sight, Katya let out her breath and scanned the street for Ayman's car. There was no sign of it, just a lone woman hurrying a young child down the pavement. *Perfect*, she thought. Her cousin was always late, and right now she needed time to think.

She could hardly believe that Nayir had just appeared on the pavement like some wayward *djinn* come to beg a wish. His face was so drawn! He had lost a lot of weight. She had never thought of him as fat, but seeing him now made her realise just how big he'd been. Guiltily, she remembered the pleasure of being around him back then. She used to feel so tiny in his presence, so encompassed, somehow. Now the wind from a passing truck might lift his scrawny body and blow him back to the mysterious, all-male desert, which is where he had existed in her dark imaginings for the past eight months.

And yet, there had been a look of pleasure on his face when she'd said she would call him, and she was utterly certain that it wasn't because he actually needed her assistance, but because it would mean that he could see her again, spend time with her like he used to—

And that was where her thoughts came to a screeching halt.

He had left her. First, he had ignored her. Then he'd gone with her to the funfair that day on what felt like their first real date, and had spent the whole time looking as if someone had asked him to swallow a pig. She had invited him to dinner with her father thinking that this, at least, might lend the 'legitimacy' to their liaison that he seemed so desperately to need, but he had gone out of his way to avoid it. She had tried to reach out to him – had left him several messages, but he never returned her phone calls. What exactly, she used to wonder, was so horrible about talking to a woman on the phone, a woman *you knew*? But she knew the answer: it wasn't proper for a good Muslim man to associate with a *na-mehram* woman. So perhaps he cared about her, but he cared about his religious prescriptions more. He had made his choice.

Which is why it was so ridiculous to feel delighted by his return. Was it too much to imagine that his weight loss, his sallow look, was a reflection of the pain he had caused himself in abandoning her?

A blue Mazda honked at her from the corner and she pulled herself together. Twice a week now Ahmad turned over his driving job to Katya's young cousin, Ayman, who had just moved to Jeddah from Beirut. When he'd come to the house that first night, she'd liked him immediately. He was fifteen, tall and bulky and not much to look at, but his humour had brought a new sense of life to the house.

Ayman drove slowly closer, pretending not to recognise her, staring at her covered face with a goofy imitation of studiousness. He pulled to a halt across the street and plucked a pair of binoculars from the seat, aiming them at Katya. She began to laugh.

Seemingly satisfied that he'd located the right woman, he tossed the binoculars in the back seat and pulled the Mazda close to the kerb.

He tumbled out of the driver's seat, his long, gangly arms swinging like those of an ape as he loped around the car. He opened the back door and hastened her inside with a monkey's *oook-ook*. He even paused to scratch his armpit and sniff his fingers, which caused her to bury her head in her hands.

'You are so shameful!' she cried. 'How can you do that in *public*?'

He cocked his head to say: *No speak human* and loped back to the driver's seat.

'Hello, monkey,' she said.

'At least I found you this time!' he said with a grin once she was seated comfortably in the back seat. His last attempt to pick her up had resulted in him approaching a strange woman on the street, who'd panicked when he'd said 'Hello, cousin', and tried to take her elbow. The woman had swatted him with her bag and started screaming. He tried to apologise but she whacked his face.

'How's the black eye?' she asked, peeking at him in the rear-view mirror.

'Much better,' he said, using a hand to raise his hair from his face. 'It's turning yellow.'

His elbow knocked the mirror out of alignment and he almost swerved off the road trying to adjust it. Katya had to shout to stop him hitting a parked car.

'Sorry,' he said sheepishly, and turned his attention to the road with a look of desperate concentration. 'I have a surprise for you.'

'You're going to get me home alive?'

'Your father and I roasted pigeons for dinner.'

'Mmmhh.' She tried to sound appreciative, even though pigeons had never been her favourite dish. 'That's very sweet.'

He cocked his head. 'I know.'

She had to laugh. It was hilarious to watch him at the wheel of the Mazda. Did cars come any smaller than this? Did men come any bigger? He was like an overgrown dog stuffed into a travel cage. If he'd had a tail, it would have been wagging.

Ever since Ayman had come to the house, her father had put him to work. It was Abu's opinion that a man was only as good as

59

the labour he could do, so in the past two months Ayman had done more than his share of the dishes, the floors, even once – to her acute embarrassment – the laundry.

It was never awkward sitting in his back seat. If Othman had been driving, or even Nayir, she would have hated it. But Ayman's irrepressible humour made it comfortable, even easy, to sit here. She felt like a queenly older sister.

'Your father said that if I get you home on time, he'll let me do your laundry again.'

She laughed. 'Stop it!' she said. 'Stop making me laugh. You are not doing my laundry ever again. Is that clear?'

'Yes, madam.' He sat up straight and clutched the wheel.

'And remember,' she said, 'when you approach a woman on the street, look at the *handbag*.' She held hers up, a red leather bag with a shiny silver buckle on each of the front pockets.

'I can never remember what yours looks like,' he said. She shook her head in exasperation.

Relaxing into the ride, her thoughts kept returning to Nayir. His scent had lodged in the back of her throat, a smell of cedar and sand. She hadn't known him long enough to fall in love with him properly – at least that's what she'd told herself when they'd stopped talking. But the truth was that in their final phone call, he'd broken her heart all over again, and so soon after her failed engagement to Othman. It was like watching a community die of the plague. She lost everyone but her father. Somehow losing Nayir hurt the worst, because he had been the one good thing she'd managed to salvage from the whole tragedy of Othman and his family, the thing she'd least expected to save.

When she'd started her new job, she'd been overjoyed – eager for the distraction and the independence. Thanks to a government initiative to get more women into the workplace, a number of positions had opened at the crime lab in the police headquarters downtown, and she had been hired. She was still holding her breath, unable to believe that she worked in a beautiful new building where she had her own lab. She'd spent the first few weeks fearing that she'd wake up one morning and find that it had all been a dream, but then she had spoken to Nayir on the phone that fateful day and realised the greater threat to her happiness. He hadn't congratulated her on the new job; his only concern had been whether she would be interacting with men or not. The censure in his voice had crushed her. The government could do what it liked to enable women, but if her father ever found out just how closely she was working with men, his reaction would be just like Nayir's. If both men had their way, she probably wouldn't be working at all.

Seeing Nayir had stirred up a dozen uncomfortable emotions. She'd been secretly happy, then traumatised by the fact that he'd only come on business, then nearly angry enough to lash out at him when she realised that he wasn't even going to mention their last conversation or make the slightest suggestion of apology. Instead, though, she'd found herself agreeing to help him because she couldn't imagine saying no, even to hurt him, and certainly not after all the pain she'd gone through at having lost him in the first place. But her disappointment and hurt were still right there, and coming back stronger every minute, especially when she thought about just how remote Nayir could be, how rigid in his beliefs. She glanced at Ayman, his goofy, smiling face looking back at her in the rear-view mirror, and resolved never to let herself get hurt like that again.

9

In the company of the crinkled take-away trays, Miriam sat at the kitchen table nursing a cup of lukewarm tea and staring at her mobile. There was still no word from Eric, and he wasn't answering his phone. Although the muezzin hadn't called noon prayer, she'd spoken to the office twice already, and both times the secretary had harped: *He is not in the office yet. Would you like to leave a message?*

What could she say: 'Tell him I'm waiting?' So what else was new? As humiliating as it was, she finally broke down and admitted to the receptionist that Eric was gone. Actually, she admitted that 'Abdullah' was gone because that's what they called him. 'Eric', it turned out, was a slang term for 'penis' in Arabic, so his boss had asked him to come up with a suitable alternative, and he'd chosen Abdullah. In Arabic, it meant 'slave of Allah', which troubled Miriam when she bothered to think about it.

The receptionist made nervous noises, the guttural equivalent of a plea to leave him out of her marital troubles, until she begged him to find Abdullah's address book and give her all the numbers in it. She already had his partner's number, but that was only because she knew Jacob's wife, Patty, who'd promised to have her over for tea but who never seemed to have the time.

'I'm afraid I can't get into his office,' the receptionist said.

Miriam fumbled. *Then find someone who can*, she wanted to say. She had never been to Eric's office, so she had no idea what it was like. Did he have a separate address book or only his Blackberry? He must have a computer somewhere, but maybe there was a password – and there was no way he would have given it to a receptionist. Or anyone else, for that matter. He was doggedly private.

'Okay, thanks,' Miriam said. 'Just let me know if he shows up.'

A short while later she called Jacob and acquired a single piece of data, not wonderfully interesting: Jacob had seen him the day before. They'd had coffee together, and everything had seemed normal. Eric hadn't mentioned that he was picking Miriam up that evening from the airport.

Once she realised that Jacob was being his usual taciturn self, Miriam agreed to speak with Patty, who had stood beside her husband for the whole conversation, inserting her indiscreet comments: *Eric's gone? Well, where on earth would he go?* and *Do you think he's been arrested?*

Patty didn't say hello, she simply gasped. 'Miriam, do you think he's run away?'

'No. What? He wouldn't do that.'

'I knew a nurse from Australia whose husband left her. He disappeared just like that.' Patty snapped her fingers like a gunshot. 'Turns out he was having an affair with his *maid*. Some girl from the Philippines.'

Miriam swallowed her anger. 'We don't have a maid.'

'It doesn't have to be a *maid*, honey.'

'I think something happened. An accident maybe. He could be—' She stopped, took a long breath. It was no good feeding her own paranoia.

'Have you called the police?' Patty asked.

'Yes. They said I had to wait two days before I could file a missing persons report. At least I think that's what they said. The guy had a pretty heavy accent.'

'What about the hospitals?'

63

'No,' Miriam admitted.

'Then call the consulate,' Patty said. 'You *have* to report this.'

Miriam didn't want to tell her about the last time he'd disappeared. 'Just call me if you hear anything, okay?'

'Sure but—'

Miriam hung up. She could handle a hundred disappointing phone calls but she couldn't handle her anxious mind, which attached itself to a problem the way something vicious in a neighbour's yard might. Visions of Eric came quickly to mind: his corpse in a sewer, bloated and drowned. An eye torn from a socket. Spurts of blood from a sucking chest wound.

She stood up and went to the pantry. It was nearly empty, but stacking the few condiments would help her relax. She tried not to think about the story Sabria's sister had told her. A Canadian man who was in Jeddah with his wife had fallen in love with a young Bedouin girl. They'd had a fling. Soon after, the girl had turned herself into the police – begging for protection. She believed that her brothers had discovered that she'd had sex before marriage and they intended to kill her. The police, believing it possible, had offered her protection and also brought the Canadian man into the station. Sure enough, that afternoon, three of the girl's brothers had shown up at the station door, threatening to kill her. The police had had to spirit the illicit lovers out of the country.

Miriam couldn't be sure how much of the story was hyperbole, but Sabria's sister had been firm on one point: it wasn't that strange for Bedouin families to react with outrage upon discovering such a tryst. Young girls had been killed before, and sometimes their lovers with them . . .

Stop, Miriam told herself. There was no reason to jump to worst-case scenarios. She remembered a story Patty had told her about an American guy who lived on the compound. His wife, who was still in the United States, had mailed him a care package containing three DVDs of porn. The censors who opened mail in Saudi had discovered the porn and had had the poor American guy arrested. He'd had to explain that his wife didn't understand Saudi culture. The police had accepted the explanation but forced the American to break the DVDs right there at the station. Apparently, they didn't want to get sued for destroying personal property. Of course, that hadn't happened to Eric, but she needed a reminder that in Jeddah, people could be arrested for the strangest reasons.

And of course, Eric had 'disappeared' before. One of his associates at work had decided to take a spontaneous trip to the desert. Eric had gone along, thinking it would only be for the day, and then had discovered that his host meant to stay for the weekend. He'd been too far out of mobile phone range to call her and let her know where he was.

Another evening, the religious police had hauled him into one of their makeshift prisons – in this case, the back room of a local mosque – to give the dumb foreigner a lesson in proper conduct. Apparently, he hadn't been wearing long sleeves, and his impatience had won him a few bruises from a bamboo cane. But that time, he had only been held for a few hours. He'd come home late that night.

Miriam took another calming breath and shut the pantry door. It was possible that the God Squad had arrested him for something. Perhaps his walk was too jaunty to qualify as pious. He would come home tomorrow, maybe bruised but unforthcoming as ever. She'd have to pry the story out of him but he'd only reassure her that everything was fine and that, yes, the religious police could be overzealous but they were just doing their jobs. The police in America pulled foreigners over all the time, didn't they? It was just something they had to put up with here, respecting other cultures, blah blah blah. The scenario was so real that it almost had to be true. At least it was the sort of explanation that Eric would devise if she had disappeared.

65

Then again, if she disappeared, Eric could probably *do* something about it.

She glanced at the phone sitting on the table. The truth was, she had thought of calling the consulate all morning, but she was afraid of making a fool of herself.

She began walking through the house, pacing really, wondering if she was ready to face the world and go to the corner shop. She got distracted by the bathroom sink, which was filthy. While cleaning it, darker possibilities began to loom in her mind. The secret police also hauled people into jails, except that the locations of these bunkers were known only to insiders and a handful of the Saudi bigwigs. The foreigners who vanished didn't reappear for months, sometimes years. They languished like women, waiting for lawyers, for trials that never came. If she went to the consulate, they'd probably zip her out of the country faster than anyone could say 'indecent'. Then Eric would be stuck in an underground bunker, waiting for a court date that would never be set . . .

Stop, she told herself. *Jesus! Think of something else.*

She went back into the kitchen. A sickly sweet smell was emanating from the broken sink disposal, so she went to work, clearing out the cabinet beneath the sink, unscrewing the trap with the torch dangling from her mouth, feeling frustrated and competent all at once. When the trap finally came down, a few weeks' worth of gunk spilled on to her hands. Tea leaves. As far as she knew, Eric had never so much as touched a cup of tea in his life before coming here, but now he spent all of his free time in the sitting room drinking tea with his friends. Not with Jacob or the other Americans he worked with. Eric hung out with Arab men who were friendly enough but who would have considered it rude to strike up a conversation with a woman. They thought it was strange that she didn't know how to make tea, that Eric boiled it himself, because he wanted to master the art of making tea Saudi-style. She even took a picture one night of Eric with a teacup in his hand. When she'd teased him about it, he'd shrugged sheepishly and said: 'It's what the guys prefer to drink.'

She watched the ease with which he adopted these new rules of manliness. Kissing other men on the cheek. Hugging. Sitting around gossiping and laughing for hours like teenage girls who shut down the moment a parent walks into the room. At first she reacted to these changes with tenderness and gratitude, even if she did think they were a little weird. It seemed that the girlish transformation applied some balm to the broken man who had come home from Iraq caged in a crushing hyper-masculinity. And for him there seemed to be something deeper still – was it good old-fashioned Protestant guilt? *I killed Muslims, now I'm redeeming myself*? Whatever the reason, despite his occasional agreement that it wasn't quite the ideal place for a woman to live, Eric had fallen hard for Saudi Arabia.

She remembered the conversation they'd had on the porch at their house in Fayetteville when he'd signed the contract for his job here. He'd popped a bottle of champagne, spilling it all over the love-seat swing, and she'd teased him about his excitement. 'Are you sure there's not another reason you're wanting to go there so badly? Maybe a female reason?'

He'd grinned devilishly and kissed her neck. 'I love you, Miriam,' he whispered in her ear. 'And you have to know that no matter what happens, you'll always be wife number one.'

She'd smacked his arm, and he'd burst out laughing. She couldn't help laughing herself. Then he'd wrapped her in his arms. 'That won't ever happen,' he'd whispered, serious now.

Yeah, yeah. She washed the tea leaves from her hands and realised belatedly that it wasn't a joke. She'd feared that some exotic beauty would snatch him away, but the real secret lover was the city itself, the countryside, the desert, and the sense of companionship he'd found among the men here. Finding another woman in Jeddah might be a natural extension of . . .

She shut the thought down immediately. It was good to see Eric so excited about a place. And his new-found companionship wasn't so different from the kind of closeness he'd always felt with his army buddies back home. Sure, their marriage wasn't doing so well, but were they doing so poorly that he would run away?

Maybe she shouldn't have been gone for so long. For weeks she had gone back and forth between thinking it was a good idea to give Eric a break, and thinking that her leaving would give him a convenient opportunity to forget about her. She had decided to trust him. And she had needed the time away.

But what if, in the month she'd been gone, Eric had grown even more addicted to this place? Perhaps even come to visualise a future here without her? They both knew she would never fit in here. She had tried very hard, for the first few months, not to complain too much. Then abruptly it had all come spilling out.

The disposal gave a pathetic whirr. She heard a crack, something shot out of the trap, and she knew without bending over that it was *really* broken. Picking up the wrench, she knelt down again to see what she could do.

10

Katya tried to avoid looking at the bloated, red and blistered skin of the woman's hands and face. She kept her eyes on the clean white walls of the new autopsy room, on the metal sinks against the wall and the locked grey cabinets where the examiner stored his textbooks.

They still hadn't identified the woman, but the police who'd brought her in had dubbed her 'Eve'. Katya alternately wondered if she would have to sit through the entire autopsy, and – if she did survive it – whether she'd ever be able to eat meat again.

It was the second time Adara had invited her into the autopsy room. The first time Katya had become sick almost immediately. She wasn't used to the sight of real corpses; she dealt with samples on slide trays, hairs and fibres, and occasionally pictures of death. Now she was being given a second chance. She didn't have to watch the full autopsy. Adara had already done it. But there were things she wanted Katya to see for herself. And the circumstances were convenient: her boss and the other men in the examiner's office had gone out for their lunches. Zainab, unofficial boss of the women's laboratory, was home tending to a sick child. The body was on the table—

Ocean fish had eaten away the woman's eyes and most of her cheeks and lips, exposing the tissue and bone beneath. Now only the forehead and the hairline edges of the face showed where she'd been burned. Where the skin remained, there were traces of blood.

Katya was already feeling light-headed. 'Why is there blood on her face?' she asked, desperate to stay focused. 'Shouldn't it have washed away in the water?'

'Perhaps,' Adara said. 'Corpses usually float face-down in the water, which causes some blood congestion in the head. It's seepage. It had to have happened post-mortem.'

It was Adara who had first drawn back the sheet and touched the naked body, taking hold of the woman's forearm and turning it gently. Eve's hands were also burned so badly that it looked as if there was no chance of fingerprints. The wounds extended up her arms in splotches.

'Let's take a few fibre samples from this,' Adara said, pointing to a spot on the lower left arm.

Katya pulled a few fibres from the skin and slipped them into a jar. She was having trouble controlling her shaking hands. She tried desperately not to look at the burns, but when she shifted her gaze, her eyes fell on the large, black autopsy scars on Eve's chest, and she felt a wave of nausea.

'There are a couple of things I'd like you to notice. First, the slight bruising on the upper right arm. It's circular. Pre-mortem.' Adara moved around to the left arm, pointing out more bruises of similar type.

Katya had to look away to collect herself.

'Katya.' Adara locked her gaze. 'Why did you agree to come here?'

'Well, you asked me and I—' She stopped short, aware suddenly that Adara wanted – or perhaps needed – the truth. 'I wanted to come.' Seeing that Adara wasn't going to interrupt, she forced herself on. 'I want to do more. I'm sick of just sitting in the lab and trying to imagine what happened to all the dead. We only get little bits of information, you know.'

'I know, I used to be a lab technician too.'

This surprised Katya; she had somehow imagined that Adara

had emerged fully formed from the womb of medical school. 'How did you come to be an examiner?'

'They needed a woman to handle some of the more sensitive matters for certain female victims.' She motioned gracefully down to the body but didn't let her eyes follow the gesture. 'They told me it was for the victims whose families requested it. The people who didn't want a strange man touching their beloved daughters or wives. But the truth is that I get to handle the cases that the male examiners don't want to bother with. Housemaids, mostly.' She looked down at the corpse now. 'I'm not saying she's a housemaid. But on the important cases there's always a male examiner standing by. They don't trust us to do our jobs, and that's the problem. One little mistake on my part justifies all of their biases against me. The good news is that the pressure has turned me into the best examiner in the building.' She said this proudly, without a trace of shame, and Katya admired her fiercely for it.

'I'm not sure I'd want to trade jobs with you,' Katya said, looking down at the victim's bruised arm and thinking about the pressure Adara was under.

'I like my job,' Adara said. 'I was placed here by Allah, but staying here has been a constant jihad. You know what the Prophet, peace be upon him, said: *The rights of women are sacred. See that women maintain the rights granted to them.*'

Katya nodded respectfully. Adara's face was firm and determined, clean of all make-up, and never hidden behind a burqa. She wore no jewellery. She was pregnant more often than not, but she had never grumbled about her long hours at work – not at three months when she couldn't eat, nor at seven when her ankles looked like pears. Even in her gestures, nothing spoke of complaint. Her practical walk, her efficient movements from one part of a room to another revealed the solid determination of a lone shrub in the desert. Katya felt like an untested schoolgirl.

71

'I can't sit still any more,' Katya said with a sudden impatience. 'I can't look at these people's lives through tissue samples and biopsies. I want to be *out*. I want to know who they knew. Where they lived. Where they died. I want to be an investigator.'

Adara regarded Katya in the same way her mother used to when she was forced to admit that the reason for Katya's refusal to marry was that the prospective groom was in fact a donkey.

'Then you will be,' Adara said. 'If you keep at it.' She returned her gaze to the corpse.

'What do you think about the bruises?' Katya asked. 'Abuse?'

'I've seen housemaids with similar bruises on the upper arms. That's where people grab them and jerk them around. However, these don't look like grab marks, they're more like wounds. I would guess that these came from fighting her attacker. They're still very light-coloured. They must have been made right around the time she died.

'Back to the face and hands,' Adara said. 'These are the kinds of burns you see with hot oils. Maybe acids. It wasn't from fire.'

'Kitchen oils maybe?' Katya was surprised by the calm in her voice. She glanced at Adara, who was looking bleak. 'Can I get a skin sample?'

'Yes, I'll do it.' While Adara removed a portion of the burned skin, Katya studied Eve's legs. There were a series of cuts on the thighs. There was no pattern in the placement of the wounds. It didn't look as if they'd been made by a fish; the cuts were too clean.

'Do you think a knife made these wounds?' Katya asked.

'Yes,' Adara replied. 'I've already checked the back of the legs, and there are no marks there, only on the front and just on the side here. I did look at her clothing and saw that they had cut through her jeans.' She pointed to a particularly large wound on Eve's left thigh. 'Anyway, whoever did this was standing in front of her. She didn't turn her back to him.'

Going to the wall, Adara switched on the display lights, revealing X-rays of Eve's legs. Adara pointed to her right leg. 'This is an older wound. A fractured tibia, probably half a year old.'

'They may be able to search hospital records to identify her then?' Katya suggested.

'Yes, and good luck with that!' Adara gave an empty smile. 'You can try, but I don't think you'll find anything. This injury didn't heal properly, so I'm guessing she never made it to a decent doctor.'

'What about this large bruise on her hip?' Katya asked. The bruise was pale, large and splotchy, beginning at the waistline and extending down to the top of the thigh.

Adara returned to the table. 'I would say she fell right before she died. Another injury from the attack. I think you should focus on the tibia. They'll want to know what made that fracture.'

They. The real investigators.

'Was she raped?' Katya asked, afraid to hear the answer.

'No,' Adara said with kindness in her voice. Grimly exposed in the fluorescent light, the body looked like a wax doll wearing bright red mittens. Katya experienced none of the weird sense of imminent awakening-of-the-dead she'd felt when gazing down at Nouf's body. Now she was afraid that the person who did this would walk into the room and do it again.

'How did she die?'

'Well, this is where it gets tricky. First of all, her neck was broken.' Adara motioned to the X-rays. 'Actually, she was burned first, stabbed, and beaten. Then she was thrown in the water. But it's going to be difficult to determine *when* her neck was broken. It's a very clean break. If it happened while she was still alive, she would have stopped breathing and died almost immediately. It could also have happened as a passive, post-mortem injury while she was in the water. She could have knocked into a piece of debris. Also, her headscarf was wrapped around her neck when

73

they found her, but it wasn't tight enough to choke her and there were no loose ends that could have become caught on something and broken her neck that way.'

'Can't you tell if she was dead when she entered the water?'

Adara gave a wry smile. 'I'm sure you know from your own work that things are never as easy as they might seem on TV shows. Here's the problem: I found traces of foam in her lungs, which is characteristic of drowning. If she was alive when she entered the water, she would have inhaled and swallowed a good quantity of water. This produces a white froth in the airways. I did find that, but not a lot. If she had a lot of sea water in her stomach, I would feel more convinced that she drowned, but again there was only a little. The truth is, this foam in the lungs, or what we call pulmonary oedema, can just as easily indicate other causes of death: a drug overdose, heart failure, or head injury. I've ruled out heart failure, but we're still waiting on blood tests for drug overdose. Given the contusions on the back of her head and the fact that her neck was broken, head injury is a distinct possibility.'

'Essentially, you think that the killer threw her body into the sea after she died?'

'It's not as clear-cut as I'd like it to be, but yes, I'm going to write in the report that she didn't drown. My primary reason for this, though, is the presence of all the other injuries. I will say there's a strong likelihood that her neck was broken after the injuries but before she was dumped into the sea.'

It took all of Katya's will to avoid imagining what the last hours of Eve's life must have been like.

'Can you establish a time of death?'

'Not precisely, but it's been a few days at least. It takes a little less than a week for a corpse to rise to the surface, given the temperature of the sea water. It could be more like five or six days. I'm sorry, I know that's not a good answer, but in a case like this, where the cause of death isn't totally clear, it's going to be up to the investigators to figure out the circumstances.'

'And no identification was found with the body?' she asked.

'Right. And obviously fingerprints are out of the question. But I have contacted a woman who specialises in facial reconstruction, based on these clever skeletal moulds she does. She's Syrian; she said she'll come in this afternoon. We may be able to get some idea of what the victim looked like.'

They both looked down at the face, a mass of unidentifiable flesh. Katya quickly looked away. She had meant to congratulate Adara on her new baby boy, but she felt it would cast a pall over the child to mention him here, to send his mother home with the memories of this body mixed with thoughts of her newborn.

'They've obliterated her identity,' Adara said. 'I'm guessing that her face was burned, too.'

DNA testing? If the killer had considered that, he would have known that there was no database against which they could compare this woman's identity. But he probably hadn't considered it at all. Given all of the injuries, it was more likely that the violence had been done in a fit of rage. Katya was determined to find the victim's identity anyway, although she had the sinking feeling that to the state, Eve would be as anonymous in death as she was in life.

11

Katya stood in the hallway outside the downstairs forensics lab and caught Majdi's eye. He smiled at her and waved her inside, but he was on the telephone and she didn't want to interrupt, so she waited. A man walked past her. Her burqa was up, her face exposed, but the man pointedly avoided looking at her face. *All the better,* she thought. Her previous boss had taught her not to wear her burqa unless she absolutely had to, so Katya kept it resting on the top of her head, ready to drape down when the next pious bureaucrat chastised her with sharp words or a withering look.

'Do you think you are so ugly,' the last one had said, 'that no man will find your face appealing? Is that why you expose it?'

No, she wanted to retort, *I just mistakenly thought that when it came to sexuality, you had some self-control.* But that had been at her last job. Since coming to this one, no one had bothered her.

There were three other cases on her desk right now – armed robberies and a suicide – and she knew she ought to be working on those, but the image of Eve's body had not left her mind. She watched Majdi through the glass. *Please, please,* she thought, *let this be one of his cases.* She could always rely on him to bring her into an important case, but until now, nothing had seemed *this* important.

Majdi was dressed in his usual jeans and wrinkled T-shirt. His sister must have cut his hair again, because the tight curls had been shorn to a thin layer that rested on his scalp like baby hairs, and the bushy goatee had been trimmed to a neat V. Even while on the phone, he buzzed happily between his workstations, completely at home. She would have loved to be his lab mate – his jittery, coffee-fuelled, boyish excitement was a nice contrast to her organised and thoughtful style. But she was a woman, so she had her own lab. How anyone could think he would be a danger to her chastity, she would never know.

'Katya!' he said when he got off the phone. 'Good afternoon.'

'Hello, Majdi.' She went inside. The lab was about the same size as her own upstairs, and although the machines here were newer, there were no windows and the overhead lighting gave the place a morgue-like feel. It was a good thing that Majdi wasn't one to care. There was a smudge on his glasses that looked like fingerprint powder. He noticed her eyeing it and took his glasses off to wash them.

'Were you working on that new case this morning?' Katya asked.

'Yeah,' he said, 'and I was looking for you.' He turned from the sink, his face beaming. Majdi tended to oscillate between two states: the first was an irrepressible, giddy enthusiasm, and the second a state of intense, almost painful concentration the likes of which she had only ever seen in children.

'I was in the autopsy room,' she said.

He spun away from the sink and fumbled to put his glasses back on. 'Did you see the body?'

'Yes.'

'Oh.' His exhalation said: *Wow*. She felt the urge to tease him; it would have been so easy. *You know, Majdi, women do autopsies, too*. And he would blush to his collar and fumble to explain his reaction. But she held the impulse in check. He went to the desk, picked up a folder and handed it to her. 'This is what we've got on the Eve case. It's not much. Osama doesn't think it's a housemaid.' He took an evidence bag from the table and held it out to her. 'Maybe you'd like to take a look at the *hijaab*?'

She nodded, trying not to seem too eager. The bag contained a black cloak and headscarf, and probably a burqa. 'I'd be happy to do it,' she said, smiling. Majdi relaxed somewhat, but she could see that he was still surprised that she'd witnessed an autopsy.

'So this is Inspector Ibrahim's case?' she asked.

'Yeah. And you can call him Osama. He hates it when we say "Inspector Ibrahim". Anyway, it's a good thing it's his case. Al-Khoury hates cases involving women ever since his wife died.' What he left unspoken, but what Katya already knew, was that the other two investigators – she couldn't remember their names – had reputations as bullies who arrested anyone who was associated with the crime, even the victim's families and friends, whether there was evidence for it or not. She always felt sorry for the innocent family members who spent time in jail while grieving the loss of a loved one, even if – more often than not – it was one of those family members who committed the crime. Osama was the only one who seemed to respect his witnesses and suspects. At least he didn't arrest them half as often as the other cops, and when he did, he made sure they were well taken care of.

'I'll get to work,' Katya said, taking the bag and leaving.

☽

Katya opened the cabinet that held the files for the department's most recent cases. Zainab hadn't bothered to alphabetise them yet. Kneeling on the floor, Katya read each of the names. She hadn't seen any of the bodies, but the clarity that lingers from speculative horror had rendered the details from each case vivid in her mind. *Roderigo, Thelma.* A skin sample. Shattered iris. Foreign blood beneath her nails. *Alvarez, Najwa.* A dismembered thumb. Fingerprints on a mobile phone. A *man's* mobile phone. And more sexually transmitted diseases than any person she'd ever seen. Of the twenty-two cases lined up in the drawer already this summer, nineteen were women. Twelve had been housemaids. It didn't matter how they died, they were represented here out of all proportion to their population in the real world.

Eve could easily have been a Saudi housewife, so why did she appear so clearly in Katya's mind as a servant?

Katya didn't believe in intuition. She believed what her father said: that the senses absorbed hundreds of thousands of bits of information, very few of which ever made it to the conscious mind. And when the unconscious mind did the thinking for you, things could sometimes go awry.

She went back to the table where Eve's cloak was laid out. Katya had already determined that there was a rip in the pelvic area closely matching the bruising pattern on Eve's hip. It looked as if the cloak had been caught on something; perhaps the killer had dragged the body.

This time, Katya looked at the label. *India Fabric*. No designer. Something you'd buy for 25 riyals at the clothing souq. The lower hem was pale and torn in places, perhaps the natural consequence of wearing an ill-fitting cloak. The fabric was worn around the cuffed wrists, which had no press studs or buttons, and which looked a little shrunken from washing. The wear was undoubtedly from Eve pushing her hands through the cuffs every time she left the house. The wrists were so worn, compared to the moderate wear and tear on the elbows and collar (which did have press studs), that she might have put the cloak on every day. For what – six months? Why not once a week for six years? No, Katya thought, in six years, the cloak would have faded much more than it had. She had owned plenty of cheap cloaks in her time, and her experience was telling her that this cloak had been worn frequently for under a year. Any longer than that and the colour would be faded, the seams coming apart.

Who wears a cloak every day? Rich women went out whenever they liked, but their worn cloaks were quickly replaced by new ones. A working woman went out, someone like Katya, but not someone with a professional job where a cloak like this would be an embarrassment. A factory worker? A grocery store employee, someone hidden in the back rooms, stocking the shelves only when the store was closed? A single mother with no family might have to go out every day to walk her children to school or do the shopping. For that matter, a married woman would go out, if her husband was too busy to take her. But an abused housemaid? She would probably not be allowed to leave the house. She would be isolated, locked in her room at night, or even during the day when she wasn't needed.

Katya bent over the cloak again, running gloved fingers slowly over every inch of the fabric as if they were an instrument waiting to register a seismic event. Eventually, she took off her gloves and began to feel with her fingertips. It was the uniformity of texture that finally struck her. There, around the knee, the fabric was smooth.

She moved her fingers to the right, shutting her eyes, feeling for irregularities. Slowly, her touch encountered a softer spot. She wanted to open her eyes to check if this was true, but she squeezed them shut and kept feeling until the worn area became an imperfect circle with a definite boundary enclosing an area the shape of a knee. Bent for what? Who prayed on one knee?

Katya opened her eyes and held the cloak to the light. It was difficult to see at first, but there it was, a spot where the fabric was slightly thinner. But only on one side.

She switched tables, focusing now on the clothing. Eve's jeans, which had been laid out on the table, had dried stiffly. Katya studied the knees. Again, it looked as if the left knee was slightly more worn than the right.

She went to the phone and called Adara.

'The Eve case,' she said. 'Were there calluses on the left knee?'

Adara put the phone down with a clunk. Katya heard her walk across the room, heard the hiss as the freezer door opened, the metal screech of a table being pulled from its frozen nest. Adara came back to the phone. 'It's hard to say,' she said. 'Neither knee is particularly callused.'

Katya was disappointed, but it didn't mean anything. The robe and jeans could have protected the knee from developing a callus.

Eve had an old wound in her lower right leg, but that wouldn't have caused her to pray on one knee. The wounded usually prayed in a chair. But what if she did try to pray on one knee, desperate to show some sign of her subservience to Allah? If she were that desperate, she might have bitten back the pain in her right leg and just gone ahead and prayed on both knees.

'The wound in her lower right leg,' Katya said. 'Would that have prevented her from kneeling on it?'

Adara thought for a moment. 'It might have caused her some soreness, but I don't think it would have made her immobile.'

'All right. Thanks.'

'By the way, Katya, the Syrian woman I told you about is here. She's working on the facial sketch now. I'll have her bring up the picture when she's done.'

Katya was surprised. 'You're not sending it to Majdi?'

'I thought you'd like to see it first. Whenever you're done with it, just give it to Zainab or Majdi.'

Katya smiled. 'Thanks, Adara.'

She went back to the tables, her mind abuzz. So when Eve left the house, she didn't go to the mosque, or she would have worn down both knees. Katya herself had never felt entirely comfortable in a mosque. It was a formal place for prayer. Her own spiritual comforts belonged to the back porch of the house, a room enclosed by shutters and cool shade where she and her mother had always done evening prayers before dinner.

But what reason would a woman have for getting on one knee when she left the house? It was possible, of course, that she hadn't left the house. That she lived in a household where she was

81

required to wear a cloak so that she could serve a room full of strange men. Bring them dinners. Kneel before them to set a coffee service on a low table. But why not bend over or squat? Getting down on one knee raised the frightening possibility of stretching the cloak in such a way that the other leg was exposed.

Finally, Katya turned to Eve's burqa and headscarf. The scarf was plain black polyester, the kind most women wore. There was no label, but one side of the fabric was lighter than the other, suggesting that it had been exposed to the sun on a regular basis. The scarf hadn't been checked for fibres yet, so Katya went over it with a magnifying glass. When they had found Eve's body, the scarf had been scrunched up and wrapped around her neck like a cord, so it was possible that there were still foreign fibres in the fabric that hadn't been loosened by her long stay in the sea. Katya found a long black hair on the inside of the scarf. It probably belonged to Eve. In the same spot, she found two shorter, paler hairs. She quickly slid them into a baggie and labelled them. They were blond. Male hairs, she guessed. This was interesting. Where would Eve encounter a blond? Where would anyone encounter a blond? And why were the hairs on the inside of the scarf?

She nearly picked up the phone to call Zainab, but she knew that her boss would not be thrilled, no matter how good the news. Zainab was all business, all the time. Her first question would be: *Did you finish looking at EVERYTHING?*

Reluctantly, Katya went to the last item of clothing: the burqa. It was just like any other face covering, a plain black rectangle of fabric with Velcro to fasten it at the back of the head and a slit for the eyes. She scanned it for hairs and found none. Two pale beige patches on the inside looked like make-up stains. Eve's face powder might have rubbed off on the fabric. Katya decided to take a sample of the stain, to double-check that it was make-up. Taking a pair of scissors, she was about to cut a small square at the edge of the stain when something in her revolted against the idea of damaging the burqa. She picked up a swab instead. Suddenly, her mobile chimed. She looked at her handbag.

Forcing herself to stay on task, she scraped some of the make-up from the fabric on to a microscope glass. Her mobile chimed again.

Katya set the burqa on the table and went to her bag. There were two Bluetooth messages, both the same. When she opened them, a picture appeared. It showed a woman's face, completely veiled except for a pair of smiling black eyes. Beneath the picture was the caption: *Smile, you're on camera!*

Katya snorted in disgust. *Even here*, she thought, *in my office*. The lab's windows were too high to see out of, but she was certain that if she climbed on a chair, she would see a group of young girls on the pavement below, making ridiculously slow progress down the street, hands working phones beneath their cloaks. One of them would be sending this message.

It wasn't the first time she'd been Bluetoothed by passing strangers. It was the preferred method of communication between flirtatious teens on the street – and sometimes the only way for a man to get a woman's attention. There was nothing like a jangling mobile to make a girl stop what she was doing and look around, even raise her burqa if she was wearing one. For Katya it was an embarrassment. Sometimes the messages came so frequently in public that she had to turn her phone off. But no one had ever sent a picture of themselves in a burqa before. What a stupid idea! She tossed the phone in her handbag and went back to the burqa.

The minute she picked the burqa back up, her phone chimed again. At the very same moment, her fingers encountered something stiff. She looked down at the burqa, not sure she could believe it.

Had the Bluetooth message come from *this*?

She quickly laid the fabric flat and picked up the magnifying glass, feeling the edges. Then she spotted it. A small silver wire woven into the side seam. The wire led to a tiny black metallic patch at the lower corner of the burqa. She touched the patch gently with a finger, and on cue, her phone chimed.

She dropped the burqa, gaping in astonishment. She grabbed the phone from her bag. There were two more messages, both the same as the first ones.

This time she couldn't stop herself from picking up the phone to call Zainab. A Bluetooth burqa! She'd read about them in fashion magazines but thought they were only for the catwalks. Who, after all, would be ridiculous enough to wear a burqa for modesty while Bluetoothing her picture to every stranger she passed? Ah, but not this one. Eve had only sent a picture of her covered face. Katya had to laugh at the mockery of it.

She touched the burqa again. The fabric was nothing fancy, but maybe that was the point. No one would ever guess that this little piece of sartorial modesty could transmit a flirtatious message to any passer-by.

Zainab wasn't answering, so Katya set the phone down. What was she going to tell her anyway – I found a picture of the victim's face, but unfortunately it was veiled? She slumped into her desk chair, staring in frustration at the messages on her phone. What was the point of sending an image of yourself which any stranger could already see? Was it only mockery, or was there something more?

Smile, you're on camera!

Katya stood up. *Pretend you're a man on the street.* She walked the length of the room. Looked at her mobile. *You've just received a cryptic message from a stranger. What do you do?* Anyone, even a woman, would look around and wonder who sent the message. It might be impossible to identify the sender. What would you do?

Katya's mobile was relatively new, but she managed to figure out how to reply to the message. She wrote back: *Show me your face.*

And like magic, another message came. Katya looked around

the room. She hadn't touched the burqa. She opened the message and let out a yelp. It was a woman's face, a beautiful one, too. She had a long, fine nose and a pair of dark brown eyes framed by thick lashes. There was something both bookish and seductive in her manner. In the centre of her forehead was a small brown bump, a birthmark most likely, but it only made her face more endearing.

The door opened and a woman came in. She introduced herself only as Um-Kareem, the Syrian facial reconstruction analyst whom Adara had mentioned. Katya welcomed her and slipped the mobile back into her bag.

The woman didn't take off her Iron Curtain of a burqa. It wasn't exactly unusual, women had come into the lab before and been reluctant to take off their face coverings for any number of reasons, the biggest one being that there were men in the building. But for some reason, Um-Kareem's burqa suddenly struck Katya as the height of pomposity. *Dear viewer*, it seemed to say, *I can read a face from a shapeless blob, but you cannot.* She handed Katya the sketch, rendered in pencil and ink on a plain sheet of art paper.

The face was touchingly pretty. Katya could see a strong resemblance to the Bluetooth picture, and her heart gave a thump. She looked up at Um-Kareem. 'Beautiful.'

'Hmmmf,' Um-Kareem said. 'I didn't *make* her that way, if that's what you're trying to suggest. My work is based on a computerised skeletal analysis and tissue depth samples. You do realise that this department has spent lavishly on your machines, and you have some of the finest computer modelling software in the world? Unfortunately, I am one of the only people who knows how to use it.' She let this comment linger so that Katya would have time to feel pummelled by its subtext: *How can you possibly be raising the standards for women in this department when you don't even know how to use your own computers?* Or perhaps she blamed Katya for the insufficient education of women in general. 'The facial interpretation,' she went on, 'is derived from a number of understood variables regarding the facial structure of any given person within a certain age and ethnicity.'

Katya was in a devilish mood, so she decided to toy with her. 'Which ethnicity was she?'

'If I had to be specific,' the woman intoned grandly, 'I'd say she was a Bedouin.'

'That's pretty specific.'

'Of course, generally I'd say she's from the greater Arabian peninsula.'

'How can you . . .?'

'Supra-orbitally, there's an excess of tissue between the nasion and glabella in a pattern consistent with certain Bedouin tribes.' Um-Kareem pointed to the picture. 'Personally, I've theorised that it developed as a reaction to the brightness of the sun. All that squinting, *generations* of squinting, the brow furrows eventually with a certain degree of permanence.' Katya imagined that Um-Kareem's face was very sleek. She would never have tolerated a glabellar anomaly. Only camels had humps. 'Based on the underlying tissue, you understand,' the woman said, 'I was able to reconstruct this fold.'

'Yes, I understand.' Katya saw that she had drawn a protrusion above the woman's forehead that probably resembled, from the side, the profile of a chimpanzee. Katya hated to tell her that the protrusion was exaggerated, that Eve was in fact quite lovely.

'What's this spot here?' She had also drawn a tiny knob in the centre of the woman's forehead, slightly above the eyebrows.

An ever so slight shifting in the burqa, right where the cheekbone would have been, revealed that Um-Kareem smiled with one side of her face. 'That, my friend, is a *zabiba*.' A 'raisin', a bump on the forehead that formed over a lifetime of prayer. Katya knew people who wore them proudly. She was grudgingly impressed that, despite Um-Kareem's biases against the Bedouin forehead, she had still managed to reconstruct a detail as fine as a *zabiba*.

'Couldn't it be a birthmark?' Katya asked.

'Yes.' Um-Kareem's eyes looked dangerously annoyed. 'But I think it is a *zabiba*. As a callus, it didn't burn away so easily.' She looked down at her sketch with an appraising eye.

'Hmm, yes.' Katya would have liked nothing more than to take the phone from her handbag and show Um-Kareem the real picture of Eve's face, but she sensed that it wouldn't take much to make an enemy of this woman, and she didn't want that.

'You're lucky you have such computers lying around,' Um-Kareem went on. 'Otherwise it would have taken me weeks to reconstruct her face, and I'm an expert.'

Katya glanced at her bag. She was getting sorely tempted. 'How old was this woman?'

Um-Kareem hesitated. 'The examiner and I have estimated twenty-four.'

'Wasn't she too young to have a *zabiba*?'

'Apparently not.' Unruffled, Um-Kareem gathered her bag and left, but not before imperiously reminding Katya that she was to give the picture to her superior just as soon as Zainab returned from her meeting.

Katya watched Um-Kareem leave, feeling a strange sense of deflation. The drawing was accurate, but it still brought them no closer to identifying Eve. The paper was thin, almost like onion skin. It was such a frail clue, and the impossibility of it washed over Katya suddenly: she was supposed to find a woman by her face. She almost laughed.

But they had one other clue: the Bluetooth burqa. There couldn't be that many of them. The police should be able to trace her through the burqa's retailer.

Katya sat down at her computer. She did a quick search on the missing persons database, looking for a female with a known birthmark on the forehead, and the result popped up on her screen so quickly that she gasped. There was one missing person in the Jeddah area with a facial birthmark. Leila Nawar. Katya's stomach did a flip. The face looking back at her was the same one from the Bluetooth photo. According to the file, Leila disappeared a week ago. She was reported missing by her brother, Abdulrahman Nawar, who owned a lingerie boutique in Jeddah. Leila herself was a filmmaker who, according to her brother, worked freelance for a local news station. So she wasn't a housewife after all.

That's really the end of first impressions, Katya thought with a strange touch of pride. And yet why should it bring her any satisfaction? She only had to look at her relationships with Othman and Nayir to feel affirmed of the point. Picking up the phone, she dialled Zainab's number again.

12

The Amirs called that morning to cancel the trip. Nayir woke to the sound of his mobile ringing. There was a hurried explanation, too many apologies. Five minutes later he stood staring at the bathroom sink, contemplating his situation. *We're sorry, but too many things have come up. Family matters – you know.* Nayir hadn't wanted to ask. He was too disappointed. And to think of all the money the family had spent on preparations. They had even bought new vehicles – twelve new Land Rovers sitting in an empty garage, each car stocked with enough supplies to last an entire Bedouin camp for the rest of the summer. The waste wouldn't trouble the Amirs, of course, but it troubled him. He decided that this morning he would say a prayer of forgiveness for the sins of profligacy.

His boat creaked unhappily when he stepped on to the pier. The paint was peeling on the hull, and the name, ~~Fatima~~, had faded to grey. It occurred to him that it might be time for a new name.

When he reached the marina car park, he found that someone had broken into his Jeep. The driver's-side door was ajar, and there was a note on the dashboard. Nayir felt the first tug of dread. *In gratitude for all of your work*, the note read. *From Mohammed Amir.* Wrapped inside the bottom half of the paper was a new set of keys. He looked and saw a Land Rover parked beside his Jeep.

It was one of the Rovers he'd packed three days before. They'd even stocked the salt tablets in the boot. There were blankets, a two-person tent, a sleeping bag, and a brand new cooler. Someone had thoughtfully filled it with ice – and recently, too. The ice cubes were growing slushy at the bottom, and the caviar and non-alcoholic beer were still cold. There was even a new canteen, one of the expensive Brookstone kinds, along with a folder of unopened topographic maps. He went to the front seat and saw a GPS navigation system on the instrument panel. A CD player. And the Quran on the dashboard was so new that its gold-rimmed pages crackled and stuck together when he opened it.

Before he knew what he was doing, he was behind the wheel and driving the Land Rover out of the car park. Having become accustomed to the thumping rhythms of the Jeep, he was amazed by the smoothness of the ride. It was going to break his heart.

Twenty minutes later, he reached the Amirs' garage. He pulled inside, parked the Rover beside the others and went looking for one of the Amirs, but only servants lingered in the air-conditioned office, smoking and drinking coffee. He gave them the keys and instructions to thank Mohammed Amir for his extraordinary kindness, but to explain to him that Nayir could not accept such a fine gift. *For what?* He wondered. *For having spent two weeks doing a job for which I've already been paid generously?* The servants understood, and one of them offered Nayir a ride back to the marina.

It was only after *dhuhr* prayers that he began to regret his decision. He was back at his boat, coiling ropes on the pier and broiling in the midday heat, desperately wishing he could go for a ride in anything air-conditioned. A woman walked by with a small dog on a lead. He'd never seen her before. She wasn't even wearing a headscarf, and her black, frizzy hair seemed to blow around her head despite the notable absence of a breeze. Her dog, small and equally black and frizzy, began to yip at Nayir as they passed. The woman laughed, bent over, and scooped the dog into her arms.

'He's afraid of tall, handsome men,' she said.

Nayir didn't look at her. He kept his attention on the ropes. As the woman walked off, he made a mental note to complain to the residential office. He could have sworn that ever since the kingdom's ban on walking cats and dogs in public – under the not-so-inaccurate pretext that pets were a means of flirtation (or was it more that they were a showy accessory, like a Gucci bag or a pair of high heels, he couldn't remember) – more people than ever were actually walking dogs. There were definitely more cats lurking around the piers at night, too. The city was beginning to feel foreign, and that was always a sign that he needed the simplicity of the desert again.

His plans had fallen through, but that didn't mean he couldn't go there himself. He already had all of the supplies at hand. He had money in the bank. And although not perfect, his Jeep was still running.

Half an hour later, he was on the motorway to Wadi Khulais. Boring, yes, but it wasn't so far out that he couldn't receive phone calls, or, if his Jeep decided to give out on him, that he couldn't catch a ride home with someone else. He had just spotted his first glimpse of open space when his phone rang, setting off a small explosion in his chest. *Katya*. He pulled to the roadside and checked the caller ID. He didn't recognise the number, but it could be her. He fumbled to answer it, trying not to sound breathless.

'Hello, Nayir, it's me.' She sounded casual, almost bored, as if they talked every day.

He felt the first tug of discomfort. In the short time since he'd seen her, he had managed to hold on to the feeling that had overcome him at their meeting – that he was being given another chance and that he'd do anything not to mess it up. But the practicality in her voice weakened his confidence, and a sudden, automatic anxiety didn't help. *Katya*. Should he be saying her name? Wouldn't it be more proper if he reverted to calling her

Miss Hijazi? Figuring that she might be offended by that, he said simply: 'Hello.'

'What are you doing tomorrow night?'

Camping, he should have said, or: *I'm heading out of town.* Instead he found that magic spot that was neither a lie nor the truth. 'Tomorrow night? I had some plans, but I'm not sure yet. Why?'

'So you could be free?'

He hesitated. 'Yes.'

'Then I'd like you to come over for dinner – at say, seven o'clock?'

It was happening too quickly. She gave him no time to back away, and he had the sense that she had planned it like this. And that he deserved it, after all of his previous waffling. Sweat was trickling down his scalp and on to the phone, running in rivulets down his arms and back. His determination had vanished, and all that was left was automatic courtesy.

'I'd like that,' he said, knowing that somewhere deep down he *would* like to go to her house for dinner, even if he didn't know it right now, even if the thought of meeting her father and having to acknowledge his previous relationship with Katya made him feel as if someone were drilling nails into his neck. 'Seven o'clock then.'

'Let me give you our address.'

He fumbled for a pen, couldn't find one, tried desperately to memorise what she was saying, all the while remaining stuck on that single word 'our'. Our address. Me and my father. The gate-keeper.

He was too embarrassed to ask if she had found out anything more about Samir's friend, Qadhi, and she hadn't offered the information. It remained unspoken, but he imagined the words: *Come and I'll tell you. Don't come, and you'll never find out.*

Once the phone call was over, he spun a U-turn on the road and went straight back to the marina. He wasn't sure exactly why he was heading home. He had a whole day before he had to be at her apartment, and getting ready might take as much as fifteen minutes. He just knew that he had to get back to the boat.

Pulling into the car park, he saw at once that the Land Rover was parked just where it had been that morning. His stomach did a simultaneous plunge and whooping leap. *How could they possibly have had the nerve to return it?* And, *Allah, they returned it!*

He parked the Jeep beside it and walked around the Rover, peeking in the rear windows. It was indeed the same car. The key was in the ignition so he took it out and slid it into his pocket, telling himself that he would make at least one more attempt to return it, but not this afternoon. He knew that he would return the Rover again, and he saw just as clearly that they would bring it straight back, at which point it would become a war of attrition. He could not keep giving it back to them without risking offence, and their continued insistence was all the proof he needed that they meant for him to keep it. If he felt guilty about it later, he could always remind himself: *They practically forced me to take it.* He wondered if he would feel guilty.

13

Miriam sat at the kitchen table, phone at her ear. The consulate was on the other end of the line. They had switched her from one bureaucrat to another and now she was on hold. On the floor beside her feet, the broken sink disposal was lying in pieces. She wasn't sure whom to call about that.

Eric hadn't been missing for twenty-four hours yet, but with every hour that slipped by, Miriam's panic grew worse. She hoped that calling the consulate would soothe her nerves.

'Hello?'

It was a woman's voice, which relieved her. She sounded American, unlike the first two people Miriam had spoken with. She introduced herself and explained her situation. *My husband is missing.*

The woman gave a sympathetic mew. 'I'm so sorry to hear that, Mrs Walker. Are you in a dangerous situation right now?'

'Er, no. I'm at home.'

'Good.' It sounded as if the woman were riffling through paperwork. 'First of all, I want to assure you that we'll do everything we can to help you find your husband.'

'Thank you.' Although sceptical, Miriam felt a small implosion of relief.

'It's not uncommon for Americans to be picked up by the religious police, even here in Jeddah. Most of the time they don't know the rules of proper conduct, or they don't understand the importance of dressing modestly. I'm trying to pull up your file right now, but let me ask you, how long have you and your husband been here?'

'Six months.'

'Ah.' The woman sounded somehow disappointed by this. 'And you say that your husband went out to buy groceries when he disappeared?'

'Well, dinner actually. He came back with it – it was take-away from a local schawarma place. He left it on the kitchen table and then . . . I don't know, I was on the roof. When I came downstairs a few minutes later, he was gone.' This was the part Miriam had dreaded; she could almost hear the woman's thoughts coming down the line. *Maybe he just walked out on you. That's not uncommon either.*

'I see,' the woman said. Then her voice turned sympathetic. 'Tell me something, does your husband own a car?'

'Yes, a pick-up truck.'

'Ah. Well, did he take the pick-up when he went to buy dinner?'

'No, I don't think so. I think he went to a local place. I recognised the food, and he could easily have walked there.'

'Okay,' the woman said. 'Do you know if his car is gone as well?'

'Ah, I'm not sure,' Miriam replied, embarrassed. 'He had parked it a couple of blocks away, and I can't remember where that was.'

'I see.' The woman's voice was kind and reassuring. 'Mrs Walker, it would help us to know if anything like this has ever happened before.' Hearing Miriam's silence, the woman went on: 'I mean, have there been unexplained absences—'

'Yes,' Miriam blurted, 'he's gone missing before, but he always managed to get in touch with me. One time he was picked up by the religious police. Another time he got stuck in the desert.' A childish panic was rising in her throat as she spoke.

'Okay, Mrs Walker,' the woman said kindly. 'We'll look into this immediately. But bear in mind, it's entirely possible that the religious police have picked him up again, and they're just holding him longer than they did the last time. I know this must be very frustrating for you, but believe me, the best course of action is for us to locate him through official channels. And I'm confident that we will. The best thing you can do is try not to panic.'

The woman was speaking to her as if she were a child, but Miriam was grateful anyway.

'Meanwhile,' the woman went on, 'is there anything you need – money? Food? A ride somewhere?'

Miriam hesitated. 'No. No, thanks. I've got some cash and there's a store nearby.'

The woman continued asking questions about Eric's job, his schedule, and the people he spent time with. It was comforting to answer questions, as if somehow the simple acknowledgement of facts would bring Eric back, a cosy delusion that was reinforced when the woman said: 'Don't worry, Mrs Walker, we take disappearances very seriously. Most of the time it turns out to be a misunderstanding. I'm sure we'll get your husband back.'

☽

Miriam spent the rest of the afternoon washing the shirts that Eric hadn't managed to clean himself and hanging them on the clothesline on the roof. With a flicker of guilt, she remembered the new shirt he'd worn at the airport: he had run through so much laundry that he was forced to wear something one of his clients had given him.

The conversation with the consulate had improved her mood for a few hours, but now in the silence, the doubt was creeping back in. She was determined to stay busy. When she finished the shirts, she went downstairs, bundled up the rubbish and dumped it out the kitchen window, into the alley where most of the neighbours dumped their refuse. The women were discouraged from making the short trip to the bin at the end of the street. According to Sabria, she and her sisters were the only ones in the building who took their rubbish there. She listened, waiting for the inevitable clatter, but when her bag hit the pile, it sounded flat, as if it had hit a mattress.

She stuck her head out the window. The smell was enough to fur her tongue, but she held her breath and leaned further out, craning to see past the stairs' metal railing to the bed of rubbish below. As far as she could tell, it looked the same as always, yellow plastic shopping bags spilling with leftovers, empty tins and bottles, orange peel.

The fridge was empty. She'd eaten the last tin of fava beans for breakfast, and she knew better than to drink the desalinated sea water that came out of the tap – sometimes it was the colour of apple juice. She crept to the front room and put her ear to the door. She listened for a long time but heard only the distant sound of mothers screaming at their children, and the muted roar of the occasional car.

It was getting harder to ignore her anger. Without Eric, the flat became nearly intolerable. They really ought to have moved into the American compound, and right now their excuses for not doing so seemed ridiculously flimsy. It was too expensive and they'd come here to *save* money. It was a high-value terrorist target – but there hadn't been an attack there yet. Most of all, it was not the 'real' Saudi Arabia. It was, Miriam reflected, a place Eric would have enjoyed, but that didn't suit Abdullah at all. Unfortunately, Abdullah was still married to Miriam.

More than that, their whole reason for being in Jeddah seemed flimsy. Eric's job was not unique to Saudi Arabia, although perhaps the wages were. He could be a bodyguard anywhere. They were here because he wanted to be here. Maybe he didn't really know why, but considering how much she'd put up with, he'd better not have walked out on her.

She picked up her mobile and called the taxi service. She and Eric had an agreement that they wouldn't spend money on taxis, but fifteen minutes later, it felt devilishly good to slip into the air-conditioned car. *I had to find you!* she would probably blather later with tears in her eyes. Or, if she were feeling tougher: *You weren't home.* With a shrug. *I had to get groceries.* But it wasn't to the grocer's that they were headed. The driver knew the compound she requested – Arabian Gates – and half an hour later, they were approaching the front entrance. The rebelliousness of being in a taxi felt so good that it quelled her anger.

The taxi inched forward, and she glanced out at the street. The back seat windows were heavily tinted. In fact the taxi service sold itself as a company for 'decent' women, its motto: *Our windows are darker.* Peering through the filmy shield, Miriam saw that they were approaching the compound gates. Like the others she had seen, it looked like a prison with its street blockades, blast walls, concertina wire, video cameras dangling from every post, and armed guards patrolling the gates. It took them fifteen minutes to get clearance from security and another fifteen minutes before Patty showed up, looking concerned. Miriam paid the taxi driver and followed Patty to her villa.

☽

Conversations with Patty had always been awkward. Miriam blamed Eric for this. He was the one who'd told her about Jacob's philandering. She and Eric had just moved to Saudi, and Eric had only just met the Marxes when Jacob confessed that he preferred Arab women, virgins if he could get them, although any prostitute would do. Back then, it had disgusted Eric as well, but it hadn't stopped him from hanging out with Jacob. Miriam, on the other hand, had found it impossible to face Patty.

She recognised the irony of coming to Patty now for information, and she had to beat down an upsurge of guilt. Miriam entered the kitchen and saw a plate of fresh fried doughnuts on the kitchen table. The air smelled of warm cooking oil and powdered sugar. 'Have one!' Patty said nonchalantly. Miriam wanted to stuff the whole plate into her mouth. While Patty bustled around making coffee, Miriam seated herself carefully at the table and took a delicate bite. It was scrumptious. She hadn't realised how hungry she was. Trying as hard as she could to keep up a light conversation, she ate three doughnuts in quick succession.

'You poor thing,' Patty finally said. 'When was the last time you ate?' Not waiting for an answer, she began pulling plates of food from the fridge, offering up a buffet of leftovers, and Miriam, ravenous, began to eat.

'Miriam, I'm sure it's *nothing*.' Patty was no longer the panicked woman she had been on the phone, but her attempts to calm Miriam's fears were perversely stoking them. 'He's probably just been picked up by the religious police. I'm sure they'll let him go.' Patty poured her a cup of coffee and set it on the table. 'You know, this happens to me all the time,' she said brightly. Miriam stopped chewing. 'Okay, well, not *all* the time, but it *has* happened.'

'What has happened?' Miriam asked.

Patty came to the table and sat down, cradling a cup of coffee. She wore a look that she probably thought was sly, but which made her seem grandmotherly and quaint. 'A couple of years ago, we arranged to have our anniversary dinner at a posh new restaurant downtown. I had to talk him into it, you know, since Jacob's idea of a nice dinner is something over a campfire. Preferably something he killed himself.' She took a sip of coffee and narrowed her eyes, obviously enjoying drawing out the suspense. 'So he was supposed to come straight home from work and pick me up. We had a seven o'clock reservation, but he didn't show up. By eight o'clock I had to call the restaurant to apologise. Meanwhile, I had called his work, his cell, half a dozen friends and compound security on top of it, but nobody knew where he was! You know, he didn't come home that night at all. So I know exactly how you feel. It's horrible not knowing and fearing the worst.'

'What happened to him?' Miriam asked.

'Oh! He was fine. Turned out the police had pulled him over for running a red light. Well, you know Jacob. He hadn't run the red light, but when he told the officer that, the officer got angry. I think Jacob lost his temper a little bit. In any event, they hauled him off to jail. He spent the night in prison for a traffic violation, can you believe it?'

Miriam nodded, mindlessly eating. She wanted to believe that something like that had happened to Eric, but somehow she couldn't.

'How long was he gone?' she asked.

'Only a day,' Patty said. 'But you know, a few months later, we found out from a guy who's lived here for something like twenty years that at this one traffic light where Jacob was pulled over – guess what? The police can actually control the timing of the light! So they sit at the corner and switch the light whenever a foreigner drives through the intersection. I mean, they're *targeting* Americans.'

Miriam wasn't sure whether she felt comforted by this.

'My biggest fear,' Patty went on, 'is not that something will happen to him, but that – well, this is really personal, but I'm only telling you because I think you'll understand.' She gazed at Miriam, her blue eyes glittering with meaning. 'I've always been afraid that Jacob would bring home a second wife.'

Miriam smiled to hide her reaction. 'Doesn't he have to be a Muslim to do that?'

'Oh, I don't know,' Patty said, waving her hand dismissively and standing up. 'There are plenty of non-Muslim women right here on the compound, but yes, he would have to be Muslim to have a co-wife. I don't think it would ever happen. It's just me being irrational.'

Miriam's appetite had fled. She kept eating a piece of bread so that Patty wouldn't become suspicious, but the words bubbled right there beneath the surface: *Patty, he's a jerk. He's been cheating on you for years. Why don't you get out?* Patty dumped her fresh coffee in the sink, then seemed to realise what she'd done. She gave a nervous laugh. 'What on earth am I doing?' she said, quickly pouring herself another cup. Miriam felt an impulse to stand up and hug her.

She had to admit that she understood Patty's fears. It wasn't that Eric might bring home a second wife, it was just that he spent so much of his time blowing freely through a world she had little access to and very little knowledge of. There had been plenty of times she'd wondered if he was cheating on her. It would have been so easy for him to get away with it.

'I know what it feels like,' Miriam said. Patty stopped stirring her coffee. 'But I'll tell you what keeps me from worrying too much is the knowledge that, in this town, women are extremely difficult to meet.'

She had hoped the remark would at least win a wry smile, but Patty simply picked up her coffee and said: 'Have you called the consulate yet?'

'Yes. They said they'd help find him.'

'Oh, good. They'll find him, you'll see.' The front door opened with a squeak and Patty went into a kind of fit of excitement and nerves. She set the coffee mug down so hard that its contents splashed on to the counter, and she practically went racing into the living room to greet her husband. Miriam heard Patty's voice and winced. 'You're back early! Is everything okay at work?' Jacob grumbled a response and came into the kitchen and saw Miriam.

'Ah,' he said. 'The husbandless woman.'

Miriam couldn't be bothered to figure out why it was insulting – she simply didn't like the comment, but then she didn't like Jacob and anything he said might have had the same effect. 'Hi,' she said, picking up her coffee in case he said something worse and she needed to distract herself.

Jacob came to the table and took the mug from her hands. 'A woman in your situation should be drinking something stronger.'

'No thanks,' she said, but Jacob was already dumping the coffee in the sink. He set the mug on the countertop with a *crack*, and pulled a beer from the fridge, opening it on the edge of the counter like some college kid and sliding it across the formica table so that she was forced to catch it or let it land on her lap.

Drink it, she thought. *In a few minutes, you'll be glad you did*. She took a long slug and set the bottle on the table with a thunk. Patty looked upset.

'How was work?' she chimed, going back to the sink. She didn't wait for an answer. 'I wasn't expecting you so early or I would have had dinner ready. I was going to make a roast.'

Miriam had only seen them together a few times, twice at parties here on the compound, and once at a private beach for a picnic that had ended when the temperature had gone above 110. The two of them had lived here for seven years and had no plans to leave. Their house might have been a little less tense if they'd had kids or pets, but their one daughter, Amanda, had been sent to a boarding school in New Hampshire. She suspected it was Jacob's idea.

Miriam had always felt intimidated by him. He seemed to enjoy making her quail. She wondered how Patty put up with it, but Patty was all about nervous chatter and that seemed to shut him up.

To hear Eric tell it, Jacob was only a convenient friend. They worked at the same company. They were both former military. They liked to do the same things: fishing, scuba diving, camping

102

in the desert. Not that they ever did much except work, but at least they had something to talk about.

She watched Jacob now; his thin face was slightly sunburned and grizzly even when he shaved. He had limpid hazel eyes that she couldn't look into without thinking of warm Vaseline. Like Eric, he was a security specialist, and his body showed it – it was well-developed, meaty, tough. His gestures had the kind of precision that came from watching peripheries, guarding other people, and handling dangerous weapons for a living. Maybe that's what kept Patty enthralled. Miriam could certainly sympathise. Yet ever since meeting Jacob, she'd had the uneasy feeling that he was the kind of man who had been drawn to Saudi Arabia because he appreciated its worst stereotypes: the treatment of women primary among them. Or perhaps she was being harsh, it was only the segregation of women that appealed to him. How can you cheat on your wife if she's always in your hair? Miriam had learned early on that Jacob didn't want the women around when he hung out with Eric. At first she'd thought it was a work thing, that they'd had business to discuss, but Eric finally told her that Jacob was a man's man who didn't really like spending time with his wife in the way that Eric did with Miriam. That is, the way he had until they came here.

Patty was still talking.

'So Miriam,' Jacob said, interrupting his wife and swinging his attention to Miriam like an interrogation light. Patty fell silent. 'Did you find your husband?' he asked.

Miriam shook her head, feeling an ominous tickle on the back of her neck. She took another swig of beer. 'He wasn't at work today?'

'I don't know. I wasn't in the office,' Jacob said, all the while keeping his eyes on her face. 'I'm sure he'll turn up.'

'You said you saw him before he came to the airport to pick me up?' Miriam asked.

'Yeah, but only for coffee. He seemed normal.' Jacob's gaze narrowed. 'Why? You think I had something to do with it?'

'With what?' she asked, attempting to look arch.

Jacob gave her a cold, eerie look that made her insides convulse.

'I thought you might be able to tell me if there was something strange going on,' she said. 'If he said anything to you . . .'

'He said nothing.' Jacob's tone was insulting, but at that moment Patty dropped a metal spatula on the floor, accidentally intervening. It startled everyone. She apologised, picked up the spatula and set it in the sink.

Miriam stood and collected her handbag. 'Patty, thanks so much for the food. The doughnuts were delicious.'

'He's probably just been picked up by the religious police,' Jacob said, his eyes still boring into Miriam. 'You live in that kind of neighbourhood, you know.'

I know, she wanted to snap. 'I'll see myself out. Patty, thanks again.'

Patty looked awkward and stricken, as if she wasn't sure what to do. It was Jacob who followed Miriam into the living room. She passed a side table in the foyer and glanced down at the framed pictures. She hadn't noticed them when she came in, but one of them caught her attention now. It was a picture of Jacob and Eric. She stopped to look at it.

Jacob stood a little too close behind her. 'Did he tell you we went camping?' he asked in a tone that said: *Bet he didn't tell you anything.*

Miriam felt herself flushing with anger. Eric hadn't mentioned a camping trip. 'Yes,' she said, 'sounds like you guys got into your usual trouble.'

She could see from his face that Jacob wasn't buying it.

The table was strange. All of the pictures showed Jacob and his friends doing guy things – fishing, surfing, hunting in the desert.

No pictures of Patty or their daughter. Even the frames were masculine, grainy wood in dark browns and greens.

At the back she saw a picture that stopped her heart for a beat. Three men were in it. Each one was holding a hunting rifle, and behind them the mountains of southern Arabia were draped in a yellowing light. Eric was on the left, looking pleased with himself. There was a cut on his chin. Jacob looked thuggish in the centre, and on the right stood a man she recognised as Apollo Mabus.

'How do you know this guy?' she said, pointing.

'Mabus? Met him through a guy at work a few years ago. He's a Brit. Kinda stuffy until you get him out to the desert. Why do you ask?'

'He looks familiar.' She kept her eyes on the picture so she wouldn't give anything away. She knew she looked nervous. All she needed now was for Jacob to start thinking that she was cheating on her husband.

It shocked her to realise that Mabus had lied. He wasn't from New York, he was British. He'd spoken English just like an American.

'You met him here?' she asked, confirming.

'Yeah.'

'And you're sure he's British?'

'Pretty damn sure,' Jacob replied.

'Then it can't be the same guy I'm thinking of,' she lied. 'When was *this* hunting trip?'

'Why do you want to know?' Jacob was moving closer again, so she shrugged, although it looked more like a nervous tic. When he saw that she wasn't going to answer, he said: 'We went out to Mabus's place. Did some camping on the dunes.'

'Hmm.' Smiling feebly, clutching her bag, she went straight to the front door and pulled it open, but Jacob followed her on to the lawn.

'Later,' she said, walking briskly away. He stood in the front yard, watching her leave, but she didn't turn around. She walked, trying not to seem hurried, until she was out of sight of the villa. Then she took her mobile from her bag and called the taxi driver again, relieved to hear that he wasn't so far away. They arranged to meet at the gate.

She already knew how old the picture was, because the cut on Eric's chin had happened right before she'd left for the States. The picture had to have been taken not long after she'd left. She didn't mind, really. He had a right to his friends, especially when she was out of town, but they'd spoken on the phone a few times that week and he hadn't mentioned it once. Normally he told her when he was going somewhere.

And, she wondered suddenly, *who had taken the picture?*

14

Faiza sat beside Osama in the front seat, laughing at a comic display of gesticulation between two young boys fighting over a football on the street. Osama steered carefully around the football players, smiling to himself. He enjoyed her laughter and let it wash over him. He had never been bothered by her forwardness, the sloppy way she wore her *hijaab*, or the simple banter that sprang up between them on the rare occasions they went on interviews together. In a different woman these things might have seemed like efforts at seduction, but in Faiza they were as natural as air and sand and stone. She was older, at thirty-seven just reaching the age where immodesty was forgiven, where women passed into the sanctuary of perceived sexlessness. Yet he found her attractive in a simple, old-fashioned way; the flat, broad gestures of her hands, the way her shoulders shook when she laughed, and the plainness of her features, which – on the occasions that he saw them – she wore with unabashed frankness. She was wholesome and comforting precisely because she had no idea of her own sexuality and he suspected that this had been as much the case with her at sixteen as it would someday be at forty.

She let out a sigh, the kind that said *My, that was satisfying, now back to serious*. They were heading to talk to the victim's brother, Abdulrahman Nawar, who owned a lingerie shop. If there was even a possibility that they would have to interview a woman,

Osama had to bring a female officer along. A lingerie shop was strange, tricky territory. He had brought Faiza on the off chance that this would be one of the 250-odd lingerie boutiques in Jeddah that had actually managed to comply with the Labour Ministry's new edict enforcing the hiring of women. 'Encouraging more women into the workplace' they called it, but it was really a bid to clamp down on one of the few places where men had access to women, where women could confer with men in whispers about their panty preferences and cup sizes and which of the dazzling variety of erotic 'looks' they preferred in the bedroom.

The religious establishment had been scrutinising and pressuring the industry for years, but until recently shop owners had always managed a successful defence, arguing that they couldn't hire women, because most of their customers were actually men shopping for their wives. Since women had a more difficult time getting out of the house, they sent their husbands to buy for them – hence the need for male sales assistants. When the Labour Ministry issued their new law – only women should work in lingerie shops – the religious establishment roared. The idea of male employees handling brassieres and thongs sent the imams into a lather, but apparently the threat of women abandoning childrearing and cooking to find outside work was even more depraved.

Faiza's hand plunged into her paper bag. They had stopped for coffee and doughnuts and she was eating without any of the delicacy he'd come to expect from someone wearing a burqa – the gentle angling of the sticky doughnut beneath the fabric, the careful biting to avoid dropping crumbs in the collar. She simply went at it. He watched surreptitiously for lapses of technique but she didn't so much as smear icing on her thumb.

'That was impressive,' he said.

She chuckled. 'Twenty-five years of practice, I'd better be good. Who are you taking me to see today?'

'The owner of a lingerie shop. He's a man, but we might have to get past some women first.'

'You've never got past a woman by yourself?'

'I thought I could use your help.'

'You know I appreciate it.'

He pulled into a petrol station and got out to refill. As he was finishing up, a patrol car drove by, triggering a small worry when the officers glanced his way. He checked to see if they recognised him, if they noticed Faiza. Being with her wasn't wrong, it was just that he had been with her more and more often in the past few weeks. For her sake, he dreaded the day that people started putting them together in their minds. The rumour mill, always efficient, would begin churning out lies, and the first career to get pulverised would be hers.

He had often wondered why she had chosen to become an officer. The few times he'd asked, she'd answered vaguely (A shrug. 'I don't know. I was interested.') without any of the impassioned rhetoric that the department's other women tended to use. With Faiza there was something mysteriously apt about the choice, as if she'd been drawn to this career not by logic or careful planning, but by some deep, inarticulate suitability.

He got back in the car and drove off, grateful when the patrol car slipped out of view. Normally, he would have been sitting in the passenger seat, and Rafiq, his partner, would have been driving. If Faiza were along, she would be in the back. But three months ago, Rafiq and Osama had walked into an abortion clinic and one of the patients' boyfriends had pulled out a gun and shot Rafiq in the chest. They'd been looking for a suspect in the murder of a young girl and their investigation had led them inexorably back to the small clinic. It was passing itself off as a fertility centre, but turned out to be a place where children were killed every day, Osama thought with a cringe of disgust even now. Rafiq had survived the wounds but had taken six months' sick leave to recuperate.

In the long term, it was probably good that this break had been enforced on them. Rafiq, the older and more experienced of the two, had always been the alpha male, boldly and proudly leading Osama from crime scene to interrogation room, from courtroom to prison, schooling him in the nuances of policing a city as vast and lawless and recklessly impious as this one. This relationship had gone on long after Osama had become a competent officer in his own right because Osama – his father-figure complex brought to majestic, swelling blossom – had turned to Rafiq the way a frail flower turns to the sun.

The accusations had started slowly. First, that Rafiq had taken bribes on a case involving a battered housemaid. Then that he had beaten a young Somali man who'd been begging at a bus station for a ticket fare back to Riyadh. About six months ago, like flocking birds, the charges began sailing in, coming from different places but all resembling one another and all heading south.

Osama defended his partner with fierce conviction, feeling certain that Rafiq was being maligned. It was going to take a sledgehammer to break his faith, but in fact it only took a whisper, something Osama's wife Nuha told him about Rafiq's marriage. After that, strangely, he began to have doubts about his partner. Then they entered the abortion clinic and everything changed.

For the past two and a half months Osama had been on his own, and he still felt slightly uncomfortable with the isolation and the independence. He could have partnered up with Abdullatif or Abu-Haitham, but he had never liked the former's brashness or the latter's cold silences and if he'd had a choice at all, he would have picked Faiza above any of the men in the department. God willing, he thought, some day this country will be modern enough to accept that every homicide investigator needs a woman, and that male–female partnerships should in fact be *enforced*, because what homicide investigation involved only men?

The lingerie shop was a large, brash affair, the stucco façade painted bright pink and gold. Six enormous front windows displayed mannequins in corsets and garters, one holding a whip above a second who wore a burqa (but nothing else) and was kneeling abjectly on the floor. There was a residue of black around the window's edges where no doubt some religious policeman had spray-painted the glass to cover the atrocity, and where the owners had removed the paint incompletely. Osama touched the black spots with his finger, and noticed they were somewhat fresh.

The next window exhibited three mannequins standing in a row. Behind them a neon green poster announced: *Latest Syrian Thrills!* The mannequins were wearing technology treats: a bra made of power cords, a mobile phone covering each breast, a BlackBerry thong. It wasn't the ridiculousness of it that made him laugh, it was the knowledge that Faiza was standing beside him, staring at two computer mice strapped to a mannequin's firm buttocks beneath a sign that read *Click me, baby!*

She turned away, looking unimpressed, and followed him into the shop.

Almost at once, his forearms bristled with goosebumps. The air conditioning was overzealous, a nice deterrent to getting naked, but it made the place feel hostile. Inside, they found an enormous, warehouse-like space split into themed sections: Romantic, Flashy, Barely There, and Hardcore. In the centre of the room was a cash desk staffed by three young men who looked as if they were fresh out of business school with trim little moustaches and neat button-down shirts. Osama went to the cash desk, Faiza walking beside him and scanning the room. At this time of day the shop wasn't very crowded, but a lone man was wandering through the aisles on one side, and a young couple was heading into the Hardcore section but promptly stopped when Osama flashed his badge.

'I need to speak to Abdulrahman Nawar,' he said.

'He's in the back,' one of the sales assistants replied, glancing at his cohorts who were frozen in aspects of silent panic. Osama gave them each a good study, enough to make them nervous. It was something Rafiq had taught him: always intimidate men in a lingerie shop. They needed to be reminded that cops didn't always wear uniforms, that any customer could be an officer, and that everybody had better be on their guard. 'There is too much sexuality around them all the time,' Rafiq had said. 'Don't think they don't get ideas just as often.' Osama couldn't imagine them *not* getting ideas.

'Uh . . . I'll go get him for you,' the boy said.

'No need,' Osama replied, practically scowling at the three of them. 'We can find it ourselves.'

The three men glanced at Faiza with looks that ranged from incomprehension to amazement. One of them asked: 'May I ask what this is about?'

'No,' Osama said, motioning Faiza around the cash desk to the back of the shop, where a pair of double doors were held open by mannequins, each wearing a brown leather get-up that looked like something you'd use to subdue a falcon. An immense workshop was visible through the doors. They saw men, but no women.

Faiza didn't complain or back down. It was one of the things he liked about her, this steadfast resolve. As they went into the studio, he saw himself suddenly as if from a distance, an investigator leading his protégée into a room – only this protégée was bold enough to pause at the door and lift her burqa without even glancing his way for approval. She was ready to face them, literally, while Osama wanted to turn around and walk away. He hated breaking the bad news to families.

One of the men inside saw him coming and approached. The man's movements were careful and when he spoke, he had the crisp tones of a man used to dealing with idiots. 'How can I help you?'

'Are you Abdulrahman Nawar?'

'No, I'm his assistant. Who are you?' the man asked. Osama flashed his badge but before he could introduce himself, the man said: 'What is this about?'

'His sister.'

The man's face seemed to open with concern. 'Oh,' he said. 'Please come in.'

The room was brightly lit and cool, with distinct currents of smell drifting through the air: stale coffee, body odour, the sour stench of industrial fabrics being unwound from their bolts. There were large white tables where patterns were laid out, where scissors and pincushions waited patiently for their masters, and between the tables, headless mannequins stood in poses of defiance. Hands on hips or arms held in a pugilist's stance. Men were standing around or bent over tables of fabrics. They were young, probably in their twenties. One was sitting on a stool, winding a ball of stringed sequins. The older man in the room – whom Osama presumed to be the victim's brother – was fussing over a mannequin with one arm outstretched, so that it looked, from the side, as if it were slapping his face. Each of the mannequins wore a lavishly sexy piece of lingerie.

'Abdulrahman.' Something in the way the assistant said the name made Osama think that he already knew what was happening, that Leila was dead and that they'd come here to break the news. He glanced at Faiza, who seemed to notice it too, for she met his eyes with a silent look of concern.

Abdulrahman responded to the strange intimacy of the tone. He immediately stopped his fussing and turned with a hostile expression.

'What is it?' he asked.

'Mr Nawar,' Osama said. 'I'm Detective Inspector Osama Ibrahim and this is Officer Shanbari. Is there somewhere we can talk?'

113

Abdulrahman stood frozen by the slapping mannequin. His 'yes' was more like a gasp for air. He attempted to lead Osama and Faiza to the small, glass-walled office across the room, but he'd only gone two steps when he stumbled, and his assistant and Osama lurched to his rescue.

Abdulrahman knocked the assistant's hand away. 'I'm fine,' he growled. 'What happened?' But he already knew, Osama could see it on his face.

'I think you'd better sit down,' the assistant said.

Abdulrahman glared at him. 'Just get me some water.' Then he went into the office, sat heavily on the room's plump yellow sofa, and promptly turned white.

His assistant returned with a glass of water, and Abdulrahman took it with shaking hands. The workers outside had stopped their activity and were gathering a few feet away from the office door. Osama didn't want to tell them to leave, but thankfully the assistant went out to meet them. 'All right,' he said, 'you all have a break. Go on.'

They dispersed obediently, but one man remained behind, moving into step beside the assistant as he came back into the office. Nobody protested, and Osama judged that the young man was a member of the family. He looked frightened.

'She's dead, isn't she?' Abdulrahman asked, his expression a mixture of fury and woe. The assistant and the young man hovered beside the sofa.

'*Is she dead?*' he demanded again, impatient for the news.

'Mr Nawar, we'd like to speak to you alone, if you don't mind,' Osama said.

'This is my nephew Ra'id, and my assistant Fuad.' Abdulrahman motioned to the two men in turn. 'I say they can stay. Now tell me what happened.'

'I'm sorry,' Osama said, 'we found a body at the beach yesterday, and we think it's your sister, Leila.'

Abdulrahman remained rigid, but the young nephew Ra'id let out his breath as if he'd been stabbed. He began shaking, tears plunged down his cheeks.

'Where is she?' Fuad asked briskly. 'Can we see her?'

Osama thought of the body and inwardly cringed. 'She's with our doctors,' he said quietly, then added: 'Female doctors.'

'But you're *not* sure it's her,' Fuad snapped. 'You only *think* it's her?'

'Fuad, shut up.' Abdulrahman was glaring at the floor.

Osama was starting to feel awkward standing next to the sofa, so he pulled up a roller chair from the desk for Faiza, and perched himself on a folding metal chair that was sitting in the corner. The nephew Ra'id didn't move to wipe the tears from his face. His eyes were locked on the centre of Osama's shirt, but Fuad gave him a nudge and he sat himself on the first thing he could reach, the arm of the sofa. Fuad continued to hover.

Osama took out his notepad and pen. He noticed that Faiza was relaxed, hands crossed on her lap, staring at Leila's brother in a disconcerting way. Abdulrahman ignored her completely.

'We've identified your sister based on the photograph you submitted to Missing Persons,' Osama said. He didn't want to tell them what had happened to her face. 'We matched it to a picture we found . . . in her burqa.'

Apparently, Ra'id knew just what he meant; the uniqueness of the burqa was enough to convince him, because a knowing look stole over his face. 'But how could she have – how could . . .' When Abdulrahman and Fuad gave him quizzical looks, Ra'id said: 'She had a Bluetooth in her burqa. But I thought it only showed a picture of her *veiled* face.' He emphasised these last words, looking at his uncle with a fearful expression. 'It was sort of a joke . . . I thought no one could *see* her face?'

'We did,' Osama said. Fuad looked disgusted.

Abdulrahman shut his eyes, clasped a hand to his mouth and

raised his face to the ceiling, although Osama couldn't tell if his expression was one of suffering or fury.

Osama forced himself to study the men as objectively as possible. Abdulrahman had a large, round face that was dominated by a black moustache and the bushiest pair of eyebrows Osama had ever seen. He might have been old enough to be Leila's father; his hair was rough like Brillo, greying at the temples, and his voice was an earth-shaking baritone that was growing gritty with age.

His nephew Ra'id was short and scrawny, probably in his teens; his pointed face had a scurrilous look. Right now he was bent forward, shaking slightly, hands gripping his knees. A lock of greasy hair fell into his face. The assistant, Fuad, was probably in his late twenties, tall and well-built with sharp edges to his jaw, cheekbones, shoulders. He looked like the sort of man who paid attention to detail. His suit was crisp, his cufflinks shiny, and every time someone moved, he glanced automatically in their direction with a look that indicated he was prepared to come to their aid, or tell them what they were doing wrong, or otherwise assist in perfecting the universe.

Abdulrahman faced Osama. 'Tell me what happened.' When Fuad went to protest, Abdulrahman raised a hand and interrupted sharply. 'Tell me what happened.'

'I'm afraid it looks as if she was murdered,' Osama said, watching the men's reactions carefully. Fuad shook his head.

'What did they do to her?' Abdulrahman breathed, shooting a warning look at Fuad. 'Tell me. *What did they do to her?*'

'Her neck was broken,' Osama said carefully, avoiding a glance at Faiza. 'She died very quickly.' *And before that she was brutally stabbed and beaten, and her hands and face were dunked in burning oil.* He would never tell them the truth, but he didn't have to. Abdulrahman's face conveyed that he didn't believe a word Osama said. At least he was smart enough not to ask for more detail.

'It sounds as if you have some idea of who killed her?' Faiza said. Fuad looked insulted but Faiza kept her attention on the brother. 'You said: "What did they do to her?" If there's anything you can tell us – any suspicions you may—'

Abdulrahman was still pretending that there was not a woman in the room. It was Ra'id who let out a derisive snort. 'You think we had something to do with it?'

Faiza didn't respond.

'She was attacked once before,' Fuad intervened.

'When was this?' Osama asked.

'Six months ago,' Fuad replied.

Osama didn't look over. 'What were the circumstances, Mr Nawar?'

'He's right,' Abdulrahman said, but from the firm set of his mouth, he clearly wasn't saying anything else.

'Occasionally, she worked for a local news station,' Fuad said. 'She did freelance work filming B-roll for their news segments. All the boring bits. You know what B-roll is?' Osama nodded. 'She was filming birds down at the Corniche one afternoon and some woman noticed that Leila was filming her and she sent her husband to take care of it. The husband came after her and beat her up. He destroyed her camera *and* the film.'

'He broke her leg!' Ra'id interjected. He was livid now, gripping his knees.

'According to Leila, the woman was only in the background of the shot,' Fuad said. 'And she was wearing a burqa anyway.'

Ra'id shook his head. Osama could perfectly well imagine someone becoming upset at being filmed in public without their permission. Incidents like this happened more often now that mobile phone cameras were everywhere. But they seldom resulted in physical violence – especially of the sort that had killed Leila.

'Did you find out who attacked her?' he asked.

'No,' Fuad said. 'He was gone before the police arrived.'

'What happened to the camera?'

'That monkey threw it in the ocean,' Fuad said.

Osama nodded. 'Was she alone when this happened?'

'Yes.'

Osama nodded, at the same time thinking what an easy target Leila must have made for someone looking for trouble. Not only a young woman walking around unescorted, but carrying a video camera, too.

'I'd like you to tell me what happened on the morning she disappeared,' Osama said, keeping a steady gaze on Leila's brother.

Abdulrahman looked menacingly at Osama, but it was Ra'id who spoke. 'You really think we had something to do with this?' His voice cracked at the end, betraying his anxiety.

'These questions are necessary,' Osama said bluntly. 'And I'm sure you're as eager as we are to help find her killer.' That shut him up. Osama turned to Abdulrahman. 'First I'd like to know how she disappeared.'

Abdulrahman let out his breath. 'I left for work at the usual time that morning. Leila was at home with my wife and kids.'

'She was living with you?' Osama asked.

'Yes. My wife and children went out shopping around nine o'clock. Leila left sometime after that. She didn't tell anyone where she was going. In fact, before my wife left the house, she asked Leila if she wanted to come shopping, and Leila said no. It was very hot that day, and she said she didn't feel like facing the heat. She was going to stay home and watch TV. At least that's what she told my wife, but when my wife got home, Leila was gone. This was around noon. Where she went was anybody's guess.'

'And she didn't have a driver?' Osama asked.

'No. My wife uses a taxi service, but we already checked with them. They only sent one car to the house that day, and that was to pick up my wife.'

'Had this ever happened before – Leila sneaking out like this?'

'She went out, of course, but she would always tell us where she was going. This time, she didn't even leave a note. She was simply gone. Normally, she goes out with Ra'id here. She always arranges things with him, respecting his schedule.'

Osama turned to Ra'id. 'And did she tell you she was going out that day?'

Ra'id shook his head uncertainly.

'We tried reaching her on her mobile,' Abdulrahman went on, 'but it wasn't ringing, and she didn't come back at all that night. That's when we knew something was wrong.'

'And did you call any of her friends?'

'No. I don't have their numbers. They were in Leila's phone. I presume she had it with her.'

Osama turned to the uncomfortable question he'd been avoiding until now. 'And what did you do that day?'

'I was out most of the morning,' Abdulrahman said, looking warningly at Ra'id. 'I go out once a week to shop for fabrics.'

'Anyone who can vouch for your whereabouts?'

He paused, thinking. 'The vendors at the fabric souq might remember. Fuad stayed here. The shop was open, of course.'

Osama took down the names of the vendors. Then he glanced at Ra'id, who glared back at him. 'I was here, too,' the boy said.

'When?'

'Ahh . . .' Ra'id struggled to remember. 'From about ten o'clock until five.'

Osama turned to Fuad, who was sitting at the desk in a strangely still aspect. 'I presume the sales assistants can account for your presence here?' he asked.

'Yes, if this new batch has half a brain between them.' Fuad let out his breath. 'But that morning, I was out. Our air conditioning was broken in the workshop, and I had to go to the repair shop.'

Osama gazed at him, waiting for more. When Fuad didn't

supply it, Osama was forced to ask: 'They didn't come here to fix the air conditioning?'

'No. I only needed to pick up a part.'

'How long were you gone?'

Fuad began to bristle. 'All morning. After I got the part, I went and had coffee with a friend. I didn't get back here until around noon.'

That seemed a long time to be gone. Osama wrote down the names and addresses of the friend and the air-conditioning repair shop. Faiza was sitting beside him, arms crossed defiantly, looking for all the world like she would have arrested the three of them right there and then. It gave Osama an uneasy feeling.

'Was your sister married?' Osama asked.

Annoyingly, Fuad answered. 'Yes. For two and a half months.'

Osama was beginning to think it odd and intrusive that Fuad had such easy recall of all the details of Leila's life, but the whole conversation had been punctuated by nervous glances at his boss. Fuad was searching for approval and he looked fearful of rebuke. Abdulrahman sat as still as a dry stone fountain.

'And when did the marriage end?'

'Eight months ago.'

Ra'id pressed his lips together, clearly holding back a nasty remark about Leila's ex-husband. Osama made notes of it all. 'I'm going to need the name and address of her ex-husband.'

While Fuad went to the computer to get the information, Abdulrahman remained on the sofa, gripping his knees, looking much like a boxer sitting in the corner of the ring. Osama noticed for the first time that he had a meaty build and very intimidating shoulders.

'What kind of relationship did she have with her ex-husband?' Faiza asked.

'None,' Fuad said from across the room, pre-empting the angry remark Ra'id was about to make. 'They hadn't spoken in months.'

Abdulrahman blinked furiously. 'After her divorce, she moved in with me.'

'Your sister was . . .' Osama checked his notepad, 'twenty-three years old?'

'Yes,' Abdulrahman said. 'That marriage was a bad decision from the start.'

'Why?' Osama asked.

'It was arranged. He was a cousin of ours. She didn't know him at all. Once she realised what he was really like, she divorced him. It was my mother's fault, *Allah yarhamha*.'

Faiza crossed her arms and planted a hand on her chin.

Ra'id gave a soft snort; Osama almost missed it, but he could see that the men wouldn't say anything more on the subject. 'What about the rest of your family?' he asked.

'My parents are dead,' Abdulrahman replied. 'I have four other brothers, but they live in Syria now. My mother was from Syria, but my father was from Jeddah. We grew up here. When my father died, our brothers returned to Damascus. Leila stayed here.'

'And how often did she do work for the news station?'

'About once every three weeks or so.'

'Did she usually wear modest clothing when she went out?'

'She didn't *usually* go out,' he said. 'But yes, when she did, she always wore a cloak, a headscarf and a burqa.'

'I presume she kept copies of all of her footage,' Osama said, hoping. 'Would it be possible to see it?'

'I believe we have a copy of some of her work here,' Fuad said.

He began rummaging through a desk drawer. Ra'id's eyes followed him nervously.

'How much money did she earn freelancing?' Osama asked.

Abdulrahman's face darkened. 'I'm not sure. It wasn't much. Certainly not enough for her to support herself.'

'Your business does well,' Osama said.

'Yes,' Fuad said bluntly.

Ra'id stood up abruptly and left the room. The phone rang, and although nobody answered, Osama could tell that the men were ready for them to leave. 'One last thing,' he said. 'Was there anyone who harassed her regularly? Anyone she talked about repeatedly or whom she might have known on sight?'

Abdulrahman glared at him. 'If someone had been stalking Leila, we would have known about it.' His voice was hostile now. 'We would have hired a driver for her, or asked her to find another job. We would never have let her get into trouble.'

Fuad stood up from the computer and gave Osama a pair of discs and a small slip of paper on which he'd written the address of the news station Leila worked for.

Osama glanced at the door. Ra'id had disappeared.

'Was your nephew close to your sister?' Osama asked.

Abdulrahman shot a menacing look at the doorway. 'Yes, he was.'

'I'd like you to bring him back here. We're going to have some more questions for him.'

With a flick of the hand, Abdulrahman motioned for Fuad to go after him.

Then began the tedious business of confirming the alibis. Abdulrahman remained on the sofa, staring furiously at the floor. When he made no protest about the police taking over his shop, Osama thought that they might be getting off lightly, and indeed with a couple of phone calls he was able to confirm that Abdulrahman had been at the fabric souq shopping that morning. They also checked his business records and found receipts for his purchases. Fuad's alibi held up as well. He had indeed visited the air-conditioning repair shop and then gone for coffee with a friend. But everything from there took a bad turn. Talking to the sales staff and the workers in the studio, Osama was able to confirm that Abdulrahman had come to work late, that he had spent the entire day here, that he hadn't been there at all, and that he had come and gone with frequency for most of the morning. To make matters worse, when Fuad finally returned it was to announce that Ra'id had left the premises. His car was gone from out the back, and he wasn't answering his mobile.

'I'm sorry,' Fuad said, looking angry. 'He's an impulsive boy.'

Abdulrahman looked grimly satisfied.

When Osama questioned the rest of the staff about Ra'id, he got an even bigger jumble of contradictory stories than the ones he'd heard about Abdulrahman. One of the fabric workers said: 'Ra'id is always in and out. No one ever knows where he is, even when he's here.'

Only Fuad's alibi seemed to hold up. All of the workers could recall him having been gone that morning, and they knew precisely when he had returned – just before their noon break. Fuad was apparently a taskmaster, and when he was at the shop, he made his presence felt. He had refused to let two of the fabric workers take a lunchbreak that afternoon because he wasn't satisfied with the work they'd done in his absence. Equally, the sales staff recalled him harassing them about a lock on the bathroom door which had been broken the night before when someone had handled it carelessly. Fuad had made one of the salesmen spend his lunch hour hunting down a locksmith.

Eventually, Osama called the station and requested that a forensics team meet him at Abdulrahman's house. He also requested back-up to take Abdulrahman home. He could have done it himself, but he wanted to talk to Faiza alone in the car.

Osama went back into the office, where Faiza was keeping watch over Abdulrahman.

'Mr Nawar, we're taking you back to your flat,' Osama explained. 'We'd like to have a look at Leila's room.'

'My wife is there,' Abdulrahman snarled. 'And my children are home.'

'We'll make sure they aren't disturbed,' Osama said.

'*You* are not allowed to talk to them, do you understand?'

Osama nodded, annoyed by the bullishness of his tone and its implication that Osama wanted more from the wife than a simple interview. 'We may need to ask them some questions however,' he replied evenly. 'Officer Shanbari here will talk to them.'

Abdulrahman eyed Faiza as if it were the first time he'd noticed her presence. He stared at her long and hard, then finally said: 'Fine. She may talk to my wife, but I will be present when she does.'

Once the back-up had come to collect Abdulrahman, Osama and Faiza went back to the car. Fuad saw them out, and apologised for not having offered something to drink.

It's only worse when you do, Osama thought.

Back in the car, Faiza kept her burqa up. He was beginning to realise that this was a sign that she wanted to say something unpleasant.

He started the car and drove, trying not to think about what she might say. She reached down for the paper bag, took out another doughnut and began to eat, casting him a slightly guilty look. He had to smile.

'They knew before we told them,' she said.

'Yeah, it was strange,' he replied. 'Her brother seemed to know. But it could have been common sense. Police don't usually show up unless there's something wrong.'

She nodded. 'Maybe our faces gave it away.'

'I thought you were going to tell me we should have given them a harder time,' he said, noticing that she had a dot of chocolate on her nose.

She smiled. 'You could have been a little rougher.'

'How is it that the woman in this equation is telling the man how to be tough?'

'Isn't that what always happens?' she asked. 'Think back on your parents.'

'You don't know my parents.'

'I don't have to, they're all the same.' She spoke with food in her mouth and it was somehow endearing.

'No,' he said firmly, 'they're not all the same. And my wife never tells me to be tough. It's only you, Faiza.'

This time with an even guiltier look, she reached back into the bag.

'There's a *fourth*?' he asked, incredulous. 'When did you . . .? Give me that.'

'You can have half.' She split the doughnut before he could protest and thrust one half towards him.

'No, no. I don't want it,' he said. 'I just didn't want you to eat it. That's your fourth one!'

'My husband likes me fat,' she replied in all sincerity.

He watched a tentacle of cream filling dangle above the seat. She set the half doughnut in his hand and he took it.

'Those men were lying,' she said. 'Not about their alibis, but about Ra'id.'

'You think they let him go?'

She nodded.

'I agree,' he replied through a mouthful, hoping he sounded casual enough. In fact, he hadn't suspected them of lying, and Rafiq's words rose up in a haunting symphony in his head: *If you're going to be so damn nice, Osama, at least do it to the people who deserve it. Like me.* He swallowed uncomfortably and took a swig of coffee. But he'd toughened up a lot since then. *I try not to be too mean in front of you*, he wanted to tell Faiza. *Someday you'll see it. I can be hard when I need to.*

He looked at her, but she popped the last of the doughnut in her mouth and lowered her burqa.

☾

Abdulrahman's house was one of the most lavish Osama had ever seen. It was new, perhaps only a few years old, but built in a

125

traditional style that, for all of its unusual features, smacked of Jeddah through and through. On the outside was a tall façade of coral stone, with elegant screened woodwork covering the windows and a large patio overlooking the street. Abdulrahman led Osama, Faiza, and the first of many forensics men into the house. He was still looking nervous and shaken. A servant arrived, and Abdulrahman sent the man to bring them drinks.

'Actually,' one of the forensics men said, 'we'd like it if you could wait outside.'

The servant looked to Abdulrahman for guidance. 'Very well,' Abdulrahman said. 'Do as these men say.' The servant left and Abdulrahman turned to Osama. 'My wife is out,' he said. 'I just spoke with her, though. She's at her sister's house across town.'

'We're going to need to talk to her eventually,' Osama said.

Osama and Faiza and a forensics team followed Abdulrahman into the central courtyard, an enormous indoor space radiating green from the abundance of plants and the elaborate mosaics on every wall. Below, in a sunken atrium, was a swimming pool, its bottom tiled to resemble an enormous, woven carpet. The doorways, twice the size of normal men, were arched, every surface layered with polished stone and detailed carvings reading *Allah* and *Allah Akbar.* Osama's first thought was that Abdulrahman would clearly have had no trouble supporting Leila. They walked through half a dozen gloriously decorated rooms, each bearing some evidence of a traditional style: an antique hookah sitting beside two stone benches; Bedouin antiques of all sorts, including a rifle and bandoleer hanging on the wall; and a marble slab propped against the wall. The slab was engraved with a passage from the Quran. Passing through every room took them over richly woven carpets, detailed stone tiles, or newly polished wood.

Climbing a wide flight of stairs, they entered a large sitting room, its upper balustrades rich with marble crenellations. There were sofas here, set in a large square so that three sofas sat side by side against each wall. Beyond that was a massive round sculpture that looked like a Bedouin teapot blown up to the size of an automobile. It might have been tacky but its exterior was screened metal, and inside were two chairs, both facing a large bay window. Between the chairs was a handsome telescope.

They followed Abdulrahman through the sitting room to a hallway that led to a series of upper-storey bedrooms. The doors were open. Peeking in, Osama spotted king-sized beds in each. He was beginning to think the house could sleep a hundred people.

'Was it only your family and Leila living here?' Osama asked.

Abdulrahman still looked angry. 'Ra'id is here as well. He came a year ago.'

'Where is his room?'

'There.' Abdulrahman pointed to an open doorway and Osama glanced inside, half-hoping to find Ra'id.

Leila's room was at the end of the hall, perched in a corner of the house so that her windows gave a view of the garden, which wrapped around the back and sides of the house. Abdulrahman went to the wardrobe, a mighty structure of oak that stood against the wall. Sliding a key from a wooden niche on the side, he unlocked it. 'Her wardrobe,' he said. 'Everything else should be open. There's not much to see.'

'If you wouldn't mind waiting outside,' one of the forensics men said. 'One of the officers here will escort you.' A uniformed officer motioned to Abdulrahman, and the older man went without protest.

Osama watched the forensics team sweep through the room. Faiza stood beside him, looking around.

They went to the dresser, another intimidating oak structure, and studied the pictures on top. None of them were framed, simply splashed across the wood as if they'd been dropped there. One of the forensics men gave Osama a pair of plastic gloves, and he put them on. He looked through the pictures and soon became aware that Leila and Ra'id had spent a lot of time together. There were pictures of the two of them lounging on a private beach, laughing at the bowling alley, splashing around in the swimming pool downstairs. Lots of photos of cats in various parts of the house. A few of Abdulrahman, looking hierophantic.

'He was right,' Faiza said, 'there's not much of Leila in this room.' A few clothes, a couple of school books sitting dusty on the shelf. No jewellery or make-up. The bathroom had a few essentials but was missing the small army of hair products and creams that Osama had come to associate with women. Most conspicuous of all, there was little sign that a filmmaker had ever lived in the room – no camera bags or cameras or lenses, no stacks of DVDs.

'She didn't have her camera with her when she disappeared,' Osama said, thinking out loud. 'It got destroyed at the Corniche when she was injured that day.'

'Maybe she bought another one,' Faiza said.

'Shouldn't there at least be a camera bag here?'

'You're right. There's nothing.'

'There's no computer either,' Osama said. 'I'm no expert, but wouldn't you need a computer to edit film?'

'I think so,' Faiza said. 'Or you'd need some pretty expensive equipment.'

'Her brother didn't say if she bought a new camera.'

They wandered back through the house, stopping in Ra'id's room only long enough to be disappointed again. There were clothes here, most of them scattered on the floor, and a tall shelf of CDs. A factory-issued computer box on the desk was still sealed.

They carried on, touring the house in a leisurely way, stopping to read the Quranic inscription – it was *all* Quranic inscription, everywhere words were hung – above a ceramic, wood-burning chimenea and an Ikea media shelf that was packed with CDs.

Standing above the central courtyard, Osama's thoughts shifted between competing ideas about Abdulrahman. At first he had assumed that Abdulrahman was the older Syrian bachelor type, busy snipping away at tiny scraps of lingerie for the bustling business that was practically Syria's birthright, and yet now he saw that Abdulrahman was all Jeddawi. He must have dumped millions of riyals into this house, and you wouldn't build a house like this in the first place unless you loved the city and its architecture. Abdulrahman seemed conservative. Of course, he designed and sold lingerie for a living, but that didn't mean he couldn't remain traditional in every other respect. After all, lingerie was meant to arouse a husband in the privacy of the bedroom. There was something frank and square about Abdulrahman that had caused Osama to think he was old-fashioned. The fact that he wouldn't let a male investigator talk to his wife seemed to confirm the point.

But now that Osama had seen the interior of the house, he realised that Abdulrahman fancied himself just as modern as anyone. It was in the CD rack, the satellite television, the iPod speaker system playing dulcet jazz in the sitting room. And perhaps that was what was so peculiar: that in Abdulrahman, the extremes of traditional and modern coexisted so comfortably.

They found Abdulrahman loitering outside the kitchen, watching the forensics men work with apprehension on his face.

'Mr Nawar,' Osama said, motioning him away from the kitchen door, 'did Leila buy a new camera after the old one was broken?'

'Yes,' Abdulrahman replied after a hesitation. 'Yes, she got another.'

Osama took out his notepad. 'Where did she get it?'

'I don't know.'

'What kind of camera was it?'

'A video camera . . . No, it was digital, I believe. I don't know anything about it.'

'Digital cameras are pretty expensive. Where did she get the money for one of those?'

Abdulrahman shrugged. 'Leila kept her business matters to herself.'

'And you never asked her?'

Abdulrahman turned his back on Osama and moved towards the kitchen. Osama felt insulted.

'Mr Nawar, we're not finished.' He waited for Abdulrahman to turn around.

'In order to edit film, your sister would have needed a computer, but I didn't see one in her room. Did she have one?'

'Yes,' Abdulrahman said, glowering now. 'If it's not in her room, then I don't know what happened to it.'

'Was it there after she disappeared?'

'I didn't notice,' he said. His face was like a stone mask. Osama didn't have to glance at Faiza to know that they were both thinking the same thing: that Abdulrahman was lying. Osama was getting annoyed.

'Your sister went missing and you didn't check her room?' he asked.

'Of course I checked her room!' Abdulrahman exploded. 'But I wasn't looking for a computer, I was looking for my sister!'

'It seems strange, Mr Nawar, that your sister bought herself a brand new digital camera and that you didn't ask her how she came by that kind of money? Yet you said earlier that Leila's job didn't pay well enough for her to support herself. How did she come by that money?'

'I already told you: I don't know.'

'And you never asked her?'

'No.'

'Did you ever ask her about her work? Do you know what she did when she left the house?'

'Of course!' he blurted angrily. 'She worked for the news station! And she occasionally took other jobs.'

'What kind of jobs?'

'Private work. For individuals. People she knew.'

'What was the last thing she was working on before she disappeared?'

'She was taking pictures of a religious art collection.'

'Was this for a museum?' Osama asked.

'No, a person. His name was Wahhab Nabih. He lived here in Jeddah. I'm not sure exactly where so don't ask.'

'Is that all she told you about the job?'

'Yes.'

Abdulrahman was making to leave again, but before he could turn away completely, Osama said: 'If you remember anything about the computer, you'll let me know.'

15

Katya was trying not to fall asleep from boredom. Her eyes were fixed on the computer screen. The second of Leila's discs was in the drive, and the dead woman's film footage was playing out – silent but for the typical background noises of a city street.

Majdi had already gone over the first disc but he hadn't had time for the rest of it, so he'd given it to her. Katya had imagined, after her coup with the Bluetooth burqa, that they might start giving her the really interesting evidence. Perhaps this was interesting and she just didn't know it. The footage was long and uncut, and the past forty minutes had been nothing but B-roll. Scenes of black-cloaked women walking through shopping malls, cars driving at night down a busy, nameless street, men praying at a mosque, the kinds of mind-numbing images that one could see every night on the local news.

This filler was not even part of Leila's last assignment filming B-roll for the local news station. It was dated five months ago, but Katya watched it anyway, just in case.

This morning, however, she'd had a small victory. She had managed to analyse some of the fibres that the coroner had pulled from Leila's wounds. They were goat hair, dyed black, the sort that was typically found in a man's *'iqal*. The black goat-hair cord the Bedouins used to hobble camels was the same cord men wore to fasten scarves to their heads. Unfortunately, every man in Saudi owned an *'iqal*, and the chances of being able to match the fibres to one in particular were extremely low. However, if they could find the *'iqal*, they might find traces of blood and skin on it.

She stopped fifteen minutes later and stood up to stretch her legs. The air outside was sticky and wet and it left a filmy coating on the windows. The reflected sunlight danced in watery patterns on the opposite wall. She took a bottle of orange juice from the little fridge by her desk and sat back down.

Finally, the B-roll came to an end. There was one more segment on the disc. It was shorter than the rest and titled *Games*. She opened it.

A woman's face appeared on the screen. She was in her twenties with a small pointed chin and almost grotesquely large eyes, a comic mixture that she used to wonderful effect.

'On the subject of game cards,' the woman said in formal speech, noting every short vowel with a tilt of the head, 'scientific researchers have finally proven that in fact the famous children's game, Pokémon, is indeed representative of evolutionary principles.' At the bottom of the screen a text box popped up. *Farooha Abdel Ali, Pokémon Specialist.*

Katya chuckled. 'Being of the generation of children who were briefly exposed to Pokémon in Saudi Arabia before the religious authorities banned it, I can attest to their claim that the game is a—' Here Farooha checked a note card in her hand. '"A Jewish-Darwinist theory that conflicts with the truth about humans", as they say. I can also confirm that it is a "front for Israel" that "possesses the minds of Saudi children". However, that is not to say that children don't enjoy trading the game cards and, in effect, learning the basic principles of gambling.'

Off the screen, Leila laughed – a loud, staccato burst that carried top notes of contagious glee.

Katya sat up. She stopped the disc and went back to listen to it again. It was such a beautiful laugh, and its effect was odd. Aside from the occasional exclamation, so far on the DVD there had been a conspicuous absence of Leila herself. That short, unguarded laughter had charged the room with her presence.

Katya flipped open the file and looked at the Bluetooth photo again. The look on Leila's face was self-consciously seductive. *Hi there, gorgeous*, it seemed to say. It was the same generic expression worn by models in fashion magazines.

Rewatching the segment on Pokémon, Katya wrote the name *Farooha Abdel Ali* on a sheet of paper and turned to the other computer. She did a quick people search on the police database for Farooha and found her immediately. The girl had registered with an ID card in Jeddah. *Thank Allah for ID cards*, Katya thought, snatching up the disc and leaving the room.

☽

Majdi was sitting in his lab as usual, a cup of Starbucks in one hand, the other hand clicking the computer mouse with efficiency. Katya stood behind him, dizzied by his quick scrolling through a series of digitised documents. They were photographs of old manuscripts.

'They found these in the victim's bedroom,' he said, indicating the documents. 'They were taped to the underside of a dresser drawer.'

'What are they?' Katya asked.

He shook his head. 'I've just scanned them into the computer and have been trying to figure them out. From the looks of it, they're Quranic, but I have to double-check. I don't know the Quran very well,' he added, casting a quick glance at her, checking for a reaction.

'You mean you haven't memorised the holy book?' she asked.

He gave her an appreciative smile. 'Unfortunately, I'm lacking in that area. But I am seeing references to prayers in these texts.'

The manuscripts were yellowing. The script was neat and loopy, the ink smudged in places. Katya struggled to read it but

Majdi was flipping so quickly through the pages that she only caught a word here and there.

Majdi skimmed through a few more documents before forcing himself to stop and turn to Katya. 'Anyway, what's going on upstairs?'

She told him about her discovery of Farooha. Majdi was not the sort of person who could express enthusiasm when his mind was obsessively focused on something else, but he gave a quick nod.

'Osama's out this morning,' he said, 'but I'll tell him when he gets in. Or you could tell him yourself.'

'Where is he?'

'Out looking for the victim's cousin. And the ex-husband. There's no telling when he'll be back.' Majdi finished the last of his coffee and threw the cup in the trash.

'What's the story with the ex-husband?' she asked.

'Leila hadn't seen him in months.'

It seemed a waste of resources to hunt down someone the victim hadn't seen in months. 'And her cousin?'

'A person of interest who disappeared when they were questioning the family at the lingerie shop.'

'Ah. What about her last assignment?' she said. 'There was something on the missing persons report about a photography job.'

'Yeah,' Majdi said, motioning to the computer screen. 'I've been toying with the idea that this is it. Leila's brother said she had done some film work for a man named Wahhab Nabih. The brother had no idea what kind of work Leila had done for the guy. She just told him it was a private religious art collection.'

'These documents could be considered an "art collection", don't you think?'

'Yeah, but the only problem is that I can't find anyone named Wahhab Nabih.'

'What do you mean?'

'There's no Wahhab Nabih in Saudi Arabia, and if there is, the guy has no passport, no ID card, no bank accounts, and no immigration records. The only thing I could find was a property here in Jeddah owned by a W. Nabih. So if it is the same guy, he owns a home but no ID card.'

'Maybe he's a Bedouin?'

'Believe it or not,' Majdi said, 'most male Bedouin have at least registered with the government.' He turned back to the screen. 'And anyway, Nabih isn't a Bedouin name. You don't happen to know anyone with expertise in analysing old Quranic documents, do you?'

Katya shook her head slowly. 'If this really was the last job she did, then wouldn't it be wise to send someone to find Mr Nabih?'

Majdi gave her a wry look. 'Yes, wouldn't it?'

'Will Osama—'

'Yeah, I'm sure he'll get on it once he tracks down the cousin.'

'What about sending junior officers?' she asked.

'I'm not sure he has any left,' Majdi said.

'Why would these be taped to Leila's dresser drawer?' she asked.

He shook his head. 'According to her brother, Leila preferred video, but occasionally she did photography jobs on the side. Her brother had some Quranic art in the house, but he didn't recognise the photos when we showed him these this morning.'

'I don't understand why she would hide them,' Katya said. 'Especially if they're pages from an old Quran. Her brother isn't opposed to religion, is he?'

'No,' Majdi said. 'I get the impression he's very religious. Aside from the fact that he runs a lingerie shop. But you're right, it is weird that she'd hide them. Maybe she did a job her brother had forbidden her to do for some reason. Or maybe she took the photos for someone who wanted them to stay secret; but if that's the case, then why hide them at her house?'

'I don't know,' Katya said. 'Maybe she wasn't supposed to have kept any copies of the work?'

'Perhaps.' Majdi's attention turned back to the screen. 'So do you want to tell Osama about this friend of Leila's that you found, or should I?'

'You'd better do it,' Katya said. 'I don't want to bother him if he's busy.' She felt foolish for saying it. The truth was, she just didn't have the nerve to face Osama. She knew little about him and about how direct contact with him might be received. 'But I trust you'll give me a glowing recommendation,' she added, grinning.

Majdi turned to her in surprise. 'Of course,' he said. 'I already told him you found the picture in the burqa.'

She smiled, although his earnestness had deflated the moment. Thanking him, she went back to her lab.

16

In the hallway in front of her flat, Katya struggled to unlock the front door before Ayman dropped the six shopping bags he'd managed to balance on his arms.

'What would I do without you?' she said.

'I don't know,' he grunted. 'What did you do before?'

'We didn't eat this much food.'

Ayman lurched into the flat and made straight for the kitchen.

'Hello!' Katya called to her father. The savoury smell of biryani spices greeted her a moment before Abu poked his head around the kitchen door. He was wearing an apron and there was a smear of curry on his cheek. Seeing Ayman about to collapse, he set down his ladle and helped him with the bags.

'What on earth did you buy?' Abu asked in amazement.

'A cake. Perrier and orange juice. Mangoes, in case he wants fruit.'

Abu shook his head and went back into the kitchen. Katya followed.

'Ayman,' her father said, 'I'm sending you out again. We need one more thing for dinner.'

'Oh, what?'

'Another fridge.' Abu eyed Katya with scorn. 'How big is this friend of yours?'

Katya smiled. 'Thank you for cooking,' she said, getting herself a glass of water. 'I'm going to change my clothes. Baba, remember, please be good to him. He can be awkward.'

'You've told me a dozen times.' He picked up the ladle and waved her out of the room, exchanging a glance with Ayman as she left. She knew what they were thinking: that she obviously had a crush on Nayir, and he obviously didn't deserve it.

Sweaty and sticky and hot, she took a cool shower but it did nothing to relax her. Her thoughts skipped through a silent list of worries – would Nayir like her father? What would he think of Ayman? Was he going to be silent and judgemental all through dinner, and would she have to do the talking? What could she talk about that wouldn't land her in a potential mine-field?

She couldn't decide what to wear. Nayir had never seen her in regular clothes before; he'd only ever seen her in a black cloak. But she wasn't going to wear a cloak in the house. That was one of her rules for the evening. She would dress as she always did. She'd wear a headscarf but not a burqa. Looking into her closet, everything suddenly seemed too risqué. Jeans? They were form-fitting. The only house robe she had would make her feel as if she were wearing her pyjamas. She settled for a loose pair of black trousers and a blue silk tunic with a delicate lace trim. It was a little dressy but she figured it was all right.

Standing in front of the bathroom mirror, she tried to decide if she needed make-up. Perhaps a little blusher? She didn't wear make-up during the day, only on special occasions, and this felt like one of those. Except that Nayir was going to see her face, and he probably wouldn't approve of make-up. She could still remember his reaction when she had accidentally pulled a bottle of nail varnish from her bag. '*You paint your nails?*'

She dabbed on some lip gloss and left it at that.

There was a knock on the door. She was surprised to find her friend Donia standing in the hallway outside her room. Her three little girls were lined up behind her like nesting dolls, each dressed in the same blue frock, each one as timid as the next.

'Donia, what a wonderful surprise!' Katya was sure her voice cracked. She greeted her friend with kisses and hugged each of the girls in turn, inviting them all into the room. But her mind was working frantically: *What are they doing here? Why didn't Abu tell me he'd invited them?*

'We came with my father,' Donia said, sitting at the dressing table. Katya's stomach did a plunge. 'The girls have been looking forward to wearing their new dresses.'

Katya fawned over the dresses and told them how lovely they were. The girls were clearly pleased, but they glanced meekly at their mother.

Katya had known Donia for many years. Their fathers had met at the mosque and become friends because both men worked in the chemistry field – her father at the plant, and Abu-Walid at the university. However, Katya's now-dead mother had always felt that Abu-Walid had had a negative effect on her husband. He was extremely devout, and his religious influence began to find its way into their own household. After becoming close to him, Abu began praying five times a day and following all of the niggling Wahhabi rules that seemed, to Katya's mother at least, nothing more than an outward show of religiosity. Because it was forbidden to alter your body, Abu stopped shaving. He only ate halal meat, and he gave up cigarettes completely. He began to insist that Katya and her mother wear burqas when his friends came to the house. Katya's mother reminded him that he was Lebanese, but that only made him angry. 'I am *Muslim*,' he'd say.

Donia was looking at the make-up case lying open on the dressing table. Katya could see the disapproval in her eyes. Thrown together by parental association, the two women had got along for many years by virtue of persistence. Donia was the youngest child in her family, and having been subject to the abuses of seven older brothers, she was shy to the point of obstinacy. Conversations with her tended to be slow. She liked to cook, and keeping a clean house was important to her. She expressed emotion rarely. Most of the time Katya had to strain to hear her voice.

Katya used to pity her. Donia was meek and seemingly battered, the sort of woman an ultra-devout household would naturally produce. Only when Katya was older had she come to realise that beneath the sweet, modest exterior, Donia was actually quite tough.

Katya found herself talking nervously about her job and the fun she had in the lab. She left out the details about corpses and murder for the sake of the children, but she managed to keep up a steady stream of chatter. All the while her mind was racing. Donia's father was in the men's sitting room right now, probably wondering why Abu had done the cooking and silently chastising Katya for not having done it herself. Why on earth had her father invited him tonight – and not told her? She couldn't help feeling betrayed. *He's just nervous about meeting Nayir*, she thought. After all, Katya had described Nayir's piety often enough. Perhaps he thought Nayir and Abu-Walid would have a lot in common. But a darker possibility lurked: that he had invited Abu-Walid because his presence would enforce the household's segregation. Now Katya would eat dinner in the kitchen with Donia and the girls, and the men would stay in the sitting room, the *majlis*. She could imagine her father thinking, *Yes, Katya can have her 'friend' over for dinner, but she won't be allowed to SEE him.*

They went into the empty kitchen. The food had been abandoned in a half-done state. Immediately, Donia felt more at home. She rolled up the sleeves of her cloak and began to help with the preparations. The girls all took seats at the kitchen table. The oldest one offered to help and her mother put her to work dicing tomatoes for the salad.

'But be careful not to ruin your new dress,' she said.

Fifteen minutes later, Ayman came into the room to check on the progress. Donia quickly covered her face. 'Everyone's hungry,' he said.

'Has Nayir arrived?' Katya asked.

'Yes, he's in the sitting room.' He smiled. 'You didn't tell us how big he was. I see now why you bought all this extra food.'

Katya smacked his arm. 'Don't make fun of him. You'd better not make him uncomfortable. What's my father doing?'

'It's fine,' Ayman said, serious now. 'Really!'

The meal was ready, and Ayman insisted on carrying it into the *majlis* himself. He loaded the salad, meat and rice on to an enormous platter and balanced it on one arm, then scooped another platter of side dishes into the other.

'Let me help,' Katya said.

'No.' Ayman gave her a steady look. 'I'll do it.'

She stared at him, feeling suddenly vulnerable and nervous. Donia was watching. 'All right,' Katya said. 'I'll bring in the dessert later.'

Ayman quickly left the room.

The women ate at the kitchen table. Perhaps sensing that Katya was anxious, Donia made an effort to start a conversation. She talked about a recipe she'd found online, and about her cousin's new baby. For once Katya was glad that the discussion didn't require too much thought. It gave her room to nurse the wound that was opening in her heart. Her father should have told her about inviting guests; his silence was deceitful. If she had been alone, she would have gone into the men's sitting room, like it or not. Nayir was her friend, after all. But now it would be rude to leave Donia and the girls alone in the kitchen. She thought of poor Nayir, probably doing his best to impress her father – and now her father's friend – by sitting awkwardly through a meal with strangers when he'd expected to see Katya.

Halfway through the meal, she realised it was rude of her not to greet Nayir, at least to say hello. She got up from the table, adjusted her headscarf and excused herself, saying she had to go to the bathroom. Creeping down the hallway, she heard Abu-Walid's deep, resonant voice. She stopped outside the door to the *majlis* and steeled herself to go inside. And interrupt their dinner. And see Nayir look uncomfortable. And put up with Abu-Walid's disapproving looks. Her father would probably send her out for salt, or napkins, or any contrived errand just to get her out of the room. The thought of it made her angry and redoubled her resolve, but every time she put her hand on the door, she pulled back. *Why am I acting like a child?* She had to greet Nayir – she had invited him! This whole thing was her idea. But she couldn't do it. She went back to the kitchen, sat at the table, and with a stiff smile tried to finish her meal.

After dinner, her father came into the kitchen. Donia quickly covered her face again. Abu greeted her and the children warmly.

Katya leapt up to get the cake from the fridge, but Abu took it from her and bullishly insisted on bringing it out himself. 'You stay here with Donia. We're fine in the other room.' And with that he was out the door, leaving Katya to face a sink full of dishes.

Almost two hours later, Abu returned to announce that Abu-Walid was ready to go home.

'What about Nayir?' Katya asked.

'He's still here,' her father said.

Donia looked relieved to be going. The girls were getting tired and they had school in the morning. After hugging each of them and watching them leave, Katya looked down at herself and felt like crying. She had dressed up, for what?

She wasn't going to let it get to her. Putting the water on – never mind that the men had already had tea – she prepared a tea service and brought it to the sitting room. On the way, she passed Ayman's bedroom door and saw that he was inside watching TV. It filled her with dread. The conversation in the *majlis* must have been profoundly boring to force the funniest man in the house back to his bedroom.

She paused at the *majlis* door. She heard laughter within, the great explosive sound of her father's delight. Peeking in, she saw that her father and Nayir were sitting on the sofas, talking and laughing and drinking the last of their tea. The scene filled her with anger – and beneath it a worse feeling, something like grief. She didn't want them to see it on her face, so she steeled herself and, pushing the door open with her foot, she entered the room.

They stopped talking. Nayir, whose face had held an expression of warmth a moment before, sat up and looked nervous. She couldn't bear it, so she glanced at her father and saw his eyes glimmer with – was it triumph?

'I thought you might like some tea,' she said, setting the service on the coffee table.

'Thank you,' Abu said. Katya decided then that she wasn't going to be afraid any more. He couldn't dismiss her with an easy 'thank you'. She sat down on the sofa beside her father. Leaning forward, she poured out a cup of tea and offered it to him. He declined, so she turned to Nayir, who also declined. *Fine*, she thought, taking the tea for herself. Her cheeks were beginning to flush with irritation.

Nayir avoided looking at her face, but she could feel his attention turn to her like the soft touch of a hundred invisible hands. She remembered that this was the first time he'd ever seen her out of her cloak – and in front of her father, too! – and suddenly her anger turned into anxiety. The conversation was dead and neither of the men was going to restart it. She could almost hear their thoughts. *Why isn't she wearing a cloak? What does she want?*

This is ridiculous, she thought.

'How is work?' Nayir asked. It took her a heartbeat to realise that he was talking to her, and her heart exploded with relief.

144

'It's fine,' she said. 'I really like my new job.'

He nodded. It wasn't quite the apology she'd been hoping for, but she softened anyway. 'What about you? How's the desert?'

He shrugged. 'I was supposed to be there now, but the clients cancelled. Business is always slow in summer.'

'I was just telling Nayir that he ought to change careers,' Abu said. Katya felt a stab of embarrassment, which doubled when she realised that she had told Nayir the same thing eight months ago.

Nayir seemed amused. 'Your father thinks I should be a Quranic scholar.'

Katya's insides did an uncomfortable pirouette. The thought made him seem less like the sort of man she could ever be happy with. She forced a smile.

'But we've decided,' Abu went on, 'that if he doesn't like the idea of becoming a scholar, then he really ought to consider becoming an investigator. After all, he's already solved one crime.'

Nayir looked at Katya's shoe as if he wanted to tell her something but didn't have the nerve. Privately, she fought a silent battle to dominate her disappointment. Her father had never said even this much to her – and it was she who had worked so hard to find Nouf's killer, she who in fact helped solve crimes for a living.

'I would have to agree,' she said, looking at Nayir, 'that he would make a very good investigator.'

The men picked up the conversation that she'd interrupted when she came in. She sipped her tea and listened – they were talking politics – but she couldn't help marvelling at their rapport. There was nothing false about the way her father was smiling, and Nayir, although obviously a little nervous, was comfortable enough to express his opinions.

When the conversation slowed, her father stood up and said: 'Water, anyone?'

'No, thank you,' Nayir replied, glancing at Katya, who simply shook her head. She couldn't believe the flips her stomach was doing at the prospect of being left alone with Nayir. Her father went out, and she sat up at once.

'I'm sorry I didn't come in sooner,' she said. 'I was busy in the kitchen.'

'Of course. I understand.' Nayir looked embarrassed, but she couldn't tell why. Did he think it was bold of her to assume he'd want to see her? Or was he just being awkward?

Dammit, she thought, *I'm becoming neurotic.*

'I did some checking into that friend of your uncle's,' she said, setting her teacup on the table and leaning closer to him. He didn't back away. 'The coroner had no reason to suspect foul play. Apparently, Qadhi died of a massive coronary. He'd had two heart episodes before.'

'Really?'

'Yes, and he was on medication.'

Nayir looked resigned. 'Thank you for checking.'

Her father still hadn't returned, and she suspected that he was leaving them this time on purpose. But she feared at any moment he would come back into the room. *I'm sure that's what he wants me to believe.* She had the feeling that, now that she'd told Nayir what he'd come to find out, he'd get up and go.

'There's something I wanted to ask you,' she said, not even sure that it was a good idea. It had just occurred to her in their earlier conversation. 'We're working on a new case right now. A young Saudi woman was found murdered on the beach.' It pleased her to see that, despite his natural reticence for involving himself in the lives of strange women, he was interested, so she told him what she could about Leila Nawar and the few leads the police were following. 'But there's one thing that's come up in the investigation. The homicide squad, of course, has a lot on its hands. They don't have the time to follow every lead.' She didn't tell him her own motivation, that she was hoping to get into investigating herself. 'When Leila first disappeared,' she said, 'her brother filed a police report. He said she had been photographing a private art collection. It could be completely unrelated, but they can't find the man she was working for. There's a street address, but nothing else. They think that his art collection might have included Quranic manuscripts. I would really like to try to find this guy.'

'The police aren't trying?' Nayir asked.

'Like I said, they haven't prioritised it. They're too busy with other leads. I was thinking – with your background, and your knowledge of the Quran . . .' It was a frail excuse, she realised, but he took the bait so quickly that it surprised her.

'Yes,' he said. 'I'd be glad to help.' She saw a determination in his eyes that she hadn't seen – or perhaps hadn't noticed before now.

'Would you come with me to this man's flat?' she asked. 'It might be a dead end. He owns the building, but it doesn't mean he lives there. I think it's worth a try.'

Nayir nodded. 'When do you want to go?'

'Tomorrow at noon?'

'I can meet you at your work.'

She couldn't help smiling.

Abu came back a while later, and Nayir rose to leave. He thanked them for the meal and the conversation, but when Abu made to walk their guest to the door, Katya took her father's arm and pushed him gently in the direction of the kitchen. She would escort Nayir to the street herself.

It surprised her again to see that he was pleased to be alone with her. They walked in silence.

At the bottom of the front stairs, he turned to her and said: 'I always felt that you were the one who solved Nouf's case.'

She bit her lip and smiled. 'We did it together, remember?'

'Yes,' he said softly. 'I remember it all.' He seemed to be blushing but she couldn't be sure. Then he turned and walked into the night.

17

Osama opened the front door to a ruckus – blaring television, women laughing and his three-year-old son, Muhannad, shrieking in delight. He smiled and entered the foyer.

The women's sitting room was just off the hall, and the door was open. Announcing himself with a tap on the wall, Osama took off his shoes and dropped his mobile on the hall table.

Muhannad came running into the hall and grabbed his father's knees. Osama lifted him and covered his face in kisses. 'Did you miss me?' he asked. Muhannad nodded frantically, then squirmed and kicked to be let down again. He raced back into the women's sitting room.

A door opened down the hallway and his wife's grandmother emerged, shuffling slowly like a wind-up toy, looking around with the big, blinking eyes of the lost. Her headscarf was sliding down, and her balding head, sparsely covered with thin strands of white and black hair, shone in the overhead light.

He approached and kissed her forehead, greeted her with a smile. She was deaf. She smiled back with a modest, happy look, patted him on the arm, and then seemed to forget what she was doing there or why she'd come.

'Osama.'

He turned. Behind him, Nuha stood in the doorway of the sitting room. She was wearing jeans and a thin little top that glittered with golden threads. He knew she'd put them on for him, and it made him want to take her in his arms, scoop her up right there in front of her grandmother and carry her straight to the bedroom. He wanted to ignore it all – dinner, Muhannad, everyone around them and the house itself, a sizeable duplex that they shared with his in-laws. He could see in her face that she wanted the same thing, and that although she'd been laughing with her cousins or friends, she'd also been waiting for him.

She moved past him. The smell of her shot longing through him. Nuha took her grandmother by the hand and led her towards the sitting room. 'Rafiq is coming soon,' she said over her shoulder. 'And Mona.' Mona was Rafiq's wife. On any other day he'd have been glad for their company, but he wasn't in the mood tonight.

'Jidda,' Nuha said, even though the old woman couldn't hear her, 'your scarf is falling again.' She fastened it securely and led her grandmother to the sitting room, calling over her shoulder: 'I'll be right there.'

Osama went into the kitchen and slumped down at the table. It had been a depressing day. Faiza had interviewed Abdulrahman's wife at the house that morning. Abdulrahman had insisted on being present for the interview. Faiza was an excellent observer. She could see through the wife's carefully respectful answers. Even so, her impressions were conflicting. Abdulrahman ruled his household like the average traditional guy: he expected his wife to stay at home and raise the kids. But with Leila he wasn't traditional at all. Leila went out to do whatever she liked. The wife didn't seem upset by this apparent contradiction in Abdulrahman's behaviour, rather she viewed it as the natural instinct of a man who understood that the two women were very different. His wife preferred to stay at home with the kids. Leila would have hated it, so he let her go out. The wife also claimed that there had never been any tension between Leila and anyone else in the house.

149

Osama doubted this was true. Nobody, *nobody*, lived their lives without feeling some antagonism towards a relative. But Faiza was the best interrogator they had, and if that was all she could learn in a two-hour interview, then for now they'd reached a dead end. He would have to get the truth about Leila's living situation from somebody else, although who would have access to the family that Abdulrahman guarded so jealously, Osama had no idea.

There was still no indication of where Leila's cousin Ra'id had gone. He hadn't returned to Abdulrahman's house the night before, and they'd been unable to hunt him down at friends' houses. Feeling that he'd better leave the Nawar household alone for a bit, Osama had gone in search of Leila's ex-husband, Bashir. First he'd gone to the man's flat only to find that Bashir had vacated the premises the week before. He and Faiza had managed to track down Bashir's brother, Hakim, who owned the shop on the building's ground floor. He wasn't *there*, of course. They'd had to spend the afternoon driving around the city, talking to friends, talking to strangers at last-known addresses. After six hours of this they'd finally caught up with Hakim . . . back at the shop.

Apparently, Hakim was smarter than his brother. He'd heard about Leila's disappearance – Abdulrahman had called to tell them back when she'd gone missing – at which point Hakim had counselled his brother not to leave his flat just yet. If it ever came down to a police investigation, his behaviour would be flagged as suspicious. But Bashir had a mind of his own. He'd been planning on moving for six months and he wasn't going to let a little hypothetical police investigation interfere with it.

Where had he gone? Osama wanted to know. Hakim had spread his hands to the side, shrugged his shoulders and turned his eyes to the heavens in an eloquent display of ignorance. 'We didn't get along. Aside from that conversation I just described to you, we hadn't spoken in months.' It turned out that Bashir had been sponging off his brother for the better part of a year, and Hakim was getting sick of it. What a terrible irony it was, Hakim pointed out, that after a year of suggesting – not asking, mind you, because it would have been unthinkable to actually kick his brother out of the flat – but merely *suggesting* that Bashir try to find a decent job and get a place of his own, after a whole year of this, Bashir had finally decided to move out, at which point Hakim had practically begged him to stay. For his own good, of course. Just until they found Leila.

Hakim went on and on about what a lazy man his brother had become, how Bashir had changed so much since childhood that Hakim almost couldn't believe they were related. He was so much smarter than his brother that Osama began to wonder why Hakim was still standing around when Bashir had had the good sense to flee. Oh, but Hakim was wickedly smart, Osama could tell from the outset. Every detail of his story was cleverly contrived to convey his brother's innocence. To hear it told, Bashir knew that his ex-wife was missing, knew that the police might come asking questions – but he remained untroubled by it, because he was innocent and that was what innocent people did. They didn't crumble with guilt. They went nonchalantly about their lives.

But there was one thing Hakim didn't know: Osama had heard it all before.

Osama watched the entire act with a distant sense of appreciation but mainly with growing annoyance. *But Officer, I didn't get along with my* . . . Brother. Sister. Uncle. Cousin. Whomever the police had come to arrest. Because everyone knew that if a suspect couldn't be found, the police would happily take a relative as insurance, until the suspect chose to turn themselves in. So most relatives attempted to portray an unhappy family – *But sir, I haven't spoken to my father in sixteen months* – in the hope that an officer would actually believe it. Osama sometimes had the impression that there were no happy families left in Jeddah.

They'd arrested Hakim anyway. After getting him back to the

station, they'd discovered that Bashir was actually a guest worker from Syria, and his visa had expired six months before. Hakim became indignant. 'Do you really think that selfish bastard brother of mine is going to turn himself in when his visa is expired? Do you think he would do such a thing *for me*?' His hollow laughter still rang in Osama's ears.

Osama had handed him a mobile and told him to call his brother.

'Tell him that if he turns himself in, we'll help him get his visa renewed. Unless he killed his ex-wife, of course.'

Hakim had pushed the phone back across the table. 'He's too self-serving. Nothing I say will do a damn bit of good, I guarantee it.'

He was pretty good, Osama had to admit. Most people jumped at the chance to use the phone, but Hakim was stubborn. Osama left him in the interrogation room.

Of course, not having spoken to his brother for so long, Hakim insisted he knew nothing of his whereabouts when Leila disappeared. He didn't know whether Bashir still held a grudge against his ex-wife, whether he had a reason to, or what had happened in that marriage at all. Two men living in the same house for a year and they knew nothing about one another.

The final blow had occurred after Osama went back in to offer the phone one last time. Hakim refused, looking prideful. Osama moved to leave and Hakim called after him: 'My father was always ashamed of Bashir, but if my father were still alive, Allah bless him, and he were here right now, I think he would be ashamed of *you*.' Osama hadn't even turned around, but the words had done their job.

Nuha came into the kitchen and began unwrapping the plates of food that had been waiting on the counter for him. When she saw the look in his eyes, she came closer. 'This case is a bad one, I can tell.'

'It's getting worse,' he said.

'I'm so sorry.'

He grabbed her waist, pulled her on to his lap, and kissed her hard on the lips. 'I don't want Rafiq to come tonight,' he said. 'I want to go to bed.'

'Alone?'

'I didn't say that.' He caught the side of her smile and leaned in to kiss her forehead, her temple, her cheek. She met his mouth.

An hour later, the house was quiet. Muhannad was with his grandparents. Nuha's cousins had gone to the other half of the house to watch their nightly soap opera. Nuha had cancelled with Rafiq and Mona, so the couple had gone somewhere else for the evening. Osama ate a quick dinner then went in search of Nuha.

She was in the bedroom. The room was large, but she'd turned out the lamps and lit candles by the bedside so that it seemed as if the bed were floating in a golden bubble. The force that sprang up inside him was all out of keeping with the tenderness of the scene, but it didn't frighten him, it only turned him on more. He was hard by the time he reached the bed, and when she felt the strength of his grip as he stripped off her jeans, excitement flared in her eyes.

The first time it was over too quickly, the second time was more satisfying, burying him deep in his body like an animal in a cave. This was what drugs must be like, he thought, this float-ing, subliminal, half-understood state. And somewhere in the darkness of the cave he felt himself becoming a different being, a collection of nerves, of cells and plasma and blood. Images appeared, borrowed from half-remembered college textbooks, of the strata of skin layers, of bright red blood cells furiously split-ting, and grey ganglia spreading like vines. It took him a while to realise that he also heard a beat, the distant thumping of a heart, the spill of blood rushing through ventricles. It was so extraordi-nary that he gasped.

Later, he stroked her cheek and whispered: 'I had a vision that you were pregnant.'

'Oh, lover.' She turned to him, wrapped her arms around his chest. 'I'm not pregnant, as far as I know.'

'I think you are now.'

She curled more tightly into his chest, and he fell asleep with his lips on her hair.

☽

He woke suddenly in the dark. He'd been dreaming of something but it slipped away so quickly that by the time he turned to look at the bedside clock, the dream was gone. The only thing that remained was an emotion in watercolour, sad greys and browns and pale greens, as if the evening before hadn't happened at all.

The previous few days, however, came back in sharp colour. Leila's body, the limp arm hanging over the side of a stretcher. Abdulrahman struggling with the mannequin, his hands on her waist, the sudden hollowing of his eyes when he realised that his sister was dead. Hakim's angry laugh, his sneering, self-righteous, pathetic face.

Osama looked at his wife, lying on her back, one arm splayed to the side where she'd had it buried beneath his shoulders. Delicately, without waking her, he removed a strand of hair that was stuck to her mouth. There had been a time, years ago, when he'd wake up in the night just to watch her sleep, to indulge himself, to admire her without distractions. But now on the odd nights when he woke before her, he found himself listening for her breath, watching her chest for a rise and fall, and fighting the impulse to disturb her so she would open her eyes and moan and give a sleepy half-smile or bat at him with a tired hand. Some proof of life.

Getting up quietly, he went into the bathroom and did his

ablutions. He was going to spend another day trying to track down Ra'id and Bashir. They had to profile the murderer, but their best profiler was out of town. And he could tell that it was going to be dripping hot. It was five in the morning, the air conditioning was on full, he was standing stark naked in the ceramic-tiled bathroom, and already he was sweating.

In the kitchen he found Nuha's laptop and her work papers scattered on the table. He made himself a cup of coffee and sat at the table to eat a piece of bread. Her laptop was still on, its power light was illuminated but the screen was dark. He glanced at the papers. She must have woken up in the middle of the night to finish an article. She only worked in the kitchen at night, because her office was just off the bedroom, and sometimes the sound of her typing woke him. The newspaper could be demanding, but if he'd known she'd had a deadline, he wouldn't have kept her in the bedroom for half the night.

But, he thought with a burst of pleasure, *the second time we made a baby*.

From the looks of it, she was working on a story about the kingdom's effort to encourage more women into the workplace. He picked up a print-out of her article and read over it. She was eloquent. To his small relief, he found a typo and, not seeing a pen on the table, he reached into her handbag to locate one. He corrected the mistake, adding a small heart shape in the margin for her to find later.

It was only when he put the pen back in her bag that he noticed the plastic canister. It was oddly shaped, like a flying saucer, and a strange green colour that made him think of a doctor's office. Guiltily, he removed it from her bag. It rattled slightly. He popped the lid and saw a spiral row of pills, half of them missing. Some were white, the rest blue. He stared at them stupidly. It took him a moment – not to recognise what they were but to believe he'd found them. *Nuha?* He'd seen these pills before – once belonging to a prostitute he'd interrogated and once in the hands of a violent husband who'd killed his wife over a little disc almost exactly like this one.

Contraceptive pills.

He set them on the table as his thoughts began to swarm. Had something happened – was she seeing someone else, and that's why she needed to avoid a pregnancy? She would never do that. She'd said she wanted more children. In fact, she was upset that she hadn't become pregnant again. She had even talked about going to the doctor to find out why. It had all been a lie. But why? Was it something at home? Did she hate children so much? Did she hate Muhannad? Why hadn't she told him about any of this? Did she think he was so irrational that they couldn't have a conversation about it?

He looked back inside the bag, desperately double-checking. It was definitely hers; he recognised the purse. He was overreacting and he knew it, but for an awful moment he remembered the murderous husband who'd thrown his wife out of a fifth-storey window after discovering contraceptive pills. He had thought the man was insane at the time, but here he was experiencing the same blind fury. He had a right to be angry. He'd been lied to. Osama remembered thinking how stupid it was to kill a woman over a small case of pills. Pills! They were tiny; the man was a backward fool. It was crushing him now to discover that he'd been the ignorant one, that the killer's understanding was more nuanced than his own. Discovering something like this – oh, he saw it so clearly – opened a terrifying chasm of fury and distrust.

It took a few minutes, but eventually Osama's hands stopped trembling. He stood up from the table, fighting the impulse to storm into the bedroom and confront Nuha. It wouldn't be fair. She would be vulnerable, sleepy. And he would be full of rage. Instead, he slammed his fist into the container, shattering it, crushing the pills. A tiny shard of plastic hit the laptop's keyboard and bounced to the floor.

A few minutes later he heard the toilet flush in the other room, the sound of Nuha washing herself at the bathroom sink. She'd be out any minute.

He left the pills on the table, the plastic container like a broken oyster with its pearl-like irritants destroyed.

18

Katya stood just outside the entrance to the station. It was lunchtime and her burqa was down so that no one would recognise her. She didn't want people to start asking questions if they saw her getting into Nayir's Jeep. *Is that your husband? Why do we never see him pick you up after work?* The only problem was that, with her burqa down, Nayir might not recognise her either.

The sunlight was crashing mercilessly on to the street, reflecting off the windows of the building opposite, springing up from the marble courtyard, and flashing straight into her face from the car windows zipping by. She had sunglasses on under her burqa but it wasn't enough, and she kept having to raise them anyway to squint at the faces of the drivers who were parked on the street. Her eyes were watering, she was hungry, and there was no sign of the Jeep.

What if he couldn't find her? What if he had to get out of his car and come looking for her, and someone saw them together and started asking questions? Carefully, because it was difficult to see where she walking, she made her way across the courtyard and down the three stairs to the pavement. There were people here but no one she recognised.

This whole thing was probably a bad idea. The police hadn't followed up on Leila's last job because they were too busy hunting down her ex-husband. Katya had got the address of the art collector from Majdi. The junior officers didn't seem to think it was important. Grudgingly she acknowledged that her real reason for doing this was because she had a fantasy of cracking the case. They'd be grateful if that happened. They'd be able to take all the credit and she wouldn't say a word. But they would know that she was invaluable, more than just a lab tech, and if they ever found out that she wasn't really married, they'd think twice before firing her. It had been bothering her for months, this pathetic lie. As far as she could tell, there were no other women in the department who were single and lying about it, or if they were, they did an excellent job of hiding the truth.

She could never have got the job as a single woman. The men took it for granted, and never asked about her 'husband', but the women were more dangerous. It often seemed that if the workday could be divided into ten segments, they talked about their families – and particularly their husbands – for nine, and the tenth one was simply a resting period, a necessary 'sleep' zone that enabled them to return, refreshed, to the same discussion later. On more than one occasion Katya had had to lie blatantly about her husband – that he was a businessman who spent much of his time overseas, that his family lived in Riyadh, that they had been trying to have kids but had had no luck yet. Most of the time she managed to avoid the outright lies and got by with little lies of omission, *hmmms* and *yeses* that indicated assent, shared experience, insight that she didn't really have and wasn't sure she wanted. The truth was, even if she had been married, she still wouldn't have wanted to talk about men all the time.

Five minutes later a Land Rover pulled up to the kerb. Nayir was at the wheel. He didn't look over at her, in fact he avoided looking at her at all, which struck her as ridiculous. Wasn't the whole point of wearing a cloak and headscarf and burqa so that the man could look safely at a woman without committing a sin? When he got out of the car, she knew from the tilt of his head that he'd already recognised her. It pleased her that he knew her well enough that he didn't need to see her face.

She approached the car. His eyes flickered to her burqa.

'Hello, Nayir,' she said. 'Nice car.' He ducked his head nervously and went around to the other side of the Rover to open the door for her. She followed slowly and carefully. Walking was difficult with only a single slice of vision, nearly impossible when that slice was inundated by light.

He shut her door and went around to the driver's side. In that moment she realised that he had opened the front door, that she was sitting in the front seat, and that – Nayir definitely not being the type to let a woman sit in the front – he had done it all without apparent hesitation. She wondered if he knew it would impress her.

Once he had taken off and they were out of sight of the station, she lifted her burqa. He noticed but didn't react. She glanced at him. He wore a long blue robe over a pair of white cotton trousers. Brown leather sandals. A white headscarf with no 'iqal to hold it down. The ends of the scarf were flipped up to the side, revealing his face – his equivalent, she realised, of raising the burqa – with a few curls of black hair peeking down from his crown. He was freshly shaven but his face had a rough, textured quality that probably came from spending too much time in the sun. It wasn't a handsome face, per se, but in its ruddiness and stocky squareness it was incontrovertibly masculine. He smelled of sand and engine oil and something fresh and warm like baked bread. She lost all of the teenage giddiness that energised her in the lab with Majdi. Around Nayir, she felt a deeper sensation, a kind of spiritual tremor.

'How are you?' he asked.

'Fine.'

He glanced in her direction but not quite at her. She had resolved not to keep things from him any more. She would plunge ahead, because if this was ever going to work, it had to work for the right reasons. She told him about the case, about discovering the Bluetooth burqa and the video footage of Farooha joking about the religious establishment, all of the things she hadn't told him yesterday because they might reveal Leila's impropriety, or because they would lead inevitably to the fact of her own inter-action with men like Majdi and Osama. She told him everything she could think of, describing Majdi as a youthful, distracted scientist with thick glasses and unkempt hair, hoping to make Nayir realise that he wasn't sexual in the least, but halfway through the description she realised that she was talking about Majdi with obvious affection, and she stopped.

Nayir seemed to be cogitating. She waited expectantly, think-ing, *Please, please, say something. Anything.* She knew what he was thinking: *You work alone with a man?* She turned nervously to the window, watched the shops passing by, a Hyper Panda supermar-ket, a pair of petrol stations, looking greasy in the sunlight. There were two women on the street with unveiled faces, they were laughing and talking, and one woman's headscarf was slipping down the back of her head. Nayir seemed not to notice; he was studying the car in front of him. An image popped into her mind of those crazy drivers they called drifters, which was just what this felt like. She was racing along at full speed on a flat, wide-open expanse of motorway, and she had just yanked the parking brake. Now she was skidding, skating past cars and spinning in curlicues. The last victim of drifting who had passed across the coroner's table – and consequently beneath a forensic flashbulb – had been so badly damaged by a collision with an HGV that his face looked like a pound of raw purple meat.

'So it could have been anyone who killed her,' Nayir said. Katya felt a small burst of relief. 'If she wore this Bluetooth burqa, she could have met a man on the street . . .' He waved his hand at the passing pavement in a resigned way.

'We don't have many leads,' Katya admitted. 'But here's what

I think. Leila's murder wasn't premeditated, it was a passion crime. Someone acted in the heat of the moment. That usually happens with someone who had a relationship with the victim. We didn't see any signs of long-term abuse. She had a fractured tibia. But according to her brother, those injuries happened when someone attacked her in public. However, she did have a bad relationship with her ex-husband.'

'Have they arrested him?'

'They can't find him,' she said. 'But they're holding his brother. The alternative is that the killer could be someone who was provoked by something Leila did just before she died. And there were two things she was working on: B-roll for a local news channel, and photographing a private art collection. The first assignment probably won't lead anywhere, the footage itself is intended to be boring – background stuff. But this art collector is interesting.'

'He collects old Quranic texts,' Nayir said.

'Well, that was a guess.'

They sat in silence for a while. The Rover had come to a halt at the edge of a roundabout, stopped by a tangle of traffic. They inched forward slowly in the outer lane. At the centre of the roundabout she spotted the source of the congestion: a public whipping was taking place. A young man was kneeling on the pavement, naked from the waist up. Two officers stood above him, one holding a bamboo whip and a Quran under his arm. This was to ensure that he didn't raise his arm too high in the beating, but it didn't make much difference. She caught a glimpse of the young man's back, red and raw and scorching beneath the noon sun, and the sight of it immediately brought bile to her throat, triggering an image of Leila, face burned beyond recognition, fighting furiously with an attacker and being beaten to the ground, then stabbed again and again until her body was a limp mass of flesh.

☽

162

Nayir could only catch glimpses of the whipping through the sea of heads. He heard it, however: the young man screaming for mercy, the brutal *smack* of the whip. Then he noticed Katya reaching for the air vent and he realised she was anxious. Focusing on the road, he managed to cut out of the roundabout.

Ever since she had got into the car, her smell had enfolded him in a whirling cloud of distraction. It was all he could do not to stop the car and grab her. This was the worst kind of weakness because there was nothing he could do about it, at least nothing that could put an end to the torture anytime soon, short of kicking her out of the car. They had another hour together at least, and so he immunised himself by cracking open the window, cranking up the cold air and turning his attention to a silent prayer of repentance that somehow never got past the first refrain. Since they'd made the arrangement the night before, he had been looking forward to seeing her with a kind of obsessiveness. He had expected to be nervous. But now, unable to keep his mind from producing dangerous images of kissing her, touching her neck, her face, her hands, feeling the small of her back, the curve of her hips, he felt betrayed by his body, frustrated that it would spoil an afternoon with her, frustrated with her for smelling so good.

'Do you have any other suspects?' he forced himself to ask.

She shook her head. 'Whoever killed her felt a significant rage. I mean, they desecrated her body in almost every way they could. Knife wounds, physical beating with an *'iqal*, and then the burns on the hands and face . . .'

'How do you know it was an *'iqal*?' he asked.

'I tested the fibres from her wounds and found goat hair.'

Nayir remembered as a boy confusing the word *'iqal* with *'aql*, intelligence. He thought that this was why men wore the cords around their heads, that somehow the black band bestowed a halo of wisdom. It was only recently that he had told Uncle Samir about

163

his boyhood confusion. Typically, Samir had deflated the moment by explaining that the two words were actually from the same root, which meant they were related in a subtler way: fostering intelligence was much like hobbling a camel, you had to teach focus and restraint.

'They're not exactly scarce,' Nayir said, referring to 'iqals, 'but isn't it unusual that she was beaten with one?'

Katya shook her head. 'A lot of bodies come in having been beaten with 'iqals. It's the easiest and quickest weapon most men have.'

'More proof that the killer acted in the heat of the moment,' he said.

'Yes. And the hot oil could have come from anywhere. I have this idea that Leila was in a kitchen, maybe cooking something. The guy comes in, they fight, it gets violent and he starts beating her with his 'iqal. Maybe she fights back and he gets so angry he throws hot oil in her face. At this point she's beaten and bruised, burned from hot oil, but she's still fighting furiously because he grabs a knife and starts slashing at her legs. Maybe he did it before the hot oil. But all of these things happened to her while she was still alive, and they happened in quick succession. It had to be someone strong enough to overpower her, and someone vicious enough to keep going at her even though he'd already disabled her. Someone enraged. The question is why.'

'Is it possible she was drugged?' Nayir asked.

'We're still waiting for the lab results on what was in her blood, but yes, she could have been drugged. Let's say that she was, and that whoever did this did it just out of viciousness. Being drugged, she probably wouldn't have felt as much pain. Maybe she wasn't even conscious. But if that's true, then we're dealing with a psychopath because the killer kept going at her *without provocation*. In other words, she wasn't fighting back. The killer was just . . .'

'Enjoying the kill.'

She nodded. 'But he didn't just throw hot oil in her face, he covered her whole face in it, and then he did her hands. What's so disturbing about it is that he seems to have done it to erase her identity, so that the police wouldn't be able to get her facial features or fingerprints. Yet the killer did this to her while she was still alive. It feels calculated, like he knew he was going to kill her.'

'Maybe he'd already realised how badly he'd beaten her, so he knew it was inevitable?' Nayir asked, cringing at the thought.

'But think about it – the attack was so full of rage. People usually come down from that at some point. That's when your brain starts to function again, when you start *thinking*. That's when the calculation comes in, and the killer starts to get worried. He tells himself: *Oh no, look what I've done. I'd better erase her identity, so the police will think she's just another housemaid.*'

'All right,' Nayir said. 'So at that point he kills her out of fear. He's afraid she'll survive to tell the police his identity.'

'Right,' Katya said, suddenly alert. 'It's possible the killer just finished it off by snapping her neck.'

'So you've got a killer in a rage,' Nayir said. 'Maybe a psychotic person – someone with a history of mental instability?'

'We've checked into that. No one in her family has a history of mental illness, and neither does her ex-husband, and he's our primary person of interest right now. But only because he had a temper.'

'So she probably didn't know any psychotics,' Nayir said.

'No, she probably didn't. Which raises the possibility that it was a stranger who killed her.'

'But how would it happen?' he asked. 'The scenario you described had to occur in a kitchen. If she was in her kitchen—'

'Her brother's,' Katya put in. 'She lived with her brother.'

'Even then,' he went on. 'How could someone do all those things to her in her brother's house? She would have had to know him to let him in the door. Although I suppose it could have been a burglar, or someone who broke in.'

'Or a friend of the brother,' Katya said. 'The day she was reported missing, the police went to the house and interviewed the brother. They also interviewed the neighbours, and nobody heard anything out of the ordinary – no screaming or banging around. And when my boss went to talk to the brother after we identified Leila's body, we had full access to his house. It was clean. She didn't die there.'

Nayir nodded. 'So the question is, what other kitchens did she visit?'

Katya gave a grim laugh. 'Women are always in kitchens,' she said. 'I don't know. According to her brother, she didn't have many friends.'

It hadn't occurred to him until now how the discussion of the case had made his nervousness vanish. But he'd heard the darkness in her tone that came with the words *women are always in kitchens*.

'What about someone she might have known through her job?' he asked, trying to stay on the subject.

'The police talked to the news station. The woman who hired her told us that she hadn't seen Leila in months. Apparently, Leila worked freelance. She did all of her work with them over the phone and the computer. She wasn't filming things that needed to be broadcast right away, she was only filming filler, so she uploaded everything to the station's website. When they wanted something from her, they communicated by email or called her on the phone. She had never even been to the station.'

'Then how did she get hired?'

'She responded to a newspaper ad. The woman who hired her came to her house – well, the brother's house – to do the interview. I'm thinking she also wanted to find out if Leila had all the film and computer equipment she needed to do the job.'

'That makes sense,' Nayir said. He wondered briefly if Katya could ever take a job like that, where she could work from home.

'But I don't think Leila was exactly modest,' Katya said. 'I mean, I get the impression that she was comfortable being out in the world with a video camera. I told you she was attacked once, according to her brother.'

'I remember,' he said.

They drove in silence for the last few minutes of the journey, dismayed to see that the neighbourhood they were entering was rather run-down. Bags of rubbish lay scattered on the pavement. Two men leaning against a rusty Toyota gave the Rover an appraising look, but when the Rover slowed down, the men turned their backs and began walking away.

The street was a mish-mash of old blocks of flats, some of them leaning precariously over the street, others covered with graffiti and grime. Nayir parked in front of the address.

'This doesn't seem like the kind of place an art collector would live,' Katya said.

He silently agreed. The foyer door was unlocked but its hinges were so rusty that it was difficult to open, and when they did manage to move it, it gave a shriek loud enough to alert the neighbours. He heard rustlings behind doors, indications of women peering through spy holes. The foyer stank of old cooking smells – curries and beans stuck in an airless room. The linoleum floor felt tacky against the bottoms of his shoes as he led the way up the stairs.

They found flat number six on the third floor. Before knocking, Nayir turned to her. 'In case this man – what's his name?'

'Wahhab Nabih.'

'In case Mr Nabih doesn't want to speak to a woman, what should I . . .?'

'Just ask him what he knew about Leila, what she was doing for him, that kind of thing,' Katya said. 'He probably won't mind talking to women,' she added. 'He was working with the victim, remember?'

'Right.' Nayir tapped on the door. They heard a stirring within, then a thump like a book falling to the floor. A woman's voice cried out a muffled curse. Footsteps came towards them.

'Who is it?' the woman asked. To their surprise, she spoke English.

'We're sorry to disturb you, Miss Nabih,' he said in English. 'But we're here on police business.'

This was met by silence.

'Miss Nabih?'

'You have the wrong address,' the woman said. 'I'm not Miss Nabih.'

'What did she say?' Katya asked. He translated. 'Well, tell her that this is about the murder of a young girl and that I'm a female investigator. If she's home alone, I'll come in by myself. I just need to ask a few questions and find out why we have the wrong address.'

'But you don't speak English,' he said.

Katya slumped. 'Just tell her what this is about.'

Nayir did and translated the response: 'She's never heard of anyone named Nabih.'

Katya looked crestfallen. 'This is the only address we could find for him. If this woman can't help us, we've reached a dead end.'

'I don't think she can help us,' he replied, but he translated Katya's words anyway. They were met by more silence.

They waited. Something screeched at the bottom of the stairs – probably the front door. Katya was staring in a pleading way at the spy hole.

A minute later, he heard the *clack* of a bolt. The door opened a few inches and a woman peered out. Even if he hadn't heard her voice, he would have known that she was foreign. Her burqa was pulled so tightly to her nose that she might as well not have been covering her face at all. Her eyes and forehead were completely exposed, which was probably convenient, vision-wise, but made her eyes pop. They were large and a startling, clear blue.

'I think Nabih may be the name of my landlord,' she said.

Nayir kept his gaze on the door frame. 'Do you have his address?' he asked.

The woman nodded and swung the door wide, motioning them into the flat.

☽

Nayir entered the hallway, trying not to stare. When he'd first heard her curse, he'd expected – well, he wasn't sure, but someone who was larger, rounder, and less covered up. Yet the woman who opened the door was short and slender, and even if her cloak was three inches too short and sticking a little tightly to her sweaty arms, there was an air of modesty – even awkwardness – in the way she moved, staying close to the door, her eyes searching nervously for a safe place to rest.

Walking in, Nayir turned at once for the men's sitting room. It was easy to spot, being right by the entrance. But the woman said: 'No, no, come on in.' There was no doubt she was American. She didn't have the same concepts of space. *Come in* meant come all the way in. Make yourself at home, enter any room, follow me into the kitchen, sit at the table, *both of you*, man and woman. Let's all sit in the same room.

She was clearly upset about something, and Nayir suspected that it had nothing to do with their arrival. In the glimpses he managed to steal of her eyes, he could see something bigger. Those eyes, which were a blue he'd never seen before, at least not on a human, momentarily distracted him. They were large and, he discovered with a jolt, capable of gazing at him with an astonishing frankness.

From his periphery he noticed that Katya was frowning.

Reluctantly, he followed the women into the house. They entered a central room which might have been a women's sitting room except that there was only a small, ratty sofa and an end table. There were no decorations on the walls and no windows in the room, so the only light came from a feeble lamp on the end table. There was a book on the floor, and while stepping over this, the American woman stumbled against the table and cursed again. Frustrated, she took off her burqa and turned back to Nayir and Katya. 'Watch out for the table.'

Nayir quickly averted his gaze, but he had already seen her face. It was small-featured and precise. Her profile had the delicately rounded edges of a line of script cut into a marble wall. Against the paleness of her skin, her lips were bright red and he wondered, so fleetingly it might have been a spasm, what it would be like to kiss a mouth that small. *Allah clean my mind and forgive my sins.*

Katya was staring at him and he did everything he could not to meet her gaze.

They entered a small kitchen. The woman invited them to sit at a table pressed into a corner, which they did simply to get out of her way. The three of them standing took up the whole space. The woman opened the pantry door, knelt down and began rummaging.

Katya lifted her burqa, which left him with the sense that there were even fewer safe places to rest his gaze. He studied the empty chair until he realised that Katya might think he was staring at the woman's rear, which was protruding in plain view. So he glanced at Katya's hands. And that's when he saw it: the engagement ring was still on her finger. Trace memories of Othman rose ghost-like in his mind, all the times he'd imagined them together. Apparently, Nayir's being back in her life hadn't changed her feelings about her thwarted engagement. The glittering diamond was like a needle in his eye.

'Ask her if she's home alone,' Katya said.

Nayir forced himself to translate. The American turned to them: 'Yes,' she answered. 'I'm alone.' Something in her voice made him think that the question had offended her. She brought a cardboard box to the counter and withdrew a file labelled 'Apartment'. She handed it to Nayir.

'That's our lease, I think. It's in Arabic,' she said. 'I can't read it.'

Nayir took the file. 'Do you live here alone?' he asked.

'No, with my husband . . .' she trailed off. 'He reads Arabic.'

He scanned the papers and found that she was right: their landlord was named Nabih. There was an address for him in the Al-Aziziya district. 'Thank you,' he said. 'I believe this is what we need.'

'You said you were with the police?' she asked.

'Yes.' He motioned to Katya. 'Miss Hijazi works with the police.'

'Ah.' The woman crossed her arms and leaned against the counter in a feeble attempt to look casual. 'Can I ask what this is about? You said a young girl was murdered.'

'What's she saying?' Katya asked.

'She wants to know about Leila.' He turned to the American and explained what he could. 'Have you ever heard the name before – Leila Nawar?' he asked. She shook her head. 'She was doing some photography work for your landlord,' Nayir explained. 'We just wanted to talk to him about it.'

'I didn't know this country had female cops,' she said.

'She is actually a . . . I don't know the word. She works with evidence. She's a scientist.'

'A forensic pathologist?'

'Yes, I suppose.'

'Wow.'

Katya had pulled back into herself, her expression unreadable.

'So who are you?' the woman asked. 'A driver?'

171

Nayir hesitated. 'I'm a friend. I came along because your landlord has an art collection of Quranic writing, which is something I know a little bit about. Are you sure you've never met your landlord?'

'Yes.' She turned to the stove. 'I'm really sorry, I don't have any tea or coffee in the house. Could I get you guys some water?'

'No.' Nayir avoided glancing at Katya. 'No, thank you. How is it that you rented this place but never met your landlord?'

She had begun pawing through the fridge in an effort, he suspected, to hide her face, because the fridge was almost empty. 'Oh,' she said blithely, 'my husband arranged the whole apartment thing before I got here.'

'And where is your husband?'

She closed the fridge and regarded him. He hadn't meant for the question to sound like a chastisement, but that's how she seemed to take it. 'He's not here,' she said. 'Why do you want to know?'

He glanced at Katya, who seemed to notice something odd as well. 'I was only thinking that we might ask him about Mr Nabih, in case we can't find him at this address.' He motioned to the paperwork. 'When will he be back?'

The question was simple enough, but she struggled to answer it. 'Maybe tonight.'

Nayir felt the inevitable tingling of discovery. 'Mrs . . .'

'Walker,' she said. 'Miriam Walker.'

'Mrs Walker.'

'Don't call me that. Just Miriam.'

Nayir faltered. 'I know it's not my business,' he said, hoping he got the English right, hoping his tone conveyed the right delicacy, 'but where could we find your husband?'

She stood rigidly at the counter, arms stiff at her sides, face frozen in an awful expression that could have been fear or pain or silent fury. 'I don't know,' she said finally.

Katya gave him a quizzical look but he ignored it.

'Did he leave?' Nayir asked.

Miriam shook her head and said very slowly: 'I don't know.' He had never had such an intimate view of a woman on the verge of crying before. Even the one time Katya had done it, she had been behind a burqa. Miriam's face was rigid with her attempt to control a trembling that seemed to be shaking her within. The air was pulsing with tension. She looked down and noticed that she was holding a tea towel. She set it on the stove.

'How long has he been gone?' Nayir asked gently.

'Oh, ah.' Her voice was trembling. 'It happened three nights ago. He picked me up from the airport. I'd been on vacation in the States. And then he went out to get some dinner. I wasn't really hungry – at least I didn't think so – but he insisted on going out. That wasn't odd. But then—' She waved her hand.

'Then what?' he whispered. He saw a tear spill down her cheek. She wiped it angrily away. 'He never came back?'

Miriam nodded, her lips pressed into a line so they wouldn't crinkle.

'And you haven't heard from him since then?' he asked.

She shook her head and let out an awkward bark of a laugh. She took a deep breath. 'You know what? I'm actually on my way out to visit a friend and I can't be late.' Her cheeks were scarlet, and she was standing close enough that he could see the odd red capillary beneath her strangely frail, translucent skin. He had the urge to do something, anything, to give what comfort he could, but she was wheeling back with every gesture.

Suddenly, Katya reached up and took Miriam's hand. It startled everyone, but Miriam forced a smile. 'Thanks. I'll be fine.'

Without looking at Katya, Nayir explained to her what Miriam had said.

'Has she called the police?' Katya asked. 'Or the consulate?'

'Yes, yes, I'll figure it out,' Miriam said hastily once Nayir had translated the question. She took her hand out of Katya's. 'Don't worry about me. Please.' She glanced at the kitchen door in a meaningful way, and Nayir reluctantly got to his feet. Katya stood up, a dark expression on her face.

They followed Miriam to the front door and she saw them out, not meeting either of their gazes. 'Thanks again,' she said, in a wavering voice, and then more seriously: 'I hope you find the killer.' She was about to shut the door, but Nayir stopped her.

'Mrs Walker,' he said, fumbling in the pocket of his robe. He extracted a mangy-looking, creased business card. He always kept one handy in case he met a potential client, but that rarely happened. The card was water-stained as well but it was the best he could do. He handed it to Miriam. 'This is in case you think of anything that might be helpful to us later.'

Miriam looked at the card and gave a solemn nod. 'All right,' she said. 'Thanks.'

☽

Katya had the unique sensation that she was floating on the surface of a very great lake, but that beneath it, her mind was busily at work. Any moment now a great and obvious understanding of what had just happened would pop out of the water like a monstrous whale.

She peered through the glassy water, looking for the things that should be bothering her – the missing husband, Miriam's unexplained resistance to clarifying her situation – but instead she saw the wide, slithering back of that familiar creature, jealousy. She pictured Miriam, so petite and exotically lovely with her great blue eyes, black lashes, and cheeks as white and delicate as butterfly wings. And Nayir, who had suddenly become cold to Katya and, in some perverse but appropriate twist, become uncommonly responsive to Miriam, protective and kind, not judgemental at all. Of course, one doesn't judge the infidels. They don't live by the same rules, so they can't be held to them. She had not thought Nayir capable of such a lapse of morality, but apparently a crying female stripped him of his senses.

Beside her, Nayir seemed lost in his thoughts. She wondered if he were silently chastising himself for having spoken to an American who wasn't wearing a burqa, for having given her his phone number, for having stared at her face.

He tensed under her gaze. 'Don't you think it's odd that we show up at this flat and find that the tenant is missing?' she asked.

'Yes, I'd say it's odd. Do you want to check this out now?' He held up the sheet of notepaper on which he'd written down the landlord's address, but there was nothing in his voice that suggested he actually wanted to continue this lead. He seemed in a hurry to get rid of her.

'Actually, I have to get back to work,' she said. 'I really ought to bring the address to Osama.'

'Osama?'

'The investigator who's in charge of this case,' she said.

Nayir looked as if he might have more to say but wisely refrained. He handed her the paper.

'I was hoping you'd come back with me to the station,' she said. 'Perhaps you could look at the Quranic documents we found in Leila's room.'

He didn't look at her when he replied, somewhat distractedly. 'Yes, I'd be glad to.'

A long silence filled the car.

'You know,' she said finally, 'I found two hairs on Leila's headscarf.' Nayir glanced in her general direction. 'They were blond hairs,' she added. 'Short ones.'

'So what are you saying – the victim knew a blond man?'

'Well, obviously, she'd come into pretty close contact with one.'

'And you think that this missing husband could be blond?'

'Arabs generally aren't,' she replied.

175

He ignored the sarcasm. 'But that hair could have come from anyone,' he said. 'You know how many Americans live in Jeddah?'

'Of course I know,' she said a little too tartly. 'But I'm going to have to tell Osama about the missing husband. It might be important.'

Nayir looked as if he were going to regret his words but felt compelled to say them anyway. 'You shouldn't do that. Not yet.'

'Why not?'

'You know that they'll just go and arrest her until they can find her husband.'

'Osama won't. He doesn't just arrest everyone.'

'You said he just arrested the victim's ex-husband's brother.'

Katya had to admit it was true. Nayir wore a dangerous look she'd seen on him once before, when he'd discovered that the young and innocent Nouf, now dead, had in fact been secretly planning to run away to America.

'It would be a mistake,' he said carefully, 'to make some frail connection between Miriam's missing husband and Leila Nawar based on – what? A mutual friend? The landlord isn't even really their friend. They probably met him *once*. If you send your investigators sniffing around, they'll just throw her in jail.'

She felt her anger rising but she held it in check. It took such an effort that she had trouble speaking.

'You're right,' she said. 'I don't want to frighten her. She was helpful, and I'm grateful. And the truth is, I don't know what Osama will do. He might not care at all. But the fact that her husband is missing is very odd.'

'There could be any number of reasons that her husband is gone,' he said. 'Maybe he ran off with another woman. Maybe the religious police have him in custody. But don't you think you'd better check those possibilities out first before saying anything?'

It would have been too difficult to give a reply. She simply nodded and fell silent.

19

Almost three whole days had passed. Miriam hadn't called the police a second time to report Eric's disappearance. The consulate had done it for her. The police were supposed to send someone to the house to ask questions sometime that day, but they hadn't arrived yet – at least not the police she was expecting.

The day before, she had spent part of the morning buying food, and the other part searching the neighbourhood for Eric's pick-up. She had never had much of a sense of direction, so she had been careful not to get lost. This meant that she had had to search the streets one at a time, walking as far as she thought reasonable before heading back to the flat. Then she would set off on another street. Their neighbourhood was not laid out in square blocks, it had a few winding streets, which always disoriented her. It was a tedious job, and after two hours of it, she had come home overheated, frustrated, and exhausted.

But she had forced herself to try again later that afternoon, once the worst heat of the day had passed. Walking through a scent of jasmine that hung in the air had triggered a memory: getting out of the car after their drive home from the airport, she could remember seeing a large jasmine vine growing just behind a gate in someone's front garden.

She had stopped walking then and followed her nose to the jasmine vine. It was the same one. Seeing it triggered another memory of a blue-painted window sill further down the street.

Walking a little way, she found that as well. This was the street where they'd parked. She walked up and down checking each of the cars, but Eric's pick-up was not there.

She had found her way home again, only to collapse on the sofa in despair. The pick-up was gone. Eric's keys were gone. If she'd had a better memory, and had found that spot sooner, she would have learned earlier on that he'd driven away. And she began to get angry. He'd actually *left* her.

But now the police appearing at her door raised the possibility that he'd left for a reason that had nothing to do with their marriage: he was somehow involved with a girl who had died.

Miriam tried not to panic. The minute the police were gone, she went straight back to the box in the kitchen to write down the address of their landlord. But she couldn't read Arabic and, looking at the lease, she couldn't tell which part was his address. She wanted to scream.

She went blowing through the flat, digging through drawers and hauling old boxes out of the guest-room closet. (*Guest room!* she thought. *Who were we thinking would come here for a vacation?*) There had to be an English copy of the lease somewhere in the flat. But where? She knew this flat. In the past six months, she'd spent more time between these walls than she'd spent in their last house in two years put together, and she knew that there were only three places they kept papers: the kitchen pantry, the guest-room closet and on Eric's 'desk'.

It wasn't a desk, just a wooden counter jutting out from the wall in the guest room, but inevitably his papers found their way there. She'd gone on a cleaning spree one afternoon, stacking everything neatly and putting useless miscellanea in a box. She felt strangely guilty touching his stuff. She had never cleaned his desk before – he might have been sloppy once in a while, but thanks to the US military he was usually spare and efficiently neat – but that had changed when they'd moved here. Now he was a slob.

When he discovered that she'd cleaned his desk, he had reacted with mild panic, interrogating her about the original placement of the salary stubs and bank statements. Was this chronological order? Why was one out of place? What had she done with the Arabic documents? She hadn't thought it strange at the time, but now it seemed ominous.

She hadn't touched the desk after that impulsive spree, and now it was back to disorder. There were piles of notes that he kept for his job, and she glanced at these briefly before realising they were useless, filled with a ridiculous technical jargon that might as well have been Arabic. The last sanctuary was a briefcase sitting on the floor. She lifted it on to the desk and found that it was locked. She used the letter opener to jimmy it. Inside were more notes, a recent bank statement and a single document in Arabic.

She scanned the document, futile though the gesture was. But halfway down the page her eye caught a single word. She recognised it only because Eric had brought home an Um-Kalthoum CD called *Alf Leila Wa Leila* – A Thousand and One Nights – with the title printed in English and Arabic. Apparently it was one of the most popular songs in the entire Middle East – bells clinking, the strange gramophone sound of a woman's voice, a fifty-minute epic that sounded like the results of putting an opera singer on a camel caravan and sending her off on a trek through the desert. Miriam went into the living room and retrieved the CD. Comparing the two words, she saw that they weren't exactly the same – the endings were different – but they were close enough and if she had to guess, she'd say the word on the document was indeed one of the three words she knew in Arabic: *Leila*.

☾

Sabria always answered the door with the same hesitant, fearful expression on her face. It said: *I'm too lazy to look through the spy hole or put on a burqa, so I hope you're a woman . . .?* And, seeing Miriam, she'd grin.

Today the grin didn't appear. 'Come in!' she hissed, snatching Miriam by the arm and dragging her straight to the kitchen. She shut the kitchen door and locked it.

'Let me guess,' Miriam said, 'your brother is here?'

Sabria was flushed. 'If he comes in, you may have to cover your face.'

'I won't stay long,' Miriam said, glancing at the table.

'Stay as long as you like!' Sabria said defiantly. 'He's the one who shouldn't be here. And yes, sit down. *Sit down.*' She pushed Miriam into a chair and went to the hob to make tea. 'I wish he would run away to Pakistan.'

Sabria's brother, Marwan, was a reformed jihadi. He'd been arrested two years before during one of the security sweeps of al-Qaeda militants in the kingdom. They had kept him in prison for a year then judged that he was eligible for the new reform programme to rehabilitate jihadis into normal life, using religious counselling and generous offers of cash. Marwan had taken the cash to buy a house but the counselling didn't seem to make much of a difference. For the past three months he had been as strict as ever, coming to the house once a week to make sure that his family was eating halal meat, praying on schedule, and following the rules for proper womanly conduct. According to Sabria, he still went to the same mosque and still felt the influence of the radicals who'd put him on this path in the first place.

Miriam had been alarmed to discover that Marwan had been arrested for nothing more than participating in an online chat room, but once Sabria had told her about the glee with which Marwan spoke about killing Americans, Miriam wished they'd kept him in jail a bit longer – at least until she and Eric left the country. It seemed a phenomenal oversight to have rented a flat above a man who would have liked to see them both dead, though

Eric rightly pointed out that Marwan no longer lived in the building.

Still, every time she left the house, Miriam felt a low current of dread that she might run into him in the hallway. The one time she'd seen him on the stairwell, he'd thrown all religious conventions to the wind and stared straight at her with a foul, somewhat juvenile look. She had scampered back into her flat and locked the door.

'How is he doing?' Miriam asked.

'Oh, you know . . .' Sabria dumped a handful of mint leaves into the teapot. 'I still don't think he's over it. They treat it like it's an addiction or something. Put him in a rehab programme, give him enough money to buy a house, and then they expect him to go back to normal. Every night he's angry about something. Right now it's his stupid job at the petrol station.'

'Do you think he's getting worse?'

'Well, I guess he's been angry for a long time. And I'll tell you, the government was right not to keep him in jail. That would really have turned him into a criminal. He's got a crazy temper. He could never be a real jihadi, you know, because he can't pretend. I mean, could you see him trying to go to America?' She laughed.

No, Miriam thought.

Sabria brought the tea to the table and sat down. She smiled. 'I've been wanting to see you.'

Miriam congratulated her again on the engagement. Sabria showed her the ring and Miriam oohed. She was suddenly uncertain how much to tell about her own troubles. She couldn't count the times over the past few months when she had showed up at the door desperately lonely and panicky, or feeling depressed, but unable to admit it. Sabria was always kind and hospitable, and she offered a tempting shoulder to cry on, but basic courtesy and a feeling of motherliness kept Miriam from revealing too much.

'What about you?' Sabria asked. 'How is it being back?'

181

The question was like a needle plunged straight into a water balloon. Miriam exhaled, reminded herself that she was the older woman here, but the tide was already rushing out. She felt the first drops spilling in a clumsy way, then the gushing, the explanations, beginning first with the description of Eric's disappearance and ending with the police arriving at the house and Miriam's failed attempt to find the landlord's address. Sabria listened with a stunned, frantic look on her face.

'Listen,' she said, taking Miriam's hand, 'it could be *anything*.'

'I know,' Miriam said. 'I know. He could be with the religious police. Something stupid.'

Sabria nodded. 'But you *have* to call the consulate.'

'I did,' Miriam said. 'A few times now. But I'll try again this afternoon.'

Sabria nodded and picked up the lease that Miriam had laid on the table. 'This is old information. Mr Nabih lives in Dubai, he has a local guy who manages the property now.' She stood up. 'I'm going to get you his address. Be right back.'

'Sabria—'

Sabria paused at the door and looked back meaningfully at her guest. 'Don't worry,' she said, 'I won't say anything.'

The minute she left, Miriam felt waves of calm wash over her, alternating with splashes of guilt and embarrassment. She took a sip of cold tea.

Sabria returned a few minutes later. 'My father says he can find the address for the local manager, but he has to make some calls,' she said. 'He doesn't remember it. Anyway, I told him to hurry. It shouldn't take too long. The guy's name is Mr Mabus.'

Miriam froze, teacup in mid-air. It shouldn't have shocked her; it should have clicked into place because the suggestions had already pointed her there, but naively – which was, she thought, just so typical of her – she couldn't come to terms with how boldly Mabus had lied to her on the plane, with his American accent, his claim that this was a business trip, and the casual way he'd enquired about her and Eric as if he didn't know them.

She thanked Sabria and headed back upstairs, fighting panic. It was only when she got to her flat that she remembered the strange document with the name 'Leila' on it. She'd had it in her handbag the whole time. It wasn't too late to go back down to Sabria and ask her to translate it, but now Miriam felt too scared to show it to anyone.

20

Pretending to be a scholar, Nayir sat at the laboratory table with *masahif* stacked in front of him. They were two collections of papers that contained the Holy Quran. He was sure it wasn't the entire Quran – it didn't look big enough – but a partial Quran was still holy. He had performed ablutions before touching it, because he hadn't purified himself since that morning. The lab tech Majdi had watched Nayir indelicately as he had cleansed himself at the sink in the corner.

Majdi explained the two stacks of papers. The first one, composed of maybe fifty sheets, was made up of photographs that they'd found taped to the inside of one of the dresser drawers in Leila's bedroom. Presumably, the photographs showed Mr Nabih's private collection of Quranic documents. The other stack came from the internet. There were only ten pages in this pile, but they were similar to the first documents – so similar in fact that Majdi believed they were from the same codex. He had only done a cursory comparison. He had found the second set of documents on a Kuwaiti website. Apparently, they had been up for auction.

Once Katya had introduced Nayir to Majdi, she had left for a meeting with her boss Zainab. Nayir wasn't sure what to think of Majdi. He was as Katya had described him, young and geeky, but where she found him endearing, Nayir simply felt awkward around the young man. He didn't talk much and was absorbed in his computer. Nayir quickly got to work, trying to determine whether the photos from Leila's bedroom matched the ones from the auction site.

'How's it going?' Majdi asked, not even bothering to turn around from his computer screen.

'It's fine,' Nayir replied. A preliminary study of the two stacks confirmed that Majdi was wrong: the documents from the internet did not match the photos Leila had taken. There were a few similarities, but the handwriting was different.

Nayir focused on the stack from Leila's room. This was easy reading, the pages no more than photographs of what appeared to be a very old copy of the Quran. He read slowly, recognised the verses as they came, and tried to stop his mind from wandering back to the problem of Miriam.

Katya was right – it was suspicious that Miriam's husband was missing, and that officially the landlord didn't exist. Both of those problems could easily have nothing to do with Leila's death, but put together they seemed ominous. And yet he still didn't think it was a good idea to inform the police about Miriam's situation, and to drag a frightened foreigner into a criminal investigation. She didn't even speak Arabic, which alone made him feel inexpressibly sorry for her.

He forced his attention back to the reading but soon began cutting a new path through the overgrowth of worry: why had Leila been asked to photograph these documents? They were obviously very old, and no doubt worth preserving, but the photos themselves were somewhat sloppily done, blurred at the edges and framed slightly off-centre. And why had they been hidden in her bedroom?

'Are you noticing any differences between the old texts and the modern Quran?' Majdi asked.

Nayir tore his eyes away and processed the question. 'No,' he said. 'However, the internet documents don't appear to be from the same codex as the one found in Leila's bedroom. I'm reading hers now.'

Majdi turned back to his computer. Nayir bent over his reading again as the implication of what Majdi had just asked washed over him: the Quran was the same now as it had been fourteen hundred years ago. Exactly the same. Not a single diacritic mark had been changed. The Quran said *the words of the Lord are perfect in truth and justice; there is none who can change His words*. This meant the words on the page were Allah's, exactly as they had been revealed to the Prophet Mohammed, peace be upon him.

Nayir flipped the page and kept reading. When he had first sat down to study the documents, he had recognised the Quran immediately. He had not assumed that there would be errors. In the early days of Islam, all the poorly copied texts had been destroyed.

What did surprise him was that there were no diacritic marks to indicate vowels. In its modern, printed form, the Quran contained every single vowel marking, so it was easy to comprehend a word's meaning. For someone like him, who knew the Quran so well, it wasn't difficult to read an unvowelled text. But had he been reading it carefully enough?

He was halfway down the page when he stumbled on a word. At first he thought he had misread it, the mistake was so obvious. He shook his head, thinking he had brought the confusion on himself. He went back to the beginning of the verse and read it again. Indeed, the mistake was glaring.

And we shall marry them to a companion, with beautiful, big, and lustrous eyes.

The verse was a promise that the blessed would reach Paradise and be rewarded by truth and beauty. The word 'companion' was supposed to be *hur*, a plural form of *houri*, which meant grapes. It also meant young virgins. Of course, the choice of meaning was clear, because who married a grape with beautiful eyes? But instead of *hur*, the text showed the word *ahwar*. It meant a single male companion, which didn't make sense.

186

And we shall marry them to a single male companion, with beautiful, big, and lustrous eyes?

His head was swimming. He mistrusted his eyes. 'Do you have a copy of the Quran?' he asked Majdi.

Majdi left the room and came back a few minutes later with a worn copy of the holy book. He passed it to Nayir.

Nayir opened the book to the appropriate surah, feeling ridiculous but determined to hold the real Quran side by side with the mistake. He set the book beside the paper, comparing the two with a thoroughness worthy of Sherlock Holmes.

'There's a mistake here,' he said. His voice came out pinched. Majdi came over and Nayir showed him the phrase.

Majdi looked unsurprised. 'I thought so,' he said.

'What do you mean?'

'Well, there had to be some reason Leila hid these in her dresser drawer.'

'Well, yes.' Nayir said. 'But where did she get them? And why have they been altered?'

'They weren't necessarily altered,' Majdi said. 'It's probably a bad copy. I mean, a thousand years ago they didn't have Tipp-Ex.'

'Then it should have been burned,' Nayir said.

'Burned?'

Nayir reminded himself that not everyone kept themselves up to date on fatwas. Still, it seemed like something everyone should know. 'The Hadith says that when 'Uthmaan produced the first standard and complete version of the Quran, he burned all the excess, incomplete copies. It protected them from being stepped on or desecrated.'

Majdi looked unimpressed.

'He buried them, too,' Nayir went on. 'But I think when a document contains a mistake like this – especially something that would lead to a misinterpretation – the general agreement among sheikhs is that it ought to be burned.'

Majdi was one of those people who thought with his whole body. His eyes were scrunched up, fingers drumming his chin.

Katya came in the door behind them. She looked slightly frazzled, probably from the meeting with her boss. Majdi greeted her and proceeded to explain the inconsistency in the text.

'So somebody made a mistake copying it,' Katya said. 'What does that mean?'

'Well, Nayir and I were just discussing the fact that when mistakes are made in copying the Quran, the bad copies are usually burned.'

'Do you know how old this document really is?' she asked.

'No, but I've got an archaeologist from the university coming in this afternoon. He should be able to help.'

'Okay, but we can assume they're pretty old.'

'That's what we've been assuming,' Majdi said.

'Let's say that they are, and they didn't get burned,' she said. 'Someone overlooked them, or they were hidden somewhere.'

'Or . . .' Majdi sighed and glanced nervously at Nayir. 'It might not be a mistake.'

'What do you mean?' Nayir said. An awful premonition was forming. 'It would have to be a copy mistake.' He wanted to say more, but they already knew that the published Quran in front of them was *the* Quran.

Majdi plunged ahead: 'Have you ever heard of the Yemen documents?' he asked.

They shook their heads.

'About thirty years ago, an archaeologist in Yemen came across a paper grave. It was a site where old copies of the Quran were stored; it was actually in the roof of the Great Mosque of Sana'a. The archaeologist, I can't remember his name, realised that the documents were very old, and the antiquities people brought in some German scholars to work on the preservation. There were a lot of documents – thousands of pages' worth – and it took them about twenty years to sort them all out and get everything cleaned and treated and assembled.

'Anyway, the German scholars have claimed that the documents are authentic early copies of the Quran. In fact, they're the earliest copies ever found. Except that there are many minor differences between those old pages and the modern text today. In the old codex, the verses were out of order, and the text itself was different in places. Some of the documents were palimpsests; they showed obvious signs of having been *edited*.'

'Someone edited the Quran?' Katya asked, clearly surprised.

'Yeah, well the scholars are fairly certain that because these documents were so old, they represented an earlier and more authentic version of the Quran than the one we currently have.'

Katya glanced at Nayir just as he said: 'There are no "versions" of the Quran.'

Majdi looked uncomfortably at Katya before going on: 'Obviously, this idea didn't go over too well. I don't know what's happening with their research now. I'm only telling you this because I think it's possible that these are part of the cache that was found in Sana'a – or at least, they're something very similar.'

Katya shook her head, looking slightly overwhelmed.

'And it's obvious,' Majdi went on, 'that Leila was hiding them. No matter where they came from, they wouldn't be well-received in this country if they contained mistakes – no matter what the reason for the mistakes was.'

This was met by a tense silence.

'Personally,' Majdi said, 'I don't think anyone should have a problem with it. There have obviously been variations of the holy book over the centuries, or 'Uthmaan wouldn't have had to burn anything in the first place. And if the Quran was written down in error, then it's human error.'

'The Quran says Allah corrects his errors,' Nayir replied, quoting: '*And for whatever verse we abrogate and cast into oblivion, We bring a better or the like of it; knowest thou not that Allah is powerful over everything?'*

'Right,' Majdi said. He looked as if he were making an effort not to roll his eyes. 'But as a person who cares about the Quran, shouldn't you be curious to know which version is correct? Wouldn't you want to know better what Allah really said?'

'This is what Allah said,' Nayir replied, touching the printed Quran.

Katya was quick to intervene. 'But Majdi, just because the document is old, doesn't mean it's *not* full of errors. What you're saying raises the possibility that the whole text is full of human error. But then how can you know which parts of it are authentic?'

'Exactly,' Majdi added, 'and don't forget that the Quran was originally written in Aramaic, so it was *translated* on top of everything else.'

Katya bit her lip, looking worried.

'Actually, I don't think this should matter so much,' Majdi went on, seeming immune to the tension around him. 'What's really important about the Quran is already there, isn't it? Love Allah, love your neighbour. And the idea that there's only one way to read it reduces the whole book to something flat. It's not dynamic any more. It can't keep up with the changes in humanity. It just becomes an ornament.'

Nayir stared uncomprehendingly at him. He almost couldn't believe what the young man had said – arguing that the Quran was some sort of human project was insulting enough but going on to say that one of the Quran's finest aspects – it being *mubeen*, its purity, the fact that it hadn't been altered since its inception – was actually a detriment seemed over the top.

'It all comes down to this,' Katya intervened again, 'we don't really know anything about these documents. They could have been falsified. Until we find out who their owner is, and what they were doing in Leila's bedroom, we should avoid speculation.'

21

It was too early in the morning for a stern conversation. Osama tried not to squirm. Sitting across from Chief Inspector Hassan Riyadh was the career equivalent of being beaten by an *'iqal*; it would leave marks, but it wouldn't necessarily deform you. Riyadh was a master of courtroom silences that would alternate, awkwardly, with a false paternalism. He was a man with seven children and two wives but seemingly no comprehension of how to handle people. Osama had visited him at home during past Ramadans and the man had been just as awkward in his own house. On a regular day, Osama could keep a cool façade in the face of whatever beating he was about to take, but today he felt weak.

He blamed this on the fact that he'd only slept for four hours on the unforgiving rug of his sitting-room floor. When he'd arrived home the night before, his wife Nuha had met him at the door with a terrible expression of fear and apology on her face. Obviously she'd found her contraceptive pills lying scattered on the kitchen table. He could still see it now, still feel wounded by the tears welling in her eyes and the image of himself turning away. Seeing Abu-Haitham come in the door behind him, Nuha had fled to the women's sitting room, which is just what Osama had intended by inviting the most devout man in the department over for dinner. It had ensured that Nuha would not have a chance to speak to Osama all night. Of course her mother had come in to bring dinner and to shoot him nasty looks, but otherwise he'd managed to avoid the whole family.

He and Abu-Haitham had stayed up until two in the morning making a futile and often confusing attempt to profile the Nawar killer. He had woken up this morning on the floor of the men's sitting room. The call to prayer was ringing through the neighbourhood's loudspeakers. Abu-Haitham was asleep on the sofa above him.

Even though it was the weekend, Chief Riyadh had called him in anyway. Osama dreaded the meeting, but he dreaded staying at home even more.

Across the desk, Chief Riyadh sucked on his lower lip and regarded Osama coolly. They'd been discussing the Nawar case, the chief demanding to know why they hadn't found the victim's cousin or ex-husband yet. Osama reassured him that it was still early in the investigation and that they were working on a number of promising leads, but that it was going to take some time. Now the chief was glowering at him.

'I'm cutting your support staff in half,' he said, forestalling Osama's protest by soldiering on. 'You don't need this many men if you've only got these thin leads you've mentioned, so you're going to have to make do.'

Osama heard in this a familiar criticism – that he had been foolish enough to trust his partner Rafiq, and that he might even have been in on all the dirty dealing himself. It galled him that Rafiq had been scapegoated when so many other officers were corrupt. It was doubly annoying that Riyadh was now using Osama's former partnership with Rafiq to keep him under his thumb.

'All right,' he said. 'Then I want to keep at least one woman.'

'You can have access to one, but I'm not handing any of them over permanently,' Riyadh said. 'We've got precious few of them; they get prioritised, too. Who were you working with?'

'Faiza Shanbari,' he said.

'You can't have her.'

'Why not?'

'She was let go this morning,' Riyadh said, emotionless. Osama managed not to give a visible reaction, but his mind was racing. Faiza had been fired? She couldn't have done anything to merit that.

'Turns out she wasn't really married,' the chief said. 'One of the detectives in the department met a cousin of hers at a friend's house, and he put the matter straight.'

Osama blinked, trying to believe it. 'Her cousin?' he said. 'What did Faiza say?'

'She admitted that she'd lied.'

Osama's heart dropped. He finished the meeting as quickly as he could and left the chief's office. The building was air-conditioned, and he was grateful for that, but his blood was still pumping as he made his way to the forensics lab. He wasn't sure why he was going there, just that he needed to avoid his desk, the horrible emptiness of his office, as much as he needed to avoid the squad room with the crowding and loud laughter and telephones jangling. As he walked, he felt the flickers of grief give way to anger – at Riyadh for firing Faiza for such a small, stupid lie, at Faiza for being stupid and lying in the first place, and then for being stupid again and admitting the truth to Riyadh. And most of all anger at Nuha.

Majdi was in the lab with a woman. When she turned, he saw that it was one of their more recent recruits, Katya, who had come to his attention recently for discovering the Bluetooth in Leila Nawar's burqa. He was impressed to see that she was working on a weekend. He stood outside the glass-walled office for a moment, not in the mood to face a stranger right now. But when she saw him she didn't lower her burqa and he figured it was foolish to keep standing there.

'Good morning,' Majdi said, getting up from his stool with a slumped expression that indicated he would have few new revelations to impart. Osama greeted them both.

'Glad you're in today,' Osama said. He turned to Katya: 'Congratulations on the Bluetooth discovery.'

'Thank you.' She looked pleased and a little surprised.

'I just wanted to check on things,' he said to Majdi, realising from the looks on their faces that his tension was showing. 'Any more news on the Nawar case?'

'Well,' Majdi said, 'we heard from the coroner, Adara, that the victim's blood test came back negative for drugs. It doesn't really change her report, though. She still thinks that the victim was killed before she was dumped in the ocean, and that she died from a broken neck. Meanwhile, I've been looking at the ocean current reports from the coast guard, and it's going to be impossible to figure out where the body was dumped. The problem is, we don't know the victim's time of death, and the currents vary so much on this part of the shore that we really do need to narrow it down. I've put that aside for now.'

'What about the documents we found in the victim's dresser?' Osama asked.

Majdi motioned to a computer on a corner desk. 'We had a specialist in yesterday afternoon, a friend of Katya's named Nayir Sharqi. He noticed a few errors in the text which made him think that these documents were possibly early copies of the Quran that had been written down incorrectly, in which case they should have been burned. Apparently, early versions with mistakes in them were also buried underground, so I'm thinking it's possible that if these documents are genuinely antique, they could be from one of those poorly copied Qurans which were buried instead of burned. We also had an archaeologist in this morning. He said it would be difficult to determine just how old the documents really are without seeing them. As you know, all we have are the photographs. Preliminarily, however, he thought there was a good chance they were authentic texts from early Islam. But none of this explains what the documents were doing in Leila's dresser drawer.'

Osama nodded.

'So I switched tactics,' Majdi said, 'and decided to scan them for fingerprints.'

'Did you find anything?' Katya asked.

Osama, who had opened his mouth to ask the very same question, snapped it shut.

'Only the victim's prints,' Majdi told her glumly. 'But I think I may have a partial print that isn't hers. I'm running it right now.'

Osama watched them converse, knowing he ought to add something but feeling unable to summon the energy.

Majdi sat down at the computer and then, having second thoughts, turned back to Osama. 'Katya has something. Maybe.'

She looked embarrassed. 'Majdi gave me the discs of Leila's work to look over. At the very end of one, there was a segment with a friend of hers. At least I think she was a friend.' Katya took a small piece of paper from her pocket and handed it to Osama. 'That's the girl's name and address.'

Osama received it with some embarrassment. 'Yes,' he said. 'Majdi told me about this. I'm sorry I haven't followed up on it yet.'

'Well, this girl's face was showing on the film,' Katya said nonchalantly. 'And I double-checked it with the ID photo, so I'm sure it's her.'

Osama nodded and tucked the paper in his shirt pocket. 'Good work. I'll check it out.'

Katya nodded.

Majdi said over his shoulder. 'Did you hear what happened to Faiza?'

'Yes,' Osama said.

Majdi frowned, clearly disgruntled by the news. 'That new woman they hired last month only works on Wednesdays and Thursdays. I think Maddawi may come on Monday.' Osama knew the women's schedules, for the most part. He had the feeling that Majdi was attempting to drop a hint – not to him, but to Katya. Osama glanced at her and saw that she was squeezing her hands together.

'I'll go look for someone,' Osama said. He was making to leave when Katya blurted: 'If you can't find anyone, I could go with you.'

Osama stopped. Angry as he was at everything else, he made an effort not to sound too harsh. He didn't want to crush her. 'I'm afraid we really need someone who has experience interviewing people.'

Katya kept her eyes on the tabletop, and he saw a slight blush creep its way up her cheeks. In an instant he loathed himself.

'I have experience,' she said. Her voice was calm and even. 'I helped solve a murder case a while ago.'

It was a good thing she kept her eyes on the table. He didn't want to see her face when he said 'no' again. But as if she knew his thoughts, she looked up at him. 'I know a lot about this case. I saw the body, I've watched two whole discs of the victim's work, and I've gone over all of the evidence. I might be able to help.'

He got the message: *I might know more about this case than you.* It should have ticked him off but for some reason it completely deflated his anger.

'And I'm pretty sure Maddawi won't come in until Tuesday,' she said.

He recognised the first flicker of rebelliousness in himself, and very quickly it blossomed into an outright determination. If the department wouldn't give him Faiza, then he'd do what he damn well pleased.

'All right,' he said to Katya, 'come on.'

'Now?'

'Too early for you?'

Her face broke into a smile and she followed him out the door.

☽

With some effort, Katya calmed her breathing. After months of trying so desperately to prove herself, she had finally been given the opportunity. It wasn't hard effort and determination that had brought her here, it was a lucky break, but she'd take whatever she could get.

At first, she had attempted to get into the back seat, but Osama had motioned her into the front, pointing out that, even though it wasn't a patrol car, he had grown accustomed to a world in which only criminals sat in the back. She knew that the other women who went out on these interviews sat in the back seat – she'd seen them getting out of the cars in the parking garage – but now that she thought about it, she'd never seen them with Osama.

She kept her burqa up because she felt that he could handle it and because she didn't want to put it down. She liked being out in the world and being able to see things. More discomfiting was the wedding band on her finger. It seemed to loom large in her peripheral vision, an invitation to an unpleasant conversation.

She glanced at Osama. He was sunk in his thoughts. The women in the lab discussed him with such giggly, unabashed infatuation that it had provoked in Katya a perverse dislike of him. But now, feeling more generous, she could admire that he was a well-built, well-groomed man, unselfconscious, a bit reserved but not arrogant. He had soulful brown eyes, the kind that teenage girls swoon over, but Katya suspected that he would find such reactions annoying. There was a small scar on his temple that he made no effort to hide. He kept his hair short, his cheeks shaven but slightly shadowed, and he didn't wear a headscarf. His look was that of a typical professional, slightly on the Western side – she couldn't have pictured him in a white robe – and she guessed that he wasn't religious at all, rather the kind of man who didn't pray except during Ramadan, and who thought that piety and devotion were slightly backward concepts, quaint, dangerous in a certain kind of person, but ultimately irrelevant.

The silence in the car, although broken now and then by a crackle from the radio, was beginning to make her anxious. She knew she shouldn't say anything. He might think she was nervous and change his mind. And who knew how he would interpret an effort at conversation? He didn't seem like the sort who would perceive communication from a woman as an act of flirtation, but you never could tell. You didn't have to be pious to have opinions about how women should act. She decided to play it safe and keep her mouth shut, her eyes on the window and her hands folded to the side where he wouldn't see them.

'Did you get anything else from the DVDs?' he asked.

She felt a small explosion of relief. 'No. Most of it was B-roll, probably for the news station she worked for.'

He nodded and fell silent. She glanced in his direction and saw that, despite his cold silence, there was a sadness in his eyes. She had the urge to tell him what she'd discovered with Nayir the previous day, but she refused to let her excitement get the better of her. Now was definitely not the time. Not only would Nayir be angry if he ever found out, but in his current mood, Osama might decide that it was presumptuous of her, perhaps even harmful to the investigation. She had, after all, been doing his job without his permission.

The neighbourhood was north of the city. It was a boxy place, newly built and austere, an ever-expanding grid lined with lookalike homes. Each house was white stucco, two storeys high, with a garage in front and wood-screened windows. Some of the neighbours displayed potted lemon trees by their doors or an arbour of jasmine struggling in the sun, but otherwise the street was unadorned.

They parked in the driveway and quickly determined that there were two separate entrances. A small sign indicated that the women's entrance was around the side.

'Stay with me,' Osama said, a sudden gruffness in his voice that made Katya think he was annoyed by the two entrances.

A woman answered the door, keeping the chain latched. She wore a burqa and all they could see was one eye.

'Police,' Osama said, showing her his badge. 'We need to speak to Farooha Abdel Ali.'

'About what?' the woman asked.

'A friend of hers is missing,' Osama said carefully. 'We'd like to ask her some questions.' He stepped aside so that the woman could see Katya, and when she did, that single eye went wide. 'I've brought a female officer along,' Osama said, 'to speak with Miss Abdel Ali, if we could.'

The woman gave Katya an up and down, taking in her newish *abaaya* and *hijaab*, the plain black shoes and, lastly, Katya's face, which seemed to put the woman at ease somewhat, because she opened the door saying '*Ahlan wa'sahlan*,' and then, out of modesty, made a race for the interior of the house, motioning them into the men's sitting room with a wave of the arm. 'Please make yourselves at home,' she said. 'That's the *majlis*, and the women's sitting room is over there.' She waved to the opposite side of the hall before disappearing through a doorway.

'Stay with me,' Osama said.

Katya followed him into the sitting room and glanced around. The flat was clean and elegantly furnished with a pair of ivory sofas and plush white carpets overlaid with brilliant red and orange rugs. There was a massive TV, an equally pretentious stereo system, and an entire shelf of CDs. Osama went straight to the shelf to read the spines of the CDs.

A moment later, there was a tap on the door and Katya went to answer it. The woman was standing in the hallway, her face still covered.

'You can speak to my daughter,' she said, motioning for Katya to follow her. Katya glanced back long enough to catch Osama's look of concern.

☾

Farooha was waiting in her bedroom, sitting atop a stack of books on a chair. Beside her was a desk pushed against the wall. She'd been at her computer, but the moment Katya came in, Farooha quickly darkened the screen and turned to face her inquisitor. There was ink on her thumb and she snapped up a tissue from a mother-of-pearl-encrusted Kleenex dispenser on the desk. Katya saw that she had been writing notes in a binder.

The girl stood up, nearly toppling the books in her clumsy descent from the chair. She was a very small, stocky woman; when standing, she barely reached Katya's chest. The surprise must have shown on Katya's face, because Farooha gave a wry grin. 'Yes,' she said, 'I'm short. Have a seat on the bed and the difference between us won't feel so dramatic.' She pushed aside a stack of CDs and books to make room for Katya on the rumpled sheets.

'Thank you,' Katya said. 'I didn't mean to be rude.'

'Everyone stares. I'm used to it.' Farooha leaned back against the desk, crossing her arms and gazing churlishly at her guest. 'I take it this is about Leila.'

Instantly, Katya regretted coming. In all of her excitement, she'd forgotten that Farooha probably didn't know that her friend was dead, and that the job of delivering the news would fall to her. Osama's parting look suddenly made sense.

'I'm sorry to tell you this,' Katya began. Farooha reacted immediately. Her arms seemed to freeze, and that strange frozen quality spread to the rest of her body. 'But I'm afraid that Leila is dead.'

Farooha unfroze a bit, looking as if it took some effort to shake herself free. With some awkwardness she climbed back on to her desk chair, situating herself carefully on her stack of books – among them, Katya noticed, was the Holy Quran – and she sat there, staring at the ground, although Katya had the feeling that Farooha had already suspected the worst, already run through the most gruesome possibilities in her mind to prepare herself for a moment like this. When Farooha looked up again, her eyes were clear and sharp. 'How did it happen?'

'Her neck was broken. She died instantly.'

'I don't believe that.'

Katya felt a strong wave of unease. 'She was also beaten,' she said, willing only to give that much. She wouldn't be drawn into telling her about the '*iqal* and knife wounds or the hot oil. 'I don't suppose you have any idea who might have wanted to do something like this to Leila?'

Farooha looked momentarily taken aback by the abruptness of the question. 'I can think of a dozen people,' she said, 'but I don't know their names.'

'What do you mean?' Katya said.

'You do know that Leila was a filmmaker?' Farooha asked.

Katya explained what she knew about Leila's work, and how she'd found Farooha.

'Ah, then you only know the sterilised version,' Farooha said with a certain grim set of the mouth.

Katya reached into her bag, panicking silently when she realised that she had forgotten to bring a notebook or even a pen. She found a broken pencil and an old shopping receipt at the bottom of the bag. *Oh, very professional*, she thought. Farooha eyed the pencil and smirked.

'New at investigating?' she asked.

'I left my notebook at the office,' Katya replied evenly,

although she was sure she was blushing. Without making a show of it, Farooha retrieved a pen and small notepad from her desk drawer and handed them to Katya.

'Thanks.' Katya took them gratefully.

Farooha went on. 'Leila was bold,' she said. 'She was brilliant and creative and nothing frightened her. However, she pissed a lot of people off. She only filmed B-roll to support her real passion, which was a documentary project she was working on. She called it *City of Veils*.'

'What was it about?' Katya asked.

Farooha snorted out a laugh. 'Well, mostly it was about Jeddah. She wanted to point out how strange it is that almost every pilgrim who comes to do the Hajj at some point has to pass through Jeddah. But Jeddah itself is the least religious city in the country. She loved this contradiction, the idea of sending people to Mecca through the Saudi equivalent of Monaco or Las Vegas . . .' Farooha smiled grimly. 'Uncovering all of this city's unsavoury behaviours became an obsession for her. And you have to give her credit for courage.

'It started out being tame,' Farooha went on. 'Leila caught a couple of things on camera and wanted to put them together – women eating spaghetti in burqas, those drivers doing their "drifting" thing on the motorways. But she wanted something bigger. About a year ago, maybe more, she met a woman who claimed to be a prostitute. Leila did an interview with her. It went badly, but Leila kept at it. She started visiting brothels and women's shelters. She interviewed a lot of women.'

'Did her brother know about this?'

Farooha frowned. 'Are you kidding? No one knew but Leila and her cousin, Ra'id. And me.'

'So she became interested in women's rights,' Katya said.

'Well, yeah, but she began going after anything that was controversial. Abused housemaids. Sex slaves. Men who marry twenty wives. And believe me, she had a knack for finding these things. She even filmed a drag queen show at a private villa outside the city. I don't know how she found *that*, but she did.'

'It sounds like she was interested in breaking sexual taboos,' Katya said. 'Did she ever investigate political or religious corruption?'

'No, not really, but I think she might have started if she hadn't died . . .' Farooha trailed off awkwardly. 'I'm not sure.' She took a sip of water from an Evian bottle on her desk. 'Anyway, she kept going despite the treatment she got.'

'What do you mean?' Katya asked.

'Well, she wasn't always filming things privately. Sometimes she would just wander around the city. Imagine a young woman walking around alone, pointing a video camera at anything that seems slightly embarrassing. She got attacked twice. One time some guy threw her camera in the ocean and physically assaulted her. He broke her leg. I don't think they caught the guy, but I know she filed a police report.'

'Yes, we know about that.'

'Another time, some guy grabbed her. If he'd been any bigger, he would have done some damage, but she managed to get away, although the guy followed her until she flagged down a cab. The religious police were always after her, but she could usually get away from them. I don't know how. If you ask me, she was just incredibly lucky. She also started to toughen herself up. She wore heavy metal T-shirts and jeans. She let her cloak hang open so people could see that she was the kind of person who would do whatever she liked. Maybe they would think she was a member of the royal family and they'd leave her alone.'

Katya thought of the worn spot on the knee of Leila's cloak. 'This may sound like a silly question, but did she kneel a lot?'

'Probably.' Farooha gave a wry laugh. 'She was forever hiding behind things to get a good shot of something. Why do you ask?'

'There was a worn spot around the knee of her cloak,' Katya said. 'It was only on one side, and I couldn't understand it.'

'Yes, that's probably why. In answer to your previous question, Leila was out in public a lot, pissing people off. There were plenty of people who might have wanted to harm her, aside from the larger-than-average number of men in this city who want to harm women whether they carry cameras or not.'

Katya looked down at her empty notepad. She hadn't been able to take her attention away from Farooha long enough to take notes. She scribbled a few things down. *City of Veils* and *sexual taboos* and *physical assault – check police records*. 'Let's put the strangers aside for a moment,' she said. 'All those people whom she might have angered while she was filming something. What about people she knew? Friends – maybe a boyfriend?'

Farooha's eyes glittered angrily. 'Well, first of all, her ex-husband was an arsehole. One time, he wouldn't take her to the hospital when she had a five-day fever. He left her lying on the bathroom floor and took her mobile away because his was broken. He got angry at her for not cooking his dinner and doing his laundry. And finally he just left because she was boring him. Turned out she had typhus.'

Katya was horrified, but she wrote *typhus* on her notepad to hide her shock. 'How did she end up getting to the doctor?'

'Her brother got worried and went to check on her. He had to have his assistant break down the door. They found her lying in a pool of blood and shit.' Farooha's nostrils flared and she spent a moment composing herself. 'In a way, it was a good thing. It caused her to divorce that stupid monkey.'

'And that's when she moved in with her brother?'

'Yes,' Farooha said. 'Although that was another kind of torture.'

'What do you mean?'

'They were fighting all the time before Leila disappeared. Didn't Abdulrahman tell you?'

'I didn't interview him.'

'Ah, of course.' Farooha twirled a pen between her fingers.

'What was the fighting about?' Katya asked.

'He didn't like that she was doing it, and he wanted it to stop.'

'You mean he didn't like her working for the news station?'

'Right. He didn't know the whole story, and now you can see why. If her working for a news station was enough to upset him, then she was never going to tell him about her other projects. He didn't like her being out of the house, and he thought that filming people was inappropriate. I think he considered it an invasive act. He wanted Leila to get married again, this time to a good Jeddawi man. If he'd had his way, Leila would probably be married and pregnant right now. And she would be totally miserable.'

'What did she tell you about the fights with her brother?'

'She said that he kept threatening to cut her off. You know he was supporting her. Personally, I could see him kicking her out completely.'

'Really?'

'Yeah, he could be pretty brutal. But he didn't go too far. He did stop paying for her camera equipment and the cost of all the taxis. This happened right after her camera got destroyed that day at the Corniche. Of course Leila wasn't going to stop just because of money. She kept pressuring him. Abdulrahman would get angry, and they would get into these terrible fights.'

'And what happened in these fights?'

'Well, I don't think he ever hit her, but she would come here looking pretty shaken up. When I asked her "Did he hit you?", she would never answer.' Farooha sighed in a maternal way. 'She always came when she needed a shoulder to cry on. But I told her then what I'd told her before: you shouldn't be relying on your brother anyway. She knew that financial independence was the only thing that would make her a happy person, Leila being who she was. *Financial independence.*'

'And did she eventually manage to get a new camera?'

'Yes, she did.'

'How did she get the money for that?'

Farooha sighed. 'Well, she had some saved up from her job at the news station.'

'And . . .?'

Farooha let the rest out reluctantly. 'And her cousin Ra'id gave her the rest.'

'How much did he give her?'

'Probably most of it. A thousand riyals. She didn't have that much saved up.'

'That's a lot of money,' Katya said. 'Does Ra'id get paid well by his uncle?'

Farooha shrugged. 'I only know what Leila told me, which on that subject wasn't very much. Back to your earlier question,' she went on. 'Leila also had a boyfriend of sorts. She'd met him recently, but he was American and I never met him.'

Katya froze. 'Do you know his name?'

'Walker. Eric Walker.'

Forcing herself to stay calm, Katya wrote down *Eric Walker – boyfriend?*

'Leila loved the Americans.' While she spoke, Farooha climbed down from her throne and went to the far corner of the room. She knelt beside the bed, momentarily disappearing from view. Katya heard a grunt and a few seconds later watched as Farooha hauled a metal lockbox the size of a large shoebox on to the bed. She went back to the desk for the key, which was dangling from a hook on a corkboard, and used it to open the box.

'Eric had a car and plenty of free time,' Farooha went on. 'He would take her everywhere. I mean, it was great for her, because he could get her into places that she couldn't otherwise go, like the American compound.'

Now Katya was scribbling furious notes. 'How did he and Leila meet?'

'Same way she met anyone – filming them.'

'Is that how you met her?' Katya asked.

Farooha looked as if she might decide to take offence – and Katya heard the implications in what she'd said. *A dwarf, who would want to miss filming that?* But Farooha shook her head. 'We went to school together, before my parents decided to pull me out.'

'Out of school?'

Farooha nodded. 'They were becoming too worried about me, they said, and it's true I put up with a lot of teasing, but it's more true that they were – and are – deeply ashamed of me.' She was still standing by the bedside, but now staring straight at Katya as if waiting for her to protest at such a cruel parental decision, or to make a weak, insincere, sympathetic remark. When Katya didn't respond, Farooha went back to her rummaging.

'Do you know where Leila and Eric met?'

'At a mall,' she said. 'I can't remember which one. Leila was filming something and Eric came up to her and asked if she was with the local news station. They got to talking ...' Finally, Farooha brought something to Katya. It was a square cardboard box. Inside it three dozen DVDs were lined up in hard plastic cases. 'This,' Farooha said, 'is the collected work of Leila Nawar.'

Katya accepted the box – it was practically set upon her lap – and pawed through the discs with amazement, puzzlement, and the dangerous urge to jump up and shout for joy.

'Whatever you got from her brother,' Farooha said, 'was only the clean stuff. This is the rest of it.' She jutted her chin at the box with a mixture of pride and warning. 'If someone from Leila's adventures killed her, I bet you'll find some evidence of it in there.'

'And you have these because . . .?' Katya asked.

'She was paranoid about losing her work, so I agreed to watch over her back-up discs.'

'Do you know where she kept the originals?'

'I don't know exactly. In her house somewhere, no doubt. And they'd be hidden. She wouldn't have wanted her brother or his wife to find them.'

'She must have been glad to have you as a friend.'

Farooha climbed back on to her chair. 'As I said, Leila was very lucky. Aren't you going to ask me where I was when she disappeared?'

Katya felt like smiling, but beneath Farooha's funny voice was an edge of viciousness and pain. 'Where were you?'

'Here, like I always am.'

☽

Osama sat on the white sofa. Farooha's younger brother sat on the sofa opposite, babysitting him, which was funny because the boy was six years old. He was the only male in the house at the moment, and so the de facto man of the house. The boy's mother – at least Osama figured that was who had answered the door – had brought him into the room and told him to keep their guest company. She hadn't explained who Osama was, and the boy didn't seem to care. His legs were so short that they stuck straight over the sofa's edge. He had some kind of computer game in his hands and he could scarcely take his attention off it for longer than a second, in which time he would glance at Osama, lick his lips nervously, and go back to his game with a vengeance.

The beeping and clanging were the perfect accompaniments to Osama's foul mood, which was only growing more miserable as the minutes ticked by. He was simultaneously relieved that he didn't have to watch Farooha learn about her friend's death, and disgusted that he couldn't ask her any questions himself, and that he'd brought along a woman who might or might not know what the hell she was doing.

Finally, a woman he presumed to be one of the boy's other sisters came into the room with a glass of orange juice for Osama. She set the orange juice on the coffee table and held her hand out to the young boy. He stood up, still not taking his eyes from the game, to follow her out of the room.

In the new quiet, Osama's attention went back to the CDs lining the shelves. It had been a mistake to browse the titles. Many of them were artists that Nuha loved. He'd tried segregating his thoughts of her all morning but now he could feel her slipping in, ghostly quiet, shrouded in a new obscurity.

It was crushing how proud he had always been of her and of their marriage. He admired that she worked at the newspaper, that she could write and that she got along with people so well. But every night that they'd made love over the past two years she'd let him believe that she wanted another child, that their love-making was leading up to that goal. More crucially, when the child didn't come, she'd convinced him that a woman's body was a mystery, that yes, she'd already become pregnant once, and given birth to a healthy baby boy, but with most women things didn't happen like clockwork, and sometimes stress and busyness depressed the body so that it wasn't as fertile as it should be. They'd discussed how perhaps she should cut back on her work hours, and for the first year after Muhannad was born, she'd only gone into work part-time. He didn't pester her about it, since obviously there was little he could do but what he was already doing. He had never once suspected she was using contraception.

He wondered if Rafiq knew. Had Mona told him? Before Rafiq was shot, the four of them used to get together all the time. The men would talk about work, the women would talk about their marriages.

When the allegations began coming in about Rafiq, Osama told

Nuha everything. He had thought she would be one of the few people who would understand, but instead of lending Rafiq her sympathy, she had gone strangely cold. When Osama pressed her, she told him that she thought Rafiq was cruel. Mona had told her how he had all these rules. He wanted Mona to wear an *abaaya* and *hijaab* around certain friends, then to wear casual trousers and no headscarf around others. He even made her label certain outfits so she would remember which ones to wear at which times. He gave her rules for wearing make-up (only with close friends, never with his family), rules for how to dress when they travelled to Egypt (always jeans or trousers, never a long skirt). She was allowed to take classes – she chose yoga, sewing, and a computer skills class – but Rafiq had to approve them first, and she was not allowed to go to a class if he was home, because he might need her for something.

Nuha told him all of these things with a disgust kept carefully in check – for Osama's sake – but she finished by saying how grateful she was that her own life was nowhere near as controlled, that her husband respected her for who she was. It would never have occurred to him to treat Nuha that way.

Osama had been vaguely annoyed that, in the face of Rafiq's tragedy, Nuha was criticising his marriage. On one hand, Rafiq's behaviour was normal. It was very like him to boss people around. And Osama always had the impression that Mona was a special case, one of those helpless girls who never quite became a woman. Rafiq's attraction to her had given way to annoyance over the years, and no doubt he readily imposed his will in the absence of hers. And anyway, there were plenty of men who micromanaged their wives. It didn't mean Rafiq was also a liar, a thief, an extortionist and a thug.

Osama had rationalised it in this way for a while until he realised that he couldn't stop thinking about what Nuha had said. Finally, during a conversation about women, he found the opportunity to ask Rafiq: 'Why are you always telling Mona what to do?'

Rafiq had given him a strange look that Osama hadn't understood at the time but that he was able to interpret now with frightening clarity. It said: *My wife tells you our secrets, and your wife tells us yours.* 'If you don't keep an eye on your wife,' Rafiq had said in a pointed way, 'she'll betray you one way or another.'

Osama stared miserably at the glass of orange juice, hating the fact that Rafiq had been right.

☽

Katya was just leaving Farooha's room when she heard footsteps in the hallway. As she opened the door, there was a *thump* on the wall and a man's voice said: 'Stay in your room, you little freak. You'd better not come out until I'm gone.'

Katya glanced at Farooha.

'My brother Jamal,' Farooha muttered. 'He must have just come in.' Katya was torn apart by the look on her face. She expected an expression of fury, but there was a wounded quality there, something much too raw and fresh. At the very least, Farooha's brother must have worn her down over the years.

Katya swung the door wide and went into the hall.

The man spun around with a vicious fury. 'I said *stay in your*—' But when he saw Katya, he started back. His face wore a look of horror of the fairy-tale kind, where a *djinn* slips into your house at night and replaces your ugly sister with a young princess. She might appear to be a beauty, but she'll cast a spell to switch your fingers and toes, and cause you to bleat like a sheep for the rest of your life.

He recovered quickly. 'Cover your face, woman,' he snarled.

Katya recoiled. She would have given anything for an ID badge to flash in his skinny, pathetic face. Instead, she had Osama, who poked his head out of the *majlis* door, flashed his own badge and called to Katya. 'Officer Hijazi, when you're finished, I'd like you to help me take care of this man.'

Katya nodded stiffly, watching with satisfaction as the man spun between them, trapped like a fox on a motorway between two oncoming trucks. Osama motioned him into the *majlis* with a threatening look, and the man went grudgingly.

Farooha was facing her computer, clicking idly on her mouse. 'Is that all?' she said over her shoulder. 'Because if you're done, I have work to do.'

Katya wanted to say: you spend all of your time in your room. Your parents want you locked up here, and your brother threatens you if you so much as open your bedroom door. Aren't you longing to get the hell out? Instead, she wrote her mobile number on a piece of paper from the notepad Farooha had given her and set it on the desk.

'Please call me if you think of anything that might be helpful.'

Farooha pinched the piece of paper between two fingers and looked over her shoulder at Katya. 'Please call me when you find her killer.'

))

Back in the car, with Leila's DVDs sitting heavily on her lap, Katya found herself suppressing the urge to thank Osama again for appearing in the hallway and, without even missing a beat, making her his equal. The feeling was ridiculous, swelling in her throat, making her giddy. But the more she attempted to fold it away, the more another feeling ballooned in its place, a fierce kind of loyalty rising, warm and satisfying.

After dishing out a short but heavy dose of intimidation, Osama had learned that Farooha's brother was a car mechanic, that he lived down the street with his wife, who was expecting their second child, and that he thought his parents had made a huge mistake not giving his sister up for adoption when they had the chance.

212

'You fit our profile for the killer,' Osama had said with a serious face.

He's married, Katya had to remind herself when her admiration for him threatened to burst out, *and apparently so am I*. She told him everything about the interview with Farooha, raising her biggest concern: that it was going to take forever to get through all the video footage that Farooha had given them. She was also worried about their being back-up discs.

'You didn't find the originals at her house?' she asked.

'No,' Osama said. 'And we still haven't found her computer.'

'Farooha mentioned that Leila would have hidden them well.'

'We stripped her room, but maybe they're in another part of the house,' he said. 'I'll make sure to send someone back there to broaden the search.'

When Osama asked about the girl, Katya admitted that Farooha, though intelligent and charming, was also an introverted, self-conscious homebody who seemed possessive of Leila, her gregarious, edgy, courageous friend.

'She also told me that Leila's ex-husband was abusive,' Katya went on. She took out Farooha's notepad to remind herself of the details. At the next stop light Osama asked to see the notepad, so she handed it over. As she blathered on, her mind was secretly still reeling with the news that Eric Walker knew Leila. When she reached the point of having to explain who Walker was and how Leila knew him, Osama seemed to notice the skip in her voice, because he looked at her suddenly.

She blushed, and sighed. 'There's something you should know.'

He studied her coldly, as if expecting the worst. She had to force herself to continue.

'I know this probably wasn't a good idea,' she said, 'but I heard that Chief Riyadh was planning to cut back your staff.' He looked confused by this, and stung. She had the feeling that she'd learned about it before he had, and that she'd just made a very big mistake admitting it. 'So I wanted to help. I learned from Majdi that Leila was working on two things before she died – the B-roll for the news station, and photographing a private art collection.'

Osama waited.

'Because Majdi was having trouble getting in touch with the art collector, I went with a friend of mine to the address we had for him, just to see if we could track him down. There was a woman there,' she said quickly, hoping he would catch the implication: *It's a good thing I went, because we wound up having to interview a woman.* But Osama didn't blink. 'An American woman,' Katya went on. 'It turns out the art collector was her landlord. She gave us another address for him.'

'This is the guy we *think* might be connected to the Quranic documents we found in Leila's bedroom.'

'Right,' Katya said. 'Mr Nabih. Anyway, this American woman was helpful, but she also seemed nervous. Here's where the story gets odd: we learned that her husband had disappeared. He'd been gone for three days, and she had no idea where he was. She seemed . . . scared.'

Katya, who had been unconsciously turning her wedding band in circles, stopped when she noticed him staring at her hand.

'The husband's name,' she said, 'was Eric Walker.'

All of the coldness left Osama's face, replaced by a look of meaningful surprise. 'Are you sure?'

'Yes. I didn't tell you before because I wasn't sure that it meant anything to the investigation. This art collector was only their landlord . . .'

Osama nodded. 'So Leila was probably lying to her brother. Maybe the landlord was an art collector, but it could have been a fabrication. She was actually going to meet with Eric Walker?'

'I think it's possible,' Katya said. 'Farooha said that Leila had met Eric the way she met everyone – by filming them. She met Eric at a mall, and he may have introduced her to his landlord for this photography job. In any case, I doubt she would have told her brother that she was seeing an American.'

'I'll find out,' he said, and immediately fell into an uncomfortable silence.

'I'm sorry, I know it was taking a lot of liberties—' Katya said. Osama cut her off with an impatient wave of the hand, but she blurted: 'I want you to know that I haven't done anything else, it was just the one thing.'

When Osama turned to her, she saw relief on his face. 'That's all right,' he said. 'You did the right thing telling me. But in future, be aware that every single detail is important, even the stuff that doesn't seem like it at the time. Don't ever keep secrets.'

She nodded. They were just pulling into the station, but instead of parking, he pulled up to the door. 'Take those discs to Majdi. Or actually, start looking at them yourself. He's working on a lot of things right now. But first, do you have this American woman's address?'

She fished around in her bag until she found the slip of paper, which she handed to him.

'And what about the landlord's address?'

'It's in al-Aziziya,' she said.

'All right. I'll check that out. You did very well,' he said, closing her notepad, which had been sitting on his lap. 'Mind if I borrow this?'

'Go ahead,' she said. 'I have another one in my desk.' She cringed at the presumption that he'd ever be taking her out on another interview.

Distractedly, Osama nodded.

))

Dhuhr prayers had just finished and the sky was a blinding white, draping the city in a blanket of nuclear heat. Osama was sitting in his car outside his favourite Indian restaurant when his mobile rang. It was Fuad, the assistant from the lingerie boutique. He sounded nervous, and it was difficult to hear what he was saying over the background noise of rushing cars. Osama had an image of him walking furtively down a busy street.

'I'm sorry, Mr Jamia, I can't understand what you're saying.'

'Ra'id is back,' Fuad said, finally loudly enough.

'Leila's cousin?'

'Yes.' Fuad launched into a plea. Osama could only make out every third word, but it sounded as if he were saying: *Don't tell my boss.*

'Of course not,' Osama said, but the line was dead.

22

The address that Miriam Walker had given them for Mr Nabih turned out to be useless. Katya spent half the afternoon on the computer before discovering that it was an address for a postal store in Abu Dhabi. When she finally reached them on the telephone, they told her that they didn't have a box registered to anyone named Nabih. She had reached a dead end.

She spent the rest of the day in front of her computer. She knew she ought to get to some of her other cases, but Leila's DVDs were irresistible evidence.

She slid the first one into the computer's drive half-expecting that the killer would appear on the screen with a gruesome confession, but the picture that came up was only the inside of a women's department store.

The camera was focused on a circular clothing rack that held shirts and dresses. The rack seemed to be moving but it was hard to tell because Leila had been filming the whole thing from the inside of another clothing rack across the aisle. At least that's what it looked like; there was something obstructing the left side of the frame, like the sleeve of a woman's shirt. Across the aisle, a woman was inspecting the items on the rack. Her burqa was up and Katya could see her profile. She looked very young. All of a sudden, the woman screamed and backed away. A security guard came running, and at the same time a man bolted out from the inside of the clothing rack. He took off to the left just as the security guard came from the right. And in a flash, Leila was after him, jerking out of her hiding space and galloping down the aisle. The screen went haywire for a moment, then it steadied, showing the man lying flat on his face on the carpet. Behind the camera, Leila's voice whispered 'Dammit!' Two women were standing over the perpetrator; apparently he had stumbled over their pushchairs. Leila had missed filming his fall, but the scene was still amusing. A moment later, the security guard came rushing up to arrest the peeping tom.

The disc was full of such scenes. In one, a religious policeman was chasing a woman down the street, hollering at her about the sinfulness of walking a dog in public. 'They are devices of flirtation!' he shouted. 'They are like jewellery, or make-up. The bedizenment of the time of ignorance!' Katya rolled her eyes. But the man managed to catch the woman. First he grabbed her arm, but she swung her handbag at him, so he went straight to the root of the problem: he seized her tiny dog by the neck and yanked it free of the leash. Then he ran off with it. The dog began barking. The woman screamed.

Katya told herself to start taking notes but she couldn't stop watching. She went through the whole disc, eating lunch at her desk and ignoring her mobile. There were a few more professional-looking cuts, probably work Leila had done for the local news station, filming old buildings and new construction projects and city beautification events, like tree-plantings with grade school children. She skimmed through those. Leila had done a special report for a major media network in Dubai about boy scouts serving as guides during the Hajj. But clearly her real interest was in exposing the obscenities and clashes in her favourite city, and these took up most of the next two DVDs.

Every cut had a time and date stamp in the bottom left-hand corner of the screen, and so far they had all come in chronological order, starting about a year and a half ago. Farooha had said that

Leila went out almost every day, and judging from the time stamps, she seemed to catch interesting things – things worth saving on disc – every third or fourth day.

The fourth DVD that Katya placed in the drive was different. Chronologically, it was out of sequence – there was a two-month gap between this and the previous one.

The first segment was titled *Summer of Love*. The minute it opened, a woman appeared on the screen. She was in a sunlit sitting room on a soft pink couch. Posters of Audrey Hepburn decorated the wall behind her. The woman was wearing a modish black skirt, tights, high heels, and a short pink blazer that made her look Parisian. Her hair was short, black and wavy and her face, pretty in a plain sort of way, was covered in too much white make-up. Katya figured she was trying to look European, including altering the colour of her skin.

Text appeared at the bottom of the screen reading 'Johara', the girl's pseudonym, and *Almesyaf Zawaaj*. Summer marriage. Katya groaned. The 'summer holiday marriage' was a disgusting arrangement. A man, usually a businessman, would marry a woman for the summer so he could take her as a travelling 'companion' overseas – to Egypt or Europe or America. They would pass themselves off as man and wife. Once the stay was over, the couple would return to Saudi and terminate the marriage.

Katya had seen wanted ads, Bluetoothed to her mobile from men looking for summer wives, and it was these more than anything that made her feel that the whole arrangement was dirty. The ads were almost all the same. Men were looking for women who could speak English well, who were pale-skinned, slender and sexy, and who came from good families. The pay was upwards of 100,000 riyals, sometimes even a new villa or a brand new BMW. That part always made her laugh bitterly. Giving a woman a car! It was prostitution, plain and simple.

When the religious establishment got wind of this new trend

(which was probably just an old trend that few had known about before), one notable cleric stepped forward to approve of the practice. He spelled it out: summer marriage was acceptable in Islam because it prevented men from falling into the sin of prostitution while they were spending so many months abroad without a woman. It was much more preferable for the man to bring a Saudi woman along – at least she was Muslim and his wife. The sheikh pointed to another underlying concern: the fact that so many Saudi wives didn't devote enough time to their husbands any more – because they had found jobs outside the home – necessitated the husband looking elsewhere to satisfy his needs. If that husband happened to be a businessman who travelled, well there was nothing wrong with him taking a young woman along on the journey, since he couldn't take his wife. She had to stay home and work.

Katya felt the first twinge of an emotion more violent than disgust. Not a single person she knew would approve of this kind of marriage. In fact, if the subject came up, most of her friends expressed outright fury, because to their minds it was disgusting. It cheapened both the sacred vow of marriage and Islam. It was just another way that the religious establishment used the Quran to support its own warped vision of the world.

Johara was facing the camera, her face masked with make-up and something stronger – defiance or pride. Leila was asking her to describe her latest summer marriage, and Johara was saying that she did it every year, and that she enjoyed only having to work for two months, and then having the rest of the year to herself, to spend her money as she liked.

Katya forced herself to watch the rest, the smugness of the woman's face as she took Leila on a tour of her brand new villa, showing off a teak bar, the living room's enormous cathedral windows, and a kitchen that looked like it belonged in a restaurant, not to mention three lavish bedrooms with king-sized beds and a closet full of clothes in each. Two small chihuahuas nipped at

Leila's heels as they walked. Katya had to give her some credit; Leila didn't criticise or make her subject uncomfortable. She simply recorded everything, and only once they were back at the sitting-room sofa, having tea, did Leila begin to ask the difficult questions.

'Do you think of yourself as a prostitute?'

Johara seemed prepared for this, her face remained cool. 'No,' she replied somewhat mechanically. 'This is not prostitution. Prostitutes can sleep with a man without a marriage contract, and that is not acceptable to me. I am a traditional woman.'

'Do you ever think of yourself as a slave?' Leila asked. Katya was taken aback by the strong words.

Johara looked shocked, and replied in an icy tone: 'Of course not. When I am married to these men, I am their *legitimate* wife.'

'But your marriage is only temporary,' Leila said, her voice neutral. 'And you've said it yourself: you'll never have children with these men. So you're not really a *traditional* wife.'

Johara looked as if she might stand up and leave, then she turned from Leila and glanced sharply at the camera. 'Turn that off,' she said.

Leila didn't move; the camera remained fixed on Johara's face. 'I said *turn it off*,' Johara snapped, reaching for the camera. There was a tussle and the screen went black.

Katya sat staring at the screen. She couldn't be sure who angered her more – Johara for being so smug, or Leila for going into the woman's home, nodding and oohing at her lovely house and her cute little dogs, then confronting her with critical questions that would obviously offend her host.

The next few sequences on the DVD were similar to the first. Leila was interviewing a prostitute in each one. Johara was apparently the only one who did summer marriages; the other prostitutes were more pedestrian than that. The location changed every time, and it was always the inside of somebody's house. But in each instance, Leila managed to either alienate or upset her subject, and the interviews tended to become very tense.

As Katya ran through the rest of the footage, the reality of the situation began to settle over her. Leila spent all of her time invading the privacy of others. Whether or not her work took place in public, the presence of a video camera was seldom taken lightly. There were too many people who would feel that her camera was not just a nuisance but a dangerous assault. And she did this kind of work every day. Johara had nearly punched her camera, and there were other instances of minor assault. Most likely at least one of her subjects had felt that Leila deserved worse than a public beating. They had decided that she deserved to be physically punished in a brutal way. The potential pool of killers was looking very wide. It was an investigator's worst nightmare: there was a very good chance that the killer was a stranger, one of the many Leila had encountered in the past year and a half.

It was getting late, the office was emptying – Katya heard people walking down the corridors outside her door, talking in loud, end-of-the-day voices. She checked her watch. Ayman would be here in fifteen minutes, he was on the road already, but she could feel the prickling, electric sense of a revelation about to happen, and she wasn't ready to go home. In the box beside the computer, the remaining DVDs were neatly queued. She had only gone through five and a half and it had taken most of the afternoon. Unless she took some of them home, getting through the rest of them was going to take forever. And she hadn't even *looked* at her other cases today. Slipping the next three DVDs casually into her handbag, she locked the rest in her filing cabinet and left the room.

She met Majdi on the stairs. 'Heading home?' he asked.

'Yes, my ride is waiting.'

'Lucky you,' he said. He looked exhausted. 'We just picked up Leila's cousin. He's in interrogation right now, and apparently there's more evidence to process. It looks like it's going to be a long night.'

'I'll stay if you need me.'

'Well . . . what about your ride?' he asked with concern.

'I can stay,' she said.

'No, it's okay. I think we can do—'

'I'm staying,' she said firmly, taking out her mobile to call Ayman and turning back up the stairs. 'Let me just put my bag away.' She looked back once to see Majdi's look of gratitude and relief. 'You're welcome,' she said.

He gave a smile. 'Thank you.'

Turning away, she felt a mixture of excitement and frustration. The reason he hadn't expected her to stay was because she was a woman and because, in his mind, there was a husband at home waiting for her to cook his dinner and prepare his tea and pleasure him in the bedroom. It was her fault for lying about the imaginary husband. Still, she couldn't help but feel sad. She and Majdi had been working so closely on Leila's case that she had almost – *almost* – forgotten who she was supposed to be.

23

When Osama arrived at the interrogation room, he found Abdul-rahman and Fuad standing outside the door. Both men looked upset.

'I'm sure they won't keep him,' Fuad was saying in a half-whisper. 'Just as long as he explains himself.'

'The *stupid* boy,' Abdulrahman said loudly, looked ready to burst.

Osama came upon them and Abdulrahman turned with a start.

'*Salaam aleikum*,' Osama greeted the men warily. After Fuad's phone call Osama had waited an hour, then gone with two of his most trusted men to Abdulrahman's house, their only pretext an elaborate errand that no one but forensics was likely to comprehend. Ra'id must have seen their cars pull up in front of the house, because he'd attempted to escape through the back garden. They had caught him and arrested him promptly.

They'd done a search of his room and found nothing, but the inspection of his car had been more fruitful: they'd found a small box of cassette tapes, the type that could be used in a video camera. Each one was labelled 'Leila Nawar'. They'd also found a computer in the boot. Forensics suspected that the computer was Leila's, but according to Majdi, the hard drive had been wiped clean.

'I understand the young man came back to your house on his

own?' Osama asked, knowing that his involvement would get Fuad into trouble if Abdulrahman ever discovered that his assistant had called him.

'He's ready to talk,' Abdulrahman said. Osama disliked his tone. There was too much aggression in it.

'Did he come to you?' Osama asked.

'Yes,' Abdulrahman said. 'He showed up this morning and explained himself. I told him he had to come to the police. He was a little nervous about it. I was about to convince him before your people showed up.'

Fuad wore a look of careful neutrality.

Inside the interrogation room sat a very forlorn-looking Ra'id, his head in his hands, his greasy hair hanging over his fingers. His shirt was rumpled and there was a long cut on his forearm that looked fresh. On the table next to his elbow was an old brown box.

When Osama came in, Ra'id quickly dropped his injured arm beneath the table and sat up.

'What happened to your arm?' Osama asked.

'Bumped it against the gate in the back garden,' he said.

Osama set a folder on the table and opened the box, glancing at the cassette tapes.

'Where did you get these?' he asked.

'Leila's bedroom,' the boy replied. His skin was grey, the bags under his eyes were a terrible dark brown.

'Are these her original cassettes?'

'Yes.'

'Where did you get them?'

'She kept them in one of the spare rooms, in a hidden panel in a wardrobe.'

'And the computer that was in the boot of your car – whose was that?'

'Leila's.'

'Where did you get it?'

'I took it from her room.'

'Is this why you ran away from the lingerie shop that day?'

Ra'id nodded and sat forward, pressing his chest against the table as if expecting a whipping. Osama studied the boy. The family photographs they'd found in Leila's room gave testimony to the fact that she and Ra'id were close.

Osama pushed the folder aside and sat down: 'Can I get you anything?'

Ra'id looked surprised.

'Coffee? Something to eat?'

'No.' Ra'id blinked, frowning, but Osama could tell he'd made a dent.

'All right,' Osama said. He reached for the tape player. 'Osama Ibrahim interviewing Ra'id Nawar. First of all, Mr Nawar, tell me why you ran away.'

Ra'id glanced at the door again. 'I knew where Leila's video stuff was – her tapes, I mean, and all the stuff on her computer. I didn't want you guys to find it.'

'Why not?'

This time his eyes met Osama's. He gave a slightly derisive sniff and seemed to relax a little. 'They're listening to us, aren't they?'

'No one is listening,' Osama said.

'What about that window?' Ra'id motioned to the one-way glass.

'No one is in there, least of all your uncle or his assistant, I promise you.'

Ra'id seemed to take forever to decide to trust him, but finally he said: 'Leila's stuff was . . . not exactly proper, you know what I mean?'

'Tell me.'

'She interviewed disgusting people. Prostitutes. Kleptomaniacs. I mean, I tried to get her to stop, but she wouldn't listen. She went ahead with it, because she was so fucking stubborn.' This last word came out breathlessly, and he lowered his gaze.

'So you thought, if you could hide the tapes, you'd be protecting her reputation?'

'I just didn't want you guys to see it all. It's going to give you this idea about Leila, make you think, I don't know, maybe she deserved what she got—' He broke off with a choke.

'We have other copies of the videos she made,' Osama said.

'What? How?'

'Do you know why she was interested in those women?'

Ra'id paused. 'She wanted to know how they got by,' he said. 'Most of the women she interviewed supported themselves. Maybe their families had cut them off. Some of them didn't have families. They didn't want to do what they were doing, but they felt they had no other choices. Leila was interested.'

'I see. How did she meet them?'

'I'm not sure. She met one woman online . . .'

'And the others?'

'I don't know.' Ra'id had begun to sweat.

'I get the impression that you and Leila were close,' Osama said. 'That she might have told you things.'

The boy nodded.

'So you, of all people, would have some idea of how she did her work. And I do understand that it was a serious pursuit for her.' For the first time, Ra'id met his eye. 'Did she walk the streets looking for these women?'

He shook his head uncertainly.

'Perhaps she knew a man who introduced her to some of them?'

Ra'id shook his head, looking beleaguered. 'Listen, I don't know exactly. She didn't tell me everything. She was the kind of person who would just get an idea in her head and follow it without stopping. She didn't know any of these women, but once she decided to start interviewing prostitutes, she wasn't going to stop until she'd found a dozen who'd be willing to talk on camera. That's just how she was.'

'Do you think she was trying to make a comment on our society?'

Ra'id looked nervous. 'Maybe, a little.'

'There's a lot to criticise here,' Osama said, 'especially for a woman. It seems like Leila was committed to making a statement.'

'Yeah, kind of.' Ra'id still looked nervous. 'She didn't like the way the women were treated, but she respected that they were taking care of themselves. She was just trying to show people that sometimes bad things happen here.'

Osama noted the delicacy of expression. The idea that Leila cared about the women wasn't exactly in keeping with the behaviour Leila had apparently shown on the clips of her interviews with them. The preliminary report that Katya had put on his desk said that Leila seemed more interested in exposing the prostitutes' flaws and hypocrisies, even humiliating them.

'Leila wasn't thinking of exposing these women, was she?' Osama asked.

'No! She was committed to their privacy.'

'But you have to admit, it would have been an ideal opportunity to create a sensation, for Leila to make a name for herself as a film-maker.'

'That's not what she wanted! She was going to blur their faces so you couldn't recognise them. And she hardly ever told anyone what she was doing.'

Osama bristled at Ra'id's innocence. He wanted to tell the boy that Leila the idealist might have been just Leila the sweet-talking girl who could convince her cousin that she was on a mission for a higher cause. He had the feeling Leila's 'higher cause' was fame, or money.

'Did Leila ever talk about what sort of hopes she had for this film project?' he asked.

'Yeah, she was going to send it to film festivals in Syria and New York. She had them all picked out. And she had all of the stuff already recorded. She just had to . . .' He stopped as if wounded by the reality that the project would never be finished. 'She had to put it all together, and make a documentary out of it. She just . . . she didn't get the chance to do it.' He exhaled heavily, fighting tears.

The boy was pitiable.

'What about her video camera?' Osama asked. 'The first one got destroyed when she was attacked at the Corniche, so she bought another one. How did she get the money for that?'

'I gave it to her,' he said somewhat nervously.

'That was very generous.'

'She needed it, and she was going to pay me back someday.'

Osama nodded. 'How much did your uncle know about her activities?'

'Nothing.' Ra'id snorted. 'If he had . . .' Ra'id seemed to think the better of finishing that thought.

'But Abdulrahman let her go out,' Osama said.

'No. He tried to keep her home, but she went out anyway. He said it was okay for her to film B-roll if she brought me along as a chaperone. She hated working for the news station. It was boring. Abdulrahman was at work all day, so he didn't know what she was doing. Occasionally, he'd find out that she wasn't home, and he'd call her mobile. She'd always tell him she was at her friend Farooha's house, and Farooha would cover for her.'

'So he never knew what Leila was really doing? He never found out, not even once, that she was going around the city filming things other than B-roll?'

'No.'

'How can you be so sure?'

'If he had found out, believe me, we would have known.'

'He has a temper,' Osama offered.

'Yeah,' Ra'id said. 'But he would never have hurt her, even if he was angry. He would have screamed at her, that's all.'

Osama nodded. 'According to witnesses, Leila and your uncle fought quite a bit.'

'Well, yeah. He was always trying to force her to stay home, and she'd go out anyway. She was always asking for more money, and he would never give her any. He thought she was just going to go out and spend it on clothes. Obviously, she never told him that she needed it for her film projects.' A cool expression settled over Ra'id's face. 'He wasn't her father. He acted like it sometimes, but he couldn't control her.'

Osama decided to change the focus. 'Where were you on the morning she disappeared?'

Ra'id sat up. 'I was at the shop all morning. Why?'

'No one at the shop seems able to verify that you were actually there.'

'I was there!' he insisted, voice rising. 'I was there all day!'

'Were you supposed to be with her – you know, being her "chaperone"?'

'I didn't go out with her every single time.'

'Did your uncle know this?'

'No.'

'So wouldn't your uncle have found it suspicious if you showed up at the shop?'

Ra'id was squirming. 'Yeah, but he wasn't going to be at the shop that morning.'

'Still, one of the staff members might have noticed and mentioned it to him. Fuad, for example.'

Ra'id was chewing his lip. 'Well, Fuad wasn't there either.' He said this with a mild look of triumph that gave Osama the idea that he'd just stumbled on the answer.

'But you would have known where Leila was going that morning,' Osama went on. 'Was it to see someone in particular?'

'I don't know. She didn't tell me.'

It was as if the conversation had hit a wall. Osama waited, watching. Ra'id sat staring at the box on the table.

Osama sat back and made a show of reflecting. 'You must have really cared about her. You gave her a lot of money. You supported what she did and kept her secrets. And you even risked becoming a murder suspect by stealing these tapes and the computer from the house to protect her reputation. You have definitely committed a crime by erasing her hard drive.' Ra'id seemed to struggle not to look panicked. 'Now these tapes may be the only evidence we have of who killed her.'

The boy had the grace to look stricken.

'So it raises the uncomfortable question,' Osama went on, sitting forward now, 'of what your real motivation was for stealing those tapes.'

Ra'id's mouth hung open, and he sputtered: 'I don't know what you mean. I told you why I did it.'

'It didn't bother you, for example, that Leila was seeing an American man?'

For just a moment, Ra'id's eyes flickered with hostility. 'Who? That Eric guy? She wasn't *seeing* him. They were friends.'

'Oh.'

'You don't believe me?' Ra'id was getting more tense by the second. 'They were friends, nothing more.'

'It seems to me she knew this Eric guy pretty well. She went out with him quite a lot.'

'They hung out sometimes, that was it.'

'Is that what she told you?'

'It's none of your business!' Ra'id shot out of his seat, surprising Osama.

'Mr Nawar, sit down.'

Ra'id remained standing a few seconds longer, then reluctantly took a seat. The look on his face told Osama that he was done cooperating.

'Was she going to meet Eric that day?' Osama asked.

'I don't know.'

'Did it upset you that she didn't want you to come along?'

Ra'id jutted out his lower lip. Despite the proliferation of coarse black hairs on his chin, it was a boy's chin and he seemed more juvenile with every minute. 'Like I said before: I don't know where she went that morning.'

Nothing more was said for a few cold minutes. Osama thought of Nuha's contraceptive pills, lying shattered on the kitchen table, and of the shameful feeling he'd had after smashing them – that he wasn't able to control himself, that there was something very traditional inside him that couldn't be so easily dismissed. Instead of thinking of it as a character flaw, however, he began to imagine that everybody had their secret trigger. Had Leila, like Nuha, done something in particular that had brought out her cousin's surprising wrath?

Osama stood up. 'Mr Nawar,' he said, leaning over the table. 'We're going to find out what's on these tapes, and we're going to put all of our information together, and I want you to know that there's simply no chance at all that we're going to let this killer get away. Is that clear?'

Ra'id didn't reply, and Osama made to leave.

'Wait,' Ra'id said. 'Are you going to let me go?'

'No,' Osama said.

'But why? I didn't do anything!'

'I'm sorry, Mr Nawar, you ran away once before, and I'm not convinced of your innocence.' Osama waited for more protest but Ra'id didn't speak, he just sat there looking furious.

24

Before *dhuhr* prayers on Sunday was the best time to catch Imam Hadi alone. It was supposed to be the hour when his older students would practise their recitations, but they always came after *'asr*, leaving him a brief period to inhabit his office and enjoy a cup of tea with those congregants who knew him well enough to know this glitch in his schedule. He was usually studying or writing, sitting behind the great oak desk, glasses perched on his nose, his *shumagh* draped on the chair behind him.

Nayir found him like this and felt guilty for intruding, but Imam Hadi welcomed him with typical bonhomie and begged him to take a seat while he went to fetch tea. Nayir found it comforting to note that nothing had changed since his last visit here two months before – not the parchment scriptures on the walls, nor the way the holy books were stacked on the shelf above their heads. Even the smell was the same, wood and leather and the cool plastery scent of stucco walls.

When the imam returned, he was carrying two cups of tea. Nayir liked that about him, that he wouldn't use a servant, that he understood what genuine modesty was. Hadi set the cup before Nayir and took a seat at the desk.

'It's been a while, Nayir,' he said. 'I've been thinking of you. My wife and I went out to the desert last week to visit a friend of ours, an old Bedouin. I know I've told you about him. He reminds me so much of you, he might have been your father.'

'Which tribe is he from?'

'Al-Murrah.'

'Ah, I know some Murrah.'

The imam's mobile rang and he switched it off. They sat in contented silence for a while, listening to the creaky metal fan in the corner spin back and forth.

'So tell me how you've been,' Imam Hadi said. There was no note of concern in his voice, none of Uncle Samir's pitying looks. If he'd noticed that Nayir had lost weight, he had chosen not to mention it.

Nayir assured him all was well, but then he explained the reason for his visit. He gave the imam a brief explanation of the documents he'd analysed at the lab, and Majdi's suggestion that they represented earlier, and somehow more authentic versions of the Quran. Yet they had contained obvious mistakes.

'What sorts of mistakes?' Imam Hadi asked.

Nayir explained. Imam Hadi sat back in his chair and crossed his hands on his belly. 'Don't trouble yourself,' he said gently. 'We know about the existence of minor differences in wording in the Quran throughout the ages. And there are a number of very simple reasons for it. When the words of Allah were first delivered to the Prophet, peace be upon him, they were transmitted orally. Of course the first Muslims wrote everything down, but those who learned the Quran in the beginning had to memorise it, and sometimes they wrote the Quran in their own way. The Prophet's companions had their own versions for personal use. But because they had already memorised the Quran, they used the written documents as a memory aid, nothing more. There are books that go into great detail about all of these things.

'You see,' he went on, 'in any human system like that, you will find imperfections. What is miraculous – what is evidence to me of the greatness of Allah – is that the true Quran has remained unchanged. And that centuries of Muslims have chosen not to alter a single diacritic mark in the holy book.'

'You're right,' Nayir said. He knew about the various 'personal' versions of the Quran, but he had assumed they had all been burned. It was hard to understand why he hadn't explained this to Majdi, why he hadn't been as calm about the whole matter as the imam was now.

'Islam has often been accused of inconsistency,' the imam said, 'or of being a mere forgery of another religion, or of being some variation of the truth, and not the whole truth. But remember the words of Allah: *When we substitute one revelation for another – and Allah knows best what he reveals in stages – they say: "Thou are but a forger!": But most of them understand not.* It means that Allah had given us guidance throughout the ages, in many forms, but the fundamental message doesn't change. The Truth is always the same.'

Nayir nodded. He felt a flood of relief and gratitude to the imam. Of course he had known all of this before, but he needed the reassurance that Majdi had indeed been too quick to judge.

'We can talk about the history of the Quran,' the imam said, 'but I would like to hear about you. Tell me what has been going on.'

Guiltily, Nayir remembered his other reason for coming. 'The truth is . . .' He felt a flush of embarrassment for not having told the imam any of this before, but he pressed ahead: 'I met a woman. A while ago, in fact.'

Hadi raised an eyebrow with a happy, expectant twitch. 'Yes?'

Nayir began to explain. He had to start at the beginning, meeting Katya at the morgue when he was picking up Nouf's body on behalf of her family. He had tried to tell the imam these things months ago, after he and Katya had stopped talking, but he hadn't had the nerve. He hated to think how the unfolding story of his relationship with Katya would change the imam's opinion of him, but worrying about that now was only stupid pride.

Hadi listened patiently, sipping his tea and nodding, occasionally letting his face reflect interest or chagrin. At the end, there was a thoughtful silence.

'Tell me,' the imam said, 'why didn't you speak to her for all those months?'

'We talked on the phone this one time,' Nayir explained again, running a hand down his neck, 'when she told me about her new job. I asked if she would be working with strange men, and I think the question upset her. She's not the sort of woman who expects that I should understand everything she does. She's a good Muslim, and there's a part of her that's traditional, too—'

'That's good.'

'Yes, but she said she worked at this job with men,' Nayir said. 'It's a new job.'

Hadi gave him a look that seemed to say: *Well, we'll have to deal with that at some point.* 'So she stopped calling you because she was upset by your reaction?'

'I think so.'

'And you didn't call her?'

'It wouldn't have been proper.'

Nayir wanted to tell him that she still wore Othman's engagement ring, that it stabbed him every time he saw it, and that he had no idea what it really meant – did she still have feelings for Othman? It would be a terrible admission, because at the very least it meant that her heart wasn't invested in a relationship with Nayir, and that he was a fool for hoping.

The imam sat back in his chair and took a breath, raising his eyes to the ceiling in a thoughtful way. 'And you believe that she's a good Muslim woman.'

'Yes.'

'Despite the phone calls.'

'Yes.'

'And despite her insistence on seeing you alone.'

She always had a driver, Nayir wanted to say, but he thought quickly of the time she'd showed up at his boat without an escort, and the time they'd eaten lunch together alone, and he bit his tongue.

Hadi sat forward again and set down his cup. 'It seems to me that you care about this woman.'

'Yes.'

'And has that always been the case?' he asked delicately.

Nayir cringed inside. *Yes*, he wanted to say. 'I would have done the right thing and asked her to marry me, but she had just broken off an engagement with another man. I felt that she wasn't ready, or maybe that she was rushing things. For herself.'

'And for you?'

Nayir shrugged nervously. He wanted to say how difficult it was to think of asking for Katya's hand in marriage when he wasn't even sure himself. He wanted to say how much he felt for her, how beautiful she seemed, how when he'd first met her she'd been very pretty, but now that he knew her better, there was a different kind of beauty about her, something both thrilling and familiar. Yet after waiting so long to marry, it would be stupid to leap into a bad decision. He wanted to be absolutely sure that it was right. He knew that the imam would tell him that he ought to have proposed to her months ago.

'Nayir,' Hadi said with a sudden rush of compassion, 'you shouldn't be afraid of rushing into a mistake. You of all people can be relied on to approach things with caution. Your mistake here will be *not* to act when you should.'

'You mean proposing marriage.'

'Yes,' Hadi said. 'It's what you should have done from the first. If this woman is important to you, then that is the only proper way. Not to let these months of silence go by.' He frowned at Nayir in a kind way. 'I don't think you want to spend your whole life alone.'

Nayir was surprised. He had felt certain that Hadi would tell him he ought to have proposed marriage, but could he recommend it now after learning what Katya was like?

'But she is not . . .' he began.

'No, she is not the Muslim you are,' Hadi interrupted, 'but you believe that she is a good Muslim. And you said that her father is devout, so you know that she is from a good family. I trust your judgement of people. And if she is pious, then she will eventually understand the impropriety of interacting with strange men. You see, many women expose themselves to strange men because they are looking for a husband. And this woman, if she is a good Muslim as you say, once she marries you, will not have that need any more. She will have you. She will begin to have children, and she will want to stay home to raise them.' Imam Hadi spread his hands. 'Everything will change once you do the right thing.'

Nayir blinked, fighting off an abrupt feeling of sadness. 'And if it doesn't?' he asked.

'Then she's not right for you.'

That's what I'm afraid of, he thought.

'Go and find out,' the imam said. 'Go and make a mistake if that's what you need to do. Because it is *haraam* for you to spend time with this woman, to yearn for her, to feel improperly towards her when she is *na-mehram* to you and you are not married.'

Nayir stayed and talked with the imam a while longer in a vain attempt, he realised, to improve his mood. But the sadness followed him back to the Rover, rooting around in his chest and swelling up now and then like the wild cry of some poor, lost animal. He couldn't figure out where the feeling came from. Something about Katya, and the image of her having children. The thought had always made him feel hopeful, but the conversation had thrown melancholy over it, and he felt, for a sad, lonely moment, that he would never be happy with her again.

25

With a treacherous sigh, Katya slid the next of Leila's DVDs into the computer's disc drive. She'd taken only a short break to help Majdi process evidence from Ra'id's car. Now she was beginning to feel that she'd been trapped in her office too long, and that if she poked her head out the high window she would see cars flying through the air, people in spacesuits, evidence that decades had passed while she'd been absorbed in one woman's obsession with prostitutes, drag queens, and public humiliations.

Not that all of it was boring. In fact, the interesting bits were becoming more frequent, and Katya could see how Leila had begun to develop her talents as an interviewer and camerawoman. In the last full interview Katya had watched, Leila had actually managed not to anger the subject, and the whole thing had ended on a note of personal triumph, with the prostitute declaring that she didn't believe she would need Allah's forgiveness because it was never a sin to make a lover smile. But the video footage had begun to give Katya the feeling that she was pursuing the wrong lead. Leila's recent behaviour had not been all that confrontational. It was looking less likely that she had provoked someone to kill her in a fit of passion. If anything, she had become more diplomatic.

But Katya kept watching the footage anyway, hoping for a find.

On the desk beside her sat the box of cassette tapes they'd found in Ra'id's car. One of the lab techs downstairs had already digitised half of them and was right now burning them on to DVDs. Katya was supposed to do the other half, but she suspected that the originals were going to be the same as the ones she'd taken from Farooha, and she didn't want to waste any more time. She was already struggling to get through the DVDs she had.

The next DVD surprised her. The screen came alive with images of Mecca and pilgrims circling the Ka'aba. At first Katya thought that she'd stumbled on more B-roll, but a title appeared on the screen: *Pilgrimage: One Man's Quest to Find the Truth about the Quran*.

Words scrolled across the screen: *Many Muslims believe that the Quran is the pure and holy word of Allah as transmitted directly to the Prophet Mohammed . . .*

A face appeared on the screen. *Sheikh Al-Arifi*, the caption said. His robe was so white and crisp that it looked as if a confectioner had iced him, applying just the right swirls around the head and hands. His skin was agonisingly soft and clear (was he wearing make-up?) and his beard was neatly trimmed with an endearing unevenness at the bottom edge, a faux carelessness. He was handsome – too handsome. He belonged on a wedding cake. As he began speaking, a mellifluous, rolling Jeddawi accent draped him in an air of professionalism. This was not a ranting madman but a strong-minded, articulate scholar.

'The Quran is pure,' he was saying. 'The book as it is printed today is the same text *exactly* that was revealed to the Prophet Mohammed, peace be upon him. The reason is that the Quran contains the true words of Allah, and they cannot be corrupted.'

He spoke as if he were having dinner with his family and was explaining something obvious to his wife: 'Yes, of course once you turn the key, the engine starts. That's how cars work, *habibti*.' Katya wanted to roll her eyes, but she was too full of contempt.

From the logo in the corner, she saw that Leila had stolen this segment from Memri TV. Of course. The station aired anything that made Islam look tawdry and ridiculous: extremists, rigidly conservative sheikhs. The last segment she'd seen on Memri had involved an imam giving a lecture on how girls in Denmark were so perverted that they regularly had sex with donkeys.

Then the picture cut to a different sort of man. He was tall and blond and deeply browned by the sun. The text on the screen identified him as *Apollo Mabus, Quranic scholar.* He wore a pair of khaki trousers and a safari jacket with bulging pockets. He was standing in the desert as if he belonged there, dust caking his neck and face, big brown eyes squinting against the over-bright sun. A strong wind kicked up clouds of sand, giving the scene a certain urgency.

Speaking less formal Arabic, and with no trace of an accent, he said, 'Most modern scholars agree that the Quran is not pure. It's not the perfect embodiment of the words of Allah, because I tell you—' here he chuckled, 'if so, then Allah is a terrible writer. The truth is, the Quran contains factual errors, grammatical errors. Fully one fourth of the book makes no sense at all. It has been rewritten and abrogated and abridged. It's so full of contradictions and mistakes that it's embarrassing to most intelligent Muslims.'

His voice betrayed that particular pitying tone that intellectuals often adopt when speaking of the irrational world around them. It was the kind of all-knowing superiority that stemmed, perversely, from an ignorance of the power of tradition and faith. And it provoked an even greater contempt in her.

A recitation came over the computer speakers while images of Quranic documents filled the screen. Katya recognised them – they were similar to the ones Majdi had been looking at in the lab. They scrolled elegantly from right to left, while faded images of minarets and city skylines lit up in blank spaces.

A voice-over began. Katya recognised Leila's voice:

Is the Quran pure? Or is it the result of editing and meddling? This question has plagued Muslim scholars for centuries, but today, the brave men and women who ask that question must fear for their lives. Even to suggest that the Quran is not pure can result in charges of apostasy, which carries a punishment of death.

Katya groaned as a film clip came on, showing the now-renowned college professor Nasser Abu Zaid being led from a hotel amidst a throng of paparazzi and flashing lights. The voice-over explained that he had been found guilty of apostasy in Cairo for publishing his opinion that the Quran is not the absolute word of Allah but rather a historical and literary text that should be interpreted like any other. The charge of apostasy resulted in Abu Zaid being forced to divorce his wife on the grounds that he was no longer a Muslim and therefore could not be married to one. It caused him and his wife to flee to the Netherlands.

There was more narration after that, but Katya wasn't listening. She was trying to untangle her reactions. Not normally offended by discussions that questioned Islam or the Quran, she was disgusted by Mr Mabus's remarks, but equally disgusted by the sheikh's pomposity and inflamed once again by the reminder of the Abu Zaid case: more proof that fundamentalists were waging their battles in the courtrooms as well as in embassy bombings and kidnappings. She had to give Leila credit for one thing: she knew how to be provocative. And maybe that was exactly what got her killed.

☽

'Well, we have prostitutes. We have public humiliation. It's not as if we need another motive exactly,' Majdi said, scratching his head.

'No, you're right.' Osama sat on the edge of the table in Majdi's lab, one hand across his chest, the other covering his mouth. He was staring at the blank computer screen, having just watched all twenty minutes of Leila's unfinished documentary, *Pilgrimage*. But he seemed withdrawn, and Katya had the sense that his thoughts were somewhere else.

'We don't need another motive,' Osama said. 'What we need is a *good* motive.'

Majdi looked over his shoulder at Osama. 'I think the prostitution angle was pretty compelling. Any one of the men involved with those prostitutes could have found out about the footage and gone after Leila. Or any one of the prostitutes, for that matter.'

'Yes,' Osama said, 'except that most of the prostitute footage was taken months ago, and I don't think her killer planned the crime. I have the feeling that whatever triggered the killer's rage happened just before her death.'

At least they had learned one thing from the documentary: a quick comparison had shown that the texts on the DVD were the same as those in the pictures Leila had hidden in her bedroom.

So Leila had photographed the texts for use in the documentary. There was still no clue about Wahhab Nabih, but Katya guessed he might be a wealthy sponsor who funded Mabus's work. The texts didn't play much of a role in the documentary itself. They were mostly used for filler. The rest of the documentary showed film clips from news sources and interviews with Mabus to focus on the tension between religious hardliners and Mabus's work.

'So Leila probably did hide the photos in her bedroom to prevent her brother from finding them,' Katya said.

'Yes,' Osama replied. 'I think he's the sort who would have noticed errors in the text and become angry about it. But on the other hand, he didn't seem to have much control over her. If he had forbidden her from working on this project, I doubt he would have enforced it.'

'What about this Mabus?' Majdi asked.

'What about him?' Osama said. 'It looks like they were working together. And judging by the quality of the cut we've just seen, she was taking this seriously and probably intending to publicise this documentary somehow.'

'Yes, it's more professional than her previous work,' Katya said. 'We have to assume that it was with Mabus's consent.'

'Then he's a real risk-taking guy,' Majdi observed. 'Personally, if I were doing the kind of research he was, I wouldn't make a fanfare about it in this country. I certainly wouldn't go on video and tell everyone all about it.'

'He must have trusted Leila,' Katya said. The men looked at her. 'You know I found blond hairs on her headscarf?'

Osama regarded her with interest. 'Yes, I'd heard. You think they could belong to Mabus?'

'Maybe,' she said. 'I think we have two blonds associated with this case: Apollo Mabus – we can see he's blond from the video – and' – she turned to Majdi – 'I hope you don't mind, but I thought I'd save you the trouble. I got a copy of Eric Walker's residency permit. It's up in my office. But I can confirm that he's blond as well.'

'By the way,' Osama said, 'I sent two men to Walker's apartment, but they couldn't track down the wife. You said she was there?'

'Yes,' Katya replied, feeling anxious at the thought of the police dragging Miriam Walker into custody. 'Maybe she was out shopping.'

'I'm sure we'll find her,' Osama said. 'But back to Mabus and Walker. Do you think the two men know each other?'

'They're both connected to Leila and to Mr Nabih,' she said. 'Eric Walker rented an apartment from Mr Nabih, and Mabus was in possession of documents that we presume belonged to Mr Nabih. I'd say the chances are good that Eric and Mabus knew each other.'

'Well, we need to find Mabus,' Osama said. 'Majdi.'

'I'm on it.' Majdi spun back to his computer.

'What do you think about all of this?' Osama asked her.

Katya hid her surprise behind a pose of reflection. 'I think

Leila was the kind of person who wanted to stir up controversy. She was going after prostitutes, but then she met Mabus and his work excited her even more. So she dropped what she'd been doing on women and started focusing on this.' She motioned to the DVD. 'All this footage of Mabus was taken in the month before she was killed. She was out in the desert with him, obviously. And from the video it looks like she was in his flat in Jeddah. She was probably spending a lot of time with him.' She paused, but Osama didn't interrupt. 'My guess,' she went on, 'is that someone else found out about what Leila was doing and became upset about it.'

'Like who?' he prompted.

'Her brother?' Katya said. 'It sounds as if he's pretty devout. But the truth is, it could have been anyone who has a strong enough feeling about the sanctity of the Quran.'

Osama kicked himself down from the table and began to pace. 'It all comes down to who would have known about the documentary. Mabus could have told someone, but let's focus on Leila.' He stopped and faced Katya. 'She probably wouldn't have told her ex-husband; she hadn't spoken to him in months. I haven't verified that yet. There's her brother, Abdulrahman. But it would have offended him and got her into trouble. We're thinking she was hiding the photos from him. That leaves her cousin, Ra'id. She would have told Ra'id, because she trusted him. He was probably one of the only people she would discuss this with, although I think he would have kept her secret.'

'Is he still in custody?' Majdi asked.

'Yes,' Osama said. 'He was possessive of her. The morning Leila disappeared, Ra'id was supposed to accompany her. He says he had no idea where she was going, because she didn't tell him, but when I suggested she was going to meet Eric Walker, Ra'id lost his temper. His own alibi is flimsy. He stole Leila's DVDs and erased her computer's hard drive to hide evidence from us.'

'You think he was jealous enough of Leila's relationship with Walker to kill her?' Katya asked.

Osama shrugged. 'I've seen this kind of thing before. It wouldn't surprise me.'

'And it would explain why this was a passion crime,' Katya added.

'But religious passions can be just as strong,' Majdi put in.

'What about her female friends?' Katya asked. 'Farooha didn't say anything about the documentary, but that may have been to protect Leila. If we come to her with the information, she might open up. I think we should go back and ask . . .'

'Yes, that's a good idea,' Osama said. 'But you don't have to go back there. Just call her.'

'I will,' Katya said, suppressing her excitement at being treated as part of the team.

'I don't think we should abandon the family entirely,' Osama said. 'Abdulrahman's alibi checks out. He was shopping at the souq, and then he had lunch with a friend. The only people who can vouch for Ra'id are the workers in the shop.'

'And the staff say he was there?' Katya asked.

'They don't remember,' Osama said. 'Some of them do, some of them don't.'

'What about in-store security cameras?' Katya asked.

'We collected them when we were there,' Majdi put in, 'but apparently the cameras had been broken for some time.'

Osama and Majdi exchanged a look that said: *That's ridiculously suspicious.*

In the hallway, one of the junior officers was motioning to Osama. He turned to the door. 'Majdi,' he said over his shoulder, 'call me the minute you find out anything about Mabus.' Without even nodding goodbye to Katya, he left the room.

26

Nayir awoke to the ringing of his mobile. He rolled out of bed and looked at the clock: 6:45. He'd slept straight through the call to prayer. Cursing at the phone, he answered it.

'Mr Sharqi?' It was the American woman's voice. He sat up.

'Yes,' he said. He had never been comfortable with phone courtesies in English.

'I'm sorry to bother you,' she said. 'I've just . . . I was wondering . . . I'm the woman you spoke with two days ago?'

'Yes, Mrs Walker, I remember you.'

'Oh, good,' she said. 'Actually, I'm calling because I have some information for you. That address I gave you for Mr Nabih? Well, it's not the right one. I checked with the neighbours and they said that he lives in Dubai now. He's been there for a long time.'

'Oh.' This would be a disappointment for Katya – a dead end. 'Thank you for telling me.'

'There's one more thing,' she said quickly. 'There is a property manager who takes care of the building. I have his address if you'd like it. I just got it from my neighbour this morning. This guy might know more about Mr Nabih.'

Nayir took down the name and address, registering the nervousness with which Miriam was giving it. He felt the impulse to warn her that the police might come back with more questions for her, but the words seemed to be tumbling together in his mind. He didn't want to upset her.

'Thank you again,' he finally said.

'Sure.'

'Mrs Walker,' he said, 'did you find your husband yet?'

There was a silence. 'No. I called the consulate again but they haven't found him either.'

'Oh, I'm sorry to hear that,' he said. 'Do you have everything you need? Food and—?'

'Actually,' she said, 'could I ask you a favour?'

'Yes,' he said automatically.

'Could I trouble you for a ride? I know it's a lot to ask, but I've got to get somewhere – here in the city actually – and the cab service has no available cars.'

All of his impulses rose up at once to say yes, of course, I'll help. But his stomach bottomed out at the very suggestion. Being alone in the car with Katya was one thing. Katya was . . . Well, what was the difference? That he cared more for Katya? That he'd known her longer? That she was a Muslim? When he'd started seeing her, she'd been engaged to another man. It occurred to him suddenly he had fallen into a trap, letting himself think it was all right to be with Katya even though they weren't married. If he let himself go with one person, then what was to stop him from letting go with another?

She was still talking. 'But if you're too far away, I'll understand . . .'

'I'd be glad to give you a ride,' he found himself saying. 'Are you at home?'

'Yes.'

'I'll be there in twenty minutes,' he said.

The drive took less time than that, just long enough for him to have a tortured series of thoughts in which he decided that he wouldn't call Katya, that he would call Katya (but later), that Miriam obviously needed his help and he was meeting with her under the pretext of helping her find her husband while secretly hoping to get more information from her, which Katya couldn't have helped with anyway, since she didn't speak English, and finally, that he had no business doing any of this because he wasn't an investigator.

Miriam was waiting for him in front of her building, and when she saw him, she waved. The minute he pulled into the kerb, she jogged up to the car, climbed into the front seat, and thanked him breathlessly for coming. He took off at once so that he didn't have to sit there looking shocked.

$$\supset$$

After giving him the address, Miriam sat back against the plush seat and tried to relax. It was awkward being in the car with this tall, silent stranger who was doing her an enormous favour. So far the only thing he had said to her was 'It's no problem,' when she'd thanked him for picking her up. God knows she was used to reserve in men, but Nayir's stony silence intimidated her, fraught as it was with implications of cultural differences so vast as to be unfathomable.

When he'd seen her standing on the kerb, his eyes had flicked quickly away from her face and landed at that mysterious point above her head that she couldn't help thinking of as her 'halo', the spot where pious men rested their eyes when they didn't want to look at a woman's face. One of the local cornershop cashiers did this to her every time she bought milk. Miriam had once complained to Sabria about it, because the gesture offended her. She thought it meant that she was ugly.

'On the contrary, dear,' Sabria had said with a smile. 'You're so beautiful that to look at your face would be a temptation for a man.'

Does anyone really believe that? Miriam wondered. Somehow she couldn't imagine Nayir having lascivious thoughts about her. His halo-gaze seemed more perfunctory than that, something he did

249

out of habit. He hadn't seemed this way the first time they'd met. He'd been nervous, yes, but his face had been open with sympathy. It was the main reason she'd dared to ask for a ride today.

Now he just looked uncomfortable.

'I didn't have the money for a cab,' she admitted. 'I've got to stop at a bank, or an ATM, if you don't mind.'

'Sure,' he said.

'And I'd be glad to pay you,' she added.

'You shouldn't even offer,' he said darkly. He seemed offended, so she left it at that.

'Are you still working with the police?' she asked.

He hesitated, then said: 'No. Don't worry about that.'

She nodded, feeling grateful. A few minutes later, he pulled up to a bank and actually got out of the car to come with her to the ATM. 'You should put your burqa down,' he said.

'I know,' she said, 'but I am, by nature, the clumsiest person you've ever met. You haven't been injured yet, so let's keep it that way.' She left him to determine the exact meaning of those words and went to the ATM. While she stood at the machine, he came and stood against the wall beside her and turned his eyes to the ground.

'Where am I taking you?' he asked.

'SynTech,' she said. 'It's where my husband works.'

He kept his gaze on the street, but she could feel his attention zero in on her in the subtle shift of his shoulders, the sudden tension in his neck. 'Is it an American company?' he asked.

'No, but one of his bosses is American. The other one is Saudi.'

'Do they know that you're coming?'

'I didn't make an appointment,' she said. 'Why?'

He looked away as she punched in her PIN code. A moment later, he said: 'Have you told them about your husband's disappearance?'

'Yes. They weren't very helpful. They didn't know anything.'

'Then why are you going there?'

She stuffed the money in her purse and retrieved her card. 'I have a feeling they know something,' she said stubbornly, heading back to the car.

Nayir waited patiently for a break in the traffic then pulled on to the highway. She watched the world speeding by, league upon league of generic blocks of flats, ugly office towers and sprawling factories. The overpass into the city gave a view of the skyline, an expanse of sleekly modern buildings, billboards and a sky that hung heavy with vehicle exhaust and industrial by-products. The smell that poured through the windows had an acrid stench that made her think of rotten rice, of things that could kill you through your bronchial tubes. A few minutes later they passed a ship graveyard and the odour intensified, greasy like a swamp. Old ships lay atop one another, splintered and decayed, the foreground coloured by the marine blue of weathered sails.

'You said your husband picked you up from the airport,' Nayir said, 'and that he disappeared right after you got home.'

'That's right.' She kept her eyes on the window.

'Don't you think it's odd . . . if he wanted to run away, why wouldn't he just leave you at the airport?'

'I don't know.' She tried to sound sufficiently uninterested in the problem, and it seemed to work because he dropped the subject at once. But she could still feel his attention warming the side of her face like a heat lamp.

As they drove, she lost all sense of direction. They coursed down long boulevards lined with palm and maple trees, where traffic flowed relentlessly like blood, seldom pausing for street signs or pedestrians but shuttling forward by an automatic impulse, as if propelled by a beating heart. They manoeuvred into side streets, cutting through capillaries to large veins beyond. Finally, on a side street that was quiet and bare, Nayir pulled into a car park in front of a plain brown office building. A shiny metal sign read *SynTech Corporation* in English and Arabic. Miriam stared at the building with interest; she had never been to Eric's office before.

'Are you going in alone?' he asked.

She looked around in a gesture meant to say: *Do you see anyone else here?* But she stopped herself midway, realising it was rude. 'Yes.'

'It might be better if you had an escort of some kind. A man.'

'Are you volunteering?' she asked. He looked perplexed. 'Are you saying that you—'

'Yes,' he said. 'I'd better come with you.'

As they got out of the car, she could feel the moral responsibility pulsing off him. It made her feel like a little girl, and she oscillated somewhere between gratitude and annoyance. As they were approaching the building, he stopped abruptly.

'I *know*,' she said, raising a hand. 'I should put on my burqa.' She sighed and spent a moment fastening it over her face. 'Just do me a favour,' she said.

'What?'

'Try to make sure I don't trip on anything.'

Looking worried, he led her into the building.

They entered through a large revolving door. Almost at once, her cloak got stuck in the turnstile and she was forced to take it off and go back round to fetch it. Inside, she checked it for rips and put it on again while Nayir stood a few feet away, eyes raised desperately to the ceiling, a blush creeping up his neck.

'Don't look at me like that,' she said. 'Not every woman gets used to these things.'

The floor was polished and smelled strongly of bleach. At the end of the lobby, a security guard sat behind a desk so high that he had to walk down three stairs to pass them a clipboard. Nayir signed his name and handed it back. Then the guard came down with a hand-held metal detector, which he passed over Nayir's body. He ignored Miriam completely. When he was finished, he said, 'Sixth floor,' and motioned vaguely to the left.

Nayir went down a corridor and Miriam followed, struggling to see through her burqa. She felt like a kid in a Halloween costume, tripping blindly along with a basket in her hands. Nayir walked six feet in front of her, and no matter how hard she tried to keep up, he managed to stay ahead. It had always seemed arrogant to her, making a wife stay behind like a duckling, another reminder of a woman's public inferiority. With grim reluctance, she could now appreciate the usefulness of having someone lead the way.

They reached a lift. There were two men waiting but, seeing Miriam, they let her and Nayir get into the next lift alone. Nayir thanked them and pushed the button.

When the door had slid shut, Miriam said wryly: 'That was nice of them.' Seeing that Nayir wasn't going to respond, she said: 'Do they really think women are that awful, that they can't be in a lift with me?'

'They did it out of respect,' he replied. He seemed pleased and a bit surprised, as if such behaviour were all too rare these days.

'It makes me feel dirty,' she said.

He kept his eyes on the glowing panel of numbers above the door. 'You're used to something different then.'

'What's that supposed to mean?' she said. 'That men don't treat women with respect in America?' He looked slightly wounded, and she hated herself for getting so angry.

'You're right,' she conceded. 'I'm used to something different.'

The door opened, but it wasn't their floor. No one stood in the hallway.

'What's your husband's name again?' he asked, pressing the button for their floor once more.

'Eric, but they call him Abdullah.' She felt foolish in her burqa, the little hem puffing forward every time she spoke. 'You know, I think I should do this myself.'

'You shouldn't,' he said bluntly, glancing at her.

This time she pulled off her burqa, nearly giving him whiplash. She knew she was pushing it, but even as she felt guilty, a part of her wanted to grab his chin and force him to look at her. 'This is about my *husband*,' she said.

The lift door finally slid shut and Nayir looked relieved.

'If they're hiding something,' he said carefully, 'they'll tell me more if I'm alone, and if they think I don't know you.'

He was right, she knew, but she also suspected that the real reason he didn't think she should be there was because she was a woman.

'What I mean to say,' he went on, 'is that they might know things that they wouldn't tell you.' His expression made it clear that he meant 'man' things.

'You think Eric was cheating on me?' she said. She gave a soft, derisive snort, but her insides felt leaden. 'Well, even if he was, why would they tell you that? Isn't it a capital crime for a man to cheat on his wife?'

He seemed to be mulling something over because he didn't reply. The lift door opened with a *bing*, and she refastened her burqa, this time to hide her entire face. 'Wherever you go,' she whispered, 'I'm coming with you.'

SynTech occupied the entire sixth floor. An enormous central office extended back to a row of panoramic windows which faced a collection of drab blocks of flats. A male secretary sat quietly behind a glass desk.

Miriam's first thought was that it didn't seem like the sort of place where bodyguards would work. She had somehow imagined that there would be more men in uniforms, a glimpse of old military fatigues, cold coffee and boxes of ammunition stacked on a shelf. The office smelled of floor polish and bleach, and the people who worked there kept it neat enough that nothing spoiled the clean lines of the modern furniture.

With a gentle nod, Nayir motioned for her to take a seat on the hard-looking sofa in a waiting area off to the right. She considered it but decided it was best not to manoeuvre around the coffee table.

Nayir approached the secretary and asked for Abdullah Walker. The man shot him a frightened look. He put up his finger and rose nervously, striding across the room to an office door on the left. He tapped on the door. There was a muffled answer and he went inside. A moment later he came out and motioned for Nayir to come forward. Miriam scurried after him despite the secretary's disapproving stare.

The office was a bright room with a thick Berber carpet and mahogany chairs. The air was cooler in here, the smell crisp and inviting. The man behind the desk looked slightly misplaced among the palatial appointments. Miriam recognised Taylor Shaw, Eric's American boss. He was a tall, burly, Paul Bunyan figure with a gigantic slab of a face, a bushy shock of blond hair, and a pair of rough-hewn hands that were always in motion. She had met him at a party on the American compound but they had been introduced only briefly. Shaw was one of those gregarious, whirlwind people who seemed capable of having three conversations at once. In his office, he was naturally more subdued, but there was still a crackling energy about him.

Shaw didn't appear to recognise her, but that did nothing for her nerves. Her hands were pale enough to telegraph to most people that she wasn't an Arab, so she tucked them into her sleeves. She lowered her head and kept her eyes on the floor in an effort to seem as devout as possible. The room was so bright, and her burqa was thin enough that, at a certain angle, Shaw might be able to see the outline of her face.

'Please have a seat,' Shaw said. Nayir and Miriam took the chairs facing the desk. Even though he was American, Shaw knew the local customs and he neither glanced at Miriam nor seemed to realise that she was there.

'I understand you're here about Eric Walker,' he said.

'Yes,' Nayir replied. 'I'm trying to find him.'

'I'm afraid we are, too,' he said. 'Eric hasn't been to work for the past month.'

It took all of Miriam's efforts not to raise her burqa and cry out: *What?*

Nayir seemed confused. 'Was he on holiday?'

'He took a leave of absence. He was supposed to have reported back to work on Thursday, but he never showed up. We've been getting phone calls from his wife. Apparently, she doesn't know where he is either.'

'Do you have any idea where he might have gone?' Nayir asked.

Shaw sat back and squinted at his guest. 'Can I ask why you're looking for him?'

'I'm part of a police investigation involving his landlord,' Nayir replied calmly. 'The only address we have on file for the landlord was Walker's. When we discovered that Walker was missing, we thought we'd better check it out. I doubt there's a connection. We're trying to be thorough.'

Shaw glanced briefly at Miriam, no doubt wondering if she was with the police as well. She marvelled at the smooth way Nayir had just made the whole thing seem innocent. Her own thoughts were racing in terrible directions.

Shaw sat forward again. 'Well, I can't tell you anything about that,' he said. 'Normally, my foreign workers live on a compound. Eric was an exception, but I don't know all the details of his living situation. Why are you investigating his landlord?'

'I'm afraid that's confidential.' Nayir's face had become the picture of authority. Shaw took the rebuff badly, gazing at Nayir with a look of amusement that managed to be condescending.

'Before he left, did Mr Walker say anything about how he would be spending his leave?' Nayir asked.

'No.'

'Is there anyone at the office who might know where he went?' Nayir continued. His whole demeanour had hardened, and a threatening aura seemed to be spreading through the room.

'Not at present,' Shaw said coolly. 'But I'll do some asking.' Miriam doubted that.

'Was there anything unusual about Walker's behaviour before he left?'

'I didn't think so at the time.' Shaw got up from his desk and went to a filing cabinet in the corner. 'But some surveillance equipment went missing – or rather, we noticed it was missing right after he went on leave. I didn't believe it had anything to do with him at the time, but now I'm not so sure.' He retrieved a file and brought it back to the desk, handing it to Nayir.

'How much equipment is missing?' Nayir asked.

'About five thousand dollars' worth – that's about twenty thousand riyals.'

'And what makes you think he might have taken it?'

Shaw shrugged, a massive gesture that lifted his jacket a good four inches. 'He was one of the only people with access to the equipment room, and the stuff disappeared right around the time he did. I never thought of Walker as the dishonest type, but greed is sometimes hard to spot.' He sat down and Miriam's heart fell with him. The word struck an awful chord: *greed*. It was one of the things she'd accused Eric of when they fought – that he'd only wanted to come here for the money, that he'd put money above their marriage. But back then she was just looking for a place to punch.

Miriam realised that she was frozen in her chair and that her fingers were gripping her wrists so tightly that it hurt. She wanted to leave the room now, but she had no way of reaching Nayir. He was on another island. The only thing she could do was kick his foot where Shaw wouldn't see. Inch by inch, she slid her foot across the

257

floor, but as she moved closer, Nayir pulled his own foot away and set the folder back on the desk.

'Would you like to report this theft to the police?' Nayir asked calmly.

Shaw considered a moment and shook his head. 'When Walker turns up, I'll talk to him. Right now I don't have any hard evidence. Anyway, I thought you were just looking for the landlord?'

Nayir regarded him. 'One more question, Mr Shaw. Do you know a woman named Leila Nawar?'

Shaw looked genuinely perplexed. 'No,' he said slowly. 'I've never heard the name. Why?'

Nayir stood, and Miriam rose with him. Shaw got to his feet. 'I've already talked to our employees about Walker,' he said, 'but I'll bring it up again, see if anyone knows where he might have gone. If you want to leave your number, I'll call if I have anything.'

As she made her way out of the office, Miriam had trouble keeping Nayir in her sights. She couldn't focus. Why hadn't Eric told her he'd taken so much time off? What had he been doing all month? Had he stolen the equipment? The document she'd found in his briefcase flashed into her mind – it was in her bag right now. She couldn't bear to think about it. Abruptly, she remembered Mabus on the plane. His words echoed back in a portentous rhythm. *Just as soon as you're ready to go home, you'll find that your husband has fallen in love with the place* . . . Now that she knew that Mabus had known Eric, those words filled her with dread.

27

Osama stood at the interrogation room window reflecting on the mysterious Leila Nawar. A woman who wore a burqa and showed her picture via Bluetooth. A woman who was courageous enough to film strangers in public. Katya's words rang true: Leila was chasing controversy.

In every investigation, he wondered randomly: 'Where would the victim be right now, if she were alive?' He closed his eyes and saw Leila in motion, not sitting quietly in the back seat of a car or on a balcony overlooking a city street. She was on a pavement, hurrying along, talking on her mobile, hitching a rucksack up her shoulder, laughing loudly. One of those female pedestrians for whom a cloak and burqa were useless accoutrements, because her presence dominated the energy on the street.

Her ex-husband was a different matter. Bashir Tabbakh sat on the other side of the interrogation room window, sipping a cup of tea and staring at the wall. He had been there for an hour, unruffled, looking slightly bored but resigned.

Bashir had turned himself in after his brother, Hakim, had managed to contact him by phone and convey the details of his imprisonment. In a touching display of brotherly affection, Bashir had come into the station before the noon prayer and apologised to his brother for the inconvenience. Osama suspected that his offer of assisting with Bashir's expired work visa had provided the proper bait.

When Osama entered the room, Bashir turned in his direction and nodded.

'Thank you for coming in, Mr Tabbakh,' Osama said, taking a seat across the table.

'Of course,' Bashir said. 'I'm sorry to hear about this. Her family must be shattered.'

Osama opened a folder, mentally noting Bashir's calm.

'Am I under suspicion?' Bashir asked.

'I just need to ask you some questions,' Osama replied. 'We want to know a little more about Leila.'

The sound of her name made Bashir stiffen for an instant. 'I don't know how much I can tell you.'

Osama took his time setting up the tape recorder and going through the protocol. Bashir watched with growing unease.

'When was the last time you saw her?' Osama asked.

'I can't remember the date exactly. She came to the shop a few weeks ago. We talked, and she left.' Osama heard the first hint of disgruntlement in the man's tone.

'You mean the shop beneath your brother's apartment?'

'Yes.'

'Did she often go there?' Osama asked.

'No. Only when she needed money.'

'Was that a frequent occurrence?'

'It felt like it, but no.'

Osama nodded, thinking. 'You were divorced by then.'

Bashir let out a soft laugh. 'Sure. When we were married, she didn't have to come begging for money. I had to hand it over.'

Osama heard the opening strains of a familiar symphony – the complaint that women always wanted money. Women were lazy. They were greedy. They nagged and nagged their husbands for money and then they spent it foolishly. So many men expected their wives to stay home, and then complained about having to support them. Was there a bigger cliché?

'Did you give her any money?'

'No.' Bashir looked disgusted. Osama could almost hear the symphony swelling. 'Her family was rich,' Bashir said. 'Her brother could have bought me as a slave, and she was coming to me for pocket change? Who does that? What kind of woman do you have to be?' His face was reddening now, but his voice was in control.

'Did the two of you have a divorce settlement?'

Bashir took a deep breath. 'Yes, well, according to the marriage contract, I was supposed to pay her something like a million riyals.' He barked out a laugh. 'But listen, we *both* wanted that divorce. She agreed to forgo any of the money. A few weeks after the divorce, she started coming to the shop to beg for cash. She tried to make me feel guilty; she even threatened to take me back to court.'

Osama nodded. 'Did that worry you?'

'No.' Bashir almost laughed. 'She could have taken me to court, but I still wouldn't have had anything to give her.' He looked tough, his arms crossed over his chest, a scowl distorting his thin face, but beneath it was all the insecurity of the penniless immigrant.

'You weren't married long – what, two and a half months?' Osama asked.

Bashir shrugged. 'About that.'

'How did you marry in the first place?'

'Her mother set it up. My mother and Leila's had known each other since childhood. They were very good friends. They both lived in Damascus, although her mother is dead now. But before she died, she wanted one thing: to see Leila married, safe and happy. Leila was her only daughter.' Bashir had spread his arms. One was resting comfortably on the table, the other on his knee. The openness of the gesture was unusual for an interrogation subject. Osama couldn't help thinking that Bashir really was as comfortable sitting here as he might have been in his own living room, talking with friends. Either Bashir was a very fine actor, or he had nothing to hide.

'This is strange to say now,' Bashir went on, 'but I think we got married to please her mother. She was dying of cancer and we just wanted her to be happy. We divorced a week after she died.'

'So it was a marriage of convenience.'

'Yes.'

'Did you get along with Leila?'

He shook his head, looking melancholic. 'Not really.'

'Personality differences?'

Bashir snorted gently. 'You could say that. She was always on a mission. She was going to save somebody. She was going to be a famous filmmaker. She was going to impress someone. It didn't matter what she set out to do, she always did it with the same attitude, like she thought she was the last hero in the world.' He pursed his lips, choosing his next words with care. 'It's admirable in a person, but it's a hard thing to live with. Let's just say the relationship was never about us, because with Leila, everything was always about Leila. You see, she was doing everything for a higher purpose. How can you argue with that?'

'Let me guess, she didn't do any housework,' Osama said, nodding conspiratorially.

'Of course not!'

'I think I know this type of woman,' Osama said. 'Liberated. Working on some scheme to start her own business, but it never comes to anything. Meanwhile, they need money all the time, and suddenly there's no time for housework, or cooking, or raising kids. And if you try to confront them, they have some pious thing to say that makes you feel guilty. And you wake up one morning and realise that you married a child.'

Bashir let out a dry, heartless laugh. 'That's exactly what it was like. I mean, was it too much to ask that she do the laundry once in a while?'

'She never did laundry?'

'Not once,' Bashir said.

At this point, Osama had clearly won Bashir's sympathy. It hadn't taken very much. Osama feigned a look of dismay. 'At least mine does the laundry every once in a while.'

'She never did a damn thing,' Bashir said. 'Except spend my money. And after the first few nights, she stopped everything, if you know what I mean. She said she just didn't feel like it.'

'You think she ever went out with another man?'

'Nah.' Bashir's lips wrinkled in a scowl and he sat forward. 'Here's the thing – she was so self-absorbed that men only served one purpose for her.'

'Money,' Osama supplied.

'Yes.'

Osama knew he ought to be pleased with himself for the little coup he'd just pulled off. It had always been one of Rafiq's favourite manoeuvres, sympathising with the beleaguered husband on the subject of selfish wives. But instead the whole thing left him feeling uneasy. Bashir and Leila had been a terrible match. Leila wanted an independence that Bashir was clearly not able to give her. Sure, he wasn't the sort who would mind if she worked outside the home. In fact, he would probably have appreciated the second income. But everything he had just revealed about Leila now had to be seen in the light of their incompatibility. Leila must have been disappointed to have married such a poor man when her own family was better off. She would have expected more generosity. She wouldn't have been truthful with him – about herself or her feelings, or perhaps even her real plans.

Osama bent over the folder he'd brought in – a prop, nothing more – and pretended to look for something to deflect an image that had just sprung at him: Nuha raising her burqa on their first night together, the way his whole body had jolted with excitement. She had remained unperturbed. She had even given him a playful smile. She didn't normally wear a burqa, and she hadn't during most of the wedding, or even before. She was one of those determined women who insisted that one didn't need to wear a burqa in Jeddah; it was an open city, it was not Riyadh. Headscarf, yes; but a burqa? Ridiculous. Only she was wearing it in the bedroom that night, their first night, and when she lifted it, he had been overcome. It was the feeling that she had just opened herself to him completely, which was crazy because by then he knew her. He already loved her. Theirs hadn't been a traditional courtship, no parents involved. They had met through friends and chosen each other. They had gone on dates, got to know one another, made the decision themselves. And there she was in a burqa. It was such a simple gesture, like taking off a shoe. She could have stripped off her dress and stockings first, and it wouldn't have come close to having that kind of effect. *Now I'll show you my true self*, it said. *And I want to give it all to you.*

He closed the folder and looked up at Bashir. 'It's never what you think it is, is it?'

Bashir shook his head grimly.

At this point, Osama was supposed to go in for the kill. *Didn't you ever just want to put her in her place? Show her who was the boss?* Looking across at Bashir, he saw a downtrodden soul. Then he remembered what they'd learned from Farooha; she had painted a very different picture of Bashir.

'Leila had typhus during your marriage,' Osama said.

Bashir nodded, for the first time looking anxious.

'How did you handle that?'

'Not very well,' he said, his discomfort growing with every second. 'I didn't realise how sick she was until her brother showed up and started threatening to kill me.' Bashir sighed and shut his eyes. 'Look, I was working three jobs and barely paying the bills. Leila was spending all of my money on stupid stuff. I just thought she had the flu . . .' He went quiet. Osama could see that he was torturing himself with the memory. 'I may not have been the best husband, but it turned out her brother wasn't any better.'

'What do you mean?'

'It's ironic that she went to him for protection when he was the one who beat the shit out of her.'

Osama tried to hide his surprise. 'When was this?'

'No one told you, did they? That's because Leila never told anyone. It only happened once. I forget what she did – something about going out when she wasn't supposed to. But in general they were always fighting.'

'How often did he hit her?'

'Only the once, as far as I know, but it was bad. She wound up in the hospital with a broken leg. See, Abdulrahman is the kind of guy who's trying really hard to pretend that he's a Saudi. He keeps his wife locked up in that prison of a house and he would have kept Leila locked up, too, but she wasn't afraid of him. I'm pretty sure she went out one day when he told her not to, and he went crazy when he found out. I know – she had lost her camera that day, that's what happened. Someone had attacked her at the beach.'

'Her brother said that that's how she broke her leg.'

'That's not what she said.'

'But if she wasn't afraid of him, why didn't she report it to the police?' Osama asked.

'Because she knew he could make her life miserable. He could send her back to Syria, have her visa revoked. She didn't want to go back there.'

'Do you think she married you to be free from him? Because of the visa?'

'Not really,' Bashir said, 'because he could have had *my* visa revoked at any time. He was my sponsor, too.'

Osama let this information sink in. Leila had married a man who was dependent on her brother. It was not strange that

Abdulrahman should have sponsored Bashir – their parents had been friends for so long that they were practically family – but it made Osama realise just how dependent on her brother Leila had been.

'Is he the reason you're having visa problems now?' Osama asked.

'Yeah. After the divorce, Abdulrahman refused to keep sponsoring me,' Bashir said. 'I don't know what Leila told him about me, but I have the feeling she blamed me for everything, and he was still angry at me because of the typhus. He cut me off. I moved in with my brother, and I've been looking for a sponsor ever since.'

Osama nodded. He had to confirm that Abdulrahman had indeed attacked Leila, but he had the feeling that despite Bashir's obvious bias against his brother-in-law, the man was telling the truth. 'All right,' he said, opening his notebook. 'For the record, I'm going to need to know where you were on the day Leila disappeared.'

28

Osama remembered shopping for Nuha's trousseau. His mother had taken him to a lingerie boutique and they'd spent three hours in the place. They'd come away with six bags of underwear. If he'd gone home right now and opened Nuha's dresser drawer, he wouldn't have been able to tell which of the garments he had bought her. The only thing he remembered about that day was the conversation with his mother. She had explained to him how important lingerie was; how women spent so much time hiding their beauty, that for most of them, marriage felt like their chance to finally show what they'd been hiding. Of course, they would come to the marriage with their own truckloads of clothing, but it was important to set the tone, his mother said. Let his fiancée know what sorts of styles he liked in the bedroom. And yet they'd spent the entire three hours befuddled by choices. What would Nuha prefer? Blue or red? Leather or satin? What kind of woman was she? He hadn't been entirely sure, but he had made decisions anyway. And later, Nuha had been so pleased that she cried. Then she threw a party for her friends to come over and look at all the goods. For a long time he had secretly congratulated himself on tailoring the trousseau so closely to her tastes. Now it crossed his mind that she didn't wear much of anything to bed, and the lingerie occupied its own dresser in a forgotten corner of the bedroom.

He was driving back to Abdulrahman's shop. Katya sat in the passenger seat, no doubt wondering why he'd asked her to come along when he was obviously in such an ill-tempered state. But to her credit, she kept quiet and didn't gaze out the window like some poor banished child. He couldn't have handled the guilt.

They pulled into the car park in front of the shop. Katya made to leave the vehicle but he told her to wait – the first words he'd said to her since they'd got in the car. So she nodded and sat back against the seat.

'By the way,' he said, 'do you have a copy of the medical report for Leila's broken leg?'

'No.' Katya looked slightly embarrassed. 'I never went looking for it. Adara said that Leila's fractured tibia hadn't properly healed, so she'd probably never made it to a decent doctor.'

Osama nodded.

'Why are you asking?' Katya asked.

'I think it may have been her brother who attacked her when he found out she'd gone out that day and lost her camera. Her ex-husband, Bashir, said that she had told him that.'

They waited until the call to *'asr* prayer rang out over the street before going in. When Osama pushed open the front door, one of the sales assistants saw him and came rushing out from behind the cash desk. He went to the front doors in an effort to look as if he were actually going to lock the doors for prayer time. Osama watched the man draw down a metal grate and flip over a sign in the window that said: *Closed for prayers, Allah akbar.* The man looked around nervously, uncertain what to do next. There were shoppers still lingering among the racks. He looked as if he would have liked to stay and continue his surveillance of the possible shoplifters in his midst; instead, he headed to the back of the shop, no doubt to perform his ablutions for Osama's benefit. Osama said nothing and also made his way to the back of the shop, Katya trailing quietly behind him.

When they reached the back room, he realised that Katya hadn't lowered her burqa, and that she was looking around with a confidence that could rival Faiza's. But just the thought of Faiza sent him into a black mood and he pushed through the swinging double doors.

The back room was quiet. It looked as if Abdulrahman gave his workers prayer breaks. One of the side doors was open and a faint line of cigarette smoke drifted into the room. In the office, Fuad was sitting at the computer, typing. Seeing Osama, he nodded nervously and rose to greet him, but when his eyes fell on Katya, he scowled.

'Detective,' he said, inclining his head slightly and glancing out at the studio floor. He ignored Katya completely. 'Please come in. Would you like some tea?'

'No, thank you.'

'What can I do for you?' Fuad asked.

'We were hoping to catch Mr Nawar,' Osama said. 'Did I interrupt—' Just then, a door against the wall opened and Abdulrahman stepped out from what looked like a bathroom. He was wiping his hands on a towel. The fresh-washed look on his face and forearms suggested that he'd just performed ablutions.

With surprising speed, Fuad stepped in front of Katya, blocking her from Abdulrahman's view. He said loudly: 'The detective and his assistant are here to see you again.'

Two thoughts hit Osama at once. First, that Fuad didn't realise that Katya was a different woman. And second, that his seeming hostility to her had not been authentic, rather her presence had made him nervous for a very particular reason: because he knew that his boss was preparing for prayers and would probably be offended, or made 'impure', by the sight of a woman. Osama watched with curiosity. Just how religious was Abdulrahman? Would the glimpse of Katya's cloak be enough to send him back to perform his ablutions again?

Abdulrahman faltered. His eyes flickered quickly from Katya's cloak to Fuad's face with a look of reproach, as if it were the assistant's fault for letting a woman into the studio. Then he turned to Osama.

'Yes, detective?' he asked curtly. 'Is there a problem?'

'We'd like to ask some more questions,' Osama said, matching his cold tone.

'Then I trust it can wait until after prayer time?'

Osama didn't like this man and would have had no trouble interrupting his schedule, but Abdulrahman was also the sort who would do what he liked, whether it was convenient for anyone else or not.

In the end, Katya decided the situation. She stepped out from behind Fuad and gazed at Abdulrahman square in the face. The man looked back, and for a moment seemed prepared to say something sharp, but instead he dropped his towel on a cutting table and ushered them stiffly into the office.

☽

Katya sat on a desk chair to the left of Osama, just behind him, where she could keep an eye on both of their subjects. She'd had to pull up the chair herself because apparently the assistant, Fuad, expected her to stand. He'd motioned Osama into a seat and then cast a dirty look in her direction, a look that said *Why don't you get out of here, since you're useless anyway?* She'd ignored him. Osama was too focused on Abdulrahman to pay attention, so she sat quietly, still reeling from the suggestion that Abdulrahman had attacked his sister. With all of the hostility radiating off him now, he seemed capable of violence.

She wondered why Osama had even brought her along. He probably knew that bringing a woman would make the men uncomfortable. She dismissed her anger. This was an opportunity she'd said she wanted.

Abdulrahman sat on the sofa opposite them. She stared blatantly at him. As long as he thought she was an officer, she would gladly play the part. Really she was looking for a resemblance to Leila. She saw only the faintest similarity in the cast of their chins. Abdulrahman's face was fleshier, older, and there was none of the quickness of expression she imagined Leila had had. Katya had always believed it was ridiculous for men in arranged marriages to predict the personalities and behaviours of their future wives by studying the girls' brothers, but here she was scrutinising Abdulrahman in search of a clue to what Leila might have been like.

He was passionate in his own way. His air of intense discomfort was affecting everyone, most notably Fuad. The assistant couldn't sit down, he stood by the door as if awaiting instructions, burning off his nervous energy by checking his mobile, monitoring the men on the studio floor, all the while keeping a sharp eye on his boss's mood.

Osama was talking. 'Did Leila tell you that she was working on a documentary about the Quran?'

Instantly, Fuad stiffened. Abdulrahman glared at Osama and shook his head. 'I suspect my sister did a lot of things without telling me.'

'Perhaps she was afraid of your reaction?'

'That would depend on what she was doing.'

'The religious art collection your sister was photographing was actually part of a larger project she was working on. She was interviewing a Western researcher for a documentary that claimed that the Quran is not the true and complete word of Allah, rather that it was altered by the early Muslims.'

Abdulrahman's nostrils flared.

'The documentary is incomplete, but it is enough to give us a sense of what she was doing. Obviously, her work was inflammatory, and if the wrong person were to have found out about it—'

'Are you accusing me of something?'

'Did you do something, Mr Nawar?'

The silence went on for so long that it began to feel threatening. Fuad was looking at his boss, but Abdulrahman was avoiding his gaze.

Finally Fuad said: 'Leila was always looking for a controversial subject.' Katya and Osama both turned to Fuad. 'It didn't mean that she believed it.'

Osama turned back to the brother. 'I think her cousin Ra'id would disagree.'

'Ra'id doesn't know anything,' Abdulrahman growled.

'So you knew about the documentary?' Katya asked.

Osama gave a slight twitch, perhaps surprised that she'd finally spoken. Abdulrahman refused to look at Katya, he kept his gaze on Osama. 'I said I know nothing.'

'Then perhaps Ra'id knows more than you think he does,' Katya suggested.

Abdulrahman gave a murderous look but still wouldn't look at her.

'Apparently,' Osama said, 'you were fighting with Leila quite a bit before she disappeared.'

'We weren't fighting.'

'According to our sources, Leila sought refuge with friends, and she was' – Osama consulted his notes – '"shaken" from these fights.'

'That had nothing to do with why she disappeared,' Abdulrahman said through clenched teeth.

'We also have info that suggests that you were responsible for fracturing her leg.'

Abdulrahman jerked with fury, nearly throwing the sofa against the wall behind him. 'That's ridiculous!' Fuad rushed over but hesitated, not certain what to do. 'Who told you that?' Abdulrahman boomed.

'Did you hit her that day she came back from the Corniche without her video camera?'

272

'That is *ridiculous*.' The rage on Abdulrahman's face made Katya's heart begin to race.

Osama had slipped into an icy calm. 'Did you hit her that day?' he asked coldly.

'I have never laid a hand on my sister!' he spat beneath his breath. '*Never*. Do you understand that?'

'Did her ex-husband tell you that?' Fuad put in calmly. The men looked over at him.

Abdulrahman was turning red. 'That fucking *bastard*,' he said.

'It's not Bashir,' Fuad said. 'It's just that Leila would have needed to tell him that. I presume she was at his shop asking for money. She would have wanted to win his sympathy, and she knew how much he hated you.'

Abdulrahman's expression slowly revealed a grudging acknowledgement and finally settled into something like gratitude. It was obvious why he kept Fuad around. Even Katya had to admit that it was clever of him to have concluded that about Leila. However, Osama did not seem so swayed.

'Did Leila go to a doctor that day for her fractured leg?'

'Yes, she did.'

'Do you have a copy of the medical report?'

Abdulrahman glanced at Fuad. 'No,' the assistant said, 'but I can give you the name of the doctor.' While he went to the computer to get the information, Osama turned back to Abdulrahman.

'You were fighting with your sister frequently,' he pushed on.

'We had some discussions.'

'More than one?'

Abdulrahman grunted in consent.

'What were the fights about, Mr Nawar?'

He seemed to be trying to remember to breathe. 'I didn't like her going out by herself. One time I found out that she'd been out alone all day. Ra'id was supposed to have been with her, but she

273

came home without him. And I already told you she was attacked. I didn't like her being out. It wasn't safe.'

'And Leila disagreed?'

'I told her that as long as she lived in my house, she would obey my rules. If she wanted to have a different lifestyle, then she was going to have to find her own way.'

'You were kicking her out?'

'Of course not.' Abdulrahman looked offended. 'I was telling her the rules.'

'It doesn't seem like she obeyed those rules,' Osama said. 'In fact, not only did she interview this Western researcher, she went out to the desert with him, quite possibly alone. We also know that she spent time in the company of a married man, an American. Her cousin has already confirmed that he wasn't around for *those* meetings.' Abdulrahman's face was turning a dangerous red. 'Did Leila tell you any of these things?'

'If you're going to keep accusing me of hurting my sister—' Abdulrahman never managed to finish the threat because Fuad intervened.

'Of course she didn't tell him what she was doing,' he said. 'She was acting like a child, and she expected Abdulrahman to be her father.'

Osama kept his eyes on Abdulrahman. 'So she didn't tell you any of this?'

Abdulrahman shook his head.

'What happened during your fights, Mr Nawar?'

'They were arguments, not fights. And nothing happened. I told her the rules, she agreed to keep them.'

'And then she broke them,' Osama said. 'And you must have found out about it or else why did you keep fighting? Because as you said yourself, it wasn't just one argument. There were many.'

'As I said before, I caught her coming home one afternoon without Ra'id.'

'Only once?' Osama asked. 'What about the other times?'

Abdulrahman gripped his knees. Katya could see that Osama was wearing down the last of the brother's patience, and she sat in rigid suspense, waiting for him to explode.

'I don't see what any of this has to do with her death,' Abdulrahman said.

'Answer the question, Mr Nawar. What did you learn about Leila that made you angry enough to confront her again? Did you find out about her meetings with the American man? Or about her trip to the desert with the researcher?' Abdulrahman's fists were white. 'Did you know about her documentary?'

A tense silence filled the room. Abdulrahman was clearly making an effort to control his temper. After an interminable pause, he said: 'No, I didn't know what she was doing. I didn't know about the American or the researcher. I had no idea. My sister was lying to me.' There was a terrible fury in his expression. 'Is there anything else you want from me?'

Osama was momentarily silenced. Fuad came over and handed them a business card with the name of Leila's doctor on it.

'Mr Nawar,' Katya said. 'You have an in-store security system, yes?'

Fuad's eyebrows went up a fraction of a centimetre. 'And *this* is related to Leila?'

The man's brisk, businesslike snootiness had already got on Katya's nerves, but now it struck her as arrogant. At the very least, when a homicide detective asked you a question, you answered yes or no before launching your own interrogation.

'Just answer the question,' she said.

'Our cameras are broken,' he said curtly.

'That's convenient,' Katya said. 'Considering it's the only way we can confirm Ra'id's alibi. Did you only have one camera?'

'We have *dozens* of cameras,' Fuad put in, 'but they're all linked to a network. It was the network that was broken. Something to do with a computer virus.'

'Are they working now?' Katya asked.

'No,' Fuad said. 'The company we hired to fix them is not reliable, so we wound up having to find someone else. It looks like we're going to have to replace the whole system.'

Katya turned back to Abdulrahman. 'It does look odd that your security system broke just before your sister disappeared.'

'I am sick of this.' Abdulrahman stood up as he said it, and suddenly all of the tension that had been building inside him came breaking out. He turned on Osama, towering over him, and pointed a finger in his face. Katya knew that the finger was actually meant for her. 'You think she was kidnapped here? You think we did this?' he said, spitting every word. 'I told you I have no idea what happened to her. Didn't you listen to me? I was the one who reported her missing. I kept calling the police for updates, and you stupid fucking people didn't even know who I was talking about.' Osama was leaning back in his chair now; Fuad was clutching his mobile, looking mortified. 'The fact that you're even here nosing around – all these stupid questions – tells me that you don't have a fucking clue who killed my sister. You're desperate? You need answers? Get the fuck out of my shop and go find your answers, because you're not going to find them here!'

He spun away from Osama and stormed out of the room. Fuad hesitated, looking as if he might apologise, then ran after his boss. Osama stood and motioned Katya out. She realised that her hands were shaking.

It wasn't until they were in the car that Osama spoke.

'He was right. We're fumbling around. But that was excellent work. You were very good.'

Katya nodded, not sure what to say. Abdulrahman's bullying had been a shock.

'Do you think he was telling the truth about not hurting her?' she asked.

Osama shrugged.

It took forever to get back to the station; traffic was sluggish, and they passed two accidents to which, thankfully, other police officers had already responded. Katya didn't think she could stand getting out of the car in the heat.

Once they'd parked the car and gone into the building, Osama went to his office. Katya realised she was hungry. She hadn't eaten breakfast. She hadn't packed a lunch either, so getting food meant heading back out into the heat. She was too tired, so she stood in the front lobby staring out at the street.

Osama found her there. 'Still no sign of Mrs Walker,' he said. 'We've got two guys posted outside her apartment. She's not at the house. She must have left early this morning and she hasn't come back yet.'

'Did you—'

'We checked with the neighbours,' he said quickly. 'No luck.'

It occurred to her belatedly that he was telling her this for a reason.

'Majdi pulled her recent mobile activity just now,' he went on. 'She called a number this morning before she left. It's not a cab company. It's an Arab name. The number is listed to a Nayir Sharqi.'

Katya wished she had her burqa down, because her face reacted before she could stop it. Osama eyed her narrowly. 'I thought there was a chance this was the same guy who came in . . .'

'Yes,' she said abruptly. 'I know him.'

Osama looked as if he might say something harsh, but he waited.

'I'll contact him right now,' she said, 'and see if he knows anything.'

Osama handed her a card. 'My number,' he explained. 'Call me when you find out.' She took the card with embarrassment and quickly went up to her lab.

29

The family section booth at Al-Baik was encased in opaque plastic so that curious fellow diners couldn't peer in. Nayir sat there with Miriam, trying not to watch her eat. She had looked so pale coming out of the SynTech building that he had felt obliged to stop to pick up some food, but in a manner he was beginning to recognise as typical of her, she insisted on coming into the restaurant herself. Once inside, she insisted on sitting at a booth, arguing that it would be preferable to spill her mustard sauce on the restaurant floor instead of the interior of his obviously brand new car. He would have liked to say that he didn't mind spills in the car, and that it was far more improper to have to sit facing her across a table while she had her burqa raised. But the truth was that he didn't want the mess in his car, and in either case she would have to raise her burqa to eat, and it was better that she did it in the privacy of a booth.

Once he'd sat down with her, he was surprised to discover that the whole situation hadn't made him too nervous to eat. Six months before he wouldn't have been able to do this; he would have stopped at a kiosk and bought her a schawarma and made her eat in the car. Yet Miriam's exposed face staring back at his made him realise that he was changing. He tried telling himself that this was only because she was a married woman, because she was American and not accustomed to the way things were done. There

278

was certainly something in her manner that made it easy to treat her like a man.

'It didn't used to be like this,' Miriam said, making an effort to sound blithe. She opened her carton of food and dug into her chicken. 'I mean, between me and Eric. He used to tell me everything. We were really partners. But ever since we came here . . .' She twirled a chicken wing in the air as if the last part of her sentence should explain itself. 'This is really good,' she added, referring to the chicken.

Nayir couldn't help asking. 'What happened when you came here?'

'Well . . .' She hesitated, eyeing him as if determining how much to tell. 'He fell in love with this place. And that's great, it's just that he really started becoming an Arab guy. He spends all his time running around with his friends. Going out to the desert, sailing, scuba diving, smoking hookah in the sitting room. I mean, even our *house* is segregated. It's not that he's given up being an American completely, it's just that when he brings me along, it's always weird. He mostly hangs out with Arab guys.' She took another bite of chicken. 'Don't get me wrong,' she said through a mouthful of food, 'in America, he had his guy time, too, but we did things together. You know, we used to go hiking. Or to the movies. Or to have dinner with friends. We don't do any of that here.'

'Why not?'

She looked as if he'd just made her chicken come back to life. 'Um, maybe because whenever we visit the neighbours, I go to one room and he goes to another? Don't you know that for most of the world, making your wife sit in a separate room is a little strange?'

'You could still go hiking together,' he said rather lamely.

'What about you?' she asked. 'You married?'

His appetite fled. 'No.'

'Oh.' She seemed surprised. 'But you have a girlfriend?'

He couldn't believe how bold she was being, but he supposed he deserved it, having already learned so much about her. 'No,' he said again.

'Oh, come on,' she said, 'that woman at the house? I could tell that you liked her.'

Nayir felt himself blushing uncontrollably.

'What was her name?' Miriam asked.

'Katya.'

A small grin played at the corners of her mouth. 'Well, Katya is very beautiful. And sweet, the way she took my hand . . .'

He was nervously wiping grease from his fingers with a half-shredded napkin.

'So I thought there wasn't really any *dating* in this country,' she said.

He looked at her then. 'It's improper, yes. But some people do it.'

'Just not you.'

'It's improper.' He was beginning to feel foolish. How could he explain?

'So when *can* you see her?' she asked.

'We work together, sometimes.'

'But you said you weren't with the police.'

'She asks for my help sometimes.'

'And that's it? Just when you drive her around . . .' Miriam's mouth hung open, showing a partially chewed piece of chicken. She swallowed. 'So that visit to my place was like a date for you guys?' He saw it all with clarity then, how it must have seemed to Miriam that his life was freakishly restrictive, backwards, even pathetic.

'Is *she* married?' Miriam asked.

'No, of course not.'

She nodded as if concluding something to herself.

'What?' he asked.

'Oh, nothing.' He frowned, and she said: 'Oh, all right. It's just that it's a shame you can't at least go out for dinner once in a while. Like this!' She spread her arms at the food. 'At least have lunch together or something.'

'We've had lunch,' he replied defensively.

'What – once?'

He didn't reply.

'I mean, you're having lunch with me now, and I'm practically a stranger.' Something about this seemed to bring her mind back to Eric. 'Well, I shouldn't be surprised. You never see Katya, and I never see Eric. There is something very wrong with this place.'

Nayir began to eat his own chicken so he wouldn't have to answer.

'You think he got sick of me or something.' She stopped chewing and swallowed hard.

'No,' he said.

'Look,' she went on, 'ever since we came here, he's been drifting away. I don't know why exactly. I've blamed myself, too. But I don't think I'm the reason.' She said this with defiance and a hint of desperation. 'In fact, I'm pretty certain that something else was going on.'

'What?'

She took a breath, wiped her hands on a napkin. 'Last night,' she said, 'I got nervous being in the house all alone, so I spent the night with my neighbour. When I went back to my apartment this morning, there was an odd smell in the house. It was a man's smell, like aftershave and soap and . . . it really freaked me out.'

'Was it your husband?' Nayir asked.

'No, it wasn't his smell. But someone had been there. That's why I left the house so early this morning. And actually,' she added, pressing her lips together, 'that's kind of why I called you. I mean, the cab company *was* busy, and that whole thing about the landlord's address being wrong – I wanted you to know that. But

281

when we were talking on the phone, I was so desperate to get out of the neighbourhood. I kept thinking, what if whoever broke into my house was still lurking around somewhere?'

Nayir's brow hurt and he realised he was frowning deeply. 'Was anything missing from your flat?'

'I didn't stay to check, but I had my purse with me, and nothing else is really worth taking.' She looked at her food and tentatively reached for another piece of chicken. 'You don't think it could have been the police in my apartment?'

Nayir shook his head. 'They probably would have checked with the neighbours if they were looking for you.'

'There's one more thing,' she said, setting down her chicken and reaching into her bag. Her hand stopped midway and she looked at him.

'Yes?' he asked.

She drew out a folded sheet of paper. 'I have to know that I can trust you.'

He nodded, not sure what to say.

'Just promise me that whatever this is,' she motioned to the piece of paper, 'you won't tell anyone unless I say it's okay?'

'What is it?' he asked.

'I don't know. It might be nothing. But please, just promise me.'

He could see that she was scared of something. 'All right,' he said. 'I promise.'

She slid the paper tentatively across the table. 'I can't read it. Could you just tell me what it says?'

He wiped his hands and opened it, reading over it briefly. It was a *misyar*, a temporary marriage licence that men and women sometimes used when they didn't want to commit to a full marriage. The groom's name was Eric Walker.

'Where did you find this?' he asked, hearing the tension in his voice.

'In Eric's briefcase. At the house. Why? What is it?'

Nayir looked down at the document. He hated to do this, given everything that Miriam had learned about her husband already, but he forced himself to say: 'It's a fake marriage document. Technically, it's legal. It's been signed by an imam. But it says here that your husband was married to a woman named Leila Nawar.'

Miriam's face had gone a frightening shade of grey. She was staring at him blankly.

'I'm sorry,' he said. 'But this woman—'

'Is the dead girl,' Miriam cut in.

'Yes.' He folded the document, made to hand it back to her then changed his mind. He wanted to tell her to shred the document, but he knew how damaging that would be to the investigation. 'This really isn't something you should—'

'He didn't do it,' she said mechanically, still frozen and unblinking.

Nayir felt certain that this was a new shade of denial, and that perhaps everything she had said about Eric until now had been tainted by the same impulse. Clearly, Eric was guilty of adultery – or at least guilty of marrying a second wife without the first one's consent. And his disappearance was making him look like a very good candidate for murderer.

'I have to get out of here,' she said, rising abruptly and pushing her way through the booth's plastic doors.

Nayir pocketed the marriage licence and went after her, relieved to see that she was heading for the Rover. He caught up with her. 'Mrs Walker . . .' She stood looking around numbly at the car park. 'Where can I take you?'

'I don't know.' Her voice was shaking but she was making an effort to control it. 'I can't go home, I don't feel safe there. I don't trust Jacob and Patty. I guess I could go to my neighbours, but if the police come looking for me . . .'

'Perhaps you should go to the police,' he said.

'No!' she burst out. 'Are you crazy? Do you know what they'll do to me?'

'They might just want to talk—'

'No, they won't!' she said. 'Look, I may not speak your language, but I know a hell of a lot about the police. They're fucking crazy. They can do whatever they want! Do you know a friend of Eric's got sent out of the country for *dating*? They caught him with a woman and – *bam!* He didn't even have twenty-four hours to pack. And – and another guy we know got picked up for wearing a cross around his neck. Don't look at me like that – he was a Catholic! It was a tiny cross. They held him in prison for six months! I mean, what the hell? And my husband is wanted in conjunction with a murder investigation. What do you think they'll do to *me*?'

'But you haven't done anything wrong,' he said quickly.

'If Eric and this girl were screwing each other, how long do you think it will take the police to decide that I might have been jealous enough to kill them both?'

'You weren't even in the country when she was murdered, yes?'

'I don't know!'

'Apparently her body was found last Wednesday.'

'All right, I wasn't here. But will they care? Do you know they arrested this one woman's housemaid because the *father* in the family had stolen some money? The housemaid was arrested and *tortured*. And it turned out the housemaid had been on *vacation* when it happened!' She looked appalled. Nayir had to admit that he was shocked too. He wanted to say that stories like that got passed around because they were so unusual, and that the police were not going to torture Miriam, or accuse her of murder when she was obviously out of the country when the murder occurred, but in truth, he couldn't be certain what the police would do.

'This information could be extremely useful to them,' he said. 'At least let me tell them about it.'

284

'I know what they do,' she said, finding refuge in her anger. 'They find a good suspect and torture them into confessing. Don't tell me they don't because I've heard it from too many people already. It's in *books* for God's sake.'

'Okay,' he said, trying not to get annoyed, 'but at least let me tell them that Eric's disappearance might have had something to do with Leila's death, and that Eric might be in jeopardy.'

And as quickly as her energy had gone frenetic, it settled back down with a sense of collapse. 'Oh,' she said more calmly. 'Yes. Yes, okay, you can tell them. But I'm staying here. I just need . . .' She put her hand on the car door and steadied herself. 'Maybe a hotel,' she said. 'Somewhere quiet. I need to think.'

'All right,' he said. 'I'll take you somewhere. Mrs Walker?' He stepped closer, thinking she might faint.

'You're not going to take me to the police, are you?'

'No,' he said. 'But it's very hot. You should get in the car.'

Warily, she allowed him to open the door. Nayir started the car and took off, half-afraid that if he didn't, she'd leap out again and run off down the street. He had no idea where to take her. Obviously, she couldn't go home. It would surprise him if the police weren't there already. She couldn't stay on his boat. It was too small and uncomfortable, and the neighbours would notice her, and if the police found her alone with him, they could charge her with indecency and hold her on that alone. The only woman he knew was Katya, and he couldn't bring Miriam to *her* – it would put Katya in an uncomfortable position. And if Miriam was afraid to go home, then bringing her straight to the police was an even worse idea.

☽

Miriam was engaged in a silent prayer: *Please God, please Jesus, please keep Eric safe.* She had enough trouble imagining him cheating on her without the added horrors of him stealing from his work, lying about his whereabouts, and then brutally murdering a—

Like an overloaded computer, her mind froze mid-thought, and she watched the houses fly past, a petrol station, a supermarket. Everything was shut down for prayer time. And she went back to her prayers. *Please God, please God* . . .

They reached the city centre, driving down a one-way street. The buildings were big and boxy, like large grey children's blocks left on a floor. There was a strip mall on the right, a couple of stunted palm trees, two men in white robes with matching white skullcaps attempting to cross the street. She knew that Eric was in trouble. He wasn't strutting around the city. He wasn't hiding somewhere. Every part of her resonated with clanging alarm bells. They passed a Hardee's restaurant and a Kentucky Fried Chicken sharing the same building, and she felt a sharp pang of home-sickness, even though she seldom went to those places back home. She glanced at Nayir. He was lost in thought, and she wondered if he was considering taking her to the police anyway. He didn't look like it; there was something big and solid and protective about his silence.

'Do you want to pray?' she asked him.

He shook his head. 'I'll do it later.'

'I'm sorry about what I said about the police,' she said. 'I know your friend works for them.'

'You have a reason,' he said. 'You don't know what they'll do, and when they become known for doing crazy things, you have no reason to trust them. That's their fault, not yours.'

'Well, I'm sorry anyway. I'm sure they're not *all* bad.'

'No, they're not,' he replied.

Fifteen minutes later noon prayers were finished. They were still driving through the city; it never seemed to end. Men were streaming from a mosque. The street sounded with the clang and clatter of vendors raising the grilles to their shops. Nearby, an

286

outdoor produce market was doing brisk business. All the shoppers were men, most in white or beige robes, having just come from the mosques; a few men wearing trousers stood here and there.

They hit a wide boulevard and drove past a roundabout covered in squat, fat palm trees. In the centre, blocked off by a corrugated fence, stood a mobile phone mast disguised as a palm tree. Houses were streaming by, the blocks of flats looked new. One was brick and overwhelmingly reminiscent of a European castle with turrets and towers and oddly shaped windows. It made her think of the Disneyland castle, and she felt another pang of longing.

She didn't know how much time had gone by before they turned down a quiet side street. On either side were high stone walls, with driveway gates every fifty feet. She felt a flicker of hope that Nayir was taking her into one of the large, quiet homes that she glimpsed through the gates. She would feel safe in one of those homes, barricaded against the world. But they drove past, entering another quiet neighbourhood and stopping finally at the end of a cul-de-sac.

In front of them stood a large villa, built like an Italian palazzo with a patio running the length of the house. An arcade hung above it, arched every few feet and supported by thick Grecian columns. Bougainvillea lay flung over the top of the arcade, like carpets that a chambermaid forgot to retrieve. French windows lined the front of the building. The whole thing was glowing in the dappled sunlight, a warm sandy colour. As they approached the front entrance, it became clear that despite its grand first impression, the house was not as large as it seemed.

'This is your house?' she asked.

'It's my uncle's,' he said.

'Do you live here?'

'No, I live on a boat.'

'Oh,' she said. 'What about your parents?'

'I never knew them,' he said.

He opened the front door and let her inside. It was cool and fragrant. A potted plant stood in the hallway, looking much healthier than any she'd ever owned. Nayir called out to his uncle and shut the door.

'Your uncle is the only one who lives here?' she asked nervously.

'Yes,' he said. 'But don't worry, he speaks English. And he's had female guests before. He works for archaeologists. People come here from many countries, including women.' He didn't look happy to be admitting this.

She gazed at the beautiful sitting room through a pair of double doors. 'It's okay with him that I stay here?'

'Of course. He would never turn a guest away. And anyway, he'll be pleased to meet you.'

She was relieved to hear that Nayir's uncle was not as pious as Nayir. It was probably why he'd brought her here instead of to his boat. But she still felt uncertain.

'Nayir?' A voice trailed down the staircase, followed by a small pair of feet wearing shiny leather loafers with gold tassels. A pair of brown trousers came next, then an elegant silk shirt tucked around a wide belly, and finally a head, which turned pleasantly in their direction.

Nayir said something in Arabic and then introduced Miriam to his uncle Samir. Samir was portly and slow with tiny brown eyes and a succulent nose; his face was filled with kindness as he studied Miriam. His black curly hair was slipping back, and what was left stood coiffed above his ears. He stood with his arms outstretched, still talking to his nephew but welcoming Miriam into the house.

'Welcome,' he said in English. 'You are welcome in my house.'

'Thank you.'

'First let me show you to a room,' he said. 'And then we'll have some tea.'

Nayir had disappeared into the kitchen. She followed Samir up the stairs, wanting to protest but feeling that it was foolish. Where else was she going to go? Samir led her to a room on the second floor. It was small and clean and neatly furnished.

'This is lovely,' she said, turning to him.

'Thank you.' Samir smiled. 'There is a bathroom through this door. Take your time washing up, if you like. Tea will be ready when you are.'

She thanked him again, watched him leave, and sat numbly on the bed.

30

For most of the day, a verse from Surah Fussilat had been running through Nayir's head. He had memorised large portions of the Quran during childhood, and they often came back to him, rising up from his memory like those strokes of dust in the desert whose invisible, suggestive sheen is only half-perceived and scarcely felt. It had taken all morning for his conscious ear to pick the familiar sounds of Ayah 39 apart from the other noises in his head: *And among His Signs is this: thou seest the earth barren and desolate; but when We send down rain to it, it is stirred to life and yields increase. Truly, He Who gives life to the dead earth can surely give life to men who are dead. For He has power over all things.*

If Imam Hadi were there, Nayir would have been able to ask him what it meant that Allah could give life to men who were dead. How dead was dead? Did it mean physically dead? Or just those with dead souls, beggared by evil deeds? He was thinking of Miriam's husband. He had the feeling that Eric was dead, physically or not.

He was waiting on his uncle's patio when the phone call came. Katya's number appeared on his screen and he answered at once. The tension was apparent in her voice when she said: 'We need to talk.'

☽

Nayir was quite comfortable having faith in the unseen, but believing that Allah could be known by His signs was much easier than knowing a woman by hers. Katya was sitting in the Land Rover's passenger seat, staring straight ahead. He glanced at her to read her eyes and wonder what expressions were hidden from him when the veil was down. He did not feel confident analysing her voice, interpreting her gaze, or deciphering the secrets of her hands, and what he suspected of these actions could not be confirmed without a great deal of awkwardness. So they drove in silence.

Glancing over, he saw the engagement ring on her finger and immediately wished he'd restrained himself. *You said we have to talk*, he wanted to say, but he dreaded the looming conversation, whatever it held. At the same time, he knew he had to tell her about Miriam and what had happened that day.

'What book are you looking for?' he asked, making another feeble effort to start a conversation. She had said that her cousin, Ayman, needed a textbook for school.

'Something about computers,' she said. 'I have it on a slip of paper.' She went rummaging through her bag, which relieved him. By the time she found it, he was parking next to a huge, square concrete building with inset glass windows between two large signs reading 'Jarir Bookstore' in Arabic and English. Getting out of the car, he braced himself.

Going into the superstore was like entering another world, with its vast aisles, overflowing shelves, and many foreign titles spread out among the Arabic ones. He followed Katya to the back of the shop and glanced at the other shoppers, watching what sort of people picked up the English titles. He saw a couple who were obviously American – the man skinny and blond, his wife's face radiating whiteness against the black of her headscarf. They were giggling about something on the magazine stand. But the others, who were they? He saw a tall, geeky boy wearing a sleek white robe and scarf that would have looked tailored on someone else but that only seemed to accentuate how small he was. He was studying a computer manual. Three children ran by, squealing and shrieking; they nearly ran into Nayir's leg but he sidestepped deftly and watched them chase one another down a long aisle of children's books. He scanned the shop for some sign of their parents but the children disappeared.

Katya led him through a large and obnoxiously colourful self-help section, whose titles immediately caused him to flush: *Fix Your Relationship, Now!* and *Why Women Are Unhappy, and What You Can Do About It.* The public admission that relationships were difficult and potentially disastrous was bad enough, but insisting that the remedies could come from a book made him wince. What did they do before books? Suffer in silence? What would the Prophet have done, with his seventeen wives? On the bottom shelf he spotted *How To Win Friends and Influence People*, not sure at first that he had read the title correctly, then feeling amazed by the blatant admission of vanity. He was distracted again as they passed a shelf of DVDs, catching sight of *Cinderella*, all cartoon blonde hair, and something called *The Fantastic Four* which had a picture on the cover of a woman with ample breasts and long flowing hair that apparently the censors had failed to ink out. For a terrible instant, he couldn't pull his eyes from the picture, revulsion and fascination sparring within him – was this a *children's* movie? – until modesty forced him to turn away.

'Doesn't your cousin have a car?' he asked, attempting desperately to keep his attention on Katya. The question he wanted to ask was: why did he ask you, a woman, to go to a bookstore for him?

'Yes,' she said rather coolly, 'he has a car. He's not one of those people who thinks that women should do everything for their men. It's just that he's really bad with directions. It's a miracle he gets to my office every evening.'

He got stuck on the words *women should do everything for their men*, which made him think that she had her men already – her father and her cousin – and that he wasn't in the category.

She found the book and headed straight to the cash registers at the front of the shop. She kept her burqa raised during the purchase, which he pretended not to notice. It seemed that every time he went outside there was another woman on the street who wasn't wearing a headscarf, or a woman who was bold enough to wear nothing but jeans and a T-shirt while bouncing happily down the pavement. He wondered if Katya would ever be like that. Two men in a nearby lane were staring blatantly at her face. He noticed, however, that she kept her eyes on the cash register, that she thanked the cashier without looking at him, and that as they left the shop, she kept her attention to herself somehow, so that she was looking around but not really seeing the world at all.

'Let's get coffee,' she said brusquely. Nayir followed her with mounting unease into the Starbucks next door. He had only been into one once before and the experience had been enervating. Samir had dragged him there – Samir, who was forever cluck-clucking about the boom in foreign restaurants, the all-pervasiveness of American chains like Applebee's and Fuddruckers, and the scarcity of decent Saudi cuisine. ('Where can you find a good biryani any more?') Crowds in any concentration made Nayir uneasy, and at the previous Starbucks he had seen too many women sitting at small bistro tables, sipping complicated coffees and clicking away at laptops in the wi-fi hotspot. It had provoked grim thoughts. What had happened to Jeddah, portal to the holy cities? This was Jeddah, but the name above the doorway seemed to make all the difference – so American-sounding, *Star* and *Buck*.

But the Starbucks next to Jarir Bookstore was quiet. There were no women inside, just two young men drinking coffee and conversing softly at a window table. Nayir ordered for himself

293

and Katya, and they went to the family section, which was empty. They sat in pouf chairs at the back of the store. The way she held her coffee pointed the engagement ring right in his direction.

'I saw Mrs Walker today,' he said. Katya's face showed such an expression of relief that it threw him into a momentary confusion. She didn't explain.

'She called me this morning,' he went on, 'because she talked to her neighbours and they gave her the name and address of the property manager.' He reached into his pocket and found the slip of paper. 'She thought we would want it.'

Katya took the paper without moving her gaze from his face. She looked at it.

'We know about Apollo Mabus,' she said. 'We think that Wahhab Nabih is either a rich benefactor of his or an alias. We're still looking into it.'

'Oh,' he said. 'So you think that Leila was doing her photography work for Mr Mabus?'

'She was definitely working with him.' Katya slid the paper into her bag and fastened the latch. She picked up her coffee again. 'You said that you saw Mrs Walker.'

'I picked her up in front of her flat.'

'To retrieve a piece of paper,' Katya said.

Nayir felt his cheeks getting hot. 'The other reason she called me is that she believed that someone had broken into her flat. She was frightened and wanted to get out of the house.'

'It was probably the police,' Katya said. 'They've been trying to find her.'

'In any case,' Nayir said, 'she wanted a ride to her husband's work, because she felt that they might know something.' He explained what they'd learned about Eric's leave of absence and the possible theft of surveillance equipment. 'Obviously,' he went on, 'Eric hadn't told her about any of this.' Then he reached into his pocket and took out the *misyar*. He paused only a fraction before handing it over to her. 'After you and I left her apartment, Miriam went looking through his other papers and found this in his briefcase.' Katya opened the paper and read it. She took a breath but didn't seem surprised.

'You should have called me,' she said.

'I'm sorry. I knew you were at work.'

She sighed and seemed to soften a bit. 'Yesterday morning,' she said, 'I went to interview one of Leila's friends, and she told me that Leila had been seeing an American named Eric Walker.' She went on to explain that Osama had finally pulled the Walkers' mobile phone records and discovered that Miriam had called Nayir this morning.

Nayir was struck with a potent admixture of guilt and betrayal. 'You told them about her?'

Katya looked at his face. 'I didn't have a choice. After what Farooha told me, I knew there was obviously a connection to the Walkers, and I had to tell Osama.'

The way she said his name made Nayir's chest feel like a meat grinder. He took a sip of coffee, found it too weak and set it down with a grimace. 'What are they going to do now?' he asked.

'The police want to talk to her,' she replied evenly. 'They know she had nothing to do with the murder. They checked her immigration records and she was out of the country when the murder occurred. But obviously, her husband was involved.'

Nayir was trying to stay rational. Deep down, somewhere, he agreed that Eric knew something about Leila's death.

'I know what you're wondering, and the truth is, I don't know what's going to happen to her,' Katya said, keeping her eyes fixed firmly on the floor. 'Probably they'll want to hold her until they find her husband.'

He pointed to the *misyar* that Katya was still holding. 'This doesn't mean that Eric and Leila were . . . together.'

'No,' she said slowly, 'but it does place them together. They obviously had some kind of relationship.'

'But a few things don't make sense,' he said.

'Like what?'

'First of all, let's say Eric killed Leila. Why would he let his wife come back into the country? She was in America when it happened. He could just as easily have let her stay there.'

'Maybe he had to make it look like everything was normal,' she suggested.

'But then the minute she gets back here, he runs away?' Nayir said. 'That doesn't make sense either.'

'Not unless he learned something at the last minute, something that made him realise he had to run, and it was too late to send his wife back to the States – that is, if he even thought that hard about it. It could be the case that he didn't care what happened to Miriam.'

'Yes,' he agreed grudgingly, 'that's possible. But what do you think he might have learned at the last minute? Let's say, while Miriam was on the plane, Eric gets what piece of information?'

'That the police have made a connection to him and Leila,' Katya said.

'Did they?' he asked. 'Did they make that connection? It sounds like you just made that connection yesterday.'

Reluctantly, she nodded. 'All right, then maybe someone else put the whole thing together. A friend of his? A colleague? They figured out that Leila was dead and they suspected Eric and threatened to go to the police. So he had to run.'

'But if he's a cold-blooded killer, why not just kill the friend or the colleague?' Nayir asked.

'Maybe he already has and we don't know it. Or maybe it was easier to run away.'

'And leave your wife to face the police alone, in a country where she doesn't speak the language?'

'If he's a killer,' Katya said, 'that might not seem so cruel to him.'

'If he did run away to avoid the law,' Nayir said, 'then why would he leave this marriage document in his briefcase where his wife could find it?'

Katya set her coffee on the table. He could tell that she was withdrawing into her thoughts, and he had the uneasy feeling that she wasn't going to share them.

'You have to admit,' he said, 'that it's equally possible that someone else killed Leila, and Eric found out who it was. Maybe Leila's killer has killed him, too.'

'In either case,' she said, looking at him in a pointed way, 'we need to talk to Miriam.'

Perhaps it was the 'we' in the sentence that riled him so much – it meant her and Osama. It took an effort to compose himself for a reply. 'Of course,' he said. 'And I think she *should* talk to you.'

'She hasn't been at her house all day,' Katya said in an eerily mechanical tone. 'Do you know where she might be right now?'

He hesitated for much too long; he wasn't going to lie to her. 'Yes.'

'So perhaps you could bring her down to the station tomorrow morning?'

'Yes,' he said. Was it anger on her face or disappointment?

'Good.' She reached into her handbag for her mobile. 'Sorry, this will just take a minute.' She placed a call to her cousin, he could tell from the conversation. Midway through, he said, 'I can give you a ride home,' but she shook her head.

'Ayman will be driving home from school,' she explained once she'd hung up. 'This is on his way home. It's just easier this way.'

I thought he was bad with directions, Nayir wanted to say, but he stood up instead, and Katya did, too, leaving her untouched coffee on the table. As they walked to the door, an enormous rift was opening between them. He realised with a crushing pain that he didn't want to lose her, but he felt her pulling away, and he was powerless to stop it.

☽

One of the things about seeing Katya – and he couldn't simply blame Starbucks for this – was that afterwards, he felt plagued by indecision. Should he go to the mosque, or pray at home? Was it all right to watch an hour of satellite TV? He couldn't even figure out what he wanted for dinner. With Katya, he was confronted with an obvious, nagging inconsistency: it was immodest and wrong to be in the company of an unmarried woman; but if it could put them on the path to a legitimate union, was it really wrong?

How, then, had his state of confusion been brought about? It wasn't just with Katya any more. Having lunch with Miriam, even agreeing to pick her up in the first place – had that been the right thing to do? Imam Hadi would have told him to take Miriam immediately to one of the women's shelters rather than keep her in *khulwa*, a sinful state of seclusion with an unrelated man. But he had brought her to Samir's house instead – double *khulwa*. Why had he done it? He'd felt he had no other choice. It seemed that his looseness with Katya had primed him for this doubt. If he had to break the rules in order to get married, then why couldn't he break the rules about less important things? How important were his little decisions anyway?

Until now, he had never realised just how much his faith had given solidity to his life. It had been as reliable and immobile as the Holy Ka'aba, which Allah had built for Adam and Eve to dwell in when they left Paradise, and which had stayed in its position throughout the ages. The Ka'aba, the fixed centre of the earthly universe, towards which all Muslims turned to pray five times a day, represented the unwavering strength and permanence of Allah. It would remain on this earth even after the end of time.

And it would probably take that long for Nayir to decide what to eat for dinner.

Nayir returned to Samir's house, but Miriam was already asleep, and Samir was chatting happily on the telephone to a friend. Nayir wasn't sure whether to return to the boat tonight or sleep on the sofa. (Boat or sofa? Boat or . . .?) He wanted to see Miriam first thing in the morning, before she got it into her head that she had to run off somewhere. And Samir would probably appreciate the company. But right now, all Nayir wanted was to be alone.

He went into Samir's study and sat down at the computer. He didn't do it very often. The internet was overwhelming – Buy this! Read that! – but desperate for a distraction, he went to Fatwa-online.com. There were updates on the latest pronouncements from sheikhs, and discussion boards on existing fatwas. Apparently, the Saudi government had created the site to legitimise various religious pronouncements, hundreds of which were made every week. But if the Saudi government had hoped to control the cacophony of clerics, then they didn't understand their own helplessness.

It was a wonderful diversion. For an hour he lost himself in the minutiae of Islam – was Viagra *halaal*? Should a man pluck the 'al-anfuqah', the hairs that grow beneath his lip but which aren't officially considered part of the beard? In which cases is it acceptable for a man to urinate while standing? Most of the recommendations were general common sense, and one or two made him feel a certain agony for the poor questioner. Was a sex change allowed? (According to one sheikh's opinion, no.) What should a mother do about her hermaphrodite child? (Pick one gender and surgically excise the rest.) And one or two of the issues threw him into reflection: was it permissible to read fiction? (No, because fiction was full of lies that occupy the writer and reader without benefit, and good Muslims should use their time wisely.) He could think of a few sharp remarks Uncle Samir would have for that. However, the fatwa writer did concede that sometimes one could indulge in books if there were a higher reason for doing so.

Just as he was wondering what a higher reason might be, the door opened and Miriam peered in.

'Hi,' she whispered. She looked as if she'd just woken up. She wasn't wearing a headscarf and her hair was tangled and loose. He lowered his gaze to the floor.

'I don't want to bother you,' she said groggily, but she came into the room anyway and shut the door.

His first thought was that she had forgotten where she was: this wasn't America, where a woman could walk into a room, her head uncovered, her face exposed, and talk comfortably with a man who was no relation to her. But he simply couldn't bring himself to point this out. She had been having this effect on him all day. If he'd had the chance to turn back and consult Fatwa-online, he knew what a sheikh would tell him: that it was his responsibility to remain pious in the face of an infidel who had no understanding of things. It was his job to stay virtuous, and if virtue failed, then it would also be his fault.

But in this case, he could not submit to the duty of dissociation, because some deep part of him had never liked the idea, and because Miriam needed him. She was more dependent than he imagined a woman should be. Muslim women at least had their families, their friends, whole networks of people. But who did Miriam have? It was strange that she should appear so vulnerable; in his mind American women were so much like men, so competent and muscular with their short hair and mannish clothing and lack of adornment. But here in the flesh was a real American, and she needed his help precisely because she was an infidel and had

300

no one else to turn to. It wasn't so much the sheikhs' words as their sensible tones that prompted the thought that sometimes one has to do things that don't agree with precepts, because there was a higher reason. And if murder was a higher reason, then shouldn't compassion be one as well?

'Stop looking at me like that,' she said.

'How am I—?' He hadn't even been looking at her.

'Like I'm the most pitiful creature in the universe.'

'You should cover your hair,' he said, motioning at her head, his eyes glued to the floor.

Looking around, she spotted a cloth napkin on an old tea service that was sitting on the desk. She unfolded it and draped it over her head. It scarcely reached her ears.

He raised a hand to his mouth to cover the nervous laugh that was forming on his lips. 'What is that?' he gruffed, attempting to pass off his covered mouth as a gesture of sternness.

'It's a napkin,' she snapped. She was standing right in front of him, looking small and frail in her rumpled tunic and trousers. Her face was puffy from sleep, and a smear of make-up trailed down from one eye. 'Something wrong with a napkin? Or does it have to be blessed by an ayatollah?'

'We don't have ayatollahs.'

'Finally,' she snorted, 'something to like about this place.'

The napkin on her head and the juvenile way she crossed her arms kept him from getting upset about the remark. For a moment, he thought that this was what it must be like to have a sister.

He kept his eyes on the bookshelf and said: 'I think you could like this place if you gave it a chance.'

She snorted and crossed her arms more tightly. He wondered how Eric would have dealt with this. Then he wanted to wring her stupid husband's neck.

'I was going to tell you something,' she said, becoming serious.

She took a seat on the room's other swivel chair. Nayir turned aside so he wouldn't have to stare at the napkin.

'I've been thinking things over,' she said with a trembling voice. 'Look, sometimes Eric did private jobs for people in the States. Escorting them, like a bodyguard. He said something to me once that made me think ... he said something about how difficult it was to protect women here because he wasn't allowed to be around them. He'd have to be married to them. He could have married that woman just on paper. Maybe to protect her?'

'Did he ever protect other women that you know of?' he asked gently.

'No. I don't know. I'm just saying he *could* have.'

'Yes, but how would he have met her?'

'Probably not through his work. I'm pretty sure Shaw was telling the truth when he said he didn't know her. Maybe privately, like through Eric's friend Jacob. And Jacob knows all kinds of people. It wouldn't surprise me if . . .'

'What?'

'If Jacob was sleeping with her,' she said. 'Or if he met her at a brothel or something. Jacob, I mean. Eric wouldn't do that.'

Nayir's look of discomfort must have shown, because she said quickly: 'Sorry. I don't know this woman, I'm just guessing. It would also explain why he might have stolen the surveillance equipment. Maybe he was using it for a private job, and just waiting for whomever to pay him back, or maybe he was even planning to return it? Because I know Eric wasn't a thief. He liked his job. He wouldn't have jeopardised it without a *really* good reason.'

Nayir didn't answer, so she went on. 'And I know for a fact that he would *never* kill someone.'

Nayir refrained from pointing out that there were obviously a lot of things she didn't know about her husband. He was struck anyway by her loyalty.

'And it doesn't make sense,' she went on. 'If Eric killed this woman and ran away, then why would he leave that marriage document in his briefcase? And why would he—'

'Pick you up from the airport,' Nayir finished. 'I know.'

She looked surprised. 'So I don't think he ran away. He must have known this woman, but maybe he—'

'Found out who killed her,' Nayir said. 'Yes, I've thought about it. But you also have to think about this: why did he lie to you about what he was doing that whole month?'

'Well, obviously, I was out of town . . .' She sat back in her chair. 'Maybe he couldn't . . .' Nayir looked sceptical. 'I don't know,' Miriam went on, her voice rising. 'Okay, maybe he *was* cheating. And of course, if that's true, then he wouldn't tell me about it. But just because they were together, *if* they really were together—'

'It doesn't mean that he killed her,' Nayir said.

They looked at one another in silent agreement. She slid the napkin off her head and used it to wipe the tears that had started running down her face. He directed his gaze back to the safety of the bookshelf.

'I have to do something. I have the feeling that he's out there and he's hurt—' She broke off.

'First thing in the morning,' he said, 'I'm going to take you down to the police station.'

'What? No!'

He raised a hand. 'You have to go. And they need your help.'

'They'll arrest me!'

'I'll be honest,' he said, 'they might do that. But regardless, they need your help finding Eric. He might be guilty, he might not, but they have to find him. And you want to find him, too.'

Her nostrils flared but she didn't say anything.

'And once you've talked to the police, I'm going to go and try to hunt down this property manager. As far as we know, this man—'

This time it was her turn to interrupt. 'This is about Katya, isn't it? She wants you to bring me in.'

'Yes,' he said. 'She's going to get in trouble if you don't go in.'

Miriam slumped. She gave him a doleful look. 'What if I give you something else?' she said. 'Something that might help the case. And in exchange, will you promise not to make me go to the police?'

'No.'

'Listen, it might be important, and if you make me go to the police, and they arrest me—'

'Don't worry about it,' he said, cutting her off.

She reached into the pocket of her jeans and took out a small piece of plastic. 'I found this in my bag when I got back from the States,' she said.

'What is it?'

'I think it's a memory card for a phone or a camera. I thought it was Eric's, but I can't imagine why he would have put it there. I don't know why anyone would, but it's not mine.'

'Who do you think it belongs to?'

She explained how she'd met Mabus on the plane and then discovered at Jacob's house that Mabus knew Eric.

'This is the same Mabus who is your property manager?' he asked.

'Obviously,' she replied. 'How many could there be?' Looking slightly self-conscious, she went on more lightly. 'All I know is that something was going on with the three of them – Eric, Jacob and Mabus. What if Mabus put this card in my bag? He would have had the opportunity, because I went to the bathroom on the airplane and left my bag behind.'

He nodded, thinking.

'When I found it,' she went on, 'I didn't think it was important. But this morning, when I knew someone had been in my house, I figured they were looking for something.' She held up the memory card. 'This was the only thing I could think of. And of course whoever it was couldn't find it because I was with the neighbours.'

'Let me see the card,' he said. She handed it over. He fished through the desk drawer and found the converter Samir used for downloading digital photos. The converter had various input slots, and the memory card fitted into one. He plugged the device into the computer and waited.

31

There was a time when Monday nights meant basketball practice, the sounds of whistles, referee horns, the squeak of trainers against a polished floor. That was before the kingdom had banned organised sports for girls, and before the girls' school where Katya had tutored chemistry students had enforced the ban. She had coached their basketball team for six years, and even if the girls ranted about the injustice of not being recognised internationally because the Saudis wouldn't send women to the Olympics, the girls still enjoyed the sport itself, playing it with a kind of churlish ferocity that helped them prove they were just as good as boys. In their complaints she heard only the uninspired echoes of their parents, immigrants from Lebanon and Syria who were appalled by Saudi culture, who felt it was backward and a shame to Islam, and who would have given anything to pick up dear Mecca, holiest of cities, and move it away from these righteous louts whose beliefs still lurked in the dark ages of the Bedouin.

The team had quietly been moved to a women's centre across town, although technically it was still illegal to play. The problem became transportation. Because so few of the girls could coerce their brothers or fathers into driving them, the team numbers fell by three-quarters, and the few who could come were inconsistent. Finally, they had disbanded.

Tonight, Katya entered the flat alone – Ayman had gone to a

friend's house to study, and her father was visiting Abu-Walid. She laid her bag on the kitchen table, helped herself to a plate of left-overs from the fridge, and stared emptily at the front of the oven. A delayed revelation had occurred to her that evening after leaving Nayir at Starbucks. *He is just like my father.* Why hadn't she seen it before? Both men were conservative. Devout. Both hid things from her – Abu failing to tell her about Abu-Walid coming to dinner the other night, and now Nayir doing all of these things with Miriam behind her back, only telling her at the end, and probably because she forced him to. She understood logically that she was the one who had brought him into the investigation, and that Miriam had called him to ask for help, but she was frustrated anyway at being left in the dark.

Finishing dinner, she went to her room. It was a terrible mess; she didn't have the time to clean. There were old coffee cups on the dresser, clothing jumbled on the closet floor. The bed hadn't been made in days, the sheets hadn't been cleaned in weeks. She went to her desk, pushing aside a stack of boxes that was leaning precariously against the wall. Waiting for the computer to power up, she cleared a space for Leila's DVDs. She didn't want to lose one in all the clutter.

That afternoon she'd called Farooha again. The girl had assured her that she didn't know anything about *Pilgrimage*. Yes, Leila had brought the disc to the house, but she had never talked about the new documentary, or even about Mabus. She only talked about Eric Walker.

'So she really liked him,' Katya had said.

Farooha had fallen quiet. 'Well, he was exciting,' she finally replied.

Katya was inclined to believe Farooha about the documentary. About Leila's feelings for Eric, she couldn't be sure how much of the truth Farooha was revealing. The girl did confirm that Leila had never mentioned anything about Abdulrahman attacking her, although Farooha seemed troubled by the suggestion that it could have been her brother.

'If it was him, I don't think she would have told me about it,' Farooha said after a heavy pause. 'It would have shamed her to admit that her brother hit her.'

Katya had also called the doctor who had treated Leila's leg injury. The doctor had remembered Leila vividly as 'the girl who'd been attacked for filming strangers in public'. She recounted Leila expressing fury at having her camera snatched away. Leila said that she had fought her attacker. Some of his blood was still on her shirt.

Katya was still no closer to knowing if Abdulrahman had hit Leila or not, but at least one thing became clear: the doctor said that the leg injury hadn't healed properly because Leila had refused physical therapy. Instead, she'd remained as active as usual. When the doctor had scolded her about it later, Leila had simply shrugged her off.

Forgetting where she'd left off, Katya picked a DVD at random and slipped it into the drive. The first cut on the disc showed a woman struggling to slip a doughnut through the eye slit of her burqa. Katya was in no mood to laugh. She watched through another half-dozen short clips, none of them terribly interesting.

Eric Walker appeared on the ninth clip. It took her a moment to realise who he was. It was night-time and three men were sitting at a patio table, two of them Arab, the other American. They were drinking from glass tumblers, and the Arab men looked unhappy. When one of them spoke, Katya realised that he was drunk. His eyes looked like red onions frying in oil. Eric was grinning and shaking his head. Drunkenly, he said something in a weird mishmash of Arabic and English that she took to mean: They can brew the stuff, but they can't drink it, can they? And from behind the camera, Leila gave a short bark of laughter. She said something in English, the only part of which Katya understood was 'Mr Johnnie Walker!'

And Walker laughed.

The next scene showed Walker in his flat. Katya's chest tightened when she recognised the dingy lamp on the end table. Had he really brought Leila into his *house*? She checked the date stamp and saw that indeed, this had happened a full three weeks before Miriam had returned. Walker was speaking in Arabic now, describing his flat in a mock-grandiose style. He pointed to a book lying on the floor and said: 'And that belongs to Miriam. She's coming back in twenty-one days.'

For a man who was courting a beautiful young woman in his living room, it seemed a tactless thing to say. Leila's camera zoomed in on the book and then expertly back out to Eric.

Then another man waltzed into the room. He was tall with dark hair. The camera turned to him, focusing in on his face. It was handsome but there was something mean about his eyes. The men were talking in English and she couldn't understand a word, she simply watched the dark-haired man's expressions shift from attentiveness to discomfort. Finally, he stared straight at the camera. It was an unnerving, predatory look.

The disc ended and Katya removed it from the drive. She labelled it with a Post-it note: *Eric Walker*. Over the next few hours she scanned through the other DVDs, going faster now that she knew what she was looking for: any sign of the Americans. They made no more appearances. As far as she could tell, there were only those two little segments.

☽

She awoke a few hours later, her computer screen flickering. Before falling asleep, she had given up watching the DVDs and started watching television online. Now an infomercial for Islamic bathing suits was playing. '*The Aquaburqa!*' the announcer proclaimed.

'*Reasonable solutions for Muslim women*.' She sat up, rubbed her stiff neck and watched two women walking along a beach in three-piece swimsuits that covered their whole bodies. The draping tunics had colourful tropical patterns, the black trousers were sleek, and the headpiece was a simple plastic hood that covered the hair and neck with a drawstring around the face so it wouldn't fall off in the water. She wondered what it would be like wearing such a suit, which the announcer described as a *burqa bikini, also called a burkini!*

For a while, she'd had a fantasy of going sailing with Nayir, of him teaching her to scuba dive, of harpooning a shark. It was such a thrilling fantasy because it might have been real: of course he would approve, he loved sailing and diving, and no one would see her out in the middle of the ocean, so she'd be free to swim around. She had the feeling, however, that Nayir would not approve of the burkini. He would think of it as Islam Lite, the sort of fake piety that was everywhere now. He would tell any woman in a burkini to go back to the Hadith where it says no wearing 'form-fitting' clothing, full stop.

She wasn't tired any more. Instead, there was a dangerous energy rising inside her. It had been building up for days, and now, at two in the morning, she was ready to play a whole basketball game herself. Or clean the entire house. Or finally take care of those boxes that were stacked against the wall, the trousseau Othman had given her before she'd called off the engagement. She didn't know what had prevented her from sending them back before, but tucking into the task, she sorted through everything, folded every last piece of underwear neatly, organised all of the shirts by colour, and packed every single dress and suit coat and shimmery negligee back into their boxes, taping them firmly shut and carrying them out into the hallway, where they would annoy her father and Ayman and force her to get rid of them once and for all.

310

32

For what felt like the thousandth time, Nayir lay in bed just before dawn, pondering marriage. In particular, whether it was truly as bad as it often seemed to be. He had a long list of miserable married friends – whose wives badgered and harassed them; spent all their money; failed to cook, clean the house, or raise their children properly; stopped taking care of themselves and grew ugly, lost teeth, became depressed, bored, or even suicidal. To that very long list of miserable men he now had a new addition: Miriam, whose husband had married another woman, possibly killed her and then disappeared, while Miriam herself remained firmly attached to the idea that he was completely innocent. He wondered how he could possibly want something so much when all around him was proof of its disappointments.

It was no comfort that even the Americans were miserable in marriage, although he had the notion that Eric had come here and failed to understand that when a woman stays cloistered, your duties to her multiply a dozen-fold. And he had clearly failed to comprehend that just because your wife was safely tucked away at home did not mean that you could seize any woman who happened to cross your path. *Misyar* marriage or not, it was forbidden for an infidel to marry a Muslim woman.

The night before, he and Miriam had been unable to crack the username and password that would have let them view whatever was on the memory card Miriam had found. Samir had even become involved, but their efforts had ended in frustration. Nayir had come back to his boat after promising her that he'd pick her up first thing in the morning, and quietly telling his uncle to keep an eye on her.

His alarm clock went off, ringing an imam's call to prayer in a squealing electronic voice that was becoming more tinny every week. He turned it off and went to the bathroom to perform his ablutions just as the marina's own loudspeakers blared the official call. He knelt on the floor with a deep sense of gratitude for morning prayer, for the chance to take his mind off his worries and turn his thoughts to greater things. He prayed for lighthearted blessings, for the happiness of strangers, the safety of travellers, good health to the elderly and a dozen other wishes that came into his mind, and when he stood up, forty minutes had gone by and he felt refreshed.

He ate a leisurely breakfast and managed to clean up the interior of the boat before heading out for the day with a feeling of completion. It all ended very abruptly when he came topside and saw a man standing on the pier next to his boat.

'Mr Sharqi?' He spoke in a kind way, but Nayir's instincts told him that he meant no good at all.

'Yes,' Nayir said.

'I'm Detective Inspector Osama Ibrahim,' the man replied. 'I'd like to have a word.'

Nayir didn't suppose he had much of a choice. 'Please come in,' he said, motioning to the ramp that led to the boat.

'Thank you,' Osama said. 'But I'd prefer if you'd come with me.'

So this was what it came to. He should have known better, getting involved in something that wasn't his business. He felt a flash of anger at Katya. He shouldn't have put the burden on her anyway, telling her about Miriam. Of course she would have to tell the police. His palms were clammy as he hauled himself on to the ramp and walked numbly up to the pier. 'May I ask what this is about?'

'I'm sure you know already,' Osama said. His tone was frighteningly polite. Nayir realised belatedly that this was *the* Osama that Katya kept talking about, and while it provided him with a glimmer of hope that he wouldn't be arrested, interrogated or humiliated too badly, his mind was filling with unpleasant revelations: that Katya had told him where Nayir's boat was docked, had told him all about the *misyar*, and about his promise to bring Miriam in for questioning. And evidently it hadn't been enough for Osama to trust a stranger like Nayir, so he had come here to speed things along.

They were just approaching a black, unmarked car parked in the marina lot when Osama said: 'By the way, congratulations on your success with the Nouf Shrawi case.'

Nayir was taken aback but made a polite response. He got into the car, grudgingly grateful that it wasn't a squad car, and that the neighbours wouldn't notice that the police had picked him up. He found it difficult to judge Osama kindly however. He was a classically good-looking man sporting neatly trimmed moustaches and baby-doll eyes. He wore a well-tailored suit and a businesslike air. Little things made him seem arrogant: manicured nails, a gold watch. This was the man Katya worked with, the man she saw every day and who saw her. The smell of aftershave and cologne that came wafting off him once they'd shut the door made Nayir feel sick, but the false politeness really was the crowning touch.

'So I understand you may know where we can find Miriam Walker,' Osama said, putting the car into gear and taking off slowly, as if waiting for Nayir to direct him. Nayir wanted to say no, every part of him was shouting it, but he had already told Katya that he would bring Miriam in. He wanted to ask what they were planning to do to her, but he sensed that admitting his concern for her would only make matters worse.

Osama took a left and cut into traffic. He didn't seem to mind Nayir's rebellious silence, but then he wasn't the sort to let a little sincerity get in the way of seeming composed.

They encountered traffic at once, which was unusual. Osama rolled down the window and asked a pedestrian what was going on. The man informed them that a motorbike show was in town, and that the distant roar of what sounded like aeroplanes was actually belched from the tailpipes of hundreds of Harley-Davidsons, or what the Americans liked to call 'hogs'. Osama thanked him and rolled up the window.

'Hog,' he mused.

'Isn't that another word for pig?' Nayir asked.

Osama glanced at him, apparently taking the comment to mean that he was one of those ridiculously conservative men who took offence at everything. Nayir remained quiet. When traffic began moving again, they saw that the real cause of the hang-up was an accident involving a pedestrian. A man was lying on his side on the street. The paramedics were bent over him. The poor soul was moving so at least he wasn't dead.

A few blocks later, traffic stopped again and the roar of bike engines grew louder. When the Harley-Davidsons finally came into sight, everything seemed to slow down. Cars stopped. Pedestrians froze. A woman on the pavement scooped her son into her arms and lifted her burqa, pointing at the bikers. Her son began to cry, a great wail of fear that was cut off by the roar. A pair of squat black motorbikes rode past on the cross street, riders bedizened in skin-tight leather and sleeveless shirts. Their arms and necks were pink from the blazing sun. Nayir began to sweat just looking at them. Then more bikers came, clustered in groups like vultures descending on a carcass. Some African men, a few Arabs, mostly Europeans and Americans, all processing through clouds of sweat and exhaust and rippling heat waves, making enough noise to drown a call to prayer. Riding a motorbike would have been

314

difficult in a robe; there was not a single one in sight, only leather and skin, the rippling flesh of muscled arms. The bikes paraded slowly, somehow gruff and flamboyant at once. But the blinding flashes of sunlight on chrome and the thunderous noise made Nayir wish they would hurry out of sight, drive on and be forgotten, this spectacle of American culture.

Once they were driving again, Osama seemed more relaxed.

'We've done a background check on Eric Walker,' he said casually. 'Enough to realise that he and Leila were calling one another frequently up until two days before she disappeared.'

They drove past a roundabout. 'And we also know that Miriam was not in the country when Leila died,' Osama went on. 'So we'd just like to bring her in for questioning. Your wife has told me . . .'

Nayir didn't hear the rest. *Your wife?*

Osama had finished talking and was looking at him.

'Katya told you that?' Nayir asked.

A small frown played on the corners of Osama's mouth. 'Yes,' he said. 'She's been very open. She cares about this case a lot.'

Everything was clicking horribly into place: that must be why Katya wore the wedding ring. She had to make her boss believe she was married. She'd obviously had to tell them about Nayir, but how could she explain how she knew him if he wasn't related to her? He would have to be a relative – but had she really told them that he was her husband? Aside from an undercurrent of glee, he was appalled by the blatancy of the lie.

'Mr Sharqi, is something wrong?'

Nayir realised at once that he couldn't break Katya's cover. How could he have been so stupid? Of course the police wouldn't have hired her if she were single. There would have to be a law about these things, and the police of all people wouldn't be inclined to break it.

'No,' he said quickly. 'I was only thinking.'

'About?'

Nayir couldn't come up with a suitable lie, but he was saved from doing so by the sudden crackle of the radio. A man's voice came over the speaker. Nayir didn't understand his strangely coded language but he noticed Osama's look of discomfort. A moment later, the inspector's mobile rang.

Osama answered it and listened for a moment, grunting 'yes' and 'all right'. His face showed anxiety. When he was finished, he pulled quickly back into traffic and took off with a rush.

'There's an emergency,' he said. 'It's close to here.'

'What kind of emergency?' Nayir asked.

'Domestic dispute,' Osama grunted, skidding into a sharp left that left tyre marks on the road. They merged on to a boulevard that was wide open, and Osama sped up. 'Some guys' wives are trying to kill each other.'

'Oh.'

'Technically,' Osama said, 'it's *haraam* to send a man in to break up a woman's fight. We have female officers who are trained to handle domestic problems.'

'So why are we going?' Nayir said.

'None of the women are on duty right now. Hopefully, by the time we get there, there won't be another bunch of bodies for my squad.'

Nayir was quietly surprised. 'If it's *haraam*, I still don't understand why they called you,' he said.

'I gave orders to the emergency services to notify me when situations like this come up. They want to do something about it, too, but there aren't many cops who are willing to get involved. Only me and a few others.'

'But clearly, you have the husband's permission,' Nayir said, 'if he's the one who made the call.'

Osama nodded. 'But it's still *haraam* and illegal, and I could lose my job.'

They pulled into a car park facing a tall block of flats. Just before Osama leapt out of the car, he turned to Nayir and said: 'I might need your help, if you're willing to give it.'

Nayir got out at once, anxiety, remorse, and stubbornness knocking him around in equal measure. He followed Osama into the building, Osama saying over his shoulder: 'Just stay behind me and do what I say.'

He wanted to ask Osama if he had a gun, and if so, why he wasn't brandishing it. Nayir's heart was racing despite his over-riding feeling that this could all turn out to be very foolish. The next scene put the feeling to rest. Osama pounded on the door, a man answered immediately, looking frantic and terrified, and quickly ushered six crying children out of the house and into the hallway. Nayir, anguished, watched them pass – they looked terrified. The man, obviously the husband, was just as scared. 'They're in there,' he said uselessly, pointing into the flat, from where the sound of screaming was bursting forth at intervals. They heard the crash of a plate, the horrible wail of a baby, and women yelling at one another – one woman crying, shouting raggedly through tears, then another shrieking so viciously that Nayir wanted to clap his hands to his ears.

Everything happened at once. Osama shot through the house and entered the kitchen. Nayir was right behind him, no longer afraid, only anxious that one of the women would attack Osama first, the shorter of the two men. Once through the kitchen door, Nayir moved to the side. He caught sight of blood splattered on the wall, the fridge. One woman was lying on the ground, unmoving, face-down, her back covered in blood. Another two were standing on opposite sides of the room, a kitchen table between them. Both were holding knives. On the counter, apparently for-gotten, was an infant in a bassinet, screeching at the top of its lungs.

Nayir thought for a moment that the husband had been pathetic to let things get this far out of control. But even the

317

presence of the police did nothing to stop them. The woman closest to the sink hurled a knife at the other one, who hurled a breadboard back. The two objects clattered against the opposite walls as the women ducked to avoid them. The woman nearest the sink was panting with fury, her eyes terrifying in their wildness. She picked up another steak knife. There was blood on her hand.

'Put it down!' Nayir and Osama both boomed at once.

The woman hurled it at her rival. Osama seized the opportunity to close in and grab the woman, gripping her wrists and lashing on the handcuffs he'd loosed from his belt. Nayir had no choice but to block the other woman. The minute Osama had grabbed the first one, the second had come bolting around the kitchen table, knife in hand. She thudded into Nayir's chest and he managed to grab her just seconds before the knife would have plunged into his arm. He twisted her wrist and the knife fell. She shrieked and pounded his chest with her free arm until he grabbed that hand, too, and somehow found himself pinning her to the wall, her face pressed into the tacky flowered wallpaper.

Osama was pushing him aside and slipping a pair of handcuffs on the second woman. 'Ambulance is on its way,' he said. Then he knelt beside the woman on the floor, who stirred and groaned. 'Don't move,' he told her, kneeling beside her and resting a hand on her back. 'Help is coming.'

'*Bism'allah, ar-rahman, ar-rahim.*' The prayer flew from Nayir's mouth in small muttered phrases. Time was fractured, and images clicked oddly around him like the shutter of an old-fashioned camera. Osama lifting the baby from the bassinet and shushing it. One of the women falling to her knees in tears. Another officer coming in. Nayir came to and saw that he was standing in the middle of the kitchen, holding one woman's upper arm in a vice grip and keeping the other one directly in his line of sight. She had been dragged up from her knees and was now standing next to the

318

fridge, hands cuffed behind her back, staring blindly at his face. There was blood in her hair and her eye was swollen shut.

Fifteen minutes later they were loading the women into the back of two ambulances. Osama returned to his own car, nursing a cut on the back of his hand that was bleeding profusely. Nayir followed him.

Osama fished a towel from the trunk and pressed it into the wound. Nayir noticed that the officer's hands were shaking, but it was probably leftover adrenalin. Osama eyed him sharply. 'It may be *haraam* to break up a women's dispute, but I think it's more *haraam* to let people kill each other, don't you?'

After a hesitation, Nayir said: 'Yes, I do.'

Osama nodded sharply, the fury rising off him in waves. He lifted the towel and saw that the cut was still bleeding. 'Now, about Mrs Walker?'

'I'll show you how to get there,' Nayir said.

33

Miriam sat at the computer. Samir was in the shower, she could hear the water running upstairs. She had spent most of the morning making futile attempts to guess the username and password on the memory card, but she'd had no luck. Nayir had said he'd be here at eight o'clock, but it was nearly noon and he still hadn't arrived. She'd tried calling his mobile a dozen times but he wasn't answering, and that, combined with the computer frustration, was enough to make her scream.

When her phone finally rang she answered it promptly. 'Where are you?' she demanded. But it wasn't Nayir, it was Jacob.

'Miriam,' he said, sounding more nervous than she'd ever heard him. 'Where are you?'

'Jacob?'

'Are you at home?'

'No. Jacob, what's wrong?'

'Miriam, goddammit, just tell me where you are.'

'I'm at a friend's house,' she said impatiently.

'An American friend?'

'No, an Arab.'

'All right, you *have* to get out of there.'

'What? Why?'

'Did you see the paper this morning?' he asked.

'I . . .' She stood up and went into the kitchen, the living room. Apparently, Samir didn't get a daily paper. Her heart was pounding in her throat and she had trouble getting the words out: 'What's in the paper?'

'There's an article about a dead girl named Leila,' Jacob said. 'They're suggesting that Eric may have had something to do with it.'

'What?' she shrieked. 'This is in the *paper*?'

'Yes. Now listen, you've got to get to the consulate *immediately*. If the police are convinced enough of Eric's guilt to leak it to the press, then there's no way you're going to be able to tell them otherwise. By the end of the day, this whole country is going to be frothing at the mouth to kill the American son-of-a-bitch who slaughtered some young Arab girl. And if they can't find Eric, they'll be glad to settle for you. You *have* to get to the consulate.'

'Oh God, Jacob, you don't think he had anything to do with this, do you?'

Jacob was quiet a second too long.

'What the *hell* is going on?' she snapped. 'You knew this girl. You both knew this girl.' She felt tears sting her eyes but she wasn't going to cry. 'They said Eric was married to her.' Her voice cracked and she stamped her foot.

'Miriam,' Jacob said with a tenderness so uncharacteristic that it stopped her crying. 'We both know that Eric had nothing to do with this. I'm going to check something out. You just get yourself to the—'

'What?' she interrupted. 'What are you going to check out?'

'I'll explain later. What's important right now is—'

'This is my husband!' she screeched. 'Now what the hell are you hiding? Goddammit, Jacob! I know about Mabus, all right? I know you're in on it!'

'Mabus? What are you talking about, Miriam?' He sounded genuinely perplexed.

'I know you're doing something illegal. The police shouldn't be after Eric. They should be after *you* and *Mabus*.'

Jacob seemed stunned. 'What do you mean?'

'I know that Mabus slipped a memory card into my bag on the plane.'

'What? He was on the plane with you?' Jacob sounded alarmed. 'What's on this memory card?'

'I don't know. I can't break the password.'

There was a long pause before Jacob said: 'Miriam, destroy the card.'

'What? Why?'

'Just destroy it. I don't know what's on it either but I have a very bad feeling that that memory card can get you into more trouble than you're already in. Just *trust* me.'

'How can I trust you when you won't tell me anything?'

'I'm going to the desert,' he said shortly. 'I'm going to check something out. I might be gone for a few days, but once I figure out what's going on, I'll let you know.'

'Jacob, tell me what's happening!'

'Just get yourself to the consulate *immediately*.' He hung up. She tried calling back but it went straight to voice mail. She was so angry that she couldn't breathe and had to sit on a chair and put her head between her legs.

34

When Nayir and Osama arrived at Samir's house, Miriam was gone. It was almost one by the time they got there. Samir was lounging on the patio, enjoying the unusually crisp air. Seeing Nayir and Osama come barrelling in, he stood up with some alarm and informed them that she had left half an hour before. Because Samir couldn't drive, Miriam had had to call for a taxi. When Nayir pressed his uncle about where she had gone, Samir could only say that she had spoken to a friend on the phone before leaving, so he'd been under the impression that she'd gone to see her friend. He hadn't thought it was a problem. He had tried calling Nayir twice, but he hadn't answered his phone. Apparently Miriam had tried calling him as well. Since Nayir had not bothered to keep his appointment with her, Samir couldn't be expected to keep her prisoner in the house.

Nayir realised that he hadn't switched on his mobile all morning. Inwardly cursing himself, and cursing mobiles in general, he followed Osama back to the car.

'Do you think she'll come back here?' Osama asked.

'I'm not sure,' he replied. 'She's impulsive.'

Osama motioned him into the car. While he was driving, he called the station and requested that they pull Miriam's mobile phone activity from that morning. Nayir had images of banks of sleek computers and men in crisp suits getting results within seconds, but the minute Osama got off the phone he announced:

'That may take a couple of hours, so until then, let's try to figure it out. Did she tell you anything about her friends?'

Nayir explained that she didn't have many friends – at least no one she trusted enough to stay with, and that that was why she had been staying with his uncle. The only people she had mentioned were her downstairs neighbours and an American friend who lived on a compound. He couldn't remember the woman's name, but her husband, Jacob, was a friend of Eric's. Miriam seemed to have trusted her neighbour more, but she didn't want to stay there because she feared the police would find her and arrest her.

Osama didn't contradict the statement, didn't leap to defend himself. Instead, he drove straight to Miriam's flat.

'I was there yesterday, hoping to find her,' he explained. 'We had the forensics team out there, too.'

'Did they find anything?'

'They found plenty, but I'm not sure any of it will be useful.'

Having climbed the stairs to Miriam's flat, Nayir was surprised to see crime scene tape blocking the door. Osama went inside and did a quick scan of the house but came back looking annoyed. 'She's not here. Let's check the neighbours.'

Fortunately, Mr Assad was home. He let them into the house and obligingly brought his daughter, Sabria, in for questioning. It turned out to be brief. She had seen Miriam the morning before but hadn't heard from her since. She explained that she'd given Miriam the landlord's address in Dubai, and the address of the property manager as well. Mr Assad confirmed the story. No one could remember Miriam having any friends on an American compound. She had gone there once or twice, but had never mentioned any names. Sabria said she was worried about Miriam and had tried calling her house phone, but Sabria was preparing for her wedding and had been too busy to track her friend down.

Heading back to the car, Osama's mobile rang. He listened grimly, cursed, and hung up. 'Bad news,' he said, looking as if he'd swallowed a cactus. 'There was an article in the paper this morning about the Nawar case. And they mention Eric Walker as a possible suspect.'

Nayir felt as if he'd been punched. 'How did they – did you—?'

'I have no idea who leaked the story to the press,' he cut in. 'But believe me, no one at the station wanted anyone to know. We're floundering on this one. *Fuck!*' He slammed the steering wheel with his fist, a gesture that Nayir found vaguely comforting. 'All right, we have to *find* her.'

'I have an idea,' Nayir said, aware that once he said it, he was going to have a lot of explaining to do. 'She might have gone in search of Apollo Mabus.'

Osama looked surprised.

'I gave the address to Katya last night,' Nayir said. 'Didn't she . . .?'

'No. How did you get it?'

'Miriam gave it to me. She got it from her neighbours. Apollo Mabus is the property manager of her building.'

'We know that Eric and Leila met at the mall,' Osama said. 'Eric probably introduced Leila to Mabus. Then she got involved in Mabus's project.'

'What project?'

Osama explained the contents of Leila's documentary, *Pilgrimage*. Nayir was disturbed. 'There's one more thing,' Nayir said. 'At some point Mabus left the country, because he was on the plane with Miriam coming back to Jeddah. She didn't know who he was at the time, but they were seated next to each other on the plane. He didn't tell her he knew her husband. She believes he slipped something into her handbag.'

Osama looked alarmed. 'What?'

'A memory card.'

'Where is it now?'

Nayir cringed. He had forgotten to ask his uncle about it. Making a quick phone call, he discovered that the memory card was still in the converter.

'It's back at the house,' he said.

'And there was nothing on it?' Osama asked.

'I'm sure there was something on it, we just couldn't break the password.'

Osama nodded, looking grave. 'Tell your uncle we're coming to pick it up.'

Nayir did so while Osama spun a U-turn on the road. Osama got back on the phone with the station and spent a long time explaining what Nayir had told him. Nayir listened, alternately hoping that he hadn't been an idiot for sharing all of this information, and that he hadn't been an idiot for not sharing it sooner.

35

The taxi took a left down a narrow alley and came to a halt in front of an immense cedar door. It was only one o'clock, but the sky was darkening ominously and the smell in the air indicated – unbelievably – *rain*.

Before getting out, Miriam asked the driver: 'You're sure this is number fifty-six?'

He nodded approvingly. 'Go ahead. Is right one.'

'You're going to wait?'

'Yes.'

He wouldn't meet her gaze, or even turn in her direction, which made her nervous, but she got out anyway and approached the door. The building was lavish, some remnant of the Turkish occupation. White stucco and brown wooden beams faced the street, and decorative wooden grille-work hung from the eaves. There were no windows on to the street.

She rang the bell. Deep inside she heard a faint trill. The taxi drove down the alley to let another car pass. She waited for the car to go by, watched to see that the taxi's tail lights hadn't disappeared at the end of the block.

She checked the slip of paper for the tenth time. Number fifty-six. Mabus's address, which Sabria had given her what felt like a million years ago.

She rang again. This time she heard something. It sounded like a ball falling off a chair and rolling a bit before hitting a wall. She strained to hear clearly but a car going past her ruined the silence. She rang the bell yet again, then banged on the door with an old metal knocker that echoed loudly in the entrance hall.

She pushed on the door firmly and it opened.

'Hello?' she said. She glanced up and down the street. The taxi's tail lights were just visible at the end of the block, but otherwise there was no one. She scanned the windows of the buildings around her, looking for signs of curious neighbours. The windows were all shuttered tight. Certain that no one was watching, she swung the door open.

'Hi! It's me!' she said brightly, entering the building.

She shut the door behind her and immediately regretted the decision. The room was pitch black. She groped around, feeling a chair back, a table beside it. She felt along the wall for a light switch but couldn't find one. Finally, her hand encountered a door frame and she reached down and found the knob. She turned it slowly.

The door swung outward and she stepped into an enormous courtyard that was littered with giant slabs of stone and wood. They looked like archaeological relics. She crossed a small patio and stopped beside one of the columns that supported the arcade, looking up to make sure no one was watching from an upstairs window.

Careful not to trip on the blocks of stone, she picked her way through the courtyard. The air was cool and fresh. A small fountain in the corner was bubbling murky water. Suddenly, she heard a noise behind her. She stopped to listen. It was nothing.

There were four doors at the end of the courtyard, and she opened each one. The first led into a dining area, the second into a sitting room. Behind the third she found another darkened room. She spent a good five minutes looking for a light switch without success. She tried to open the window. It was locked, but beside it, she spotted the outline of a table lamp. Fumbling, she managed to switch it on.

There was a desk in the middle of the room, an elaborate computer system, and a whole wall of books. The far end of the room was wide open and appeared to lead deeper into the darkened house.

She went to the desk and opened the drawers, hoping to find a clue, any clue at all about where Mabus and Jacob and Eric had gone on their camping trip. She was sure that was where Jacob was heading right now. He had said that they'd gone to Mabus's place for their trip. As far as she knew, it was the only place the three of them had in common.

The drawers were empty, but to the right of the desk was a corkboard, and here Miriam's heart skipped. The same photo she'd seen at Jacob's house, showing the three men in the desert, was pinned to the lower corner of the board. She almost couldn't bear to look at Eric's face, but she could see that he was genuinely happy in the shot, and it nearly brought tears to her eyes.

Hanging from the wall beside that was a framed satellite photo of the desert, blown up to poster size. There were several sand dunes and, in the centre, a faint grid of white stones with the words *Qaryat al-Faw* written in block letters. Various signatures, some in Arabic, were scrawled along the edges of the print, which gave her the idea that the photo showed an archaeological excavation of some sort, and that the people who had worked on the dig had created this commemorative poster for Mabus. She couldn't make out any of the names.

She pulled a pen and paper from her bag and scribbled down the words 'Qaryat al-Faw'. At least this would give her something.

She went back to the desk and attempted to turn on the computer, but it wouldn't start. As she was fussing with it, she heard a noise. It was coming from deeper inside the house. It sounded like footsteps, slow and deliberate.

She swung around and stared into the darkness. A rush of

adrenalin coursed through her when she realised that the footsteps were actually coming from the courtyard. She stepped back, but the sounds came closer.

Clutching her bag, she stumbled into the darkness of a hallway. Her foot caught on a power cord and she fell forward, cracking her knee on a table. Pain shot through her leg. The footsteps were approaching faster now. Biting back the pain, she got to her feet. It was darker in the hallway. She felt along the wall for a door. Locating a latch, she pushed it and plunged through a doorway into another hall. She shut the door behind her and tried to calm the rushing in her head long enough to listen.

She had the horrible feeling that she'd be trapped forever in this dark, confusing house, groping for safety, followed by an unknown assailant. She moved forward slightly and the door behind her opened, very slowly, letting in the smallest crack of light. She sprang forward and ran to the opposite wall, fingers desperately searching for an exit. She found a metal doorknob and twisted it open.

She tumbled on to the street. It was not the same street she'd been on when she arrived. It was another alley, wider and darker. A droplet of rain touched her face and she jumped.

Disoriented, she walked towards the light of the main road, praying that the taxi would be there. But it wasn't at the corner. With shaking hands, she draped the burqa over her face.

Was it prayer time? She hadn't heard a call to prayer but the street was deserted. The shops looked run-down and there were no signs in English. She decided to go around the block. At the next corner two men were standing by a truck. When they saw her, they stopped talking. They were young, African, each wearing wildly coloured polyester shirts. One of them opened his shirt and said: 'Voulez-vous fuck me?' The other one laughed.

Miriam turned the corner immediately and saw with dismay that the street veered off to the right. She had to go left to get around to the front of the house, but there was no alley connecting to it. The men on the corner were staring after her, and when she looked back, they began to walk in her direction. She picked up her pace and kept walking forward.

She fished in her bag for her mobile but couldn't find it. A sudden jolt of nerves. She stumbled on her robe. She wanted to run but she didn't know where to go.

'Hey!' a man's voice called out behind her. 'Hey, *marra*!' Woman! She began to jog. Finally finding her mobile, she dialled the taxi service, speed-walking now. A car stopped beside her on the street. She couldn't help slowing, turning to see through the front of her burqa. A car door slammed. Footsteps on the pavement, marching towards her. She glimpsed a man's face, a reptilian stare seeking her own. She broke into a run.

She sprinted for ten feet but she was no match for the man. Encumbered by her robe and burqa, she stumbled just as he seized her shoulder and yanked her backwards. She screamed, but he grabbed her mouth, his other arm gripping her waist, and drew her backwards – all squirming, clawing limbs – and shoved her into the car.

36

After picking up the memory card from Samir and dropping it off at the station, Nayir and Osama went to Mabus's house. They arrived as the sky was darkening with clouds. No one answered and the front door was unlocked. Osama drew his gun before entering. 'Police!' he called out. 'Is anyone home?'

They did a quick once-over of the house. No one was there, but the back door was wide open. There was nothing of interest inside. The computer seemed to be broken, and it looked as if the desk had been cleaned out long ago; the thin layer of dust on its wooden surface was undisturbed. Osama called the station and asked for a forensics team, then motioned Nayir back outside.

While they were waiting for forensics, Osama's mobile rang. He answered it and listened intently for a few minutes before hanging up.

'They finally got hold of Miriam's mobile activity from this morning,' he reported. 'She received a call from a man named Jacob Marx.'

'That's probably the same Jacob she talked about,' Nayir said.

They decided to abandon waiting for forensics and head over to the Arabian Gates compound, which wasn't that far. Nayir was surprised to notice that it was getting dark. The rain had stopped and the sky was an iron grey.

'What did Miriam say about this man, Jacob Marx?' Osama asked.

'She said that he was a philanderer and that if anyone was sleeping with Leila it would have been him, not Eric. Apparently, he slept with Arab women all the time.'

Osama didn't seem the least startled by this information. 'But this *misyar* document said that Eric and Leila were married,' he pointed out.

Nayir nodded.

'Jacob was in the desert with Eric and Mabus?' Osama asked.

'Yes,' Nayir said. 'Miriam saw a picture of the three of them out there. It was a recent photo. She'd seen it at Jacob's house.'

Osama fell to reflection. Just before they reached the compound gates he said: 'The quickest way to get information from someone is usually the least pleasant way.'

Nayir had images of someone strapped to a chair, an interrogation light flooding their face, and a small, twisted man holding a scalpel to the victim's ear. He had only heard stories of police brutality, conveyed by word of mouth and successive retellings, which of course rendered the details more disproportionate. He couldn't say if any one detail was correct, but the sheer volume of stories, the surprising number of friends and acquaintances who had something horrible to say about a loved one's unfortunate encounter with the police, was enough to convince him that the police were not always working in the public's best interest. All of the admiration for Osama that had sprung up so fiercely inside him after the events of this morning threatened to vanish as quickly as it had come.

'What do you mean?' Nayir asked calmly.

Osama glanced at him. 'I was just observing,' he said. 'But I'm going to play it by ear with Jacob. What I'm trying to tell you is that whatever I do, just go with it, all right?'

Nayir didn't respond. He wasn't going to 'go with it' if Osama started sawing off somebody's toes.

Seeing Nayir's face, Osama let out a bark of a laugh.

☾

They had little difficulty getting through the compound gates. The guard gave them Jacob's address, but he must have called the house to warn the occupants, because when they knocked on the door, Jacob's wife opened it as if she'd been standing right behind it.

'Excuse us for the intrusion,' Osama said in English, 'but I'm Detective Inspector—'

'I know,' she said. 'Come in.' Although her face was exposed, she was wearing a black headscarf and a long black *abaaya*. Nayir surmised that she'd put on the garments just for them. The head-scarf kept slipping back from her forehead and she had to adjust it twice before they even reached the kitchen.

Nayir thought it must be an American convention to invite guests straight into the kitchen, because it's exactly what Miriam had done. Once they were seated at the table, he realised that she felt more comfortable here. She pottered about making coffee and setting dates on a tray. Osama looked as if he'd have liked to protest at all the fuss and get straight down to business, but out of politeness he refrained. 'You're Mrs Marx?' he asked.

'What? Oh! Yes, I'm Jacob's wife. Patty Marx.' She had stopped pottering and now stood staring at them anxiously. Behind her, the coffee pot beeped and she spun back round, poured coffee hastily, and set two mugs on the table in front of them.

'Mrs Marx,' Osama said. 'We're here about Miriam Walker.'

Mrs Marx froze, leaning over the table.

'You don't happen to know where we can find her, do you?'

She shook her head, looking more frightened than ever. 'She was here last Thursday, but I haven't seen her since.'

Osama nodded and scribbled something in his notebook.

'Has she done something wrong?' she asked.

Osama gave her a peculiar look. 'No, we'd just like to talk to her about her husband's disappearance.'

'Well, I haven't seen her,' Mrs Marx said with a blatant tone of finality that managed to say: *So you can leave my house right now*.

The whole conversation was going much too slowly for Nayir. 'We think she might have gone to meet your husband some-where,' he said. 'She spoke with him on the phone this morning. She was with my uncle at the time, and she told him that she was going to meet a friend. We believe that friend was your husband.'

Panic was apparent in the woman's eyes now. 'My husband's not here,' was all she could bring herself to say. She turned back to the coffee pot and took a glass cup from the shelf, obviously lost in thought. After a moment, she looked at the glass strangely and exchanged it for a mug. She poured herself a cup of coffee and turned to face them, leaving the coffee untouched on the counter.

Osama, who had been watching her behaviour with a falcon's eye, said: 'Mrs Marx, where is your husband?'

'I – I don't know.' Her voice cracked. 'He was here this morn-ing, and then he said he was going out. I didn't ask where.'

'What time did he leave?'

'About – I don't know, noon?' She cringed as if hoping it was the right answer.

'Where do you think he went?' Nayir asked on a sudden impulse.

Her eyes flickered nervously to Nayir but she turned back to the counter and picked up the sugar bowl. 'Well,' she said, 'if he said he went to meet Miriam, then that's where he went.'

'He didn't say that,' Osama said.

'Oh.' Mrs Marx nodded.

Osama was looking discouraged. There was even a trace of anger in his eyes now. 'Mrs Marx, the reason we're looking for

Miriam is that we believe she may be in danger.' Mrs Marx rounded on them. Her mouth formed a small 'o'.

'You saw her on Thursday,' Osama went on, 'so you probably know that her husband is missing. What you might not know is that there was an article in the paper today linking her husband with the murder of a young Saudi woman here in Jeddah.'

She let out her breath in surprise. A subtle change in her expression made Nayir think that this information had triggered an important understanding for her. She brought her coffee to the opposite end of the table from them and took a seat, balancing herself on the edge of the chair as if preparing at any moment to spring up again.

'So if there's anything you can tell us about where your husband might have gone—'

'Well, I think he went to the desert. But you don't think he's any kind of danger to Miriam, do you?' she scoffed. 'Even if he had gone off to meet her somewhere – which I highly doubt – he would never hurt her!'

'Why would he go to the desert?' Osama asked.

'Well, because he likes to go camping!' Patty said.

'Would he really go camping in the middle of the week?' he asked.

Just then, Osama's mobile gave a jingle. He looked startled, took it out of his pocket and frowned. He glanced at Nayir momentarily before answering.

Mrs Marx looked at her coffee cup, obviously discomfited by the interruption. Nayir watched her fingers twitch nervously at the mug's rim. It occurred to him that he had no trouble studying the woman's face, even imagining he understood the expressions there. It gave him a heady rush of power.

Listening to something on the phone, Osama stood up from the table and went to the kitchen door. He lingered there, partially turned away from them.

Patty didn't seem to understand what he was saying, but when she heard the words 'Miriam Walker' she looked up.

'Is he talking about Miriam?' she asked in a panic.

'Yes.'

'What's he saying?'

Nayir wasn't sure. He hadn't overheard.

Osama laid his hand over the mouthpiece and said in English: 'We have reason to think Mrs Walker may have gone to the desert.'

Mrs Marx's face was the very picture of fear. 'But how would she get *out* there? You don't think Jacob took her, do you? He would never do that!'

Osama shrugged. 'We have no idea, but it's a very dangerous journey, even with a companion.'

'You can't possibly think Jacob or Miriam had anything to do with this girl's death,' Mrs Marx said in alarm. 'Do you really think that?'

'Mrs Marx, we're not after your husband,' Osama said. He listened to something on the phone and then turned to Mrs Marx and Nayir again. 'Does the name Mabus mean anything to you?'

'Mabus!' Mrs Marx hissed. 'That horrible friend of Jacob's!' She was clutching her coffee mug in a death grip. 'A horrible man! He's always doing something secretive. Probably illegal! Is he involved in this?'

Osama grunted, thanked the caller and hung up the phone. 'Mabus is one of our primary suspects,' Osama said. 'We've been looking for him for a couple of days and we suspect that he's fled to the desert.'

Nayir marvelled at the smoothness with which Osama had lied. Mrs Marx didn't seem to notice any change at all.

'We have reason to believe that Mabus may be carrying a weapon,' Osama went on, 'and that he may be dangerous.'

'*Mabus.*' Patty looked at the floor, her face taking on an obvious expression of deliberation.

'Mrs Marx,' Osama said. 'If there's anything that you can tell us that will help us track down your husband and Miriam before they get hurt, it would be an enormous help.'

'He's a dangerous man, I always said it. Jacob should have known better than to get involved with him.' She looked up at the men, her face resolved. 'Jacob went to the desert this morning. He'd found out that the police were after Eric and he knew Eric couldn't have killed that woman. He had the idea that Eric was hiding out in the desert, but it didn't make sense!' Her voice rose into a shrieking kind of pitch. 'I told him, why would Eric march out to the desert and leave his wife stranded here? Jacob didn't have an answer. I really don't think Eric is the type to do something like that, but you just never know. And now Jacob's gone after him . . .' She swallowed hard. 'What if Mabus is in the desert? You have to go after him. Jacob could be out there!' She took a few steps closer to the men.

'Where exactly did your husband go?' Osama asked.

'I don't know – I—' Her voice cracked again and she pushed past them. They followed her into the living room. There was a desk against the wall and she tore open the top drawer, scrabbling furiously through the papers and junk, turning abruptly aside to a bookshelf on the wall that held an assortment of baskets. She pulled a basket down, searched through it, tossed it aside, all the while narrating: 'Jacob kept a GPS, but he's probably taken that to the desert. It's out in the desert somewhere, that's all I know. It could be anywhere! He had a map here somewhere.' She pulled down a third basket and found the map lying on the top. She snatched it out, fumbled to unfold it, and spread it on the desk. They all bent over it, feeling the frantic energy radiating off her.

'Here!' She pointed to a spot marked in pen. There was no town, or landmark, or even a nearby road on the map, just – thanks be to Almighty God – a pair of coordinates. Nayir took a pen and paper from the desk and copied them down.

'Are you sure that this is where he went?' he asked.

'No,' she said, 'but that's where he went with Mabus the last time they went out there together. Mabus has some kind of – of *shack* or something. They go camping. They just went a few weeks ago. Oh my God, *Jacob*!'

Nayir eyed Osama, who nodded. 'Thank you, Mrs Marx,' he said. 'Trust me, we'll do everything we can to find your husband.'

She gulped, nodded and watched them leave the room.

☽

Outside, Osama hustled Nayir into the car and they took off. 'You know that wasn't really my office calling,' he said.

Nayir nodded. 'How did you manage to call yourself?'

'Actually, that was my wife.'

'Your wife?' Nayir had trouble imagining this. 'She was on the phone that whole time?'

'Yes.' Osama looked chagrined. Nayir wondered briefly what his wife had said, although perhaps she was used to such odd behaviour from her husband.

'So what are you going to do now?' Nayir asked, trying not to sound too curious.

'I'd better head back to the station and get in contact with the closest police station out there. Have them send someone to check it out. It may be that Eric Walker is hiding out there, and that Jacob has gone after him. It may also be that Mabus is out there. Whatever the case, I suspect we'll find something.'

Nayir nodded, fighting a rising anxiety. 'What do you think happened to Mrs Walker?' he asked.

'I'm not sure,' Osama said. 'We honestly don't know where she's gone. But I do want to find Jacob Marx, and see if he's had any luck finding Eric Walker. That's who we're really after.'

37

It was all Osama could do not to turn on the sirens and blow through the worst of the rush hour traffic to get back to the station. Chief Riyadh had already tried calling him twice, and there was no doubt he wanted the chance to blow up about the Nawar case showing up in the paper. Osama also had to coordinate with the police in the desert, which meant that he first had to figure out where the hell it was and which police to contact for that province. He had the sinking feeling it was in the Empty Quarter somewhere. And while all of these worries were flooding his mind, he couldn't seem to ignore the 'conversation' he'd had with Nuha.

The phone call had been a kind of torture. He couldn't talk to her, of course, not while pretending that she was someone else. Instead he was forced to listen to her. She hadn't paid any attention to his charade; if anything, she'd assumed he was ignoring her again. But it hadn't mattered, because she had his ear. And what she'd said had murdered him. That she was sorry, so sorry that she'd lied for so long, but that there were things she had wanted to say to him before now that she could never bring herself to say. That she was overwhelmed. That she couldn't find it in her to be a mother and a journalist and a wife and lover, and a daughter, and a friend, cousin, aunt, sister and all the other things she was every day, because it was just too much. She was tired of pretending that she had what it took to impress everyone all the time. She was

340

exhausted. And the funny thing was, she had thought that Osama wanted her to be this way. She knew from the beginning that he wanted her to work, wanted the second income, wanted to be able to tell his friends that his wife did something important, that they were a modern couple and perfectly successful. But now she realised that she had failed him because she had lied. And the truth: what she really wanted was to have no more family bearing down on her. No more responsibilities.

Osama had fought hard not to reply, not to break the charade and reach out to her and say anything to stop her tears. He could hardly remember why he'd been angry at her. He only knew that he wanted to get home and hold her in his arms and apologise for his coldness.

But he couldn't talk to her now. Nayir was still in the car with him and Osama's phone was ringing again. He answered it and listened to what Majdi had to say. When he hung up, he turned to Nayir.

'They cracked the password on the memory card from Miriam's bag. Majdi said it was pretty straightforward. The card contained a file of Quranic documents that belonged to an excavation in Yemen. Supposedly, it's the earliest version of the Quran that's ever been found. For some reason the Yemeni authorities won't release the documents to the public, so these are stolen copies.'

'Did Majdi have a chance to look at them?'

'Not in depth, but there was a file on the memory card that explained the documents. Do you want to see them?'

Nayir shook his head. He looked tired and hungry.

Osama dropped him off at the marina and went back to the station. It was getting dark. He went looking for Chief Riyadh, who wasn't in his office. Apparently, he had left early for a cousin's wedding.

With relief, Osama stopped in the second-floor hallway beneath a flickering fluorescent light and called Nuha. She didn't answer her mobile, so he called the home number. The phone rang seven times. He began to feel panicked. She answered on the eighth ring.

'Hello?'

'Nuha . . .'

She had been crying, he could hear it in her voice.

'I'm sorry I'm not there,' he said. 'I'm so sorry. I still have a few more things to do here.'

'But you're coming home?' she asked. He heard the touch of anger in her voice but didn't feel like chasing it.

'Yes, I'll be home later. Nuha, I'm sorry.'

When he hung up, his whole body gave a shake and for a moment he thought he would fall over. He braced his hand against the wall, surprised that he'd been so upset, that he'd just spent four days not speaking to his wife, and that his will to maintain his silence hadn't cracked before now.

Katya's lab was two doors down, and he tapped gently on the door before pushing it open. She was in the corner, standing on a chair and gazing through a high, narrow window to the street below. Half of the room was in darkness. A large machine was glowing with a blue light.

She didn't see him at first.

'Miss Hijazi,' he said. She spun round with such a start that she nearly fell from the chair. He went lurching forward in an empty gesture; there was no way he could have caught her if she'd fallen.

She climbed down, looking flustered, and adjusted her headscarf. 'Sorry,' she said, pushing the chair back under the desk. 'I was just watching for rain.'

'You're not married,' he said.

She froze.

'When I referred to you as Nayir's wife today, he didn't contradict me,' Osama said.

'Well,' she replied in a tremulous voice, 'he's a taciturn man, but

342

no, I'm not married.' She slid her hand into her sleeve. 'I'm sorry I lied.'

He was angry, but the emotion was stunted by the events of the past few hours. 'I suppose you didn't have much of a choice,' he said.

She looked at him in surprise. 'Do you want me to leave?'

Grudgingly, he shook his head. She nodded, clearly relieved.

'For now,' he said, 'this is between you and me. I won't tell anyone. And if anyone asks, you're married. Is that clear?'

She nodded again. Still frustrated, he turned to leave. 'And tell Nayir that he's not your husband.'

She looked as if she dreaded that conversation most of all.

☽

Nayir walked down the pier in a restless frame of mind, and it only got worse as the minutes went by, so that by the time he reached his boat, he was distracted enough to stumble on a pile of ropes.

It was only nine o'clock but it felt as if he'd lived through a few days' worth of activity. His day with the police now seemed a succession of astonishing encounters. The littlest things stood out. The way he'd grabbed the woman's arm when she'd tried to stab him. The way he'd gazed unreservedly at Patty's face. Above it all, Osama towered like a fortress in the face of a relentlessly surging sea.

Nayir had considered becoming a religious policeman once, but the thought of spending his days reminding people to pray, to cover themselves, to act modestly and decently seemed like the most depressing occupation in the world. It would serve as a constant reminder that people were full of immodesty and vice. The events of the day had made him aware that modesty was the least of society's concerns when people were killing, assaulting, and stabbing one another daily.

He was exhausted but perversely full of a wriggling, twitching energy. He tried calling Miriam but her phone didn't ring at all. The line simply went dead, an ominous sign. He called Samir to ask about Miriam, but she hadn't shown up there either. He knew he'd never sleep so he went to the kitchenette and ate a token meal of hummus and pita, staring at the cabin walls and trying not to think.

He kept having to remind himself that Miriam had left the house freely. She had probably panicked and decided not to talk to the police after all. The thought stung him. He wouldn't have forced her to go. But there was always the possibility that something worse had happened. A small voice insisted that she might really have gone out to the desert.

On top of that, he couldn't stop thinking about Katya. Had she told Osama directly – 'Nayir is my husband' – or had Osama simply inferred it? Did she tell the administration that she was married, or had they assumed it just because she wore the engagement ring? He tried to reprieve her by imagining that she hadn't intended to lie to anyone, and that she only wore the ring out of nostalgia for Othman, but that thought only made him feel worse.

After eating, he went to the bathroom and performed his ablutions, grateful for the respite. The minute he finished, his phone rang. He nearly switched it off but saw that it was Osama.

'Did Mrs Walker show up at your boat?' he asked by way of greeting.

'No,' Nayir said. 'She hasn't contacted my uncle either.'

'Same thing over here. I called her neighbours again, and they haven't seen her. I have a bad feeling about this.'

'I do, too.'

'We got in touch with the police in the desert. It's near Qaryat al-Faw,' Osama said. 'I gave them the coordinates. They said they'd send someone to check it out.'

'How long do you think it will take?'

Osama snorted. 'I'm not going to wait up for it.'

Nayir went back into the bathroom after the phone call, seeking a return to the fragile state of purity and calm he'd established. The second round of ablutions didn't help. By the time he was kneeling on his prayer rug, he was actively struggling to keep his mind in order. After the second *rakat*, he gave up fighting and simply prayed for her safety: . . . *and wherever she is, Allah, please let her think to call me.*

☽

Nayir woke with a start in the quiet hours of the night. He hadn't been dreaming. He hadn't heard a noise. Instead it felt as if all the anxiety of the day had wound itself up so tightly inside him that it had finally popped.

Of the many burdens that the past week had heaped on his shoulders, the one that seemed most grotesque in the moonlight was the juvenile, harshly stated opinion that Majdi had expressed in the lab. *The idea that there's only one way to read it reduces the whole book to something flat . . . It can't keep up . . . It just becomes an ornament.* He had been talking about the Quran but now it felt that he had been talking about Nayir, about men like Nayir, about a good portion of society, and that Majdi had taken everything Nayir held dear and crushed it between the great stones of logic and progress.

Without really stopping to consider why, Nayir found himself getting dressed and slipping on his hiking boots. He packed his necessities – headscarf, binoculars, favourite canteen, and an Altoids tin filled with emergency survival tools such as matches and a needle and thread – and took them out to the car. In the car park, he hauled his largest petrol and water drums from the boot of the Jeep and transferred them to the Rover. Ten minutes later he was on the road.

38

Osama sat at the kitchen table watching Nuha boil the coffee. He tried to grab hold of the feeling he'd had on the phone: that everything was going to be all right. But for the first time in his life, he felt that the kitchen was a foreign place, that the whole house belonged to someone else.

Nuha brought the coffee to the table and set it down. There were tears in her eyes, and that was the biggest part of his discomfort. She'd started crying, softly, the moment he'd walked in the door. He had hugged her, kissed her forehead, led her into the kitchen. He was exhausted, but suddenly it had burned off in a pulse of adrenalin and now he was nervous.

He reached over and took her hand. 'Nuha, *hayati*, we're going to be all right.'

She had been staring at his chest; now she shut her eyes and slowly withdrew her hand from his. 'There are some other things I have to tell you,' she said. The words dropped in him like an anchor.

'Go ahead,' he managed. 'I'm listening.' He couldn't listen any more. This wasn't an interrogation room. He wouldn't bring that crap here. But she began to talk, her voice soft, her head held low. She told him all the things she had wanted to confess before but had been afraid to say. How she spent their money frivolously on clothes and lunches with friends, then borrowed more from her parents so that he would never know how much she spent. How she didn't actually like the Indian restaurant they went to, the one he loved so much. The food there made her sick. Sometimes she would come home and throw up. And all those Wednesday nights when he thought she was visiting her cousins? She was actually out in the desert with her brother, learning to drive. 'Of course I couldn't tell you,' she said. 'You're a police officer. I didn't want to put you in that position, knowing that your wife was breaking the law.' He didn't hear everything, it went by in a blur as he waited for her to tell him the one thing he couldn't forgive: that she'd met someone else, that she'd fallen in love with another man. But she never got there. She stopped talking and looked at him. Obviously his lack of reaction was frightening her.

'Thank you for telling me,' was all he could manage.

She went on. The anchor was pulling him ever deeper; he was floundering in her confession. Now she was saying that she didn't actually like being a mother. Muhannad was the most amazing thing that had ever happened to her, of course, but all the work, the worry, the strain of parenting. It was too much. She couldn't focus, her mind was always on her career. It wasn't fair for Muhannad when all she could think about was her writing.

'That's what I really care about,' she said.

'It's important,' he said numbly.

She nodded, took a deep breath, and said, 'This has all been a horrible few days, Osama. I've hated keeping these secrets from you, and I hate that you found the pills. But I think in the end, it has been a good thing because I've come to a decision. I have to tell you what's really in my heart.' She wouldn't meet his eye, but when she pushed ahead, he saw the determination in her face. 'I've decided,' she said, 'that I don't want to have any more children.'

It took him a moment to register the weight of what she'd said. He felt something breaking inside him as he remembered the conversations they'd had about children over the past three years, the times they'd lain in bed picking baby names, discussing how they would handle sibling rivalry, how they'd have to buy a bigger car. It had all been a lie.

'But you . . . Nuha . . .' He forced a grim smile. 'You're twenty-three. You've got a long life ahead of you. You shouldn't make a dramatic decision like this. You might change your mind.'

She didn't dispute it, but the look on her face told him everything. She wasn't going to change her mind. And the fresh tears in her eyes told him exactly how sorry she was.

Osama sat back. All he could think was that his son would never have siblings. He tried to imagine himself today without his brothers and sisters, and the image was miserable. It flashed in front of him in an instant: how lonely his life would have been. He saw his son alone. Then it occurred to him that Muhannad wouldn't have parents either. They'd both be working. They'd spend their lives working. They might even be divorced. *Divorce*. The word landed like a rock on the floor. He would have to remarry if he wanted more kids. He didn't believe in taking a second wife. Nuha would never put up with it anyway. He couldn't imagine even finding one.

'Osama?' She was looking worried.

'I need some time,' he said. He resisted the urge to leave her there. To stand up and stalk coldly off. He wasn't going to follow that instinct any more; it had done too much damage already. So instead he just sat there, unable to speak.

'I'm sorry,' she whispered.

He nodded. He let a few more minutes go by before reaching for her hand and squeezing it. He stood up, bending down to lay a kiss on her forehead. The familiar smell of her hair nearly brought him to his knees. He ignored it. Looking at her one more time, he repeated what he'd said.

'I'm going to need some time.'

39

'Miriam?'

A groan.

'Miriam? Can you hear me?'

Another groan.

'Wake up.'

She struggled to open her eyes but her lids were as heavy as bricks. Her head was throbbing painfully where she'd been struck. The rest of her body was numb. It begged her to return to unconsciousness but the harsh voice continued prodding.

'Miriam.'

She thought it was Eric but the voice was all wrong. Too guttural, too deep. She tried to respond but it felt as if the inside of her mouth had been caulked.

There was a clatter nearby. Her eyelashes fluttered and she took a deep breath. A musty smell hit her throat and she gagged. Coughed.

'Eric?'

'Eric's not here.' This time the voice was a hot whisper in her ear. 'But you'll see him soon.' A hand crawled beneath the back of her neck and raised her head. She tried to open her eyes again but the lamp at her foot was too bright. The man was lifting her, sitting her upright and propping her against something warm and hard.

It felt as if her head was full of sand, and every movement sent it shifting like grains in an hourglass. She became aware of her body part by part. Her arms were twisted behind her back, tied tightly at the wrists. Her hands were asleep. The numbness was somehow painful.

'You need to drink this.' The man was nudging something into her mouth. A drop of water touched her lips. She forced them open, began to drink. It went down her throat burning like whisky.

'Who are you?'

'Keep drinking.'

She had to shut her eyes to focus on the water, but it felt good now. She was thirsty.

'Who are you?'

He didn't answer. She opened her eyes. Somewhere along the way she'd lost a contact lens and now all she could see was a half-blurry picture, nothing but darkness beyond the single lamp that sat on an end table at the foot of the bed. She flailed but only managed to fall to her side. Her head hit the mattress, causing her captor to lean over and set her upright again. She tried to remember where she was but all she could remember was the street, the two African men, Mabus's apartment—

'Mabus?' she croaked.

A figured moved past the lamplight, a man wearing a white shirt that shimmered at the edges of the light. He moved back into the darkness.

Black thoughts filled her head – not panic, but a distant awareness of his intention, mingled with despair. She was too weak to fight. She was exhausted, starving, aching all over. There was darkness beyond the lamp, the swell of midnight over the room. She was powerless.

'Miriam, he told you everything, didn't he?' he asked. His voice was soothing, like the voice of a father who wanted to know that his daughter had been lying, who wanted the truth.

'Eric?' she slurred, trying to buy herself some time, to make

350

Mabus believe she was incoherent, because it was Mabus, she was sure of it now. Where was the memory card? It had been in her bag. No, she had left it at Samir's house.

A long silence followed, broken by the sound of Mabus setting a glass on a table. She heard him breathing.

'Eric?'

'Eric isn't here.'

She opened her eyes and fought the grinding in her head. Mabus paced the darkness behind the lamp like a wild cat stalking. She could feel his frustration.

She wanted to hurt him, bite him, scream from the pit of her stomach, but the most she could manage was to sit up straighter and force her eyes to focus.

'Miriam, where's the memory card?'

She looked around the room. Shadows played on one wall. There was a recliner, the ugly wallpaper of a shabby hotel. Where was the door?

'I don't know,' she grogged.

'Think.' His voice was edged with anger. '*The memory card.*'

His exasperated sigh managed to frighten her more than anything else. A bounce. He knelt on the bed, his hands gripping her shoulders. 'Try to remember,' he hissed. 'Did you give it to someone?'

She tried not to inhale his scent – it was making her gag – but she had to breathe. She fluttered her eyelids as if she were half-dead and sloped to the side. He gripped her more tightly, yanked her back upright and pushed her hard into the wall. The pain in her wrists was almost unbearable.

The adrenalin was waking her, making it more difficult to play dead. His hand gripped her neck; he put his face close to hers.

'Where is the card?'

'I don't know.' She was whimpering. 'I don't know what you're talking about.'

Crack. His palm was like a steel bar slamming into her cheek. The other hand gripping her neck was pressing tighter. She could feel the air thinning, feel her chest convulsing as she struggled to breathe. '*You gave it to the police, didn't you?*'

'No,' she gasped.

He smacked her again. 'Tell me!'

She couldn't breathe. 'Okay,' she gasped. He released her neck ever so slightly. She realised she was crying. 'They came looking for you,' she wheezed.

'And what did you tell them?'

'Noth—' She saw him raise his hand. 'I didn't tell them anything. I just gave them your address.'

'And where is the card?'

'I gave it to the police.'

He seemed to believe her because he released her throat completely, shoved her hard against the wall, and stood up. '*Fuck.*'

40

The trip to Qaryat al-Faw was a long one. He'd had to head south on the 15 to Abha then back up on the 10, which had taken the better part of a day. He passed wadis, which had been a stark, shocking, verdant green after the white and golds of the coral desert. Cows had been grazing on the banks of the river, shallow enough for them to cross to the other side, and in the distance, the mountains had been a series of lightening khakis and army greens. Then the mountains themselves, pin-turn roads and sweeping vistas of grey and beige stone. Samir always called it 'baboon country' because the monkeys clustered in every jungle valley and dangled from the escarpments. Some had even been known to lay traps on the motorway to stop passing motorists. Nayir could only enjoy the view for a while. There was too much greenery, too many nooks and crags. The mountains seemed to cut out half of the sky. It was because of these mountains that Saudi was mostly desert. They kept the monsoon rains that fell here from reaching the rest of the country. They always felt like a gateway one had to pass to reach the true goal: the wide, barren, unforgiving Empty Quarter.

He'd spent the night in his car outside Abha, catching a few hours of sleep before being wakened by a frightening wind and the threat of rain. He stopped at a roadside market and stocked up on food and water. The vendor had a camel-driven sesame oil press, and Nayir went to greet the beast, but it made an ugly gurgling noise from the back of its throat and he backed away. After performing his ablutions with a bottle of water in the parking area, and kneeling by the side of his car to pray, he ate a quick meal of tinned fava beans and set off.

It was only when he began to see camel crossing signs that his heart softened in his chest, his worries lifted and he felt his body breathing again. Religious signs appeared by the side of the road, and when he passed an *Allah Akbar*, he said aloud: 'God is great indeed!'

Stopping to figure out how the car's navigation system worked, he punched in the coordinates Patty had given them, thinking as he did so that he was under-prepared to go into the Empty Quarter itself. The coordinates weren't really in Qaryat al-Faw, a small town on the 177. They were out in the dunes east of the road that led there. The Amirs might have failed him with the desert trip, but they hadn't failed him with supplies. The boot was still stocked with their generous gifts, although he had taken the non-alcoholic beer out of the icebox and filled it with water instead. All the same, he was heading into the great sandy waste of the Rub al-Khali, where even the Bedouin would warn him against travelling alone.

As the landscape grew sparser, his thoughts became richer. He remembered his first night sleeping on the dunes. He must have been five years old. He and Samir had slept in a tent that was completely sealed off from the world. His uncle had given him a canteen and a pillow; it was too hot for a blanket. The canteen was full of water and Nayir had fallen asleep clutching it, having the notion that he had been charged with protecting it. Throughout the night, a burning dryness in his throat woke him every few hours, and he sipped guiltily from the canteen. No call to prayer stirred him from sleep the next morning, just his uncle sitting up and groaning about the heat. The sun was cresting the horizon when Samir led him outside and showed him the hundreds of tiny tracks in the sand where scorpions and ten-legged desert spiders had tried every avenue they could to penetrate the tent. Nayir had stared at the tracks in awe, feeling for the first time that there was danger in the world.

His thoughts turned to Katya. He still found it difficult to believe that she'd lied about having a husband, but where his shock had once been mixed with pleasure at the thought of her pretending they were married, now he only felt a familiar sadness. Katya had probably been forced to lie in order to get her job. This wasn't so different from his own habit, a year ago, of carrying around a *misyar*. In case he ever found himself alone with a woman, he could write her name in the document to pretend that he and the woman were married. It had never happened, but he had carried that *misyar* in his pocket with every intention of lying. And wasn't Katya's engagement ring the same sort of falsehood? They were both trying to deceive those who would punish them for sinning. But the greatest sin of their lying was in failing to acknowledge that Allah sees all things. *He knows the eyes' deceit, and what people's breasts conceal.*

Nayir had burned his *misyar*. He wondered now what Katya would do with her ring.

41

When Miriam woke up again, she was being dragged out of the back seat of an SUV. She landed on her feet, saw Mabus standing beside her, gripping her arm. Panic set in at once. She was woozy and had the feeling she'd been drugged.

She looked around and saw a house ten yards away. It was small, sand-coloured, pale against a backdrop of dunes. The sun was up and the heat was intense.

'Where are we?' she asked, but he was already dragging her towards the house. She stumbled along, her feet still loosely tied with rope. She still had on her cloak but her headscarf and burqa were gone. She noticed a garage off to the left, its door wide open. Down the hill was a smaller building, but she only caught a glimpse before Mabus yanked her up to the house.

He shoved her through the front door and into the relatively cool space inside. The front room was tiny, with a large desk and a whole wall of books making it feel even more crowded. Above the desk was an old fan plugged into a generator on the floor.

He led her off to the left, to a room beside the garage. There was a narrow bed here but nothing else. Throwing her face-down on to the bed, he untied her wrists, flipped her over like a squealing pig and re-tied her wrists in front. 'Don't try to leave,' he said. 'You'll die before you reach the nearest town.' Then he strode back out, locking the door.

She sat up and struggled to free her hands, but it was too

difficult. She could work on her feet, though, and within a few seconds she had managed to unwind the ropes from her ankles.

From behind the house came a sound like someone scuffling in the dirt. She went to the room's only window, which was covered by a wooden grille. It was impossible to see through. She heard Mabus's heavy footsteps walk across the kitchen floor and on to the back steps. A muffled cry of surprise from Mabus, then another man's voice.

'You fuck! I ought to put a bullet in your head.'

She strained to see through the grille. All she could make out was shadowy movement, but she thought she recognised Jacob's voice.

'Jacob, I didn't do it.'

'Bullshit. You killed him!' Jacob said. 'You fucking *killed* him.'

Miriam felt the room bottom out. She clutched the window frame for support.

'I didn't kill him,' Mabus said. 'Jacob, believe me, it—'

'What was he doing out here?' Jacob sounded frighteningly cold.

'He came to help me with something,' Mabus said.

'Bullshit. He would have told me if he was coming out here!'

'I asked him not to.'

There was a grunt, a tussle. It sounded as if they were fighting. The dull thud of a body hitting a wall, shoes scrabbling on gravel and dirt, the sharp crack of a punch.

Clap. A gunshot. She started. It frightened her so much that she began beating on the wooden grille.

'Jacob!' she cried. 'Help!' She ran to the door and began pounding. 'Help!'

The door remained shut.

'Dammit!' The sound of Mabus's voice froze her. It startled her that he had overpowered and possibly just shot Jacob, a highly

357

trained bodyguard. Eric had always said he spent more time in bedrooms than he did at the gym, but Jacob had had a *gun*.

She heard him come into the house. Miriam's blood was thundering in her head. She grabbed the doorknob and yanked, but the door only rattled in its frame. Mabus crossed through the house and into the backyard. This time she heard him dragging something around the side of the house. She ran back to the window. Mabus was struggling, stopping every few feet, his breathing laboured. From the crack at the edge of the grille she could just make out that he was pulling a man's body. She clapped her hands to her mouth in horror. She had recognised the bright blue of Eric's new shirt. Not breathing, she stood suspended in shock. Eric was dead.

She stumbled backwards, terrified. Her legs were shaking and she sat on the bed. Awful minutes ticked by before Mabus came back into the house. He went through to the backyard and she heard him fumbling and grunting. She knew he was dragging Jacob's body around to the front of the house.

She stood up unsteadily. He was coming for her next. She looked around for something to defend herself with, but the bedroom was empty of all furniture but the bed.

A car door slammed, then another. When Mabus came back inside, his footsteps stopped in the living room. He stood there for a long time. She couldn't breathe, and she stared at the door, willing it to stay shut, willing herself to survive.

Finally, Mabus went back outside. The front door slammed and a moment later she heard the car door shut with a *thud*. The engine started, the car took off, kicking up gravel. She heard it driving away and slowly became aware of her body again.

She ran at the door, impacting with a thunderous *whack*. It didn't give. She stood back and began kicking the door handle, first once, then again, with a force she didn't know she had. The handle gave way with a loud *crack* and the door finally flew open.

She stumbled through the main room and into the kitchen, pulling drawers open until she found a knife, then sawed away at the rope that bound her wrists. She tucked the knife in her back pocket and went racing outside.

Mabus's car was gone. She ran round to the back and saw the blood spatter on the ground where Jacob had been shot. There was a tool shed back here, the door wide open. It was empty; drag marks in the dirt indicated that Mabus had dragged Eric's body from here.

Eric's body.

She thought she might throw up. She stumbled back into the house. There was a giant container of water in the fridge. She took it out, nearly dropping it, and poured out a glass. She poured two more, drinking as much as she could. When she was finished, she left the house.

The garage was empty. In a panic, she ran down to the only other building near the house. It was fifty yards away and by the time she reached it, she was heaving with exhaustion, dripping with sweat. The air smelled heavily of manure. She guessed it was a stable.

Jacob had to have come in a vehicle, but where was it? She found it to the left of the stable, half-hidden beneath an old tarpaulin. She stripped off the tarpaulin and there was Jacob's pick-up truck.

She flung open its door and searched desperately for keys with no success. She went back to the house and scoured the ground near the kitchen door, thinking Jacob might have dropped the keys in the attack. But she couldn't find anything, and every fibre of her body was telling her to get the hell out of there before Mabus came back. Five minutes turned into ten and she couldn't wait any more.

She ran back to the stable. There was a large door on the side and she swung it open, stepping into the cool interior. There was a camel standing there, looking remarkably as if it were smiling at her. She approached it with caution, untied its reins from a peg on the wall, and led it out of the stable. The camel made a noise like a grunt, but it seemed happy enough.

'You ready to get out of here?' she said, her voice hoarse and shaky. The camel was much too high for her to mount, so she grabbed its reins and motioned it down. It grunted dissent but after a few more yanks, it sat down, front legs first. She hauled herself on to the skimpy cloth saddle and gave the camel a good kick. It stood up slowly, its back legs rising first. The motion nearly threw her forward over the camel's head but she managed to grab on to a peg on the saddle and steady herself as the camel pushed up on its front legs. Once it was standing, it made an excited snorting noise. 'You're my ticket out of here,' she whispered. 'Come on baby.' She gave it a gentle kick and it took off with a surprising lurch, trotting away from the house, away from the driveway and off towards the dunes.

'Wait!' she cried. 'Wrong direction!' She struggled to turn the beast back towards the road but no amount of jerking at the reins seemed to affect it. It was running along with determination. Miriam was terrified. The camel was going too fast for her to jump off, and she seemed to be dangerously high above the ground, twice as high as she might have been on a horse. There was no way to get down without hurting herself. In fact all of her energy was directed at making sure she didn't fall off. Desperately, she glanced over her shoulder and saw the house growing smaller in the distance.

42

The coordinates led Nayir to a barren strip of road. The road itself was paved, and aside from the sun-bleached asphalt, nothing human marred the wilderness. When the car's navigation told him that he had reached the right spot, he got out and checked the location against his own GPS. It was correct, although there was nothing but flat, sandy desert on either side of him. There were dunes to the west, but to the east they rose in mountainous peaks, slicing sword-like across the land.

He took his binoculars from the passenger seat and scanned the terrain. Strange depressions in the land, small whirls of blowing sand, rising waves of mirage-producing heat could all obscure a small campsite or trailer or house, especially if it were white or gold-toned. Standing next to the car, his body was happily soaked in the heat. This was not the tropical wetness of Jeddah, the sticky sweatiness that made him want to shower all the time; this heat was dry and smooth, and the forceful wind whipped the sand against his skin like some giant, industrial cleaning machine.

To the south-east he spotted it. What he had first mistaken for a false wadi – a narrow rivulet snaking its way through the flat land – was actually a trail of some sort. Before getting back in the car, he checked the tyres. They were fuller than normal because of the heat, and a rough drive on hot sand would fill them to bursting. He let a bit of air out of each, gauging it with the ease of old habit. Then he got in the car and drove off the road, into the lumpy desert where the sand was gently mounded like frozen ocean waves. The Rover handled itself well as he crossed the valley to the point where the trail wound into his sight. He got out of the car and looked: it was a vehicle trail, originating even further south on the main road, heading east towards the dunes and curling north to avoid a large depression of sand that might have been too soft to drive on. From there the trail swung south-east again, disappearing behind a hill.

He set the Rover on the trail and followed it for another kilometre. As he rounded a dune, he encountered a surprising vista. There was a nook among the dunes, a small valley of sorts that was protected from the wind by a large group of boulders. A small, rectangular house stood in the centre of the valley, and the tyre tracks led right up to the garage.

It looked like no one was home. He approached slowly, gazing around at the sky and the crevice where a canyon of sorts cut a path between the dunes. He looked for dust clouds, any sign of someone coming or going. Dust rose in spurts from the dunes above, swept upwards by the insistent wind. He parked in front of the house and waited for a few minutes, but no one appeared.

He draped his binoculars around his neck and approached the front door. The sound of his footsteps on the gravelly dirt in front of the house was announcement enough. He knocked anyway. There was no reply.

The front door was open. Inside, he found a small room, an even smaller bedroom, and a kitchen. It seemed claustrophobic after the sweeping vista outside the door, but this was a desert dwelling, the small rooms and thick mud walls designed to keep out the heat as well as the night chills. He wandered through it. The cupboards were stocked with canned and dried goods. There was nothing in the fridge. A five-gallon jug of water stood open on the counter, the water inside evaporating. He sealed it, noticed a cup on the counter. The cup was dry, but he could make out the vague imprint of lips on the rim of the glass.

Miriam appeared in his mind as if she'd been sent there. He felt the first stirrings of unease. Whoever lived here – and it was probably Mabus – would have had the common sense to close up the water jug. But someone in a rush might have forgotten.

Going back out to the front, he scanned the road with his binoculars but a rising cloud of sand blanketed the view. The wind was picking up now, and an unusual redness was tinging the eastern sky. If someone was coming, he wouldn't be able to see them, much less hear them above the wind.

He went back inside, feeling anxious. The wooden floor creaked heavily beneath his weight, and he suspected that it was hollow. Walking slowly around the edges of the room, he found a trap door cut out of the floorboards. With his pocket knife, he was able to pry it open, revealing a small metal ladder that led to a cellar.

Descending slowly, relishing the coolness no matter how stuffy it was, he entered a tiny room. It was half the size of the already small main room above him. There was a desk here, two filing cabinets, and a low shelf of books. On the desk was a neat stack of papers. Nayir glanced through these and immediately stopped to read the second paper in the stack.

It looked like a journal article but it wasn't bound. At the top, a professional logo read *Journal of Criticism*. It seemed ludicrous that an entire journal would be devoted to criticism. The article's title bothered him more: 'The Qur'aan Unveiled: How the World's Most Influential Book Has Been Built on a Lie'. He scanned the article, stumbling on several passages of long, unfamiliar words, but catching phrases here and there: *abandoning the convention . . . Islam was a social movement with no true religious core . . . the Qur'aan as it is today was not as it was revealed to the prophet Mohammed . . . wholly one-fifth of the Qur'aan is incomprehensible . . .*

The paper's author was Wahhab Nabih.

Beneath this were other, similar papers, also written by Nabih. 'The Qur'aan and the Erroneous Notions of "Salvation History"' and 'Rethinking Qur'aan: How Mohammed Was Wronged by his Editors'.

So this was Mabus's hidden workshop, maybe just a storehouse for his blasphemous ideas and those of his sponsor – although it was seeming more likely that Nabih was an alias. It was a good idea to stash this work out in the desert where no one would find it, but from the looks of it, the papers had not been confined to the desert. They had been published in journals. They were being read by the world.

Feeling disgusted, Nayir picked up the whole stack of them and climbed back up the ladder. On his way up, he caught sight of something shiny beneath the stairs. He went back down and set the papers on the desk. Beneath the ladder, he found a wooden case with a glass cover, almost like a display case for a book. Inside was a stack of old documents. He thought he recognised them from Majdi's lab, but he didn't have time to take them all out and inspect them. Anyway, the case was locked, and he didn't want to risk damaging the documents.

He set the journal articles on top of the case and carried the whole lot back up the stairs. If it was evidence, he didn't want to leave it behind. A small voice inside him was saying that a man had a right to blaspheme whatever he wanted, that the price for it would be paid in the afterlife, that it wasn't his job to mete out punishment. But it enraged him that Mabus, a Westerner, had come here to study this country, its language and writing, its history and religion, for the sole, obsessive purpose of tearing it all down – or, at the very least, of making it seem foolish in the eyes of non-Muslims. Nayir didn't give a lizard's tail for the academic nonsense his uncle was constantly engaged in, but he knew enough about it to recognise their tools of attack, the cold, calculated way men destroyed ideas with the rational language of 'science'. But this wasn't science, not as Allah had created it, it was not a natural event but a contrived cruelty.

He went back to the car and set the wooden case and the papers on the floor of the back seat. Sweat was trickling down his back and he pulled a water bottle from the boot, drinking it all at once. Then he went back into the house. He shut the trap door and returned to the kitchen. He couldn't bring himself to open the water jug again and deprive Mabus of what might be his only means of survival here, but he was sorely tempted. Instead he went out the back door.

He came to a sudden halt. In front of a tool shed, the ground showed evidence of activity. Scuffle marks and little brown clumps of dirt looking very much like blood splatter. He squatted and gently touched one of the clumps. The moisture had not completely dried and a reddish hue stained his fingers. It was blood. He stood up, trying to make sense of what had happened. There were drag marks leading around the house. He followed them.

They took him past the bedroom window and all the way to the front of the house. Here the ground showed even more activity. Someone had come out the front door and gone down a slight incline on the eastern side of the house. There was a building down there, and when he reached it, he found a stable. There was a clipboard by the door with a note on it for Mabus: *Came by this afternoon. All is well with your beauty, but she'll be needing some more ointment for that shoulder laceration*. It was signed in a scribble he couldn't decipher. A camel keeper, no doubt, probably a man from the nearest town.

He went back outside and found a truck by the side of the building. It was hard to tell how long it had been there. On the floor of the front seat he found a book in English and a notepad with English writing on it, scribbles that meant nothing to him. He flipped open the glove compartment and found that the truck had been registered to SynTech. Could it be Eric's? If so, where was Eric?

He went back outside and studied the ground. Camel footprints led away from the building and due east into the dunes. He saw human footprints mingled with the camel's. The shoe size was small. It was possible that the camel had run off on its own. Or been set free by its owner. But the footprints indicated that someone had come out of the house and approached the camel. They had not released the animal and walked back up to the house. They had probably climbed on the camel and taken off.

He wished he were a Murrah; the men he knew from that tribe could have told him for sure whether the camel was carrying a burden. He bent over the footprints, pressed his palm into the sand as he'd seen the Murrah men do. The sand was hard-packed and not so easily indented. He couldn't tell how much weight it would have taken to make this print, but to him it seemed deep. And it must have been relatively recently, too, because the wind was only just blowing the topmost layer of sand away.

He walked back up to his car and looked at the ground around it. Unfortunately, the Rover had run over the other tracks that were there, and with the wind blowing up the looser sand, it was going to be impossible to tell how recently the last person had driven off. But what mattered was the absence of tracks: no one drove off into the desert. Whoever had come here had driven in on the trail Nayir himself had come in on and driven back out the same way. He turned back towards the stables. So who had taken the camel?

Quickly, before the wind obscured the tracks entirely, Nayir got back in the Rover and took off to the east, in the direction the camel had gone. The sky was growing darker now, still tinged with the same deep, ominous red. He drove through a gap between two high dunes. The sand was rippling down the edges, rising from the crests in sweeps. The air itself was gritty with particles.

He stopped at the base of the next dune and got out of the car. The camel prints led relentlessly forward, as far as his eye could see. The wind was slowly dusting them in sand from above. He had to get to higher ground, if only for a moment. From the back seat, he took his *shumagh* and wrapped it around his face, leaving his eyes exposed. He tied the canteen to his belt and stowed his emergency survival tin in his robe pocket, then set off for the top of the dune.

The wind was rising furiously, whipping his robe so harshly against his legs that he had difficulty climbing. The dune was too steep. He couldn't seem to make progress; for every step upwards he took, he seemed to sink a few feet lower. His heart was pounding with exertion, and the fiery wind was heating him like flame. Halfway up, he stumbled when a sheet of sand lashed his face, and before he knew it he was sliding back down the dune.

He promptly got back into the car and drove on, looking for a better dune. He just needed a little altitude to try to spot the camel. But the further he drove, the higher the dunes seemed to get. They were steep, some sheer like cliffs. The valley he was driving through began to get narrower, partly because of all the sand pouring down from the dunes. Soon there would be no more space for his Rover. It occurred to him that if anyone had come this way, eventually they would have had to scale a dune.

By now the wind had completely obscured the camel tracks and so he followed an invisible trajectory. Turning around a slight bend, he saw that the valley came to an end. Or rather, it narrowed enough to prohibit a car driving through, but not a camel. Now there was no choice but to drive back in reverse – it was too narrow to turn around – or head over the dune. It was a dangerous thing to do. The dune had a high, sharp peak. He wouldn't be able to stop at the top for fear of getting the Rover stuck on the zenith. How many times had he seen it, some giant SUV at the top of a dune, its wheels dangling uselessly on either side above the sand?

He backed up to get some space, then accelerated. He drove at an angle up the side of the dune. Twice, the car began to slip backwards, but he finessed it, giving the accelerator just the right touch and praying the entire time. *Traction, Allah, give me power and traction*. When he was just about to reach the peak, the Rover gave a groan. It was hanging at a forty-five degree angle and threatening to tip. It was impossible to see what lay on the other side of the dune, but it was equally impossible for him to get out of the car to check. In the time it would take him, the Rover's wheels could easily become buried in sand. He touched the accelerator gently, and with a jolt he shot forward, cresting the dune's peak, lurching forward down the other side, and gasping as he took in a horrifying landscape view: undulating dunes in the foreground, crashing like waves on a high sea, and beyond them a giant, pulsing, red wall of sand rising hundreds of metres into the sky and moving towards him like a desert tsunami.

He dropped over the edge of the dune, fighting panic. He was certain that he'd never done anything more stupid than this and equally certain that he was the only chance for whoever was on that camel. He quickly scanned the landscape and spotted something – a flicker of black in the descending orange and red glow. It could have been the shadow of a dust devil or a random piece of rubbish, but he had the feeling it wasn't.

The Rover surfed down the dune, skidding at the bottom. He saw with relief that there was enough space between dunes for him to drive for a while, at least long enough to build up enough speed to climb the next one. He gunned the engine as much as he dared; too much and he'd only dig trenches with the wheels. He kept the direction of the shadow he'd seen fixed in his mind, unmoving like the centre of the universe, and headed up the next dune.

This time he reached the peak without as much trouble, and coming down the other side he saw the shadow again, only this time closer. It was a camel after all, heading towards him down the side of a dune. There was someone on the camel's back but they were so hunched over, shrouded against the lashing wind and sand, that he couldn't make out if it was a man or a woman. For all he knew, it was Mabus he was racing off to rescue. But then it crossed his mind that only Miriam would be foolish enough to head into a sandstorm on the back of a camel – perversely, he hoped that it was true. He tried to stop the car to see the camel more clearly, but the Rover was sliding uncontrollably down the dune. At least he was getting closer.

The third dune proved impossible to scale. It was long, two hundred yards at least, and steeper than the ones he'd already gone over. Every time he tried to climb it, no matter the angle, the Rover slid sideways, forcing him back down. He zig-zagged up and down five times before he stopped. He couldn't turn around to try it again, and when he put the car in reverse and tried to drive backwards, he only found himself getting entrenched in sand. He had the feeling that if he kept going forward, he would lose his sense of direction, lose sight of the camel. Had its rider seen him? Probably not through all the dust and sand. He or she was only on the other side of the enormous dune.

Steeling himself, he got out of the car and stood for a moment at the bottom of the dune. From this vantage point, it was much steeper than it had seemed from behind the wheel. He went to the boot and took out the ropes, hanging them on his shoulder as he fished around for the pick-axe. He thought it had been among his supplies, but apparently not. He shut the boot and headed quickly up the dune.

It was faster going than the previous time. Despite the dune's angle, despite the pounding of his heart and the lashing wind – now so full of sand that it was almost impossible to keep his eyes open – he had a burst of adrenalin that sent him climbing like a goat. He forced his way to the crest and scanned the other side.

The camel was climbing towards him, slipping in the sand but making a desperate, valiant effort. On its back, the rider was crouched low, clutching the camel's neck with both arms. He saw a strand of brown hair and a flash of white arm. Miriam.

Nayir shouted but she couldn't hear him over the wind. He unwound the rope at his shoulder and shouted again. This time she looked up, squinting. Great sheets of sand blew between them, and the wind was so fierce at the top of the dune that Nayir was stumbling sideways. He shouted again.

He tied the rope end in a circle and slid the first few feet down the side of the dune. He had to get close enough to lasso the camel's neck, but not so far down that he would lose control and begin sliding. Miriam saw him, tried calling something, but all he heard was the faint strain of a woman's voice lost among the wind.

He fought against the wind to move to the right, then he threw the lasso. It missed, so he dragged it back and threw it twice again. The camel was slipping backwards now, Miriam gripping its neck in panic. He slid lower, stopping himself a few feet down, and threw the rope again. It hit Miriam's head and she sat up, grabbed it but missed. He threw it again. This time she caught it. She fumbled to put it around the camel's neck.

Nayir didn't see the rest. He glanced only once at the storm that was looming above them. The centre of the mass was a yellowish darkness, and above it, a tremendous red wall had been moving steadily closer so that its core was nearly upon them. It looked like a bright belt of fire shooting tongues of flame in every direction, deep scarlet and a few hundred feet wide.

He scrambled back to the top of the dune, a razor's edge now shooting sand straight into the sky. He slid down the other side, tugging with all his might, feeling the drag of the camel on the other side. He dug his legs into the sand and hung on to the rope, pulling and pulling until the camel appeared at the edge. It gave a jerk of surprise but found its footing and angled a path down the dune.

Nayir ran to meet it, holding tightly on to the rope. Miriam was shaking all over, clutching the beast's neck. He led the camel down the dune and for a panicked moment lost sight of his car. But the sand, falling in sheets, lifted and he saw the dim outline of the Rover. He made quickly for it, dragging the camel and Miriam in tow.

43

Face and arms raw from the burning wind, Nayir unwound his *shu-magh* and turned to Miriam. She was in the Rover's passenger seat, coughing and gagging, tears streaming down her face.

'Just breathe, Miriam,' he said, reaching quickly to the back seat for a spare headscarf and handing it to her. 'Here, use this.'

She took the scarf and coughed into it, breathing in ragged wheezes. She finally sat up, her whole torso still shaking from the effort of breathing. She put a hand on her chest and tried to talk but cringed in pain.

He reached back to find a water bottle. 'Drink some water. As much as you can.'

She took the bottle, wiped the tears from her cheeks with the back of her sleeve and took a tentative drink. She winced as she swallowed, blinking furiously.

'You'll be okay,' he said. 'Just keep coughing.'

She gave another obedient cough. It brought more tears to her eyes.

'I thought you were Mabus,' she croaked.

'Don't talk,' he said. 'Just keep drinking.'

He put the car in gear and began to pray, *Bism'allah, ar-rahman, ar-rahim* . . . When he touched the pedals, the wheels gave a jolt, but the car didn't move. He pressed harder on the accelerator. Again, nothing happened. He pressed a little harder and heard the wheels slip, spinning uselessly in the sand. 'Dammit.'

Miriam gave a soft moan of dismay.

His hands were shaking as he took them from the wheel. They had two choices now. Either try to push the car out of its rut, or stay where they were and wait out the storm. He looked past Miriam to the window. As the storm bore down, columns of swirling sand rose around them like angry geysers. Between heavy gusts of lentil-thick air, he saw the camel still standing there, taking its meagre shelter by the side of the car.

☽

Still blinking through tears, Miriam watched Nayir move with fluid strength as he collected a rope from the back seat and a frightening-looking knife in a black sheath which he belted to his waist. Then he climbed completely into the back seat and leaned over into the rear, hauling all of his gear forward. She watched him put on a pair of hiking boots.

'We're going to have to wait here until the storm blows past,' he said. 'It might be a long wait, but you can't be afraid, all right?' She nodded. 'Just relax,' he said. 'Breathe slowly, and you won't pass out.'

'Okay.'

'And whatever you do,' he said, looking straight at her, 'don't get out of the car.'

She nodded. He handed her another headscarf.

'What's this for?' she gurgled, coughing again.

'Help me get the camel into the boot.'

'What? Why?'

'Once the storm is over, the Rover is going to be stuck. It's going to take more than you and me to get it out. That camel will be our only way of getting back to the road by Mabus's house. We may even have to go further, to the next town. And who knows what the dunes are going to look like once this is over.' He motioned to the window. 'We might need the camel just to get out of here.'

'Okay. But is it going to fit?'

'It will be tight. Put this around your head. Tie it tightly and then wind this one around your face – including your eyes. Just leave a tiny slit. Take shallow breaths, and don't faint. Keep breathing no matter what.'

He bent into the rear once again and brought out a box of tissues. He tore one into strips and handed them to her. 'Put this in your ears. Get as much in there as you can. Hurry.'

He wrapped a piece of cloth over his nose and mouth and knotted it securely at the back of his head.

'I'll get out,' he said. 'But I want you to climb back here. I'll push the camel in, and you pull. Okay?'

'Okay.'

He covered his face and slipped out into the storm.

She balled the tissue and forced it into her ears, ignoring the pain and pressure of adjustment. She tightened the scarf around her head then tied the other one around her face as she'd seen Nayir do. Then she scrambled into the rear, climbing over the heaps of gear in the back seat.

The boot seemed much too small to hold a camel. With a wild roar and a flurry of sand, the door swung open, letting in a maelstrom. She squinted through it enough to see Nayir haul out two large jugs of fluid, probably petrol, and set them on the ground. The camel was standing beside him, the skinny old thing being lashed about like a kite in the wind. Nayir handed her the camel's reins and she took them and began pulling, but the beast only reared away. Miriam pulled harder.

The camel resisted. Nayir bent over, trying to force her to step on to the petrol canister, but the beast shook its head in an obvious sign of reluctance. The sand was blowing violently into the car. They were so close to the bottom of the dune that it was as if a line of men were standing just behind Nayir, tossing buckets of sand into the boot. Miriam noticed with alarm that the camel's legs were buried in sand to the knee, and that she was dancing to free her feet.

Miriam scrambled forward. All her pulling was doing nothing. She got out of the car on the camel's other side and they both bent down, grabbing the camel's legs, making a vain effort to lift it into the trunk, but they only managed to frighten the beast more. It was jumping up and down, shaking its head and making a terrible noise at the pit of its throat. Miriam went to grab the camel's reins again, but it kicked her hard in the leg and she fell backwards, into a churning pool of sand.

She screamed but only managed to let in a mouthful of sand. Struggling to sit up before the sand swallowed her, she flailed and turned over, getting more sand into her headscarf. It poured in like water, and she scrambled to her knees, spitting and blinking. She couldn't see anything. She stood up, but the wind lashed her so roughly that she lost her sense of direction. Moving blindly forward, hands outstretched, she tried to open her eyes but immediately regretted it. The sand cut her a new prescription in the one eye that didn't have a contact lens. She lurched forward, the sand rising to her knees. It was like swimming in rapids, untethered to land. Sand came in sheets from both sides, shifting like a pack of dogs on a lead. It blew particles up her nose. She couldn't breathe except in spasmodic gasps when her body forced her to take in air. She gasped, but her lungs rejected the fine granules of dirt and dust, closing off her throat, choking her. She wheezed. *Short little breaths, don't faint.*

A hand on her back. Nayir clutched her shoulder, wrapped his arm around her torso before she had the chance to blow away. He leaned against the solid air, forging brutal strides. Miriam's mind was far from thought, lost in the body; now she was her nose, pressing out sand. Now her hand, gripping Nayir's arm in the darkness.

Something dribbled over the ridge of her lip and slid into her

375

mouth at a jagged angle from the pressure of the wind. She tasted it. Blood. The sand whipped her like a million fragments of glass. Minuscule bullets of crystal and rock had torn into those parts of her face where the scarf had blown away. Her eyebrows and her nose were both wet with blood. She squeezed Nayir's arm to remind herself that he was there, that she hadn't slipped away and gone numb. She felt the strength of his hand, the solidity of his grip.

An eternity later and just when she was about to black out, she felt a sharp yank and was thrust into the car. The door slammed behind her as buckets of sand blasted on to her lap, across her face, and down the collar of her robe. She tore off her scarf and blinked, seeing fragments of light and darkness, the red of blood, grains of sand in her eyes. With her tongue, she stroked the inside of her cheek. Down in the gum line she extracted a coin of grit, spat it out. She used her fingers to scrape the rest of the sand from her mouth. She coughed again, then sneezed, ejecting a bitter muck on to her sleeve.

She opened one eye, tender and filling with tears, then the other. She was alone in the back seat.

She scrambled into the front. Sand was rising up the front window as if it were a turned hourglass. Had Nayir gone after the camel? Was he out there somewhere, suffocating in sand? She climbed across to the opposite window. She could see nothing. The light was dark red, turning to brown. She manoeuvred into the back seat and then into the boot. No matter where she went, she could only see sand.

She slumped on to the floor of the boot, her eyes stinging badly. She wiped them gingerly and felt wetness on her face. Her sleeve came away with blood and the pain was so sharp that she wanted to cry. She didn't resist. The tears, she thought, would at least clear the grit from her eyes.

She heard a sharp thud on the roof of the car, like a footstep.

Then another series of thuds, like a few people clattering about. She looked up. The car roof was slightly indented by the weight, so she climbed back towards the front, scrambling over the seat and falling to the floor, unable to move.

☽

A pounding above made her open her eyes. She saw the edge of a knife slice through the roof, get stuck and retract. Another thunderclap. More feet? The knife came in again and this time it stuck. She swallowed and felt a river of sand cut new grooves in her throat.

☽

Nayir waited for the sand to rise high enough so that he and the camel could climb on to the top of the car. It didn't take long. In that time, he tied another swatch of fabric round his face, then another, covering his eyes. He knew he had to work by touch alone. He tied the camel's reins to his torso, fastening them with a slip knot in case the poor beast got sucked beneath the sand.

Once the sand had begun to close its mouth around the Rover, he climbed from the hood on to the roof and took the knife from its sheath. It took some effort, but he managed to tie the rope to the end of the knife. All the while, the wind whipped torrents around him. He knelt down. With repeated jabs, he dug the knife into the car roof until it cut a thin hole and became wedged there. He pushed it in as deep as it would go, hoping Miriam had the sense to leave it alone.

The sand continued to climb. Every minute, he had to pull his feet out of the sand that had gathered around them. He packed the new sand beneath his shoes and made sure that the rope was still tied to his waist and that the camel's reins hadn't slipped away. As the minutes went by, he felt his clothing being shredded, felt the wind strip an old layer of skin from his body. He oscillated between feeling numbness and a raw, burning pain.

More than that, he prayed that the camel would last at least until the worst of the storm had passed. Not only was the camel his main protection from the wind, but if it fell, it would be impossible to lift her above the new layers of sand that formed every moment. Nayir pulled himself close to the camel's face and felt for the mouth. Despite choking on a fistful of sand, the camel seemed well. Nayir pried open the sides of its mouth to swipe out the dirt but only succeeded in letting more in. The camel sputtered and clucked. It stood perfectly still, an animal in fright, snorting mechanically through large sticky nostrils caked with a layer of sand and snot.

☽

Below, Miriam stared at the knife tip poking down from the roof. She figured it was an anchor of sorts, a means of finding her once the sandstorm had ended. But she had no faith that Nayir was surviving above her, that he wasn't being strangled by sand.

A few minutes later, she noticed a thin layer of sand pouring in around the edges of the knife. It formed a small mountain in the backseat. She touched the sand around the knife with her hand, and it spilled to the side, letting in more.

She climbed up from the floor, awakened by panic. Reaching up, she tried pinching the hole in the roof shut with her fingers. It took two hands to stop the downpour. Five minutes of exertion and she dropped her arms.

She pulled the tissue from her ears and stuffed it into the edges. It wasn't as strong as her finger and it held for less than thirty seconds before popping out, sending sand shooting into her hair. She rummaged through the equipment for something sturdy and found a roll of electrical tape. Scraping her nail along the roll, she found the end and pulled a strip. She stuffed the tissue back into

378

the hole then patched the whole thing with what must have been six feet of tape. It seemed to hold.

She climbed into the front seat. She wasn't sure why she felt more comfortable there – perhaps because it was the most open space in the car. She fidgeted, wiping her eyes, trying not to think about how long she had left, how much oxygen remained. Occasionally, she stared up at the knife, now bundled in tape, wishing it could resonate and bring her news from above.

☽

Nayir climbed higher. Small notches in the rope marked the places where it had been bent in its packaging. He counted them with his hands, feeling each curve, ticking off numbers as he passed. He guessed that he had risen two feet. They hadn't even seen the worst of it yet. The wind, although powerful, was still directionless and choppy. The heart of the storm would be fierce, lashing him from one direction with a force capable of lifting a car. The rope that tied him to the camel was cutting into his skin and now soaked in blood. He hoped that when they hit the centre of the storm, he would still have the strength to hold on.

☽

Miriam wondered if Nayir was always this brave, or if he only switched on in dangerous situations. She closed her eyes. She felt suddenly hot, so she stripped off her cloak. A minute later, almost all of her clothing came off and she lay across the front seat, gasping for air in the sand-choked car, and in the odd moments of lucidity, wondering why everything was so dark.

☽

Nayir was fighting unconsciousness when the vortex hit. Even though he had slipped into a dreamlike state, all orifices plugged by the deluge of sand, he could sense that the worst was upon them. The wind seized him like a large, clumsy hand and carried him up, way beyond the pinnacles of the mosques and the noble cube of the Ka'aba. He felt his body at a slant, anchored only by the cord around his chest. He was a carpet, sailing in a fairy-tale dream. A thrashing kite. Between the moments of vertigo, he was aware of a certain dead weight by his side. The camel, free-floating and whipping around him like the sand itself. He kept his eyes closed and prayed for the sky.

44

The hand that gripped the rope awakened and squeezed. He felt his shoulder respond. He was still strapped to the rope.

He lifted his head, shook it. The sand fell away. Eyes came open. Darkness became bluish, he blinked and felt the tears chasing crust from his eyes.

When he tried to move his legs, he could feel that they were buried in the ground. He wiggled his arms instead, freed the right one that was tangled in the rope and busied himself kicking and struggling until he managed to climb on to the new layer of earth.

It was dark, but the landscape was bathed in moonlight. He peeled the scarves from his face and saw that they were wet and dark: blood-stained. He continued blinking, letting the tears clean his eyes, and found the spot where the rope was sunk in the ground. He knelt unsteadily and began digging away, but the sand was too loose. Every cavern he dug only filled up again.

The camel was lying some distance away, its head poking out of the sand like a gravestone. Nayir's eyes were still blurry but he went to the animal. It was dead. Sticking his arms in the sand, he could feel that the beast was lying on its side. Reaching even deeper, he was able to find the animal's pack and retrieve the Swiss army knife he'd stowed there after he'd tried, unsuccessfully, to coax the camel into the boot of the car. Using the knife, he made a thin cut along the camel's neck. The trickle of blood that came out was enough to dampen the sand, and he was able to excavate the animal's trunk so that the stomach was half-exposed to the sky.

The sight of the blood gave him a crazy idea, something he'd heard from a Bedouin once. He released the pack and hauled it on to the sand. He removed the canteen and took a long drink. Then he picked up the knife.

Slicing deep through fur, peeling back skin and muscle, he exposed the camel's belly. Now that his eyes had adjusted, the moonlight seemed sufficient and he was able to liberate a long section of the animal's intestines, scooping them out with care and laying them on the canvas of the pack. It took him a while to unwind them and find the ends, but when he did, he sliced them off cleanly and turned back to the heart. A minute later, he was drawing the animal's blood into the safe channels of the intestines by sucking through one end like a straw. When he started to taste blood in his mouth, he spat, knotted both ends, laid the length of guts out like a rope and dragged it to the place where he had dug himself free.

Yanking gently at the rope, he swept away the sand, and, cutting a hole in the end of the intestines, squeezed them to spray blood on the sides of the small hole, aiming it like a garden hose, patting it firm, pushing it back, widening the hole wherever possible.

He dug with relentless concentration, throwing bloody sand to the surface in handfuls, until he felt the hard metal of the Rover beneath his feet. He looked around. The top of the hole he had dug barely reached his hip. He scraped enough sand from the roof of the car to kneel down there. He banged on the roof. 'Miriam!' he shouted. 'Miriam!!' He wiggled the knife and felt the roof of the car shudder slightly.

Jerking out the knife, he plunged it in again and began to saw, grunting with the effort, all the while shouting Miriam's name and getting no response. He wasn't strong enough to cut into the roof, and neither was the knife. It snapped, the handle breaking cleanly away. Cursing, he stood up and fumbled for the intestines. There was a little blood left, and he began to work on the sides of the trench, widening it towards what he hoped was the rear of the car. He finally reached the side window. Digging down far enough, he took out his Swiss army knife and began banging on the glass. It took three tries before it cracked. He pushed the pieces in, careful not to let in too much sand.

He stuck his head in first and looked around. A crumpled form lay on the front seat. He could see the faint white of her skin in the darkness. He dived in quickly, ploughing through the heap of sand on the floor, bending into the front seat. Miriam was lying there in her underclothes. He placed a hand on her neck, felt the soft thump of blood. A pause. *Thump.*

He rummaged for his canvas tarpaulin. He shoved his gear off the seat and spread the canvas there. Angling his hands beneath Miriam's shoulders, he lifted her over the front seat and laid her gently on the canvas. He wrapped the ends around her and tied them in a knot. She didn't stir. The air around him smelled of her scent, not unappealing, green like trees in a morning dew.

A few minutes later, he had her out of the car and was lifting her up, pulling her to the surface until her body hit the moonlight and rolled on to the ground with a thud. Then, before the tunnel collapsed, he went back below, pulling up water and rations, her clothing, his mobile, and the tent. He poured water down Miriam's throat, just a small trickle, but she didn't respond.

Face caked red with blood, hair sprinkled white, he wandered off to perform a different kind of ablution, to scrape the dirt from his clothing and body with sand and spit, if he had any left.

45

There were two aspects of silence, one transcendent, eliminating the ego and filling a person with sensations of connecting to a universal spirit of consciousness. The other was a negation of everything, a frightening loss of one's sense of time and identity, a cruel sensory deprivation. He was experiencing the latter now.

Beside him, Miriam lay in a semi-conscious daze, a sheet of wet canvas rolling around her head, intermittently moaning or asking for water, but mostly unresponsive. The periods of silence were filled with the worrying whisper of the *djinn*.

By the time she'd woken, the sun had come up. She'd drunk water and fallen asleep again. Now she lay beneath the tent he had pitched to protect them from the sun. He didn't have the strength to carry her back to Mabus's house, and he didn't want to leave her alone. She was too weak. Anyway, he wasn't even sure where Mabus's house was, or if Mabus would be there, and in what state. But they couldn't stay here. According to his keychain thermometer, the temperature was already reaching thirty-nine Celsius, and it was only eight o'clock. The problem was that they didn't have transportable water; they had a five-gallon jug, which was too big to carry. Anyway, he would be carrying Miriam. Otherwise, they only had the small canteen and a few plastic bottles in the Rover, not enough to last them. In daylight, with the water they could carry, they could walk maybe seven kilometres before collapsing; by night they could do forty. They would strike west at nightfall, a little sooner if the wind picked up. Hopefully, they could reach the main road.

The tent was a canvas tarpaulin with four poles; it formed a three-sided enclosure like the Bedouin tents he loved so well, and he was grateful to the Amirs for having thought to pack it. The open side of the tent was covered in a dark blue screen that rolled down from the top and let in the air. It was sweltering, but it would have been worse without the screen.

'No one's coming,' she rasped, lifting her head.

'They know I'm out here,' he said, sitting up at the sound of her voice. 'They have the coordinates.' But as he said it, he felt the shame of lying. No one knew where he was, not even Samir. He ought to have at least called his uncle before leaving, but it had been too early in the morning, and by the time he'd thought it would have been prudent – namely, right as he'd reached Mabus's house – he'd been too far out of mobile range. The chances of anyone stumbling on this part of the desert were close to zero.

He glanced at the sand outside the tent door. The ridges of their footprints were just beginning to move in the first stirring of wind. The fairy tales he'd heard as a child always began with the words *kan ya ma kan* – it was, and it was not. He'd come to associate those words with the desert. One moment a foot would break the sand, and the next it would be gone, wiped away by an oblivious wind. Like his Rover, now sitting beneath three feet of sand. Like the camel, blackening in the sun. And like some part of himself that, two days ago, had thought prayer and propriety were antidote enough to what ailed the world.

'Where are we?' she asked.

'We're in the desert,' he said.

She shut her mouth and closed her eyes. Nayir did the same. He fancied he could hear something coming from the west, but after a moment of silence, he decided it was only his imagination.

Outside, a noise.

Nayir scrambled out of the tent. If it was a plane, any sound would indicate that it had already gone past. He had one flare, and he didn't want to waste it. He began systematically scanning the sky.

Suddenly, a Toyota Land Cruiser bounded over the dune in front of him. Nayir reached for the flare, his only weapon in case it was Mabus, but as the truck came closer, he saw two uniformed officers sitting in the front. They both looked relieved, and one of them leaned out the window.

'*Salaam aleikum!*' the man yelled. 'Nayir Sharqi?'

A few minutes later, Nayir was lifting Miriam into the SUV.

46

Osama stared across the interrogation table at Apollo Mabus. The suspect had his hands at his temples in an aspect of prayer. He certainly wasn't a Muslim, but that's what it looked like. His eyes were shut, his mouth moved as if muttering to angels on his shoulders, and every now and then his head fell forward as if in submission.

He didn't seem so tough any more. Fortunately, the police in Qaryat al-Faw had caught up with him just before the sandstorm struck, and just after Mabus had unloaded two bodies from his boot and left them lying in the desert. The police actually spotted him driving away from the site. The tracks his truck left in the sand were enough to indicate that he was the only one who could have dumped the bodies there. When they'd arrested him, he'd first of all claimed he had no idea what they were talking about, then that he'd only gone out there to find the bodies because he'd received an anonymous phone call saying they were there. A forensics sweep of his boot proved that he was lying.

After the sandstorm, they had done a thorough search of his desert house as well. The storm hadn't damaged the interior of the house; it had only blown a truckload of sand into the garage. Osama hadn't gone out, but he had seen the photos of the sad little shed that stood behind the house, with one of the local forensics guys bent over the dirt floor. Mabus claimed he had no idea that Eric had been held there, but the hair and fibres they'd collected showed that he had.

'It was an accident,' Mabus said softly.

'An accident?' Osama breathed. 'You left Eric Walker in a shack in the middle of the Empty Quarter. You can't call—'

'I mean hitting him,' Mabus said. 'It was an accident.'

Osama was quiet. The autopsy had been unable to determine exactly when Walker died, but Mabus didn't know that. 'Well, you see,' Osama said, 'on a normal day, you can hit a man on the head and he just needs a few days of rest to get over it. But when you hit him like that and then you take him to the desert, his blood volume goes up, the heat swells the body, and the blood vessels start to burst.'

'He was dead when I brought him out there.'

Osama made a note.

'I didn't mean for him to die.'

'And Jacob? Did you mean to kill *him*?'

'That was self-defence. He was the one with the gun.'

Mabus was right; the gun had belonged to Jacob. Osama looked hard at the man across the table. At his desert house they'd found two Swiss bank account statements and the deeds to a block of flats in Jeddah under the name of Wahhab Nabih. Mabus had already confessed to using the alias. He had also revealed that he had a British mother and an Egyptian father. Apollo's real name was Apollo Mabus Mansour, but he'd dropped his surname when his father had left – twenty-five years ago, when Apollo was sixteen. The father had run off and taken a second wife, leaving his first wife with a large sum of money. She hadn't used it, though. She'd died of cancer two years later, and the money had been left to Mabus. This had all come out in the preliminary interrogation. He'd also stated that he'd grown up in London, New York and Jeddah, but that none of those places had ever felt like home. He preferred being in the desert.

Again Mabus shut his eyes and pressed his fingers to his temples. Nayir had brought most of Mabus's academic work from the desert house. Thankfully he'd thought to carry it out of his Land Rover before leaving the site where the SUV had been buried. From a colleague of Mabus's in London, Osama had learned that Mabus's work was not fashionable in academic circles, and that these days most critical scholars were reluctant to publish his articles, fearing a backlash from Islamic sources. The colleague also said that Mabus was not religious. He described Apollo as an intellectual 'crusader' whose research had pushed him to the fringes of the academic world. He'd lost his teaching post in Britain the year before, and there did seem to be a zealotry in his ambition. He had devoted himself quietly for many years to a single goal: trying to show that the Muslim holy texts were not as pure as people believed.

'Let's talk about Leila,' Osama said.

For the first time, Mabus met his eye. 'I had nothing to do with that. That was all your people. Hell, that was why I fought with Eric in the first place.'

Osama narrowed his eyes, listened.

'Haven't you figured out yet why they got to Leila?'

'Tell me.'

'Because she was working with *me*. Because a Muslim woman shouldn't touch what I'm doing. That's why Leila was killed. They got to her.' He had a mad look in his eye now.

'Who got to her?'

'Who the fuck do you think? The religious freaks that run this country.'

'Are you talking about someone in particular, Mr Mabus?'

Mabus looked at him as if he were a total idiot. 'Don't tell me you don't know how these men think. Someone steps out of line, someone breaks their little rules, and they go for the jugular. That's all. That's their answer.'

389

Osama cut him off. 'Did anyone ever threaten you because of your work?'

'They didn't have to—'

'Did anyone ever threaten Leila?'

'I don't know. Sure, she was threatened all the time!'

'Because of your work?'

'Probably!'

'Do you have any proof – any proof at all – that anyone else even knew about what you were doing?'

'I didn't need proof!' Mabus exploded. 'Leila's death was proof!'

Osama felt sorry for the man. He was totally paranoid. It was true that his work was deeply blasphemous, and if some fiery cleric found out about it, he might have felt it his duty to silence Mabus. But why target Leila? Just because she was a Muslim?

He just couldn't bring himself to believe it. The whole thing seemed ludicrous. Yes, occasionally there was violence in the name of religion here, but in his experience, there was more violence in the name of everyday things: a broken wedding vow, a quiet theft. What was it with these foreigners? They could live here for years and still only think the worst of the place.

Mabus had been alienated from his academic peers because his work did not please fashionable British scholars and because it might upset Muslim scholars as well. At the same time, Mabus was an Arab man who seemed to feel more at home in the Saudi desert than in the cool libraries of a Western university. Yet he acted as if the Saudi establishment were out to get him. He holed himself up in the desert and conducted secretive research. He was a man without allies, and Osama pitied him.

But for someone so reclusive, Mabus had been surprisingly bold in allowing Leila to film him in the hope that one day his work would be made public.

'I warned Eric and Jacob,' Mabus said, 'I warned them both that if they told anyone about my work, they'd be in danger. I guess I warned the wrong people, because the freaks went for Leila instead.'

'Let's go back a little bit,' Osama said. 'How did you first meet Leila?'

The sudden shift to a practical question took Mabus by surprise. He tried to make a casual gesture but his hands were still shaking. 'I met her through Eric.'

'And how did you meet Eric?'

'Jacob introduced us. I'd known Jacob for years. I met Eric when he first came here; he needed an apartment and I own a building here in Jeddah, so I rented him a place.'

'And you became friends with him?'

'No. I didn't see him at all until just about five weeks ago. Jacob brought him over. Eric's wife had just left town and they wanted to spend a week at my house in the desert.'

'I see.' Osama glanced at his notes. 'So the three of you planned a trip to the desert?'

'Yes.'

'And how did Leila get involved?'

'Eric wanted to bring her along. He had just met her. He described her as this young, passionate woman who wanted adventure and couldn't seem to get enough of it in Jeddah. I said it was all right, so she came with him to the desert. That's how we met.'

'And how did the documentary idea come about?'

Mabus sighed. 'Eric was right – she was passionate. I'd only known her for a couple of hours before she started asking about my work. Most people don't give a shit – except highly righteous idiots who get paranoid that I'm going to insult their religion. She wasn't like that at all. She was damn smart and curious and she wanted to know everything. She was fascinated, that was obvious. After our first conversation, she was already planning the documentary.'

'And you agreed to it?'

'Yes, I agreed to it. I was sick of being sidelined by conservatives and by the academic cowards who are afraid to look at the truth. I decided it was time to take the whole thing in a different direction – to the public. Making a documentary was the perfect way to do it. And all those academic bastards? I figured they could go to hell. They're just afraid of pissing off the Muslim world anyway. They live in fear, and you can't find the truth when you live in fear.'

'Is that why you live here?'

'I don't live here. I live in different places.'

'Fine,' Osama said. 'Then why do you come here – probably the one place your theories could get you into trouble?'

It took Mabus a minute to gather his thoughts. 'I come here for research. And to check on my properties. But I also come because I have to know – I have to *prove to myself* that I'm not afraid of this bullshit . . .' He trailed off. Osama sensed that the real reason Mabus came back here would be forever out of his ken, and that even if he did comprehend it one day, he had too much pride to articulate it. It wasn't a tough reason, whatever it was. It felt soft, like nostalgia for a mother's caress.

'So Leila started filming you in the desert,' Osama said.

Mabus nodded firmly. 'I wanted to do most of the filming there.'

'Why?'

'It was safer that way. Nobody was going to come nosing around.' He looked to Osama as if expecting he would finally see sense, that he would come to understand, through this simple discussion of pragmatic detail, that Mabus's view of the world was justified. Osama wanted to tell him that he might be able to claim insanity.

'Was Jacob there that weekend?' Osama asked.

'Yeah. Eric really wanted to get out to the Empty Quarter. I think Jacob just came because he was attracted to Leila and because he never says no to a trip to the desert.'

'So Leila filmed you and then what?'

'She came back here, to Jeddah. We did some more filming the next weekend at my flat. She took pictures of the codex.' He paused, swallowed hard. 'She was *supposed* to put together a sample cut of the documentary, but she never got back to me. A week later, I called her. She said it was taking longer than expected but she'd have it for me soon. The next week she disappeared.'

'How did you find out that she had disappeared?'

'Eric told me. He kept calling her mobile but it wasn't working so he called her cousin. He told Eric she was missing. You can imagine I freaked out. Eric had no idea where she was. He was closer to her than I was, and *he* couldn't find her. He seemed to think it was my fault and gave me an earful on the phone.'

'Why did he think it was your fault?'

'Because he knew what I was doing and I'd warned him it was dangerous. But you know what I think? He didn't listen to my warning. He'd told somebody and he was feeling guilty about it and so he went off on me – I mean, that night at his house, he got really angry, started accusing me of endangering his wife. But it was all to hide the fact that it was *his* fault for blabbing.'

'So you got angry at him?'

Mabus sat back and crossed his arms. 'This is bullshit,' he said. 'I'm not admitting to murder.'

Osama tried a different tack. 'Were Eric, Jacob, and Leila the only ones who knew about your work?'

'Yeah, and whoever else Eric told.'

'Did you suspect Jacob of revealing your secrets?'

'No, Jacob wasn't smart enough to get it, and he didn't give a shit about the implications.'

393

'And you trusted Leila,' Osama said.

'Yes. Leila respected my work. She believed in what I was doing. I knew she would never tell anyone until she was ready – I mean, until the documentary was ready.'

'But you have to admit that it's possible she could have—'

'No.' Mabus shook his head resolutely. 'She would never have told anyone.'

'Why did you trust Eric?' Osama asked. 'His wife says he would never have supported anything that would denigrate Islam.'

Mabus let out a sarcastic *Ha!* 'What does she know about anything?' he barked. 'I'll tell you this, I only knew Eric for a month, but I knew more about her husband than she did.'

'Apparently, Eric was very sympathetic to Saudi culture, and to Islam,' Osama said. 'He didn't like anyone speaking ill of it. So tell me this, Mr Mabus, what happened when this sympathetic man came with you to the desert, spent a weekend watching Leila film you while you explained what exactly your research was all about?'

'He got disgusted, that's what happened!' Mabus snarled. 'I see where you're going with this, but you've got it wrong. He didn't threaten to expose me, he *did* expose me. And as I just said, that's probably what set this whole horrible thing in motion.'

'Why did you leave the country?'

Mabus hesitated, still looking flushed. 'I had planned that trip for a long time,' he said carefully. 'I figured it was better if I left anyway. In case something was up – you know, they might come after me next.'

Osama regarded him. 'Yet you came back from New York a few days later and sat next to Miriam Walker on the plane.'

Mabus looked angry again, his face was reddening and his shoulders tightened. He lowered his head bullishly. 'What's your point?'

'You slipped something into her bag.' Osama pulled the memory card out of the folder and held it up. Mabus didn't say a word. 'We know what's on this card. You were bringing false copies of the Quran into the country illegally.'

Mabus glowered at him. 'I purchased some research materials that I'd been wanting to get my hands on for a long time. And they are not false copies of the Quran. They are authentic, early copies – the earliest copies ever found – and just because it doesn't agree with *your* perspective doesn't mean it's wrong.' His tone had all the juvenile defensiveness of a man who knew he was guilty but would never admit it.

'And you bought these in New York?' Osama asked with just the right tone of disbelief.

'That's where the seller chose to do the transaction,' Mabus barked. 'And it had nothing to do with Leila, okay? Nothing. It was something I'd been trying to get my hands on for a long time.'

'You already had similar documents in your desert house.'

'These were very different,' Mabus said, motioning to the memory card. 'They're from a totally different cache from the ones at the house. I was comparing the two sets. Like I keep telling you – *this was for my research*. It had nothing to do with Leila.'

'And how is it that you got them into Miriam's bag?'

'I couldn't risk being caught with it at the airport, and I knew Miriam was coming back from the States. I figured I'd use her.'

'How did you know when Miriam was coming back?'

'Eric told me.' Mabus scowled in frustration, as if Osama should have figured this out himself. 'I realised she was coming back around the same time that I would be flying back from New York. I knew I could use her to get the documents into the country. I was going to make it look like a coincidence. I'd slip the card into her bag and get it back from her once she went through customs.'

'So you arranged to sit next to her on the plane?'

'Yes, yes.' Mabus waved his hand in annoyance. 'I arranged everything. It wasn't that hard to figure out, and I wasn't going to pass up the opportunity.'

'I'm just wondering, Mr Mabus, why you thought it was a good idea to put these documents in the possession of Eric's wife? What if he'd found out?'

'I did appreciate the irony of the situation, yes.'

'Irony? It seems a bit spiteful to me, considering that you knew how Eric felt about your work. It also seems like an enormous risk. Because if he had found out about these documents, and he was indeed the one who had exposed you, who knows what would have happened if he found out you were using his wife as a mule?'

Mabus exhaled slowly. 'Like I said, it was an opportunity.'

'And how were you planning to get the materials back from her?'

'It didn't matter. I'd steal her bag or something. What mattered was that the card was safe and I knew where it was.'

Osama sat back and regarded Mabus with disgust. 'You didn't intend for her to take the memory card home?'

'No! But after she got out of customs, she got pulled into security, that special room they have for unescorted women, so I didn't have a choice. Eric would have to get her out of there, and he wasn't there. I waited outside the airport until I saw Eric going in. I followed him and Miriam home. Right after they got home, Eric left again, so I went upstairs. I had to get that memory card. It was more valuable to me than anything else in the world. I knocked twice, but no one answered.'

'So you kidnapped Eric to get the memory card back?' Osama asked.

'No.' Mabus ran a hand through his hair. 'No, he came back just as I was leaving. He caught me on the stairs and freaked out. He thought I was going for his wife or something. I swear to God he was a loose cannon. He threatened to call the *police*.' Mabus said this with complete disbelief and a touch of self-righteousness. 'He still thought I had something to do with Leila's disappearance.'

'And that's when you hit him?'

'It was an accident. We were on the landing outside his flat. He was a strong guy, and he was grabbing my shirt.' Mabus motioned to his chest. 'He threw me up against the wall and started threatening me in a soft voice, like he was going to kill me right then. I didn't know what was happening. I really thought he was going to kill me. I was trying to talk some sense into him, but he wouldn't listen.'

Abruptly, Mabus shut up. He sat back and crossed his arms. Osama knew that he wanted to say more, but this was the part where – in Mabus's mind at least – he would be admitting to murder.

'So you hit him back,' Osama said.

'Yeah, I hit him back.'

'How?'

'I waited until he released me then I sprang at him. Knocked him backwards. I didn't see what I was doing, I just wanted to get him out of the way, so I could get to the stairs. I was hoping to knock him out, but I accidentally knocked him towards the stairs. He fell down them. He must have hit his head on the concrete steps. I heard a crack, and I knew immediately that it was bad. I went down, saw that he wasn't breathing. He was staring at the ceiling. He was dead.' Mabus looked around in confusion, as if he still couldn't grasp how quickly a man could die.

'So you tried to rouse him?'

'He wouldn't wake up. He was dead, I'm telling you. I was going to leave him there, but I knew that if anyone had seen me, they'd be able to identify me too easily.' He gestured pathetically to his head of blond hair. His hands were shaking. 'I had to get him out of there. So I picked him up and put my arm around his chest. Trying to make it down the stairs. None of the neighbours noticed. I doubt they even heard it, it sounded like everyone was watching TV. I got him down to the street and I put him in the front seat, like some passed-out friend. Then I took off.'

'And you brought him to the desert.'

'He didn't wake up,' Mabus said urgently. 'I kept telling myself he'd come to, this was my stupid panic, but I drove around for three hours and he didn't wake up.'

Osama suspected that Mabus, in a situation like that, would not have needed three hours to come to grips with his mistake, if that's how long it had really been.

'I took him to the desert,' Mabus went on more calmly. 'I had to get him out of there. So I started driving. I didn't have a plan, I just had to get him somewhere where no one would find his body. I kept stopping on the motorway, thinking I would dump him somewhere, but nowhere seemed safe and before I knew it, I was at the house in Qaryat. Nobody was going to come looking for him out there.' Mabus threw himself back against his chair. 'I'd had a bad feeling from the beginning. I should never have got involved with that guy.'

'So you hid his body in the shed?' Osama asked.

'I didn't have time to bury him. The only guy who comes out there is the camel keeper, and he had already come that week. And anyway, he never comes to the house. He goes to the stables and leaves again. Just to be safe, I locked the shed. I had to get back to Jeddah to get the memory card from Miriam, but by the time I got back, I couldn't find her.' His voice was rising again, his whole body rippling with angry heat.

'You went to her flat?'

'Yes. She wasn't home. I had a key to the place, obviously, so I let myself in. It looked like she'd left. I couldn't find the memory card. I figured she had it on her. I didn't stay in the flat that long, but I waited around outside on and off for two days.'

'And how did you catch her?'

'I was heading back to my house in the city, and when I got out of my car, I saw a woman going in my front door. I wasn't sure who it was, so I followed her.'

'And you kidnapped her?'

'I just needed to get her somewhere quiet where I could ask her about the memory card.'

'Where did you take her?'

'A hotel near Abha. She told me she'd already given the memory card to the police.' Mabus paused, clearly still angry about the loss. 'I didn't have a choice then but to take her to the desert house. If I let her go, she'd go straight to the police.'

'I see,' Osama said. 'And what about Eric's car?'

'Yeah, I had to get rid of that, too. I had to make it look like he ran away.'

'How did you find it? According to Miriam Walker, it was parked a few blocks away from the house.'

'Yeah, I know. But I figured he couldn't have parked it too far away, and I knew what it looked like. He'd driven it to the desert.'

'And how did you get the keys?'

'From Eric. He had them when he fell down the stairs, so I put them in my pocket.'

Osama nodded. 'Mr Mabus, you are responsible for the deaths of Eric Walker and Jacob Marx,' he said. 'The courts will decide your sentence, not me.'

These words seemed to have no effect on Mabus. He didn't even have the grace to look ashamed. 'I told you it was an accident. And I had nothing to do with Leila's murder. That was *you*.'

☽

Nayir exited through the hospital's sliding glass doors, feeling foolish with his arm in a sling. Somehow in the desert escapade, he'd fractured his shoulder. The air was a blast of gagging heat, but inside him was a chill left over from spending six hours in the ward. He shuddered involuntarily and looked around for Samir. Instead, he saw Osama leaning against a patrol car parked by the kerb.

'*Salaam aleikum*,' Nayir said.

Osama greeted him happily and opened the car door. 'Don't worry,' he said, 'the hog rally's left town.'

'My uncle is supposed to meet me,' Nayir said.

'I told him I'd pick you up,' Osama replied. 'He was glad not to have to take a taxi.'

Nodding, Nayir got into the car. The first question that rose to the surface of his mind – How is Katya? – disappeared with a pop. He didn't want to know whether Osama actually knew the answer. Despite feeling admiration for – and now gratitude to – Osama, Nayir still couldn't bring himself to approve of the fact that Osama saw more of Katya than he did.

'How is Miriam?' he asked. He knew she had been taken straight to a hospital in Qaryat al-Faw. After learning that she was going to be all right, Nayir had come back to Jeddah, hitching a ride with one of the Qaryat police.

'I'm bringing you to see her,' Osama said.

'Where is she?'

'She arrived in Jeddah last night.'

Nayir wondered if Katya knew any of this. She must have heard about what happened in the desert. No doubt the police officer from Qaryat had described the sandstorm, which meteorologists were already calling one of the worst of the century, and the surprising discovery of two people in a tent above a buried car. What would Katya be left to surmise from that? Would she think Nayir had been heroic? Stupid? Deceitful?

'We caught Mabus,' Osama said. 'Eric Walker and Jacob Marx are dead.'

Nayir listened as Osama described what they'd discovered and filled in the back story of Eric's disappearance.

'Do you think Mabus killed Leila?' Nayir asked.

Osama chewed this over for a while, and then answered in an uncertain voice. 'No.'

Nayir's mobile rang and he fumbled to answer it.

'Mr Sharqi?'

'Yes.' Nayir didn't recognise the voice, but it was American and that alarmed him.

'Mr Sharqi, this is Taylor Shaw from SynTech. We spoke a few days ago about Eric Walker.'

Had it only been a few days ago? It felt like weeks. 'Yes, Mr Shaw.' Nayir's mind was racing. He glanced at Osama, who gave him a quizzical look. If his right arm hadn't been in a sling, Nayir would have used the pen and notepad that was cleverly affixed to the dashboard to write out a question: *Does Eric's boss know that he's dead?*

'I'm calling because we've located that missing surveillance equipment,' said Mr Shaw. 'Apparently, the box had been stored in the wrong place.'

'Ah,' Nayir replied. 'So it wasn't stolen after all.'

'Well, we're still not sure. There were a few things in the box that didn't belong there. We do still suspect that Walker took the equipment, but I think he left something behind. I've tried calling the police, but they won't tell me how to get in touch with Eric. I was hoping you could help.'

Nayir sucked in a deep breath. 'Mr Shaw, I'm afraid I must tell you that Eric Walker is dead.'

This was met by silence. Finally, Mr Shaw cleared his throat. 'God. I'm so sorry to hear that.'

'I'd be glad to come by and collect his things,' Nayir said quickly. 'I'm sure his wife would like to have them.'

'Yes. Yes, of course.' Shaw seemed stunned. 'I'm sorry. Was it an accident?'

'Yes.' Nayir didn't feel like explaining. 'Will you be in the office later this afternoon?'

They agreed to meet the next day, since Shaw had a meeting in Riyadh that afternoon, and wouldn't fly back until tomorrow. Nayir thanked him and got off the phone.

'That was Eric's boss,' he said. 'He was trying to get answers from the police.'

Osama shook his head, obviously upset. He gave a resigned sigh. 'Good of you to tell him.'

Nayir noticed that they had arrived at a hospital. Osama pulled into an indoor car park across the street, and they got out of the car. 'Miriam's still in the hospital?' Nayir asked, trying not to sound panicked.

'She's just resting,' Osama said. 'She didn't want to go back to her flat.'

When they reached the street, Nayir felt like racing into the building, but they were distracted by a loud argument happening some twenty feet away, in front of a small clothing shop.

A woman was standing on the street with her teenage son. She was shouting loudly at what appeared to be a religious policeman. She wasn't wearing a headscarf and she had an expression of complete outrage on her face. The *mutawwa* was wearing the predictable shin-length white robe. He kept his gaze on the ground, looking up once to shoot the woman's son a silent plea.

'This is not the Najd!' the woman was shouting. 'This is not Riyadh! Do you think I have to listen to you? Do you?' She was holding a brown shopping bag and shaking it at him with every sentence. Its contents rattled and clinked.

The *mutawwa* looked as if he were controlling his temper by the thinnest of margins. 'It is sinful for a woman to be seen without a *hijaab*.'

To Nayir's dismay, Osama walked briskly towards the scene.

'Excuse me,' Osama said, flashing his badge. 'What's going on here?'

The *mutawwa* turned to him gratefully. The woman, on the other hand, seemed to regard Osama as another *mutawwa*, and she flew into a fury. She ripped open her shopping bag and dumped out its contents. A pair of brightly coloured children's toys crashed on to the pavement. Then she flung the shopping bag over her head and shouted: 'There! Are you satisfied? Are you?' She turned in a circle, arms outstretched, mimicking a blind man. 'Ahmad? Is that you? Can you take your poor mother's hand and guide her home, since she can't see a damn thing?' Nearby pedestrians who had stopped to watch the scene were now chuckling. The *mutawwa* was looking angrier every second. 'Are you sure you're Ahmad?' the woman said. 'What if you're only *saying* you're my son? You see, I can't tell. You could be anyone!'

Finally losing his cool, the *mutawwa* grabbed the woman's arm. 'You are under arrest,' he said, but the woman lashed out with her fists and everyone stepped back. Her son was looking mortified.

Osama nudged him and the son very quickly took his mother's arm, whispered something, and began leading her away, not without protest. Halfway down the block, she jerked him to a halt and said something. The boy came running back for the children's toys. At a distance, the woman snatched the bag off her head and shouted back: 'Filthy *mutawwa*!' The son reached her just in time to drag her away.

Nayir had the impression that the religious policeman might have done much worse to the woman had he not been cowering sheepishly under Osama's stern gaze. Osama finally returned his badge to his pocket, still glowering at the *mutawwa*, before motioning for him to leave. Disgruntled but intimidated, the *mutawwa* slunk off and Osama's gaze followed him threateningly. Osama wore a look of deep disgust, of anger and frustration, that Nayir would never have expected from a police officer in this situation. In fact, he had often seen police officers accompanying the *mutawwaiin* about their business.

'This *isn't* Riyadh,' Osama muttered once the man was out of sight.

Nayir's thoughts preoccupied him as they walked into the hospital. Osama was clearly not strict about the law. Not that this

403

surprised Nayir exactly, but it seemed unusual that in the handful of times Nayir had been around Osama, the latter had twice gone out of his way to intervene in a dispute, and both times he had made a decision that went against the law. Nayir felt an uneasy combination of admiration and dismay. He agreed with Osama's decisions, but he didn't like to condone the breaking of religious law. This may not have been Riyadh, but it wasn't America either.

On the ward, Osama spoke to a nurse about Miriam, and the sudden reminder of Nayir's purpose there made him cringe inwardly all the more. How could he justify his disapproval of Katya's relationship with her boss when here he was, visiting Miriam? When he had driven around the city with her, alone? When he had taken her to his uncle's house and spent an evening with her which – he had to admit it – he had enjoyed. Katya would have every right to be angry at *him*.

Osama left him alone in Miriam's room. Nayir sat down quietly next to the bed, glancing furtively at the door despite himself. Even in sleep Miriam looked anxious, her brow furrowed, the edges of her mouth turned down. Her face and hands were spotted with tiny cuts, but nothing that looked serious.

When she woke, would the sight of him trigger her worst memories of the desert? Things she was trying to forget? He had an instinct to leave while he still had the chance, but the thought of her waking up alone, looking around for comfort and finding none, filled him with sadness. He looked at her hand. An ugly purple bruise circled her wrist where she'd been bound. The hand itself looked so vulnerable draped over the side of the bed, and he wanted to hold it, squeeze it, but he satisfied himself with drawing the bed covers over her shoulders and arms, and shutting his eyes to pray.

47

Nayir tapped on the door. No one responded, so reluctantly he pressed the bell. A second later, he heard scuffling and the door opened, revealing Ayman's youthful, somewhat goofy face.

'Oh, hey!' he said. 'Come on in. Katya's here. So's my uncle.'

Relieved to hear this, Nayir let Ayman escort him to the men's sitting room, where he perched himself on the edge of a sofa and waited for Ayman to summon Katya's father.

Five minutes later, there was a tap on the door and Ayman came in looking exasperated. 'You'd better come in. Abu-monkey is out.'

'What did you call him?'

Ayman looked sheepish. 'Abu-monkey.' The father of monkey.

Nayir stood up, saying as he did so: 'You shouldn't speak ill of your uncle.'

'Well, actually, it's not my uncle who's the monkey,' Ayman replied. Nayir was in no mood to debate the finer points of the name. 'Abu-monkey. *Father* of the *monkey*,' Ayman said. 'Katya's the monkey. She's being a grouch.'

Nayir paused. 'Perhaps I'd better come back later.'

'Perhaps you'd better *not*.' Ayman's look of warning said: *Don't you dare leave me alone with that woman*.

'I just wanted to give her something,' Nayir said, feeling more anxious. 'It's about a case.'

'Oh. Sure.'

And before he could hand it to Ayman, the boy was off down the hallway.

Nayir followed with growing dread. He hadn't come this far into Katya's house the last time he was here, and entering now, when she had no warning, seemed the height of rudeness.

She was sitting at a computer in the living room. It was right off the kitchen, and the smell of coffee wafted out through the open door. She wasn't wearing a headscarf and her hair, a deep silky brown, glittered in the light of the table lamp. She was so engrossed in her work that she didn't turn round, and when she did, he realised why she hadn't done so straight away: she was wearing headphones. On the computer screen behind her, a video interview was playing out.

For a moment her expression wavered. 'Oh!' She stood up quickly, taking off her headphones and grabbing a red scarf from the desk. She fastened it around her hair, shooting an unpleasant look at Ayman, who was already scurrying out of the room. Obviously, he hadn't told Katya that he'd be bringing Nayir back with him.

'It's nice to see you,' she said. '*Ahlan*. Have a seat.' She motioned to a pair of sofas behind him. Despite the hospitable sweep of her arm, he sensed a coldness in her. He didn't sit down.

'I'm sorry to intrude,' he said.

'You're not.' But the words were formal, stiff. She was wearing a modest, light grey robe and a pair of old house slippers with fuzzy leopard stripes that somehow delighted him and also managed to make him feel more invasive than ever.

'Please sit,' she said. 'Let me get you some coffee.'

'No thank you,' he said, perhaps too abruptly.

She stood staring at him. Behind her, the computer screen flickered with images of the inside of someone's home.

'Leila's video footage,' she said by way of explanation. It was eight o'clock at night but here she was, still working. At any moment her father could walk in.

'I'm glad to see you made it back from the desert,' she said.

He wasn't sure what to say. It occurred to him that she probably knew why he'd gone out there and what he'd done to save Miriam. She seemed to be expecting an apology of some sort.

'I needed to get away,' he said. She appeared to find this answer inadequate, because her face darkened. 'And I was worried about Miriam,' he added.

She didn't reply.

'I wanted to show you something,' he said quickly. Reaching into his pocket, he removed a computer disc and handed it to her. She took it with an odd expression on her face.

'I got a phone call yesterday from SynTech,' he explained, 'the company that Eric Walker used to work for. Do you remember they accused him of stealing surveillance equipment?'

'Yes.'

'They finally managed to track down the missing equipment,' he said. 'It had been stored in a box in the equipment room, but it was hidden behind a bunch of other boxes, so they didn't see it at first. All of the equipment was still inside, and it was working properly. They found this disc wedged beneath one of the flaps at the bottom of the box.'

'I don't understand,' she said.

'The supplies disappeared when Eric went on leave. That's why they suspected him. Obviously anyone could have taken the equipment, but whoever did it also brought everything back. They just stuffed it in a box and hid it so that if anyone noticed the equipment was missing, they would later think that they had misplaced it and simply overlooked it.

'When Eric's boss, Mr Shaw, found the disc, he figured it was a clue to the thief's identity and he started asking questions of his staff. He showed them what was on the disc. Nobody knew the slightest thing about it, so he called me, hoping that I could shed some light on the subject.'

'And did you?'

'I'm not sure.' He motioned to the computer and they both sat down. Her smell wafted over him and set a hammer banging in his chest. He stole a glance at her face and saw the excitement in it. However disgruntled she might be at him for running off to the desert after Miriam, he hoped that now she might forgive him.

'Where's your father?' he asked.

'Having dinner with friends.' She took Leila's DVD out and slid the new disc into the drive. He noticed that she wasn't wearing the engagement ring, and it gave him an involuntary flutter of hope.

'Don't worry,' she added a little coolly. 'My father trusts you.'

He was spared having to reply when footage from a video surveillance camera appeared on the computer screen. It showed the inside of what looked like a department store, but it was nighttime and most of the lights were out. Only a few dim lamps at the cash register illuminated the scene.

They watched as a man walked on to the screen. Katya clapped a hand to her mouth.

'Do you recognise him?' Nayir asked.

She nodded. The man walked to the cash register, opened it and removed the cash. He stuffed it hastily into a brown zippered bag. Then he went around the store. Because he moved out of the light, it took them a while to see what he was doing, but when he came back towards the register, they saw him snatch a number of clothes items from a rack. He stuffed them into a large rubbish bag that was already bulging.

'I think it's lingerie,' Nayir said, trying not to look too flustered. Katya nodded gravely.

'It is,' she said. 'That's the inside of Abdulrahman's store. He owns a lingerie boutique.'

'I remember,' he said.

She looked at him. 'You do?'

It was the kind of detail he wouldn't be likely to forget, but he wasn't going to admit it.

'That's Fuad,' Katya said. 'He's Abdulrahman's assistant.'

'And he works at the shop?'

'Yes.' She looked at Nayir. He could tell that she was on the verge of a revelation, but her complete and sudden lack of self-consciousness made her startlingly beautiful. Unadorned, sitting here in her house robe, excited by the imminent discovery – she couldn't have been more glamorous. He fought an insane urge to lean forward and kiss her.

'So Eric must have stolen the equipment for Leila,' she said. 'They set up a surveillance of Leila's brother's store. She must have suspected that someone who worked there was stealing. But then how did this disc end up in the box that Eric returned to his office?'

Nayir had thought of this already. 'She probably made a back-up copy,' he said. 'I think it's possible she wasn't going to tell her brother about it, but she was going to bring the problem to Fuad directly. That would explain why she would have hidden the disc.'

'You're saying she was going to blackmail Fuad?'

'What if she confronted him?' Nayir asked. 'Do you think Leila knowing about his crimes would be enough motive for him to murder her?'

Slowly, Katya nodded. 'It's very possible. Fuad takes his job very seriously. And Abdulrahman is a tyrant. If he'd discovered Fuad stealing, he wouldn't have just fired him, he would have made sure he was punished . . .' She trailed off, thinking. 'But if Eric knew about this, then why didn't he do something when Leila went missing? He would have suspected Fuad.'

'He must not have known,' Nayir said. 'The disc was in the box, and it was hidden at the bottom. He probably didn't even look at it.'

409

'Which means that Leila didn't tell him about it. She just put the disc in the box for safekeeping?'

'Probably. Let's say she was going to use it to blackmail Fuad. If Eric knew about the theft, and realised later that Abdulrahman didn't fire Fuad, he might have suspected her of blackmail.'

'Sure. She didn't want anyone to know.' Katya fell silent. 'And here everyone thought Leila was killed because she was filming prostitutes and interacting with strange men.'

The imam's words came back to Nayir. *Many women expose themselves to strange men because they are looking for a husband.* However much she had softened towards him in the past five minutes, one thing remained obvious: Katya was devoted to her job. And the thought of asking her to give that up in order to raise children seemed suddenly like the most selfish thing he had ever come up with. But now that he was facing it, now that it was plain that she couldn't be happy in the role of a wife, why wasn't he walking away? Why didn't he finish the conversation and take his leave?

'Will you have dinner with me?' he asked instead, shocking them both.

'Oh.' She looked startled and embarrassed. 'I already ate, but . . .'

'No, not tonight. But soon.'

Was it fear in her eyes? 'Yes,' she said hesitantly. 'I'd like that.'

He stood up, feeling as if he had suddenly been endowed with thirteen hands. 'I'd better go.'

'Nayir, thank you.' She motioned to the computer.

'It's no problem.'

'One more thing,' she said.

He froze, about to turn and leave. 'Yes?'

'I lied about being married,' she said.

He held his breath. Her face coloured brightly, but she didn't turn away. 'I'm sorry. I didn't tell them that *you* were my husband, it's just . . . they had to think I was married or they wouldn't have hired me. They just assumed you . . .' She waved her hand. When he didn't reply, she went on. 'Osama knows the truth now.'

'Ah.'

'And I'm sorry to have involved you in this.'

He nodded. 'It's all right.' After a moment of awkwardness, he said: 'Will you be keeping your job?'

'Yes,' she replied carefully. 'For now.'

He never thought the day would come when he would be relieved to hear that news. 'That's good,' he said.

She seemed surprised by this, and gave a nervous smile.

'Well,' he said, '*tisbah al-khayr*.' Good night. And he was heading down the hallway before she could say anything more that might prompt him to kiss her – or realise what a fool he'd been.

He left the building without waiting for her to reach the door, only turning once to give a polite wave, and then noticed, with a jolt that felt like adrenalin, that the street was wet, the windows glimmering in the lamplight. A soft downy rain touched his face and hands. As he walked, the rain fell harder, splashing up at his feet, crackling around him like electric pulses, whipping against him until his shirt was plastered to his chest and he began to smile. Rain! People were coming out of their homes, children rushing into it with squeals of delight, women and men leaning from the balconies and staring up at the miraculous sky as if to ask Allah why he had waited so long, so very, very long to bless them.

48

Katya watched Fuad's thin, drawn face through the interrogation room's one-way glass. She had arrived early and planted herself at the very edge of the window, taking a chair to be less conspicuous.

Fuad had been sitting there for a few hours now, waiting for Osama, but she knew that the detective was drawing it out. She only hoped that she could remain where she was, and that none of the male techs or officers would come in and begin acting ruffled by the presence of a woman. Or worse, they might tell her to get back to the lab to begin processing the evidence they'd collected from Fuad's kitchen. This could be a very big finale to a gruesome case, and she was sure everyone would want to see it. She remained, however, determined to keep her place.

Early that morning, she had showed the video from SynTech to Osama, and he had immediately gone to arrest Fuad. The forensics team swept in and quickly found evidence that someone had been injured in Fuad's kitchen. There was blood spatter on the floor – hastily cleaned with detergent – and traces of blood on one of his cooking knives. The most damning discovery was a trace of blood on an old *'iqal*. Katya had spent the whole day waiting restlessly in the lab, but there was so much evidence to collect – blood samples, clothing fibres, knives and bottles of cooking oil, fingerprints and hairs – that forensics was no doubt still at the house and would be there for most of the night.

Half an hour later Osama poked his head in. He smiled at her. A few lab techs trailed in behind him. Before she could say anything Osama swooped back out.

When he returned, he was holding two cups of coffee. He handed one to her. 'I expected to see you here. You've done a lot on this case.'

She took that as a compliment and smiled.

'And it's all thanks to you that we have the video footage,' he said.

'That was Nayir,' she replied.

'I know, but without you, we wouldn't have Nayir.'

He left a minute later and she looked down at her coffee to hide her face from the techs. She was sure she was beaming, and the slightest hint of indiscretion between her and Osama could still jeopardise her career.

Osama entered the interrogation room. Fuad looked up with disgust. A television had been set up in the corner, hooked up to a DVD player. Other than that, they had made the room as unwelcoming as possible. Nothing but a table, two chairs and a linoleum floor. No one had offered coffee or crisps. There wasn't even a waste-paper bin. Overhead fluorescent lights cast an ugly white light directly on to the table, making Fuad's face look hollow and grey. The air vent was wide open, but the air conditioning was clearly off. Katya could feel the room's sticky heat coming through the glass.

Fuad looked worn out. His shirt was rumpled and a few strands of his neatly slicked-back hair were dangling in his face. He sat in a kind of rigid stupor.

Osama switched on the television. The surveillance video from SynTech appeared on the screen. Fuad watched the entire thing with an impassive face. When it was over, Osama switched it off and turned to Fuad.

'Obviously, you've stolen from Abdulrahman more than this

one time. Leila suspected you and that's why she set up the surveillance.'

'I didn't kill her,' Fuad said. His voice was mechanical.

Two men came into the room behind Katya. She didn't turn round, but when they came to stand in front of the viewing window, she recognised the detective they called Abu-Haitham, who was reputed to be so deeply conservative that he had once refused to take a female killer into custody because she would have to ride in the car with him alone. The other man was young and had followed Abu-Haitham into the room in a deferential way. Katya couldn't be sure, but he looked like one of the junior officers. She didn't lower her burqa. The men ignored her completely.

'How do you think he's going to handle it?' the officer asked. The tone in his voice indicated that he was referring to Osama's tactic for extracting a confession.

'Not sure,' Abu-Haitham grunted. 'He'll have figured out what he can about this guy. It doesn't hurt to make him wait, either.'

'He's been in there for what, six hours?' the officer asked. Abu-Haitham nodded.

Katya's attention returned to the interrogation room. 'It's also obvious that Leila didn't tell her brother what you'd done,' Osama said. 'Because if she had, you wouldn't still be working for him.'

'I didn't kill her,' Fuad replied in that same monotone.

'This one's going to need some convincing,' Abu-Haitham remarked. Katya felt her shoulders tingle, and a cold sensation slid through her chest. He was talking about torture. The junior officer was quiet, staring resolutely at the window.

'I don't get the feeling Abdulrahman is a very forgiving man,' Osama said.

But before Osama could finish, Fuad interjected: 'I didn't kill her.'

Katya's nerves were beginning to fray. There was still some doubt that Fuad was the killer – after all, anyone could have

414

killed Leila in his house – but he was an accessory at the very least, not to mention a thief. She wanted to march into the room and wring his neck, or maybe wrap an *'iqal* around it and strangle him until the fear bulged in his eyes and he could barely spit out a confession. He had them at an impasse. He knew – they all knew – that the evidence might not be enough. It would depend entirely on which judge heard the case. All that really mattered was a confession, and who in his right mind was going to give that up when the penalty for murder was death?

There was always the chance that Leila's family – in this case, Abdulrahman and his brothers – would agree to pardon the killer in exchange for blood money, but given that Abdulrahman was so stingy and that he would have learned by now that Fuad had been stealing from him, there was little chance he would take the high ground and pardon Fuad for murder as well. No doubt Fuad was asking himself now: could blood money get him out of this? Could he, who was probably only rich by virtue of having stolen from his boss in the first place, come up with enough money to tempt Abdulrahman into pardoning him? Given Fuad's current recalcitrance, the answer was no.

Abruptly, Osama left the interrogation room. Abu-Haitham and the officer walked out of the observation room to meet him. Katya waited until they were at the door before rising, heading for the door and reaching it just in time to slip her toe into the gap to keep it from closing. She listened to the conversation in the hall.

'I'm going to wait a few more hours,' Osama said.

'He's going to say those same four words all night if you don't do something more drastic,' Abu-Haitham said.

'I think in a few hours we'll have enough evidence to throw in his face,' Osama went on. 'Given the amount of stuff that forensics has got on him, and the condition he'll be in if we don't go in there for a while, we shouldn't have to work too hard to get a confession from the guy.'

'You don't need the evidence,' Abu-Haitham said, 'you just need to make him think you've got it. Rafiq should have taught you *that*.'

Osama didn't reply. He walked past the other two men. Katya slipped back into the room.

She was just sitting down again when Osama came in. He picked up the coffee cup he'd left on the table. Then he came to the window, crossed his arms and stood staring at his quarry.

Katya didn't know what to say. She ought to have left before he came in; he probably didn't want to face anyone right now.

'Would you mind checking in with Majdi,' he said, 'to see what we've got so far on the evidence from the kitchen?'

'Sure.' She leapt up. She was at the door when Osama stopped her.

'Wait,' he said. His jaw was firm and there was something she couldn't read in his eyes. 'Actually, I'd like your help in the interrogation room.'

He appeared to be serious.

'Look,' she said, startled, 'I may be able to question a female witness, but this . . .' She glanced back at the window, struggling to understand her sudden fear. Was she certain she would make a fool of herself? Or was she just afraid that she would get into trouble?

Whatever her fears, it was stupid – *stupid* – to deny herself this opportunity. 'All right,' she said finally. 'What do you need?'

'I just want you to sit there.'

She nodded slowly.

'Let's play it by ear,' he said. 'I have the feeling he won't like a woman being there. Do you mind?'

'No,' she lied.

She lowered her burqa and Osama led her into the interrogation room.

Fuad looked up when they came in. Katya couldn't be sure, but

416

it seemed for a moment that the look of tired defiance on his face momentarily became rancorous at the sight of her. Osama pulled out a chair and motioned Katya into it. She sat facing Fuad, the burqa still covering her face.

Without offering an explanation of who Katya was or what she was doing there, Osama went back to the television and pulled out the plug. He draped the lead on the media trolley and pushed the wheeled object out of the room. The door shut behind him with a resolute thud.

Katya could hear her own breathing. She wasn't sure if Osama wanted her to start the interrogation or simply sit there making Fuad more uncomfortable. The air was stiflingly hot and reeked of body odour. A bead of sweat appeared on his neck.

'Who are you?' he asked.

She didn't reply. Her hands were clasped on the table so they wouldn't start shaking.

'Not much of an interrogator, are you?'

She kept her silence, wrapping it around herself like a cocoon.

'Is this their idea of torture?' A mean smile cracked his face. 'At least you're staying covered,' he said.

She flipped up her burqa. His expression changed immediately to one of disgust.

Osama came back into the room and saw Katya's exposed face. 'Officer Hijazi,' he said in a careful, mock-devout voice, 'why is your burqa up?'

Suddenly, she knew what he wanted, so she went for it. 'Because this man is insulting.'

'That's no reason to spoil your virtue,' Osama replied evenly.

'I'll do what I like,' she retorted.

Osama exhaled. Fuad was still staring at her, more menacing now.

'You have no respect for women?' she asked him. 'Is that why you're staring at me?'

'You should cover your face,' Fuad replied. 'You're a police officer. You shouldn't be full of deceit and lies.'

'Is that what she did to you?' Katya asked. 'Deceit and lies?'

Fuad's eyes shifted to her headscarf, so she took that off, too.

'Officer Hijazi!' Osama said. Fuad's teeth clenched.

'Does my hair offend you?' Katya asked. 'Or is it that you actually want to touch it?'

Fuad let out a snort. His hostility sickened her. He was dripping with greasy sweat, his shirt sticking to his chest so that the little black hairs showed through the thin, blue fabric, shifting with his every move like a hill of ants. His rancid sweat was filling her nostrils and creeping down her throat.

'Your problem,' she said, 'is that you can't get a woman.' She could see she'd struck a nerve, and it only emboldened her. 'You think women should be your sex slaves. That's what Leila was to you, wasn't it? A pretty face. A cute, tight arse. Someone you thought you could fuck if you felt like it.' She couldn't believe what was pouring out of her mouth. She put all her concentration on forgetting that people were watching her, their jaws probably hanging open right now. 'So what happened? She said "no"? She met a handsome American guy?'

His face twitched at the word 'American'. He lurched forward, slamming his fists on the table. 'Shut your fucking mouth!'

She held her ground. 'She was sleeping with an American, wasn't she?' Katya went on, speaking louder to control her shaking voice. 'She was fucking Eric Walker.'

'She had no virtue!'

'And then what? She wouldn't have you? That cheap, selfish whore wouldn't give you what you wanted?'

He leapt up, his chair slamming against the wall. This time she barely flinched. Osama was one foot behind him, ready to grab him.

'Did she actually say "No, I'd rather die"?' Katya asked. 'Was that what gave you the idea?'

Fuad's fists were rhythmically clenching and unclenching, his jaw working, showing knots on his cheek.

She felt reckless now. 'Leila wasn't just beautiful, she was smart,' she went on. 'She saw you and knew right away what most women would only sense – that you're not worth it.'

'She was a *bitch*.' He lurched towards her, spraying spittle on her face.

'Maybe,' Katya said. 'But she didn't deserve to die.'

'Yes, she fucking did!' he shouted, his hands gripping the table as if preparing to flip it over. 'She fucking did deserve it!'

'The boiling oil? Did she deserve that?' Katya's voice was full of its own fury now. 'The stabbing? The beating?'

'She deserved every fucking minute!' And with horrible strength he lifted the table, shoving it forward into her chest. Osama flew at Fuad. Katya fell backwards, arms raised to protect herself, hitting the wall with a thud. The door burst open. Officers ran in. She couldn't breathe, then just as suddenly the air filled her lungs. The table fell back. The men were on the floor. She felt the urge to throw up. Shaking, she climbed to her feet, the edges of her vision going black. Osama was standing there, looking terrified.

'I'm fine,' she said. Her voice came out like a whisper. She coughed. 'I'm fine.'

Osama shoved the table aside to reach her. He took her wrist, drawing her gently away from the wall. She let him keep hold of her hand as they left the room.

49

Miriam's brother Justin was an object of fascination – tall, blond and burly, he was the opposite of Miriam in almost every respect. The only thing they shared were their big, blue American eyes. Nayir couldn't help thinking it was a good thing they were American. The old saying – that when choosing a wife, you need only look at her brother's face to see what the bride would look like – would be so hopelessly wrong in this case that a prospective husband would feel deeply misled.

Those eyes fell on Nayir more often than he liked. He and Miriam were sitting on a pair of seats at the airport; Justin was standing ten feet away to give them some privacy – at Miriam's request – but his eyes continued probing Nayir's face. A few times Nayir caught him looking over with suspicion as if it were Nayir who had cheated on Miriam, and then been kidnapped and killed in the Empty Quarter.

'I still don't know what to think about it all,' she whispered.

Not for the first time, Nayir wasn't sure how to reply. He thought of all the things the police hadn't told her – about the video footage of Eric and Leila in the desert, at his flat, drinking alcohol on the American compound. About Katya's last discovery that it was Eric's hair on the inside of Leila's burqa. He made a mental note to thank Osama for his tact.

Miriam had already told him that the police had finally managed to track down Eric's pick-up truck. Mabus had parked it on the street half a mile from their flat. Miriam had gone to the police garage to identify the truck and remove any remaining personal items. She didn't say what she'd found, but clearly it was a difficult subject, and Nayir didn't press her.

'Did they tell you that now they know for certain that Leila was killed by a man named Fuad?' Nayir said.

'Yes,' Miriam said. 'But they didn't tell me who he was.'

'He was stealing from her brother's shop. She brought the surveillance video to him. She wanted to blackmail him, I think.'

Miriam nodded and looked at her hands. A tear slid down her cheek.

'Miriam.' Her brother was standing over them now. 'We've got to get to the gate.'

Miriam turned to Nayir. 'I don't know what I'd have done without you.' She wiped her cheek with the back of her sleeve and laughed. 'Well, I'd be dead actually.'

'You survived.'

'Thanks to you.'

'I'm sorry about Eric,' he said. She nodded, and more tears started sliding down her cheeks. Nayir felt the impulse to take her hand, but her brother was looming.

Heartbroken and ragged, Miriam looked up at her brother and took his hand. Nayir stood up as well, shocked by the suddenness of the departure.

'At least one good thing came out of this,' she said.

'What's that?'

'I got to meet you.' She dropped her brother's hand and opened her arms, drawing Nayir into a fierce, warm hug. Stunned, he returned the embrace.

Watching her walk away, he felt a sense of loss. The feeling was made more painful by its permanence. *It was, and it was not.* As she disappeared from view, he stood there, mesmerised by the empty space, until he realised that she wasn't coming back.

50

After they dragged him from the interrogation room, the guards brought Fuad to another room down the hall where they could handcuff him to a table that was bolted to the floor. They cuffed his feet as well and left him alone. The attack on Katya had been like the magnificent eruption of a volcano, which now sat smoking dangerously.

When Osama went in to take a confession from him five days later, Fuad had deteriorated significantly. He looked like one of those old Hajjis who comes to Jeddah and remains in a kind of permanent limbo – never quite making it to Mecca for his religious duties, and never actually leaving. Begging for money on the street with the pretext of needing to get back to some far-flung home. Unlike the homeless Hajjis, however, Fuad had not sunk to manipulating compassion. Instead, he had broken, and now he was talking simply to finish the whole affair so he could get out of this hell.

Usually it took much longer than this. A few weeks in prison at least. But Osama suspected that Fuad had never had much tolerance for being unshaven, hungry, exhausted and hot. He preferred clean suits, a nice haircut, a fine watch. His monthly laundry bills had been outrageous. He had spent his life a bachelor, earning enough to live in unabashed comfort.

Osama took a seat at the table, set down a water bottle for Fuad, and opened his folder. The guard released Fuad's hands so he could drink, but he didn't make a move to touch the bottle.

Osama took his time assembling photographs and paperwork, seeming to ignore the man sitting opposite him, although the stench of his clothing made it almost impossible. At night, the guards came in to take him to a prison cell, where he could pray and eat a solid meal, but during the day he was kept here, in an un-air-conditioned room, waiting.

He had started confessing on day four, telling them everything through the one-way glass. But Osama had waited. They still had evidence to process and they wanted to weaken him even more for the confession.

Now he looked up at Fuad. 'Let's go over this again,' he said easily. 'You killed her.'

'Yes.'

'When?'

As the prisoner began talking, Osama noticed that Fuad's tongue was swollen. He pushed the water bottle closer but Fuad ignored it. He was in a miserable state, but he still had his pride.

'She came to your house that morning to show you the video-tape,' Osama prompted.

'I got angry.' Fuad's face showed only a twinge of remorse; he seemed more concerned with not letting the memory anger him now. 'She offered me a deal,' he went on. 'She said she'd be willing to take half the money and not tell her brother.'

'Tell him that you were stealing from him?'

'Right.' Fuad swallowed, nursed his tongue against the inside of his cheek.

'And what did you say to her offer?' Osama asked.

'I said . . .' Here he hesitated. This was the part he'd glossed over when he'd been shouting his guilt at the window. 'I said I'd think about it. She said no, she wanted an answer right away.'

Osama saw it in a flash. Leila might have been courageous enough to critique the unfairness or hypocrisy she saw in the world around her, but when it came right down to it, she was not an idealist. He thought back through all the reports he'd read, Majdi's evidence, Katya's interview notes, his own conversations with Abdulrahman and Ra'id and Bashir. Money was at the root of everything. Leila needed it. It was the primary subject in all of her interviews with women. And perhaps that's what had really interested Leila: how to get money, how to break the cycle of reliance on men. Bashir had even said it outright: all she wanted was his cash.

Had she used any other footage as blackmail? The Mabus documentary would have been a better tool than the security footage of Fuad. At least Mabus had had some assets worth stealing.

'And then what?' Osama asked.

'Then she got angry.' Fuad snorted and reached for the water. He took a long drink and water dribbled down his chin. 'She started accusing me of stealing – as if *she* had any virtue. She threatened to go to the police right then if I didn't say yes. I kept thinking: this is Abdulrahman's sister. She's a fucking liar and a user, and she thinks she's a virtuous woman. She really thinks that. But she was filthy.'

'What happened next?'

'She touched me. She pushed my arm, because I wasn't responding.' He took another drink of water. 'Then she started really threatening me. "I'm going to tell my brother. Your life is finished."'

'And that made you angry?'

'Yes,' he said forcefully. 'She was everything that was fucking wrong with the world. A spoiled girl and a liar. Always taking money from her brother, never doing anything for anyone else. We were in the kitchen. I was cooking. She came up to me, really got in my face, and said: "I'll make sure he prosecutes you." Meaning Abdulrahman. And I couldn't control it, I just picked up the frying pan and threw it in her face. All the hot oil, the aubergine, everything went crazy. She put up her hands to protect herself, but it was . . . disgusting.'

He set down the water. His hands were steady, but his face was twitching with suppressed anger. 'She started fighting, screaming. It was like the oil hadn't burned her at all. She went crazy and grabbed a pot. She threw plates and glasses. I grabbed the only thing I could find – this old *'iqal* that was hanging on a hook, and I started trying to hit her arms, to get her to drop the shit she was throwing at me. By then I was really angry. I wanted to hurt her. She came into my house to defile everything. She grabbed a knife from the counter and came at me. I grabbed another knife and I stabbed her. I don't know how many times. She was pounding at me, but I couldn't stop. I couldn't stop. I kept stabbing her. I just kept stabbing . . .' He broke off. His face showed no more than a slight confusion, as if he couldn't quite believe it himself. 'I threw her off me and realised that she was dead.'

'But she wasn't,' Osama said. 'She didn't die until you broke her neck.'

'I just wanted to make sure. She was . . . there was no going back. Her face . . .' He motioned to his own face. 'It was over.'

A long silence went by. Osama felt himself floating in a kind of mental stasis, staring numbly at Fuad. The words *her face . . . it was over* kept repeating in his mind. What did it mean? That because she was burned, ugly forever, that she would somehow need death? That without her pretty face, she no longer had a purpose for living?

Osama forced himself to ask the next question. 'How did you break her neck?'

'I just grabbed her head.' Fuad's lip curled slightly, his hands pantomiming the action. 'Jerked it like this . . .'

'And the oil burns on her hands and face? They weren't just splash marks.'

For the first time, Fuad looked slightly embarrassed. 'I heated more oil to make it even.'

'Why?'

'So no one would know who she was.'

'And then you stripped off her jeans.'

He nodded, opened his mouth, and shut it again. 'I was dragging her body out of the car and the jeans got caught on something near her hip. I heard the fabric tear. I thought I'd take the jeans off but I couldn't do it. I was too eager to get out of there, so I left it.'

'And where did you take her body?'

'A pier north of the city. It was the only place I could think of.'

Osama was quiet for a moment. 'You said you were at the air-conditioning repair shop that morning. We confirmed that you were there.'

'I lied.'

'So did the shop owner.'

'He's always got so many people in that shop,' Fuad said. 'He's always frazzled. I had gone in the day before, and I was sure he wouldn't remember which day I was there exactly.'

'You also confirmed that you'd had coffee with a friend. Was that a lie, too?'

Fuad shook his head. 'I really did go for coffee.'

He seemed remorseless. He didn't ask, as so many killers did at this juncture, whether there was any hope that the judge would treat him kindly. He simply accepted that in confessing to murder, he had condemned himself to death. He knew the system. And perhaps he now thought of himself, as he had thought of Leila, as ruined goods.

'You don't seem like a religious man,' Osama finally said. 'Do you believe in God?'

Fuad gave a soft, hollow laugh. 'Do you want to add apostasy to my other crimes?'

'No,' Osama said. 'I'm just curious.'

'No,' Fuad said. 'I don't believe in God.'

Qasama. To divide. To cleave in twain. The word kept repeating in Nayir's mind like a thousand madmen, whispering, chanting. *Qasama. Qasama.*

The indecision was back. Being in the desert had been a relief, even dealing with a sandstorm was somehow easier than fighting this uncertainty. Should he have come here today, or not? Was it right to condone another death?

Nayir had just finished Friday prayers at the Jufalli mosque and now stood in the car park amidst a sea of congregants who were milling about casually, waiting to see if the executioner would arrive. It had been a difficult business focusing on prayers while this car park loomed in Nayir's consciousness as the site of future bloodshed. He had always believed that execution was a just and necessary punishment, but now he couldn't feel the force of his previous certainty. What was right about denying someone their repentance? Didn't everyone deserve Allah's forgiveness?

Executions weren't announced in advance, but thanks to Osama, he knew to be here today. He found the detective leaning against an unmarked police car at the edge of the car park. Behind him was the lake. Its centre was a deep greyish green, but around the edges it was tinged brown and littered with Pepsi bottles and plastic bags. The water smelled unpleasant despite the city's clean-up of it a few years before.

The sky was clear, the smog had left on a morning breeze, and now the sun beat down on Nayir's head and back. Oddly enough, Osama seemed pleased to be there. It was, for him, the successful conclusion of a brutal case.

'You're not wearing a uniform,' Nayir observed. 'I thought you'd dress up.'

'I didn't want to give myself away.'

Nayir nodded. People were used to figuring out that executions would take place only when the police cars came blaring into the car park.

'We've got another half an hour,' Osama said. 'You want to wait in the shade?'

They made their way to the shady arcade at the end of the white mosque but there were too many people already claiming the prized spot, so they remained in the sunlight. It reflected off the mosque's brilliant white exterior with a nuclear intensity.

Looking about, Nayir was surprised to see how many people were already there. Surely more than had actually been praying in the mosque. He stood listening to the banter around him.

People had been reading about the Nawar case in the papers for the past two and a half weeks. They knew the killer had been caught. They knew that the victim's family had not pardoned him for the crime. Some people still suspected that it was the American man who had killed her after all, and that the poor bloke they would execute would only be a dummy, perhaps a nameless drug trafficker who'd been pinned with the crime, because somehow Americans always managed to slip free. It angered Nayir to think of Eric Walker, killed by the most selfish of men, now being maligned by strangers who had no idea what had really happened. It should have been Apollo Mabus they were dragging on to the execution platform today, but Mabus was still in prison, awaiting a trial date while the British consulate furiously attempted his extradition.

Grimly, Nayir searched for a distraction. He didn't want to think about Miriam right now. Fumbling in his pocket, he found a *miswak*. He brushed the lint from the bristles and stuck it in his mouth. The *miswak* was old; its spicy tang was almost gone, but at least it gave him something to do.

Osama stood beside him, eyes obscured behind a pair of Ray-Bans. The sun was shining directly on his head. He had already looked wilted leaning against his car, now he looked as if someone had blasted him with a fireman's hose.

'Where's your hat?' Nayir asked.

'Forgot it.'

'You could borrow my *shumagh* if you like,' Nayir said, motioning to his headscarf.

Osama snorted. 'I'm not wearing that thing.' But then he smiled. Nayir shook his head. He was finding it easier to excuse Osama for being so self-consciously unorthodox.

'So what did Fuad say?' Nayir asked.

Osama kept his eyes on the pavement. 'You know when you get a feeling about someone?'

Nayir nodded.

'I just knew he was one of those guys who hated women. He might have been a modern-looking man on the outside, he even said that he didn't believe in God, but on the inside he still thought like some fundamentalist: women exist to serve men. They're disposable.'

Nayir was offended by this slight against religious-minded people but decided to stay on the subject. 'You think he killed her just because she was a woman?'

'No, but that was a part of it. He killed her because he hated what she was. She didn't act properly. She filmed people in public. She was out all the time, against her brother's wishes. It all pissed Fuad off. Then she caught him stealing from her brother, and instead of doing the right thing and reporting it to Abdulrahman, she tried to blackmail Fuad into sharing the profits.'

'Don't you think if she'd reported him, he would have been just as angry?' Nayir asked.

'Yeah, but he wouldn't have killed her, I think,' Osama said. 'He wouldn't have had the chance. He killed her in a fit of rage. He didn't plan to do it; he just did it. I think that if she had been a man and she'd gone to confront him, he wouldn't have killed her. But she was a woman . . .' Osama shrugged cynically. 'You know what got him into the lingerie business in the first place? He used to be obsessed with porn. He had so much of it in his flat that we couldn't find his kitchen table. He got a job at Abdul-rahman's store – started out as a sales assistant – and we found out later from his brother-in-law it was because he loved handling the mannequins. To him, it was all right for a man to look at porn, but for a woman to act with liberty? What really made him angry was that Leila wasn't being moral. If you ask me, that's completely ignorant.'

Nayir prickled. 'You think because a man's a fundamentalist, he doesn't respect women?'

Osama regarded him carefully. 'What I'm saying is that he wasn't religious on the outside, but inside he had all of the hall-marks of extreme thinking.'

'About religion or about women?' Nayir asked.

'Women. But they go together, don't you think – religion and women? I mean, can you be a good Muslim if you think women should walk around uncovered?'

Nayir didn't know exactly what he thought any more, and it was getting too hot to argue.

'He's just an extreme case,' Osama went on. 'Do you know what he wrote in his will? He left all of his belongings to his brother-in-law in Libya. And to his sister? Nothing. But he did waste some paper exhorting her to remember not to wear make-up and not to act like a whore. Doesn't that sound like a fundamentalist to you?'

Nayir felt he was being baited, so he didn't reply. The word *qasama* was running through his brain again. He looked out at the plaza, but the unresolved argument hung between them more solidly than the choking, humid air.

There was a rumble from the crowd as the distant sound of sirens broke the air. Immediately people began whipping out their mobiles, no doubt to call friends and give news of the execution. Seconds later, six police cars came pouring into the car park, their lights flashing insignificantly against the greater brilliance of the sun and the mosque.

People murmured as they saw the executioner get out of the car. He was not remarkable – a forty-something black man of medium height. He wore a red-checkered *shumagh* and a crisp white robe. What made him stand out was the lavish scimitar at his side. This shining silver object, engraved with what were no doubt words from the Quran, was the cause of a lot of fussing and oohing as he passed through the crowd. His robust face wore an expression of pleasure, but it was his plainness that chilled Nayir most of all. The man who chopped off heads for a living could be his neighbour. He probably had a wife and kids.

The crowd followed the executioner like geese. There were a few women vying for space, and a white man, possibly American, his bald head shining gloriously in the sun. Nayir saw a stranger grab the American's arm. The man looked alarmed, but the stranger was smiling. 'Come,' he said, 'I'll get you a good spot.' He pushed through the crowd, and people moved aside to let the American pass.

Once the execution spot had been established, the police brought Fuad out of a waiting van. His hands were tied behind his back and he was blindfolded. He stumbled a bit as he walked. Nayir had the impression that it wasn't because he was blind. His whole body moved in a sloppy, uneasy way. Word was that the condemned were drugged before executions to avoid resistance or a dramatic show of emotion. Nayir thought it was probably true.

Fuad was brought to the stage – nothing more than a sheet of plastic laid down on the pavement and a block of stone, grooved on one edge like a crescent, where Fuad would soon be laying his head for its final bow to Allah.

Nayir stared at the stone and felt heavy, as if each molecule in his body had suddenly turned to lead. He had never seen a public execution before, and he wasn't sure he could stomach it now. The heat was bearing down. The crowd rising, jostling him. Those more determined to get a view pushed him back to the rear. He was sweating in a painful way, and the sun was like a punishment, burning the back of his neck, prickling his scalp like needles. He strained to keep his eyes on the executioner. Someone thumped his shoulder and he turned to see a woman pushing him aside with her handbag.

The crowd's shuffling stopped as one of the officers announced Fuad's crimes. Nayir heard it as if from across a great chasm. *This is Fuad al-Jamia. He was found guilty of murdering a young woman. His sentence is death.*

Nayir pushed forward again without understanding why his feet moved ahead or where he found the strength to knuckle between strangers and crush the odd toe. He had to get to the centre before the sword fell. He spotted Osama craning around to look for him and pushed in that direction, not minding cries of annoyance, until he reached the front row. Fuad was kneeling on the ground, his head over the block. Sweat was dripping from the tips of his hair.

Osama explained that the man standing beside one of the officers was Leila's brother, Abdulrahman. Beside him was a young man, Leila's cousin Ra'id. The boy looked pale and withdrawn.

The executioner said to the brother: 'Mr Nawar, you have one more chance to pardon this man. Will you do it?'

Abdulrahman regarded Fuad, crouched on the pavement like some small, blind animal poised in a frozen aspect of fear. He watched him for a long time while the crowd waited breathlessly, taking in Abdulrahman's tortured face.

'No,' he said finally. 'I will not.'

The executioner nodded as briskly as a waiter who's been told to fetch the bill. He turned back to Fuad and commanded him to recite the *shahada*. 'There is no God but one God, and Mohammed is his prophet.' Halfway through, Fuad broke off his muttering and didn't finish.

With a practised, easy hand, the executioner dug the tip of his scimitar into Fuad's lower back, forcing Fuad's head up. And then, with a smooth, dramatic sweep, he raised the sword above his head. Nayir stared at the sword, *qasama* spinning wildly through his brain. It came down. A glint of light. A shattering of metal on stone. Some gasping and a brief cry of shock. Fuad's head dropped to the ground.

Blood spurted from the neck, spraying the plastic sheet. Someone behind them fainted, causing a disturbance in the crowd and forcing Nayir to turn around. He saw nothing but the backs of a dozen white robes, a blinding field of white.

There was no sound any more. The word had stopped repeating. Nayir stared at the ground, at the men stooping over to retrieve the severed head, at the doctor uselessly bending over Fuad's body to confirm the death. Nayir felt his breathing normalise again. Felt a cool chill wash over his body. A new word appeared. Not *qasama* this time but its close cousin *qismah*. Fate. Your portion. Your half of that which was divided.

He decided that Fuad had got what he deserved.

52

Nayir walked beside Katya, their progress slowed now and then by the fact that she was wearing a burqa and that occasionally she would stop, lift the burqa, and gaze at the sunset over the Red Sea. He had to keep an eye on her. More than once already he'd turned to discover that he'd left her behind. The little jolt it gave him to realise that he'd lost her, however momentarily, led him to wonder about all the married men walking around, those who marched confidently down the pavements with their wives an obedient ten paces behind them. How did they know that their wives were actually following? That they didn't stop to glance in shop windows or secretly raise their burqas and wink at strange men?

Katya was quieter than usual tonight. While it filled him with dread, he felt a fierce, unstoppable current of generosity flowing out of him and he imagined that this retreat into silence was the feminine equivalent of going to the desert for a month, an act he had often undertaken himself and therefore could not begrudge her. He wished that she would help keep up the conversation, and answer his questions with more than an *aywa* or a *laa*. As the sun dipped below the horizon, an eruption of colour broke him out of these thoughts, and just for a moment the pink and gold light and the green-smelling breeze conspired to make the view from the Corniche as stirring as a Ramadan prayer.

It seemed obvious that food was on everyone's mind. The weather was unseasonably cool, thirty degrees at most, and half of

Jeddah had come out to picnic. They laid carpets on the beaches, on roads and in the car parks. They pitched their tents on the pavement. Four metres wide, stretching to the horizon, the Corniche pavement could probably have accommodated the entire nation. The less well-prepared sat on the sand beside fast-food kiosks selling *balela*. The warm smell of chickpeas and barbecued lamb wafted over the pavement every few feet. Although there was a respectful distance between families, the whole scene seemed as busy as a coral reef.

'How is work?' he asked, hoping that this was the problem, that it wasn't something worse – or something about him.

'Good,' she said, another pat answer which naturally invited a suspicious riposte. But he didn't want to pressure her.

They walked in silence another ten minutes until they reached the restaurant. It was a quiet family place where you could dine in your own little bungalow, cloistered from prying eyes. He had been here a few times with Samir, and the food had always been excellent.

'This is nice!' Katya exclaimed. 'How did you find this place?'

'There's a popular dive site out there.' He motioned to the water some ten metres down the shore from the restaurant. She looked as if she wanted to say something but didn't.

A waiter led them to a bungalow just big enough for two. The walls were dark bamboo in a Tiki shack style, but one side of the shack was open, giving them a view of a rocky beach and beyond that, the Red Sea sparkling in the sunset. There was a rolling screen at the top of the wall that they could let down if they wanted more privacy.

They sat on cushions, and beneath them was a roll-out mat. The waiter returned with water and menus. Katya asked questions about the different types of fish, and Nayir gave his advice while his mind drifted silently to the events of the afternoon.

He had gone to her house while she was still at work. Her

father had welcomed him warily at first; he seemed to know from the look on Nayir's face what he'd come for. After escorting Nayir into the sitting room, Abu had brought a generous pot of tea and some dates, sat down across from his guest and said: 'So how have you been, Mr Sharqi?'

The use of his surname had made the ensuing conversation seem all the more stiff. Nayir forced himself through a discussion of the weather, growing more and more tense as he realised that Abu wasn't going to make it any easier for him. Finally, when he felt he'd done enough chatting, Nayir said: 'I've come to ask your permission for Katya's hand in marriage.'

Abu had sat back on the sofa and regarded him evenly. Nayir tried not to squirm. He set his teacup on the table. He met Abu's gaze. In the growing silence, he felt he ought to say more, explain at least why he wanted to marry her, but the reasons fell flat on his tongue. It would have meant admitting that he had spent enough time with her to know the many reasons to love her, and while Abu must have undoubtedly suspected that much, Nayir wasn't prepared to admit it.

The horrible silence was broken when Abu sat forward again. 'You are a good Muslim man, Nayir. I think you would make an excellent match for my daughter.'

And that was it. Taken by surprise, Nayir had let out a happy breath. Seeing Abu's stern face, he quickly sobered up, but the relief and the thrill of having Abu's blessing was enough to float him out the door. Even Abu seemed pleased by the end and shook his hand with a congratulatory vigour.

At the door, Abu said one last thing: 'I will tell her you have my blessing, but I would prefer it if you talk to her yourself before I say anything.'

'Yes,' Nayir said, feeling perplexed. 'I will.' As he left, he felt dread settling over him. The decision was in Katya's hands now. Of course, Nayir knew that this moment would come. Traditionally, the parents would handle the negotiations. But Abu had just thrown the whole thing on Nayir's lap. If Katya said no, she would tell Nayir herself. Was it only his pride that made the idea seem so horrific?

Nayir suspected, although he couldn't be sure, that Abu was doing this because of Katya, and not because he was a careless or cowardly man; but why he was doing it, what it meant about her, Nayir couldn't be sure.

These thoughts weighed on him once the waiter had left and he sat facing Katya. She seemed inexplicably different this evening; she was changing right in front of him, no longer the woman he had yearned for but a woman he might marry, who might become his wife, lover, friend, and as they drank fresh mango juice and ate their grouper, he found himself looking at her face more often, really studying its contours as if to make sure they hadn't really changed. They talked about the Nawar case again, but only briefly before she switched to the other cases she was working on now. He was reminded once again that she loved her job, and that marriage and children might not be in her plans, but the question that had been percolating inside him for the past two weeks – or, if he was honest, for the past nine months – was now exploding in his head. He thought of Omran leaping over the edge of a dune as he put down his fork and said:

'Katya, will you marry me?'

She froze in the process of setting her glass on the mat. She didn't look at him at first, but he was watching her intently, enough to notice the discomfort steal across her face. She set the glass down all the way and took a breath.

'Nayir . . .'

She was struggling. He wanted to tell her that the reason he hadn't spoken to her for those months was that he'd been afraid, and that the fear was overwhelming, huge and amorphous, too much to explain even to himself. But seeing her again had made him realise that he wanted her. He only hoped that it wasn't too late. He felt a momentary weakness, then a whooshing sensation as certainty filled him.

'Katya,' he said, 'I know I'm not perfect, and I might not be right for you. I know you love your job. And it might be difficult to have children when you work so much. But I think we can do it. We can find a way.' She still wasn't looking at him. He lowered his head to the level of hers, trying to encourage her to meet his gaze, but she kept staring resolutely at the mat.

'Katya.'

She swallowed, looking scared. And without knowing how it happened, he reached a hand to her cheek, turning her face to his. Her cheek was warm, and soft. She didn't resist. When her eyes met his, he saw that they were wet, that she looked frightened. An impulse that came from every part of his body made him lean closer, pausing as their noses touched in case she backed away, but she didn't, so he kissed her, gently at first, their dry lips touching, then more insistently, while pinpoints of light exploded inside him.

☽

Katya was the first to pull away from the kiss.

'Nayir,' she said softly, amazed at herself but even more amazed at *him*. So it was true what they said: too much repression will lead a man straight into sin. She put a hand to her mouth and gave a short, nervous laugh of surprise.

Five minutes before, she had been vaguely uncomfortable, not certain that Nayir was enjoying himself. He'd looked, at one moment, spectacularly anxious. And now she knew why. Of course she should have seen it coming. He would never have asked her out on a date for any other reason. Her first thought had been resentful, but the softness of his voice, the touch of his hand on her cheek had unleashed a kind of frenzied rebelliousness in both of them. She didn't know what she was doing any more, only that her body was doing it and that her mind seemed to have become lost in a dust storm.

She sat up, picked up her juice glass, set it down again. *I'm sorry*, she almost blurted, but she wasn't sorry, she was scared. Marriage? To Nayir? Visions of her mother flashed through her mind, the disappointments, the frustrations. Ummi had thought she had married a more open-minded man. Katya, on the other hand, knew just what she was dealing with.

'Nayir,' she began. 'I don't . . .'

'You're afraid,' he said. 'I am, too.'

Surprised, she pushed on. 'I need to know that you'll respect me. My job. And everything else I might want to do.' She met his eyes as she said it, and he didn't look away. 'I just need to know—'

'I shall not lose sight,' he whispered. It was a tender sound, and the tone of his voice made her realise that he was quoting Quran. '*I shall not lose sight of the labour of any of you . . .*' She recognised the quote then; he didn't have to finish it: *. . . who labours in My way, be it man or woman; each of you is equal to the other.*

She felt a tear threatening to spill on to her cheek. 'I can't make this decision right away,' she said.

'You don't have to answer today,' he said.

When she drew up the nerve to look into his eyes again, she saw that he understood.

They walked back along the pavement to Nayir's car, uncertain what to say to one another. Katya was outside of thought, and as the silence dragged on, another power took hold. Chemical stimuli, the warmth of the breeze associating their bodies, picnicking families hanging about them like charms. Fertile, messy bliss. She felt an inkling of hope that she might find happiness after all. She drew up beside him and carefully, so that no one would notice, brushed her arm against his.

He smiled and kept walking.

GLOSSARY

abaaya – a long, loose black cloak worn by women in Saudi Arabia.

Ahlan wa'sahlan – 'welcome' (hard to translate – loosely it's something like 'family and familiar comforts'). Slightly more formal than *marhaba*.

Allah akbar – 'God is great'.

Allah yarhamha – loosely translated, 'God rest her soul'.

'aql – 'intelligence'.

'asr – the third of the five daily Muslim prayers.

aywa – 'yes'.

balela – a salad of chickpeas, black beans and spices.

barzakh – an intermediate state after physical death when the soul separates from the body.

biryani – a rice- and meat-based dish cooked with spices.

Bism'allah, ar-rahman, ar-rahim – 'In the name of Allah, most gracious, most merciful', the opening phrase of a Muslim prayer.

burqa (also *niqaab*) – in the Gulf countries, burqa refers to a veil that covers a woman's face. Not to be confused with the enveloping outer garment, also called a burqa, worn by women in other Muslim countries.

dhuhr – the fourth of the five daily Muslim prayers.

djinn – a genie. Plural *djinni*.

fatwa – a religious opinion or edict issued by a Muslim cleric.

habibti (also *hubibti*) – (to a woman) 'my love'.

Hadith – the collected narratives about the Prophet Mohammed.

Hajj – the pilgrimage to Mecca.

Hajji – a person who has made the pilgrimage.

halaal – kosher, permissible under Islamic law.

haraam – forbidden by Islamic law.

hayati – 'my life', a term of endearment.

hijaab – the headscarf worn by Muslim women to cover their hair. Also: Muslim women's dress in general.

hookah (also *sheeshah*) – a water pipe used for smoking tobacco.

hur – plural of *houri*, an alluring, beautiful woman.

'iqal – a loop of black cord used to fix the male headscarf onto the head.

istiqara – a type of prayer that asks for guidance in difficult matters.

Ka'aba – the black monument in the centre of the holy mosque, the Masjid Al-Haram, in Mecca.

khulwa – a state of seclusion.

laa – 'no'.

majlis – literally 'a place of sitting'. Any gathering place, typically a living room or an assembly hall.

marra – 'woman'.

masahif – plural of *mashaf*, a codex.

miswak – twigs or roots of the arak tree used for natural tooth cleansing.

misyar – a marriage institution in Islam whereby a man can have a wife without financial responsibility.

mubeen – 'purity'.

mujahideen – freedom fighters.

mutawwa – a religious policeman from the Committee for the Protection of Virtue and the Prevention of Vice in Saudi Arabia. Plural *mutawwaiin*.

Najd – the central region of Saudi Arabia.

na-mehram – 'unfamiliar'.

qasama – to divide.

qismah – 'fate' or kismet.

rakat – a verse of prayer.

Ramadan – the month of fasting, occurring once a year in Islamic religious tradition.

Salaam aleikum – a greeting, literally 'peace be with you'.

Sallā llahu' alayhi wa sallam – 'peace be upon him', said when mentioning the name of the Prophet Mohammed.

shahada – the phrase 'There is no God but Allah, and Mohammed is his prophet', the recitation of which is required for Muslims.

schawarma – a sandwich of slices of shaved rotisserie meat, lettuce, cucumber, tomato and sauce folded together in a pita bread.

sharwaya – 'shepherds'.

shaytin – a kind of evil genie.

shumagh – a red-and-white checkered headscarf worn by men.

souq – an outdoor market, any commercial marketplace.

surah – a chapter of the Quran.

Tisbah al-khayr – 'goodnight'.

zabiba – a raisin-shaped bump or callus on the forehead that develops after a lifetime of touching one's forehead to the ground during prayer.

zina – a type of crime in Islamic law involving extramarital sex.